OUT OF PHAZE

By Piers Anthony

Chthon

Phthor

Anthonology

Macroscope

Prostho Plus

Race Against Time

Rings of Ice

Triple Detente

Steppe

But What of Earth?

Hasan

Mute

Shade of the Tree

Ghost

Series by Piers Anthony

THE APPRENTICE ADEPT SERIES
Split Infinity * Blue Adept * Juxtaposition * Out of Phaze

INCARNATIONS OF IMMORTALITY SERIES
On a Pale Horse * Bearing an Hourglass * With a Tangled Skein * Wielding a Red Sword * Being a Green Mother

BIO OF A SPACE TYRANT SERIES
Refugee * Mercenary * Politician * Executive * Statesman

THE MAGIC OF XANTH SERIES
A Spell for Chameleon * The Source of Magic * Castle Roogna * Centaur Aisle * Ogre, Ogre * Night Mare * Dragon on a Pedestal * Crewel Lye * Golem in the Gears

TAROT SERIES
God of Tarot * Vision of Tarot * Faith of Tarot

THE CLUSTER SERIES
Cluster * Chaining the Lady * Kirlian Quest * Thousandstar * Viscous Circle

OF MAN AND MANTA SERIES
Omnivore * Orn * Ox

BATTLE CIRCLE SERIES
Sos the Rope * Var the Stick * Neg the Sword

OUT OF PHAZE

Piers Anthony

NEW ENGLISH LIBRARY

British Library Cataloguing in Publication Data

Anthony, Piers, *1934–*
   Out of Phaze.
   I. Title
   813′.54[F]

   ISBN 0–450–42924–5
   ISBN 0–450–42930–X Pbk

First published in Great Britain 1989

Reproduced by arrangement with
G. P. Putnam's Sons, New York, USA
Published by New English Library,
a hardcover imprint of Hodder and Stoughton,
a division of Hodder and Stoughton Ltd,
Mill Road, Dunton Green, Sevenoaks, Kent TN13 2YE
Editorial Office: 47 Bedford Square, London WC1B 3DP

Printed and bound in Great Britain by
Biddles Limited, Guildford and King's Lynn

Contents

ACKNOWLEDGMENTS

The author wishes to acknowledge
the suggestion of Dana Fond
that caused this novel to
come into existence after the series
was believed to be closed.

Giants

Goblins

Yellow Demesnes

Demo

Ogres

West Pole

Black Demesnes

Oracle's Palace

Translucent Demesnes

Green Demesnes

Harpies

Orange Demesnes

Animal Heads

Dragons

Purple Mountains

© 1987 STORRINGS

White Mountains

Brown River

Red River

White
Demesnes

Lattice

Vampires

East Pole

ake

Blue
Demesnes

Red
Demesnes

nicorns

Mound Folk

Werewolves

Brown
Demesnes

Trolls

PHAZE

Giadom

West Pole

Gobdom

Lake

Anidom

Hardom

Purple Mountains

© 1987 STORRINGS

1

Mach

The two young men dived into the pool. Mach struck the water more precisely and got the lead, but Rory splashed harder and caught him a third of the way along, then drove ahead for the victory. Panting and ruddy-faced with his effort, he laughed as Mach finished. "Slowpoke!"

Mach shrugged. He had expected to lose, because his power was produced evenly; he could not put forth that extra surge of energy for a spot activity. However, neither did he tire; he could maintain a similar pace indefinitely. Had the race been longer, he would have won.

Rory knew that, of course; it was only the luck of the grid that had given him the victory. He liked to tease Mach about his supposed unwillingness to try harder. It was his human way, for he was fully human. Mach was, of course, unhuman in all but form and consciousness.

They shook themselves dry and watched while two girls lined up at the far end of the pool for their own contest. Both were young and well-formed, with tresses that fell down about their breasts with the provocative suggestion of clothing. One waved.

"Hey, I think they're following us!" Rory exclaimed. "Let's wait for them!"

"Yes, they collaborated to match our choice of contest," Mach agreed.

Rory squinted as the two young women dived in, wincing as one made a bad entry. "Android," he muttered. "They're clumsy."

"Less so than prior generations," Mach said. "Soon the androids will be up to the human norm in coordination and intellect."

"I'd rather have them clumsy and stupid," Rory said.

"So you can love them and leave them," Mach agreed. They had been over this before. The human male was easily aroused, but also easily satisfied. Mach himself could invoke his arousal circuit, and could also nullify it, but preferred to do neither. He wished that his body could move his mind in the involuntary natural human fashion, but it never happened.

The girls completed their race and heaved themselves dripping from the pool. The breasts of the android bounced as she shook herself. The other girl was more diffident, standing somewhat awkwardly, so that her body did not show to advantage.

"Looking for company?" Rory asked, his eyes traveling up and down the android's body.

"You're human, aren't you?" the android inquired. "I'd like to trade."

"Favors?" Rory asked, licking his lips.

"Companions."

Rory nodded. "Sure, why not! Here's Mach." He hauled on Mach's elbow.

"Here's Agape," the android said, giving the other girl a little shove. "I'm Narda."

"I'm Rory. Let's go somewhere."

The two walked away, leaving Mach with Agape. He had not sought her company, but found himself thus abruptly committed.

"I don't believe I have seen you before," he said to the girl. Actually, he was sure of it; his memory for detail was of course infallible.

"I'm new," she agreed, speaking with an odd accent. "I just arrived yesterday. Narda was showing me the Game."

And now Mach was obliged to take over the task the android had been assigned. Well, he really had nothing better to do. "I will show you whatever you wish, Agape," he said, carefully pronouncing her name the way the android had, three syllables with the accent on the first. "But I should advise you at the outset that I already have a liaison with one of your sex."

"My apology if I am violating a custom," Agape said. "Are liaisons required?"

"They are not. But sometimes they are expected." He studied her more closely. "Are you android? You seem different."

"I am—alien," she said. "This is not my natural form. But I was advised that if I wished to participate in this experiment, it was best to assume it. Have I given offense?"

Alien! No wonder! "No offense." Mach became more interested as his circuits grappled with the shift of concept. He had never interacted this closely with a humanoid alien before. The experimental community consisted of human beings, robots, androids and cyborgs, all in perfect human form, and in the course of the past year there had been a number of changes as individuals were shifted from one city to another. The purpose was to create a new, egalitarian society in which no serfs were ghettoized. It seemed to be working, and now these integrated serfs were being spread about the planet of Proton so as to bring the enlightened attitude to all. Whether that latest effort was to be successful remained in doubt; the wider society of Citizens and serfs clung to its prejudices as if they were points in the Tourney.

Now aliens were being included. This was ambitious indeed. Mach perceived the input of his father in that. Citizen Blue had been laboring for twenty years to revamp the society of Proton, and had accomplished a great deal. Obviously the effort was not slackening.

"Is my presence a burden to you?" Agape inquired.

"It is not. I was merely assessing the implications."

"I am concerned that I merge inadequately."

"This is to be expected at the beginning," Mach said. "I will show you the premises."

"This is appreciated."

He took her through the stations of the Game Annex, explaining how any legitimate resident was free to play any of the games of the grid. He told her how many serfs, including himself, practiced the Game diligently, because each year there was a Game Tourney whose winner was granted Citizenship and became a member of the ruling class. Apparently Narda had simply brought her along without explanation, and dumped her at the first opportunity. This was not proper behavior, but allowances had to be made for androids. They tended to be less socially aware than others were.

He brought her to a cubicle and showed her the two panels. "This is the selection mechanism," he explained. "You stand at one, and I stand at the other. Each panel presents the primary grid, with the numbered terms across the top, and the lettered ones down the side. One player chooses from the numbers, the other from the letters. On my grid the letters are highlighted, so I must choose from them. On yours it will be the numbers."

"Yes," she agreed. "They read '1. PHYSICAL, 2. MENTAL, 3. CHANCE, 4. ARTS.' But I do not grasp what they mean."

"You must select one. If you wish to indulge in a physical competition, touch 1. If you prefer mental, touch 2. I will touch one of mine, and where they intersect will define the nature of our game."

"How very clever," she said. "I shall touch the first."

"It is not necessary to tell me your choice. It is the mystery of it that provides much of the appeal." But since this was only a demonstration, Mach checked his choices of A. NAKED, B. TOOL, C. MACHINE and D. ANIMAL, and touched B. He was of course a machine himself, but that made no difference here. Citizen Blue had given the self-willed machines serf status, which meant they could play the Game.

The square for PHYSICAL/TOOL brightened, then expanded into a new pattern. "This is the secondary grid," Mach explained. "It helps to define the tool-assisted physical games. We must choose again—you from the lettered ones, I from the numbered ones, this time."

"E. EARTH, F. FIRE, G. GAS, H. H20," she read. "I don't believe I understand."

"They really stand for the type of surface on which the game is to be played," Mach said. "Flat, Variable, Discontinuous or Liquid. Some programmer decided to get clever with the letters, matching them up with words. It is true that the earth is normally a flat surface, and fire forms a variable surface, and gas is discontinuous if you seek to stand on it, and H2O stands for water, which is a liquid. All you need be concerned about is the nature of the surface upon which you prefer to play, whether flat, or like a mountain, or—"

"Thank you," she said, and touched her choice.

His own choices were 5. SEPARATE, 6. INTERACTIVE, 7. COMBAT and 8. COOPERATIVE. He touched the second.

The square for FLAT SURFACE/INTERACTIVE brightened. Now the grid became a smaller one of nine boxes, with a list of terms at the side. "We get to fill in this one ourselves," he explained. "Choose any game that you like."

"I do not know these games," she protested. "Marbles, earthball, *Jeu de boules*—"

Because she was alien. All the common flat-surface ball games were unknown to her.

"We'll simplify it," he said. "We'll fill the entire subgrid with one game, tiddlywinks. Then I'll show you how to play that."

And so they did. Their selection made, they adjourned to a chamber with a table, and thereon was the tiddlywinks set. Mach showed her how to make one chip jump when pressured by another, and she was delighted. They played the game, and he won, but she was quite satisfied. Now she had a notion how things were done on the Planet of Proton.

They exited the Game Annex. Mach would have preferred to go his own way, but was uncertain how to dispose of Agape. He had been given a commitment to assist her, and though he knew the basis for that assignment was largely spurious, he also knew that she needed guidance, and that he was a more responsible guide than the android Narda had been. Thus he could not let it go as casually as he had undertaken it.

"Am I now becoming a burden to you, Mach?" she inquired nervously.

"This is true," he agreed. "But I conclude that I should assist you further, so that you will be able to handle our society alone."

She made an uncertain laugh, as though both the act and the basis for it were novelties. "You are unlike Narda."

"She is an android. I am a robot."

She turned her head to gaze at him with perplexity. "I had assumed you were android or human, like the others. You resemble those."

"I am crafted to resemble them, just as you are. But my interior operations are no more human than are yours." He spotted a dining region. "Do you wish to eat?"

"That is appealing," she agreed.

He guided her to one of the food dispensers. "You may describe whatever you wish, and it will craft it for you," he said.

"I am incompletely familiar with local custom. Perhaps I should attempt whatever you choose to consume."

Mach smiled. "Oh, I don't have to eat. My power cell takes care of my energy needs."

"Yes, of course; you are a machine. Perhaps we should dispense with this activity, in that case."

Mach considered. He suspected that she was hungry, but so anxious about making an error of custom that she was afraid to make her own choice. "I *can* eat," he said. "I merely do not need to. Suppose I order nutro-drink for each of us?"

"My gratitude." Indeed, she was almost fawning.

He placed the order, and in a moment they had two tall containers of the beverage, complete with straws.

"Is it permissible to be private?" she asked.

"Certainly." He showed the way to a booth, and the curtain closed about them, cutting off all sight and sound of the remainder of the dining alcove.

Mach sipped his drink, using the straw. Agape hesitated. "It is a matter of generating a partial vacuum in the mouth," he explained. "That causes the pressure of the air to push the fluid up through the straw."

"My concern is not of that nature," she said. "I am an alien, amoebic in nature. I can maintain the human form for ordinary pursuits, but am unable to do so for imbibation. I am concerned that my mode of assimilation would be a social indiscretion in your presence."

"I will of course leave the booth if you prefer," Mach said. "But I am scientifically interested in your biology, and I am not subject to annoyance because of differing modes of operation."

Still she hesitated. "Narda termed it 'gross.' I believe that is why she preferred to separate herself from me."

Androids were notorious for their crudities of behavior and humor. What could Narda have found gross? "Please be reassured, Agape. I am a machine. I have no emotion not programmed, and even those can be evoked or revoked at will. Nothing you might do would dismay me."

"You are certain?"

"I am certain."

"Then I shall assimilate this material."

She put her hands to the container and stretched it wide, so that it gradually reformed into a broad, shallow dish. Mach had known how malleable the material was, as the empty containers were normally compacted into balls and rolled into the recycling hopper, but he had never before seen a person reform one while it was full of fluid.

Now she leaned forward, bringing her head directly over the dish. Her features melted, the nose, eyes, ears and mouth disappearing. Her head receded into her neck, and her breasts lifted to join it, forming a single globular mass above the table. This mass flattened and descended until it covered the full dish. The flesh dipped into the beverage.

In the course of the next few minutes the beverage disappeared, absorbed into the pancake-shaped mass of flesh. The amoeba was assimilating nourishment in the fashion of its kind.

Then the mass lifted, forming another glob. The glob stretched out, narrowing to form the neck, bulging below to fashion breasts, and shaping gradually back into the human features above. The configuration he recognized as Agape returned, features clean, eyes and mouth closed.

The eyes opened, and then the mouth. "Do you wish to depart my presence now?" she asked.

"No. I find your process of assimilation fascinating."

"It is not gross to you?"

"It is educational to me. I appreciate being shown it."

She looked at him without further comment. He remembered to resume work on his own drink.

"If I may inquire without offense," she said, "how is it that you, a machine, have been crafted in human form? I have seen other machines in other forms, suited to their tasks."

"I am what is known as a humanoid robot. I have been crafted to resemble a living human being as closely as is feasible, in both the physical and mental states. It is part of my father's effort to integrate the self-willed machines into the society of Proton. If humanoid ones can be successful at this, then the nonhumanoid ones can follow."

"But do not human beings grow from small creatures formed within the bodies of their parents? Surely you have a maker, not a father."

"I have a father and a mother," Mach said firmly. "My father is Citizen Blue, an immigrant from the frame of Phaze. My mother is Sheen, a female robot. It is possible for a female robot to be implanted with a human egg-cell that can be fertilized internally by a human male, and for her to nourish that cell in the laboratory of her body and birth it in the human fashion, becoming a surrogate mother to his child. But Sheen elected not to be modified to accommodate this; she preferred to have a robot baby, like herself. Therefore I am a robot, but my basic programming makes my awareness and intellectual quotient very similar to those of my father."

"But then you were constructed as an adult, fully formed as you are now."

"I was crafted as a robot baby, incontinent and untrained. I was adjusted for growth on a weekly basis, trained and educated by hand. Periodically my metal skeletal structure was replaced, and my wiring revamped, but I never changed size or appearance in any large step. In this manner I proceeded in the course of sixteen years to my present size, and thereafter have remained constant. I was put through normal human schooling, along with the androids, cyborgs and human beings of my group. I regard myself as a human being in all except flesh."

"You are very like a human being," she agreed. "I did not realize your nature until you advised me. But what is the point of this significant effort?"

"To demonstrate that complete integration of the diverse intelligent elements of our society is feasible," he replied. "In the past there has been discrimination against robots, cyborgs and androids. In the future all will participate on an equal basis."

"And perhaps aliens too," she agreed. "Now the rationale behind my own participation becomes clear. I was not informed by my own planetary authorities; I was simply given my assignment. Your father is a perceptive being."

"This is true. But the job is not yet complete, and there is substantial opposition. We must all be careful."

"Opposition? I did not realize."

"The majority of Citizens would have preferred to retain the prior system, in which only chosen human beings had power, and only human beings were eligible to compete for Citizenship."

"You mentioned this before. What is a Citizen?"

"A member of the governing class of Proton. Citizens have enormous power, and the right to wear clothing. We serfs must address any Citizen as 'sir' and obey any directive he gives."

"But I had understood that serfs had opportunity to achieve power. That if I succeeded in accommodating myself to this society, such opportunity would become mine."

"This is true, but such opportunity is limited. A Citizen can confer an inheritance of his position on a designated heir, the new Citizen to exist when the old Citizen dies or abdicates. It is understood that when my father dies, I will assume his Citizen status, and be perhaps the first robot Citizen. But there is doubt that this will come to pass, because the Council of Citizens may succeed in outlawing such accession. It is also possible for any serf to win Citizenship through the annual Tourney, as I mentioned; this is in effect how Blue obtained his position, though it was actually won by his alternate self."

"Alternate self? Is this an aspect of human existence?"

Mach smiled. "In a manner. Most residents of Proton have an analog in the sister-frame of Phaze, wherein science is supposed to be inoperative and magic is operative. I find this difficult to credit, but my father claims it is so, and I am not programmed to believe him to be in error. It is at any rate academic, as there is no access to Phaze."

Agape brightened. "A human myth!" she exclaimed. "A thing known to be untrue, but believed regardless."

"That seems to be a reasonable view of the matter," he agreed.

"Do you, a machine, have any desire for the future?"

"None that can be realized."

"But perhaps a myth? A hope you would possess if it were reasonable?"

"I would desire to be alive," Mach said.

"Yet you are not, and can never be."

"Therefore it is pointless to desire it," he concluded.

Again she gazed at him in her somewhat disconcertingly alien manner. "I think that I shall now be able to exist in this society. I thank you for your assistance. Perhaps at some point I may be able to render you a similar favor of comprehension."

"There is no need."

They stood and left the booth.

"Ha!" a young woman cried, spotting them. She had hair that was almost orange, that flounced about her shoulders as she moved. "So it's true!"

Mach knew that he was in for a difficult scene. "Doris, allow me to explain—" he began.

"Shut in a booth with another woman!" she flared. "With the privacy curtain in place! I don't need any explanation for that!"

"But we weren't doing anything," he protested. "Agape required assistance—"

"I can guess what kind!" Doris cried, eying Agape's torso. "Just couldn't wait to get your hands on some alien flesh, could you!"

"I do not understand," Agape said. "Have I committed an error of protocol?"

"Protocol!" Doris said. "Is that what you call it? Melting in his arms?"

"She didn't—" Mach began.

"I did melt," Agape agreed. "But not for his arms."

"Don't tell me for what part of him you melted!" Doris cried. She whirled to confront Mach. "And I thought *I* was your girl! You're just like any other male! The moment you see a chance to grab something new—"

"You misunderstand—" Mach said.

"Not any more! You and I are through!"

"Please listen," Mach said, reaching out to her. "I never—"

Doris stepped in and slapped him resoundingly on the cheek. "Don't lie to me, metal-heart!"

By this time a small crowd had gathered to admire the proceedings. One young man stepped up. "Is this machine bothering you, Doris?"

"Stay out of this, Ware!" Mach snapped, allowing his emotional circuits to govern in the human manner. Ware was an android, and Mach had had enough android-sponsored trouble for this day.

"Yeah? Make me!"

Doris' gaze passed from one to the other appraisingly. She was a cyborg, and by all accounts there were ghosts in those machines. A person could never be quite certain what a cyborg would do. "Yes, why don't you make him?" she asked Mach.

She was trying to promote a combat between them! Mach had to head that off, in the interest of species harmony; he knew how his father would react to any such episode.

"The Game," Mach said. "We'll settle this in the Game."

Ware laughed coarsely. "The Game? Why should I bother? Why not just settle it right here?"

Naturally the android didn't care what kind of a scene he made; he had nothing to lose, and perhaps a lot to gain. He had no chance at future Citizenship, because he wasn't the son of a Citizen or an expert Gamesman himself, but he could interfere with Mach's chance—for himself and his kind.

"For a prize," Mach said. "To make it worthwhile."

"What worthwhile prize could you have to offer? You're just a serf, like me!"

Doris smiled. "I'll be the prize," she said. "Winner gets my favor."

"No—" Mach began.

But Ware's eyes were lighting. He had always had a hankering for Doris, but until this moment she had not given him any positive signal. "Good enough! For Doris!" he agreed.

"Can a person be a trophy?" Agape asked, perplexed.

"Why not?" Doris asked with satisfaction. "*You* were!"

Mach wished he had the circuitry for a human sigh. He would have to put his relationship with Doris, which had been generally a good one, on the line. She was angry with him for insufficient cause, but had found a way to hurt him. He would have to go through with it.

They went to the Game Annex. They stood at opposite grid stations and touched their choices. Mach had the numbers, so selected 2. MENTAL, to nullify the android's advantage of temporary strength and throw it into the android's weakness of intellect. Ware selected B. TOOL, throwing it into the huge general category of tool-assisted mental games. Mach was strong here, so his prospects were brightening.

The subgrid for this category differed from that for the physical games. Mach had the numbers again: 5. SEPARATE, 6. INTERACTIVE, 7. PUZZLE, 8. COOPERATIVE. Ware had the letters: E. BOARD, F. CARDS, G. PAPER, H. GENERAL.

Mach chose 7. PUZZLE, trusting that his wit was quicker than the android's. Ware chose H. GENERAL, which broadened the range of choices.

They filled in the sub-subgrid with various types of mechanical puzzles: jigsaw, matches, string, knots, cube assembly, Rubic cube and a labyrinth. When the final choices were paired, the result was the labyrinth. Well, Mach should be able to solve that faster than the android could.

"Hey, didn't you run that one this morning, Ware?" a bystander called.

"Yeah," Ware replied, satisfied.

Oh-oh. The format of the labyrinth was changed on a daily basis. A player never could know which variant or detail it would have—unless that player had experienced it on the same day. Ware had gotten a major break.

Or had he made his own break, knowing that Mach preferred mental or tool-assisted games, and liked puzzles? Had he somehow planned for this encounter? If so, he was smarter or more determined than Mach had credited.

Still, Mach had run the labyrinth many times, and was familiar with most of its variants. He might not be at as great a disadvantage as he feared. There were interactive properties that could nullify advance knowledge.

They adjourned to the labyrinth chamber. This time it was set up in the form of a huge circle with three entrances. Doris was designated the Damsel in Distress, and Mach was the Rescuing Hero, and Ware was the Monster. Mach's object was to find and rescue the Damsel before the Monster found her and dragged her away to his lair. If Mach could bring her out his entrance, he would be the victor; if Ware brought her out his, he was. The Damsel was required to go with whomever touched her first. In a double sense, Mach realized.

He had kept company with her because, as a cyborg, she had the body of a robot and the mind of a human being. She had originally been human, but an accident to her body had rendered it inoperable, so her brain had been transplanted to the machine, where it was maintained in a bath of nutrients and connected to the machine's perceptive and operating units. Such mergers had always been problematical, for no human brain could align perfectly with anything other than a human body, but as cyborgs went she had been more sensible than most. She had been given the finest of bodies, which she delighted to use for every purpose, and because she was both human and machine, she understood Mach's ambivalence. He had one human and one machine parent; having experienced the machine existence, he longed for the human one, the other face of his coin. Doris had actually known both, and that made her endlessly fascinating. But she did have that erratic streak, which could make her difficult to deal with at times. Evidently she was toying with the notion of having physical relations with a flesh creature, having satisfied herself about those with a nonflesh creature. Now that she was angry with him, she was using this notion to force him to respond.

All because he had tried to help the alien female get adjusted. Yet Agape had been in genuine need; what else could he have done? A machine could have ignored her plight, but a human being would have helped, and it was the human model he preferred to emulate.

They entered at their doors. The game was on.

It was gloomy inside, but his vision adjusted automatically to the changed conditions. He could see well enough. The passage curved and recurved and divided. There was no way to be sure which passage would lead most directly to intersect with Doris' door; he would have to depend on speed and memory, learning the maze as he went. For the trick was not merely to find the Damsel first, it was to bring her back out. If he got her, but then the Monster intercepted them, he would probably be lost, because the Monster was by definition the stronger of the two males, and would win any direct encounter. This was counterbalanced by the Damsel's established preference for the Hero; she would try to help him find her, and would even search for him, while trying to avoid the Monster. If the Hero touched her first, she would go quietly wherever he led; if the Monster caught her, she would go with him, but would scream all the way, making it easier for the Hero to intercept them and perhaps prevent the Monster from making his exit.

Now Mach heard her screams. The Monster had caught her already! How could it have happened so quickly?

But as he moved on, he realized that the sounds were wrong. Doris was still alone. She wasn't exactly screaming, she was calling. "Hero! Hero!" she called. "Come find me!"

The fool! Didn't she realize that the Monster could hear her just as well as the Hero could? Since Ware was already familiar with this variant of the maze, the advantage would be his; he could go directly to her without false detours.

Then Mach heard his rival, pounding along a nearby passage. Ware knew where he was going, certainly!

Well, there was one way to even things up: he could follow the Monster! Mach ducked into a cul-de-sac, hiding, as the android passed, then emerged and pursued him quietly. Soon they both arrived at the Damsel's site. As Ware closed on her, she neither screamed nor fled as she was supposed to; she simply waited for him. Had she forgotten all the conventions of this game?

Ware slowed, approaching her. He reached out his hand to tag her, and she extended her hand to him.

Something very like human emotion took Mach. *Doris was trying to give the victory to Ware!*

Mach launched himself at the back of the Monster. By striking by surprise, at the moment the rival's attention was distracted by imminent victory, he might score against him; the Game Computer allowed for such tactics. All he had to do was touch Ware from behind—

"Look out!" Doris cried.

Ware, alerted, swung around to meet Mach's charge. They collided, face to face.

"Hero killed," the voice of the Game Computer announced.

Thanks to Doris' betrayal, Mach had lost the game—and her favor.

Back in his private serf chamber, Mach pondered the ramifications. He had thought that Doris' anger with him was a misunderstanding, spawned by his appearance with the alien female. Now he realized that he had misjudged the cyborg. She had grown tired of him, but preferred a pretext to separate. After all, if she formally broke up with him, others might conclude that she liked breaking hearts (or power cells, as the case might be) and be wary of her, leaving her without male company. She was not the sort to risk that. So she had engineered it so that another male had taken her away from Mach. That left her nominally innocent. She had had her prospective companion, the android Ware, get his fellow android Narda to set Mach up with Agape, then had sought out the pair and made a scene—with Ware handily near. How cunning! Then she had worked to ensure Ware's victory, by "misplaying" her part, and finally openly betraying Mach. Thus he, Mach, had become the butt of the play. Had he "won" her, then there would have been no onus on her, and she could have tried another ploy at another time.

So he was without a girlfriend—and perhaps had been for longer than he had realized. What was he, after all, except a machine—that could not even experience the grief that a human or android or even alien being would at such a situation! No wonder Doris had grown tired of him. Living creatures had genuine emotions that made them less predictable and more interesting. How he wished he could be alive!

He lay on his bed, which he didn't really need because it was not necessary for him to sleep, and invoked his creative circuit. This was newly developed, and had been installed only a few months ago. He had taken to playing with it at odd moments, savoring the illusion of erratic thought. It had random factors included, so that the same starting thought could lead to different results, some of them only marginally logical. Living creatures were capable of illogic, and that was part of their appeal. Even the cyborg Doris, with her inanimate body and living brain, could be marvelously illogical when she chose. Mach wanted that capacity for himself, but so far had never been able to originate a truly illogical thought process. The circuit was only a circuit; he could reflect on it, but it did not govern him. He always knew the illogic for what it was, and that prevented him from being truly alive.

Now he tried a special variant. He tried to imagine himself in the mysterious frame of Phaze, where magic supposedly operated and science did not. That was so illogical that it would represent a monumental leap of belief on his part. If he could successfully believe that, he could believe almost anything—including the possibility of somehow coming alive.

He imagined having a living brother his own age, there in Phaze. No, not a brother—an alternate self, who bore the same relation to him that Stile did to Citizen Blue. The same person he was, only split apart from his reality, existing in that nonreality of Phaze. It was of course nonsensical to postulate a robot having an alternate self—but no more so than the notion of a land of magic. How convenient that that land was forever sealed off from Proton, according to his father's story! No way to prove or disprove it! What *had* happened, a generation ago? Had Stile exchanged places with another Galactic called Blue, who had been raised on another planet in the galaxy? Called it "a fantastic world" and that was how the idea of fantasy started? But now Mach concentrated, trying to believe in the literal magic, in the living boy just like himself, with whom he might establish rapport. He tried to force the delusion on himself, to make himself irrational. If only he could believe!

Then, almost, it seemed that he achieved it. Something like a thought came to him: *Who are you?* A thought he might not have originated. A living thought.

I am Mach! he thought back. *Let's exchange places!* As the android girl had done, boldly offering to change companions, and succeeding.

All right—for a moment, the thought came back. His imagination was achieving a new level! It really seemed like another person thinking.

Mach made a special effort of concentration and longing—and suddenly experienced a strange wrenching. Alarmed, he eased off; had he blown a circuit? He felt quite strange.

Then he opened his eyes.

His room had changed.

2

Fleta

Room? It was no longer a room at all! It was a forest glade. He was sitting on a rock in its center.

Mach blinked. Sometimes dust fouled his lenses and distorted his vision; the act of blinking normally cleared it.

The glade remained. Late afternoon sunlight slanted down to touch the thickly braided vines and leaves at one side, and grass grew ankle-deep in the center. None of this existed, of course, in his room.

Mach got up and went to the edge, intrigued to discover how far this illusion carried. He touched a broad leaf—and it felt genuine. He pulled on a vine, and it resisted his effort, being springy.

He had tried to switch places with his phantom twin—and found himself here. Was there really a twin, and had he really switched—or had he merely succeeded in establishing his belief in the impossible? Surely the latter—but this still represented a significant victory. He had achieved illogic!

Moved by the wonder of it, he walked around the edge of the

glade. He found a path leading from it, twisting like a serpent between the large trees until it disappeared in the distance. Should he follow this?

He looked down at himself, considering—and made another phenomenal discovery. He was clothed! He wore boots, trousers and a long-sleeved shirt—all blue. He had been so distracted by the living glade that he had not noticed his own condition!

His first reaction was shock. He was impersonating a Citizen! That could get him ejected from the planet! Only in very special situations, such as in costumed drama in the Game, were serfs permitted apparel.

His second was wonder. How had he come by such an outfit? Had he taken it from his father's collection? Citizen Blue did prefer this color. But Mach would have had to be crazy to do such a thing, and that was a state a robot was incapable of achieving.

Or was it? Wasn't believing the impossible a condition of insanity? If he could convince himself that he was in a glade instead of his room, could he likewise garb himself in his father's clothing without realizing? If so, this effect was dangerous!

Quickly he removed the clothing. But he discovered as he did so that it fit him perfectly. This was odd, because Mach was five centimeters taller than Citizen Blue. The Citizen was a very small man whose enormous political power more than made up for his lack of physical stature. Mach could have been any height he chose, but did not want to create any awkwardness for his father, so he had compromised by assuming his mother's height. This put him in the low-average range for women, and well below average for men. But he had long since realized that physical height was not the most important aspect of individual importance, so he was satisfied. But now—how could he have worn his father's clothing without it binding on him? This clothing seemed to have been fitted specifically for his own body.

His thoughts were interrupted by an appearance in the sky. It seemed to be a huge, grotesque bird—but what a bird! Mach stared disbelievingly. He had studied birds, learning the major types, because Birdwatching was one of the events in the Game. No bird like this was listed. This one had a huge, misshapen head, and dangling breasts like those of an old woman.

A what, and *what?* Mach shook his head and looked again, but the creature had already disappeared.

He knew what it was, however. The description fit that of a harpy—a mythical construct, part avian, part human. The appearance of such a creature was of course another impossibility. Even if some sinister laboratory had crafted an android in that guise, the dynamics of flight would have rendered the harpy groundbound. The necessary wingspan and muscular attachments—

Mach found his heart beating rapidly. The implausibilities of his situation were threatening to overwhelm his equilibrium! He was not encountering just one unbelievable thing, but a complex of them! Trees, clothing, mythology—

His *heart?* He *had* no heart! He was a robot!

Mach set his right palm at his chest. He felt the beating of it. He lifted his left hand, set his right fingers against the wrist beside the large tendon and pressed in. Again he felt that steady beat.

He was breathing, too. He had always been able to breathe, so as to be able to talk, but it had been optional, never necessary, and he normally didn't bother unless in company. Now he held his breath—and in moments was uncomfortable, exactly as if becoming starved for oxygen.

He reached under his left arm, seeking the stud that opened a panel there. He found none. Slowly he moved his fingers to his forearm. He pinched the skin there, hard.

Pain flared, and in a moment a red spot appeared where his fingernail had dug into the skin.

Mach had to lean against a tree to keep from reeling. *He was alive!* His body was fashioned of flesh; it had a heart, and it felt direct pain.

Now he knew that he had suffered a far greater breakthrough than he had anticipated. He had made his belief in the impossible total, and stepped into the realm of the living. Of course this could not be literal, but even as a dream it was astonishing, for robots did not dream. That new circuit had really performed! He had achieved what no robot had ever done before: fashioned a total illusion of life.

But now that he had done this, what had he really accomplished? Metallic insanity? Was his body lying on the bed while his brain was locked into its own program of fantasy? That could be fun for a while, but after a few hours he would be in trouble, because his mother would discover him and bring in a technician to repair the glitch. If the case were judged to be too extreme, they would reprogram his brain unit, wiping out everything he had accomplished here, including the memory of it. He would be forever after bound to his natural robotic state.

That, he realized, would be disaster. He was delighted to have achieved this breakthrough. To generate even the facsimile of life, even within his dream—in fact, the mere fact of the dream was extraordinary. He had to preserve and improve this ability—which meant he had to master the technique of releasing himself from it. It would be best if no one else know of this accomplishment, until he had perfected it.

He concentrated, trying to release the dream. Nothing happened. He remained in the glade, his heart still beating, his breath still breathing.

He didn't know how to turn off the dream. But perhaps he wasn't helpless. His dream had to have limits; if he explored beyond those limits, he might force it to abort.

He started down the path. He didn't care where it went; he just meant to follow it beyond the definition that it had. To force the issue.

The path wound through the forest, following a contour. Parts of it were rocky, and he discovered that his feet were tender. Since he had gone barefoot for all his existence, and his soles had been of toughened pseudoflesh, this was a surprise. But it was consistent with the illusion of living flesh, especially if it was supposed to have used boots.

He came to a fork in the path. Which way should he go? One path led downward, the other upward. He felt thirsty, which was another aspect of the verisimilitude of this dream, so he took the one leading down. There might be a river there.

There was indeed a stream. The water wended lazily through a swampy region. The path descended into this and disappeared. Mach considered, then got down flat and put his lips to the closest clear water he spied. He sucked, employing the physics that he had described to Agape.

Agape? How far away the alien female seemed now!

There was a sudden snort behind him. He jerked his head up, twisting about to look back. It was a man—with the head of a pig. The snout was flattened in the porcine manner, and cruel tusks glinted at the sides of the mouth.

Mach scrambled up. The pighead stepped aggressively forward. Somehow it reminded him of Ware, the android.

"Now look, creature," Mach said nervously. "I don't want to bother you. I just want to drink." For the mouthful he had taken in wasn't enough.

"Zdringk!" the pighead snorted. "Owrs!"

He was claiming this drinking-spot? "Then I'll drink farther along," Mach said, trying to edge around the creature.

"Zrriverr owrs!" the pighead proclaimed.

"The whole *river* is yours? But that's unreasonable!"

The pighead lowered his head and ground his tusks together. It seemed that he was not about to be reasonable. He reminded Mach even more strongly of the android.

Mach considered again. He was thirsty, and this seemed to be the only reasonable source of water. If he gave this up, he wasn't sure where or when he would find another drinking place. He would have to stand his ground.

"I feel that I have about as much right to drink as you do," he said. "Please allow me to—"

The pighead squealed with rage. Immediately there was a rustling in the vicinity, and the sound of feet striking the ground. Several other pigmen appeared—and several pigwomen too. All were naked and completely humanoid, the females quite attractively so, except for the heads. All looked menacing.

The pigheads blocked off the path. Mach had to retreat into the water. He discovered that the path continued under the surface, firm though slippery; he could proceed without getting dunked, as it was only knee-deep.

The pigheads followed him a little way, but then halted, snorting angrily. Mach went on—and abruptly stepped off the edge and landed up to his waist in water-covered muck. He should have watched where he was going!

There was a hiss. He looked—and spied a man swimming

toward him. Relieved, but cautious, he scrambled back to the firm path, and stood knee-deep as the man came close.

And the man turned out to be only the head of a man. The body was that of a monstrous python, undulating through the water.

Mach had thought this was a dream. But he had never heard or read of either pigmen or snakemen, and his computer-type brain was not strong on creative imagination. If he had tried to populate this dream, he would have done it with conventional monsters. In fact, he would not have used monsters at all; he would have made it a completely satisfactory setting, for his own delight. This did not make sense.

"Ourss!" the snakeman hissed, his head lifting above the water. Beyond him, other heads appeared in the water.

Mach realized why the pigheads had stopped their pursuit. Their territory ended where that of the snakefolk began.

He looked back, but saw the pigheads still clustered at the edge of the swamp. He would have to proceed forward.

"I'm going!" he said, and sloshed along the path. He had to slide his bare feet forward under the water to make sure the firm path continued, lest he get dunked again. He wasn't sure what the snakes would do to him if they caught him, but didn't care to find out.

Fortunately there was no pursuit. As he moved he continued to ponder. If this was not the kind of situation his robot brain would or could have created, how could he account for his dream? The answer was that he could not. But the alternative was to assume that it was not a dream. That suggested that it was reality.

Had he really been transported to the land he had sought, Phaze? By switching places with his twin? Of course a physical exchange could not have occurred. But a mental one—that did seem plausible. His consciousness was in the body of his twin— and his twin's consciousness must be in Mach's own body.

Mach's lips pursed in a soundless whistle. This thesis was reasonable—but what would a human person do in the body of a machine?

The path led to an island rising out of the swamp. Relieved, Mach sloshed toward it—and stepped off the path again, taking another messy dunking. The path curved about, as it had on land, and he had to check for it constantly.

He drew himself out of the muck, then proceeded to the island. It was thickly overgrown with reeds and brush and small trees, but the path was clear. This was certainly better than the water.

Mach rounded a bend—and came across a worse monster than before. It was a man—with the head of a giant roach. The antennae waved and the complicated insectoid mouth-parts quivered. The thing looked hungry.

Mach backed away—but another roach-head came onto the path behind him. He was trapped.

Well, not quite. He leaped into the brush to the side. Too late he discovered that it was solid brambles; the thorns raked along his legs and torso stingingly. Yet the roach-heads were blocking the path, their ugly mandibles working. He had not been programmed to abhor roaches; indeed, they did not exist in the natural state in the frame of Proton. But his living body evidently loathed the notion of contact with such creatures, and certainly he didn't want those mandibles chewing into his tender flesh.

Trapped between unacceptable alternatives, Mach let his body govern. His head went back and he screamed. "Heeelp!"

There was a distant sound of music. Then an approaching beat. It sounded as if a horse were approaching.

Mach screamed again. He knew how to ride a horse; that was one of the Game challenges. If the creature were tame, or even if it weren't—if he could somehow get on it—but of course it was tame, for he heard the music of the rider.

In a very brief time the beat became splashing. The horse was charging through the water. Maybe there was a patrol whose duty was to come to the aid of distressed travelers. Mach called again, making sure the rider could find him.

Now it thundered onto the island, the music of its rider becoming loud. It sounded as though a flute were playing, or several of them. The roach-heads abruptly scuttled into the brush, apparently not bothered by the brambles.

"Here!" Mach cried.

The horse came into sight.

It bore no rider. It was glossy black, with golden socklike

coloration on the two hind legs. From the forehead sprouted a long spiraled horn.

This was a unicorn.

Mach was beyond caring at this point. "I beg you, beautiful creature—carry me from here!" he called.

The unicorn stopped. It was a mare, not large for a horse, but in fit condition. Her head turned toward Mach. She sounded a double note of query.

The horn was making the music! Citizen Blue had mentioned this, long ago, but Mach had assumed this was mere embellishment of a tale told to a child. Now he realized that it was literal. His father had come from this frame, and had known unicorns.

Mach pulled himself painfully from the brambles. His body was bleeding in several places. "If you will carry me—" he repeated, afraid the mare would bolt before he could mount her.

But she made an acquiescent note. He came up to her and scrambled onto her back, taking firm hold of her glossy mane. "My gratitude to you, lovely creature!" he gasped.

She started walking, then trotting, wending her way on along the narrow path with sure-footed confidence. As she moved, she played a pretty double melody on her marvelous horn. Mach was good at music, both because he had been programmed for perfect pitch and because it was a useful talent in the Game; he knew quality when he heard it, and that horn was as good as an instrument could be. To think that a mere animal could do it so well! There was no further sign of the roach-heads; evidently the music warned them away.

The path proceeded to the other side of the island and back into the water. The animal trod it with confidence, evidently knowing exactly where to place her hooves. The water swirled with fish, some of them large; three vertical fins cut through the ripples toward them. The unicorn pointed her horn at the largest and blew a triple-note chord of warning; the fin altered course immediately, approaching no closer, and the other two did likewise.

Farther along a thing like a crocodile lifted its long snout, hissing. Again the unicorn blew her chord, and the thing backpedaled. Mach was impressed; it was evident that this equine creature was not to be trifled with. How fortunate that she had come to his rescue!

But why had she done so? Mach remembered that his father had spoken of associating with a unicorn. Or his alternate self had done so. But he had never provided any details. "That life is past," was all he would ever say. Mach had gathered that unicorns were not necessarily friendly to man; apparently it had been a remarkable thing for a man to befriend one. Yet this one had come right to him, a stranger, and rescued him.

The water-path was finally headed for solid land again. Here the footing seemed to be especially intricate; the unicorn was almost doing a four-footed dance as she stepped along it. And here it was that a more formidable menace appeared.

From the deep water to the side emerged a huge and mottled reptilian head. It had two curling horns and greenish scales and widely spreading whiskers. Then the mouth opened, to reveal an array of teeth as formidable as any Mach had known of. Jets of steam issued from the metallic nostrils, forming swirling little clouds as they cooled and expanded.

The unicorn paused. It was evident that this was a threat she did not dismiss lightly. Indeed, as the monster lifted itself higher, Mach could see why. This was a literal dragon!

The dragon leaned forward, extending two front legs with ferocious talons. Its head swung on a sinuous neck. More steam issued, forming cloudlets bathing Mach with hot vapor. Viscous saliva dripped from the mouth.

The unicorn tilted her head so that her right eye bore directly on Mach, as if questioning him. He shrugged nervously. "If you don't know what to do, I certainly don't!" he said. He had been gaining confidence as the animal bore him to safety; now that confidence was rapidly draining away. He realized that the unicorn could not readily back away; the footing was so tricky that she probably had to move forward to achieve it. On land she could have fled the dragon; here she could not. Since it evidently had no fear of her horn, and appeared to be quite capable of destroying her in combat, this was a formidable threat.

The unicorn made something very like a shrug; the skin of her shoulders rippled. Then she faced the dragon and blew a new chord. This seemed to have about four notes, with a quaver and an especially penetrating quality; it made a shiver run down Mach's back.

The dragon paused. Then it snorted more steam and cranked its jaws farther open. The gape of that mouth was horrendous; Mach realized that the dragon could snap off half his body with one bite, and perhaps intended to do just that. The unicorn's chord of warning had not dissuaded it. This monster knew it commanded the situation, and it was hungry, and it intended to feed. Mach's living heart was beating at a fast rate, and his living breathing was becoming noisy. He was afraid—and this was an emotion he had never before experienced. He did not enjoy it.

The unicorn blew her chord again, louder. Again the dragon paused, the little ears below its horns swiveling to orient on that sound. Evidently the chord was a special type of signal, that did have some effect—but not enough to put this monster off entirely.

The dragon brought its head slowly down. The big nostrils pointed at Mach like the barrels of twin rifles. The torso expanded; evidently the dragon was taking a deep breath, getting ready to issue a blast of steam that would cook man and unicorn in place.

The unicorn took her own deep breath. She set herself, pointed her horn straight up, and stretched out her neck. The hairs of her mane lifted, almost like the hackles of an angry dog. There was going to be one phenomenally loud sound!

Abruptly the dragon backed away. Its head traveled to the side and down to the water, and under the surface, and the sinuous neck and body followed. In a moment it was gone.

Mach relaxed quiveringly. The mare had bluffed the dragon away! For some reason the monster had feared the threatened loud sound more than the lesser sounds.

The unicorn resumed her motion along the path, picking her way toward the land. While she did this, Mach pondered the matter further. Surely the louder chord could not have hurt the dragon, if the fainter ones had not. Why, then, had it retreated?

His living brain was not as straightforward about logic as his robot brain had been, but this was not a difficult process. Obviously the chord was not a weapon in itself, but a signal—a call for help. Thus a faint one served as a warning, while a loud one would be heard all over the forest and bring reinforcements. Other unicorns, perhaps. One dragon might overcome one immobilized unicorn, but suppose several unicorns came? Yet the dragon had disappeared so swiftly and completely into the water that it was hard to see how other unicorns could have come in time to help, or how they could have located the dragon for revenge if they came too late to save their companion. So this didn't make complete sense.

The unicorn reached land and picked up speed, resuming her trot. She resumed her melody; evidently she liked trotting to music. Where was she taking him? And *why?* She had put herself in real jeopardy to help him; why do this for a stranger? His logical mind struggled to make sense of things.

The path divided; without hesitation the animal selected one fork and trotted on. The forest was thinning now, with larger glades appearing, and finally open fields. They were ascending a slope that seemed to have no end; the unicorn's body became warmer from the exertion, but she did not sweat.

Now the land fell away on either side; the path was mounting a ridge, perhaps a glacial moraine. It was hard to tell, because time had passed and dusk was closing; he could not see clearly to the base of the slopes. In due course they reached a ragged cliff; the path cut its way through to an interior crater that was open to the sky but otherwise closed. Here at last they stopped.

Mach slid off, glad to return to his own feet. He winced as he landed; he had forgotten the abrasion his soles had incurred. Also, his scratches stung. The interest of the ride had distracted him from such details, but now they intruded.

"Well, we are evidently here," he said. "But I don't know why you brought me, and I don't suppose you can explain."

The unicorn eyed him—and suddenly he had an ugly thought. Horses grazed on grass and ate grain and hay. What did unicorns eat? He had seen enough to know that their metabolism was not at all like that of mundane equines. Had this one brought him here—as prey?

The unicorn lowered her horn and stepped toward him. Abruptly terrified, Mach tried to run. But there was nowhere to run to; this was a closed region, with the unicorn blocking the only exit. He tried to climb the wall, but found no suitable handholds. He scraped his fingers against the stone in his desperate effort, incurring more scratches. He knew he was reacting foolishly, only making himself seem more like prey, but he had no automatic control over the emotion of this living body.

It was no use. If he was here to be eaten, he would just have to accept it. Defeated, he slumped against the stone wall, waiting for whatever was to come.

Nothing came. After a moment he turned around. The unicorn was gone.

She had brought him here—and left him. What did that mean? He wasn't sure that he cared to guess.

His palpitating bodily processes settled down somewhat. His more sensible mind reasserted itself. He explored his prison. There was a mound of soft brush and hay at one side, evidently a sleeping place. This must be the unicorn's lair, protected from most other creatures. He was relieved to discover no bones; if she brought victims here for leisurely consumption, there should be bones.

He considered trying to escape, but he was now so tired that he knew he would not get far. Tiredness was another new phenomenon for him, and he didn't like it. And what was there for him outside? A jagged path, and a series of predatory monsters! Better to remain here and get some rest, and hope that the unicorn was after all beneficent.

He sat on the nest of brush. It was surprisingly comfortable. He leaned back against it. Before he knew it, he was asleep.

He woke in starry darkness. Something was wrong with his abdominal circuitry. He felt bloated. Had an oil valve clogged?

He checked at a service aperture, but found none; his fingers slid across unbroken skin. Then he remembered: he was in a living body!

That meant that he needed to release fluid, in the living manner. His robot body could eat and drink, but did not eliminate in the biological way; it simply regurgitated the material at a convenient time. Now he would have to perform in the fashion he had observed in human beings and androids.

He got up—and discovered that he was not alone. His hand brushed across the torso of another living creature. The unicorn?

He peered, and made out the vague outline. Not an animal, but a man! His hand helped define the leg, arm, breast—

It was female!

Mach withdrew. Evidently he had not awakened her, and that was probably best. How had she come here?

She must have walked up the path, arriving after he was asleep. Perhaps this was where she regularly spent the night. She had seen him, and had simply settled down beside.

That seemed too simple, but it would have to do for now. He needed to find a suitable place to relieve himself.

He felt about with his feet, but knew that there was no place within this enclosure. He would have to go outside. So he walked carefully in the direction he remembered the entrance to be, and found the wall. The starlight from above did help. He moved along the wall, finding the exit. A gentle breeze gusted through it, refreshingly cool. In the distance was the sound of some night bird.

He established himself at the edge of the path, aimed his liquid-disposal appendage, and let go down the mountainside. It was a great relief. However, this reminded him of his thirst, which had not really been slaked at the swamp, and this now manifested with renewed force. Another problem of the living state!

He returned inside the crater. He would just have to sleep until morning, and then see what offered. Perhaps the human female would know where there was water. And food—he would be hungry soon.

But as he came to the brush pile, he realized that the female was awake. Indeed, she was sitting up, peering at him.

"I—I was uncomfortable," he said awkwardly. Natural functions were normally not discussed between the sexes in Proton, and he assumed it was the same here.

"Bane," she said. Her voice was pleasant, having an almost flutelike quality.

"I don't understand."

"Bane—is thy game over?" she asked.

"Game?"

She sighed. "Not over. Then I will play it on with thee. Do thou kiss me, and we shall sleep."

"Kiss?" he asked, perplexed.

She stood, rising lithely to her feet. She approached him, reached up, took hold of his head with both her hands, and brought her face to his. She kissed him on the mouth. "Long has it been since we played thus," she said. "Come, now; sleep." She tugged him toward the nest.

Mach followed, bemused. This girl seemed to know him, and she wanted to sleep. There were several meanings for that word, and he was not sure which one applied, so he simply lay down in the fragrant brush beside her, as she seemed to want. If she intended sexual expression, he could do that; as a robot he had the hardware, and was programmed to—but no, he wasn't a robot anymore! Still, as a living man he had similar capacities, and she seemed to be an attractive girl; he could do whatever seemed to be called for.

She squeezed his hand, turned her head to the side, and slept. In a moment her gentle breathing signaled her condition.

Relieved, Mach did the same. He wondered whether she would still be there when morning came.

As it happened, she was. He woke to the pressure of her little hand, tousling his hair. "Wake, Bane!" she exclaimed. "What is the game today? Naked through the swamp again?"

That made him realize that though he was properly naked, she was not. She wore a black cloak that covered her body from neck to ankle. He remembered, now, that he had felt cloth about her body in the night; he had assumed it was a cover, not clothing.

Now he had to ascertain the situation. He had three alternatives. First, she might be in costume, considering this to be a play; indeed she had mentioned a game. Second, she might be a serf masquerading as a Citizen. That was of course dangerous. Third, she might actually *be* a Citizen.

He had to know. A Citizen always had to be addressed with the proper forms of respect. But a serf in Citizen garb had to be set straight immediately, before real trouble came of it.

"Sir, I must know," he said, erring on the safe side. "What is your status?"

She looked at him, her green eyes seeming to twinkle. " 'Sir'? What speech be this, Bane?"

So she was not a Citizen. Just as well! "Then you are a serf?"

"Serf? Bane, if thou willst but tell me thy game, I will play it with thee. But I know not the rules of it."

"What is this 'thee' business?" he asked.

She smiled. Her black hair framed her face, and she wore a pearl at her forehead; she was lovely in her joy. "A game of language!" she exclaimed, clapping her hands.

"No game. I just don't understand. Who are you? Where did you come from? Why do you use the archaic forms? Why are you garbed?"

She cocked her head at him cannily. "So we call it not a game. That can I do. As for who I be, as if thou dost not know: I am Fleta, thy companion of yore. I speak as thy kind does; wouldst rather have me neigh? As for my garb why there be no need for it, if this be the game!" And she reached down, caught hold of the hem of her cloak, and drew it up over her head. In a moment she stood before him naked, for she wore no underclothing. "Be that better, Bane?"

"Yes," he agreed. She was a most comely figure of a young woman, perfectly formed and standing just slightly shorter than he. "But why are you calling me Bane? Do you know me?"

"What wouldst thou be called, then?" she inquired merrily.

"My name is Mach."

She laughed. "What a stupid name!"

He frowned. "Is Fleta a more intelligent name?"

"Certainly! But I will try to keep my laughter down while I call thee Mach." Indeed, she did try, but the laughter bubbled up from her stomach, caused her breasts to bounce, and finally burst out of her mouth. She flung her arms about him and kissed him, as she had in the night. "O, Bane—I mean Ma-Ma—" A giggle overcame her, but she fought through it. "Mach! What a romp have we here! I feared thou hadst forgotten me in thy serious studies of blue magic; how glad I be to learn not!"

"Fleta, I have to say that I do not know you. What's this about magic?"

"Ah, wait till I tell the fillies of the herd of this! Never played we music like this!"

"If you would just answer my questions," Mach said somewhat stiffly.

"As thou dost wish," she agreed. "But first may we eat? and O, I see thou art all scratched! Why dost thou not heal thyself?"

"Heal myself?" he asked blankly. "I think only time can do that."

"With thy magic," she explained. "Surely the game be not such that thou must suffer such smarts!"

"I don't know anything about magic!" he protested.

She made a moue. "Or wouldst thou have the unicorn heal thee instead?"

"The unicorn!" he exclaimed, alarmed. "What do you know about that?"

She stared at him, then smiled again, dismissing his supposed ignorance. "Thy memory seems brief, lately!"

"A unicorn brought me here last night, after rescuing me from monsters in the swamp. I don't know why; do you?"

She shook her head so that the lustrous hair swirled. "Who can know the mind of a 'corn!" she exclaimed, laughing again. "Mayhap she thought thou didst call for help."

"I *did* call for help," he agreed. "But—but why should an animal do me any favor?"

"An animal," Fleta repeated thoughtfully. "An thou hadst called her that, mayhap she'd have left thee in the swamp indeed!"

"Oh—are they sensitive about that sort of thing? Good thing she didn't understand my speech."

"Aye, so," she agreed, twinkling again. "So thou dost not desire the 'corn to heal thy trifling wounds with her horn?"

"With her horn?"

"Adepts be not the only ones who do magic!" she exclaimed. "Dost thou not remember the healing of the horn?"

"You mean—that unicorn—when she approached me with her horn lowered—only wanted to—to touch my scratches and heal them magically?"

"Lo, now he remembers!" she exclaimed. "What else would she be about?"

"I wasn't sure," he confessed. "I was relieved when she left."

Fleta frowned. "There be aspects of this game I understand not," she said. "Thou dost not wish the return of the unicorn?"

"True," he agreed. "But of course I cannot prevent it. Maybe we should get away from here before she arrives."

She sighed. "Be that the way thou dost want it, so let it be. I had not thought to hear thee say the like, though."

"Well, I'm sure unicorns can be perfectly good animals, and I do appreciate what she did for me yesterday. But I must admit I feel safer with you."

"And thou dost not propose to conjure up a repast for us both?"

"What makes you think I could do such a thing?"

She laughed her merry laugh. "Sheer foolishness, Mach!" she said. "Come, I shall find us food." She led him from the crater.

3

Bane

Bane found himself in a chamber, sitting on a bed. A moment
before he had been in the forest glade, seeking rapport with his
other self. He had sung a spell to facilitate the exchange of
identities—and it seemed that it had worked! Here he was in
the other frame, while his alternate had to be in Phaze. Wait till
he told his father of this success!

He looked about, trying to fix as much of this locale in his
mind as possible before he reverted to his own frame. It was not
that Adept Stile would doubt him, but that he wanted to have
information that would establish the case beyond question. This
was the first genuine contact with the frame of Proton since the
two had separated twenty years ago. Of course no one else had
seriously sought such contact; it had been generally agreed that
total separation of the frames was best. But Bane had regarded
it as a challenge, and when he had tuned in on the sendings of
his other self, he had jumped at the chance to intensify the
contact.

This was definitely Proton! Everything about the room was

unmagical. The bed was formed of some substance unknown in Phaze, hard like wood but with no grain, and the mattress on it was like one big white sponge. There was a cabinet against the wall with a window in it that opened on blankness. Beside it were several books—no, they seemed to have no pages. But perhaps the folk of this frame didn't read books. His father would know.

He looked down at his body. It was naked. That, too, aligned; Stile had mentioned that the folk of Proton went naked, all except the rulers. He was really here, in the body of his other self.

But he decided to make sure. If this were Proton, magic would not work here. "Make me rise, to realize," he sang, composing a ditty on the spot, as he had been trained to do from childhood. It was his mind that really governed the spell, but it had to be in the right form: singsong and rhymed.

Nothing happened. He remained firmly planted on the bed. In Phaze he would now be floating above it. This was the final proof: he was definitely out of Phaze.

He clapped his hands, expressing the sheer joy of the accomplishment. What a breakthrough! To transport himself to the other frame, when others had believed it to be impossible. And he would be able to do it again, now that he knew exactly how. What a tremendous opportunity loomed!

But now he had better switch back, so they could each report their accomplishment to their folks. Bane sat on the bed, concentrated—and nothing happened.

Oops! He had used magic to facilitate the exchange—but here magic didn't work. His other self would have to perform the spell—and would his other self *know* the spell?

Well, he could explain. All he needed to do was use their rapport to make it clear.

He concentrated again—and discovered, to his horror, that the rapport was gone.

The two selves had to occupy the same site in their respective frames, for the rapport to be achieved. They had to unify in their fashion, seeming almost as one. It had taken Bane a long time to discover the place where he could overlap his Proton self, and to be there when his other self was ready for that rapport. This was that occasion—but now the other self had moved off the spot.

Bane got up, casting desperately about for the other. He knew he could sense the other if he overlapped, or even if he came close—but where *was* the other?

He moved around the room, seeking that intangible spoor, the otherframe presence of the other self. There was no sign of it. He needed to cast a wider net, but the room restrained him. Where was the door? There seemed to be none.

Baffled, he studied the walls. Finally he decided that the one blank section he saw had to be it. There was no knob, no evidence of any aperture, but this was the strange scientific frame, so there could be another mechanism. He walked toward it, putting out his hand as if to push a door open.

It worked. The wall before him fogged and disappeared. He stepped out into a metallic hall.

Naked—outside the room? He didn't trust this! He turned to go back into the room—but the wall behind him was now opaque and unbroken. He put his hand out, but it didn't fog. He pushed against it, and it remained firm. It seemed that some other technique was required to enter, similar to a spell that limited access to only those folk who had the counterspell. A scientific spell— and he didn't have it.

A person rounded a corner and came toward him. It was a woman—naked! *Now* what was he to do?

He fought to control himself, and found it much easier than he had anticipated. It seemed that folk really did go naked in Proton, male and female. So he should be all right. All he had to do was act natural.

The young woman approached him. "Hi, Mach!" she said brightly. "Looking for a game?"

A game. What did she mean? She was a voluptuous creature, as well formed as any he had seen, though of course he had not seen many naked before. Was it safe to say no? She evidently expected him to agree, so that seemed best. Then, after it was done, he could resume his quest for his other self, who had to be somewhere close.

"A game—yes," he agreed. He remembered the games he had

played as a child with Fleta. Some of them had become pretty intimate; it embarrassed him to remember, now. Fleta had a nonhuman sense of humor, of course.

"Well, then, let's go!" she agreed. "I'm going to take you this time, Mach!"

Mach. That was evidently his other self's name. That was helpful to know. But who was this attractive girl? She seemed to be his own age, nineteen, but that could be deceptive. Well, perhaps he would find out.

They walked down the hall. Bane followed her lead, hoping that his own ignorance didn't show. He also tried to note the route they took, so he could return to the original spot. He was good at that sort of thing, but he had never tried it in a huge building like this. Was there no end to it? Where was the forest?

They threaded a virtual labyrinth, arriving at last at a strange complex. The girl took a stance before a kind of pedestal with a blank window set into it.

She glanced at Bane. "Well, get on over there, Mach," she said. "You scared to play me?"

He went to the other side of the pedestal, where a similar window was set. But he did not know what was expected of him next.

The window lighted. A crosshatch of lines appeared. Across the top was written a combination of numbers and words, and down the side were letters and words. The top ones were brighter: 1. PHYSICAL, 2. MENTAL, 3. CHANCE, 4. ARTS.

"What's keeping you?" the girl demanded.

Bane didn't want to admit that he had no idea what to do, because obviously his other self understood this business, and he didn't want to give away the fact that he was not Mach. "Why dost thou not make a suggestion?" he inquired.

She smiled. "Oho! The fish is eager! Well, I'll be direct, Mach. The news is fresh that the cyborg dumped you, so I figure maybe you'll fare better with your own kind. I don't want to beat you, I want to win you. If you've got any interest, give me the physical. You won't regret it."

Her words were indecipherable, but her manner suggested intimacy. This girl wanted romance! Bane didn't want to get his other self into anything he might regret upon his return, but feared that turning down this offer could be awkward. "Just tell me what to do."

She licked her lips. "So it's that way, is it?" Her voice lowered. "Touch the one, lover."

Bane realized that she referred to the print. He brought his finger to the lighted number 1 and pressed it.

Abruptly the first square of the pattern became bright, and the words PHYSICAL and NAKED. This was like the paper game, that his father had shown him, wherein one person chose from one border, and the other from the other, and where their choices intersected was the decision. The challenge was to out-guess the opponent, so that what he thought would bring him success actually brought him defeat.

But what did PHYSICAL/NAKED mean? The girl's attitude suggested one thing, but since they were already naked, he hesitated to assume too much.

The square expanded to fill the window. A new crosshatch appeared, and new numbers and words. Across the top was written 5. SEPARATE, 6. INTERACTIVE, 7. COMBAT, 8. CO-OPERATIVE, and down the left side, more brightly, E. EARTH, F. FIRE, G. GAS, H. H2O. He recognized the four elements, earth, fire, air and water, which were fundamental to the various types of magic. Of course there was another element, more important—

"Come on, Mach," the girl urged. "Make your play."

So he touched a lighted word at random: GAS.

A new square illuminated, on the line he had selected, and in the second column. INTERACTIVE/GAS. He wasn't sure he liked the notion. Then a smaller pattern of nine squares appeared, with a list of words down the side: PILLOW-FIGHTING, SEX, TAG, TRAPEZE . . .

"You know what Tilly wants!" the girl said. In the center square appeared the word SEX. "Make your pick, Macho!"

Uncertainly, he touched the word PILLOW. Immediately it brightened. Then, catching on, he touched a corner square, and the word jumped into it. Who said there was no magic in the science frame!

Tilly put SEX into another corner. So it went, with Bane selecting a variety of terms, she only one. Then they touched their lighted sides, and the chosen square appeared: PILLOW-FIGHTING.

"Oh, damn!" Tilly swore. "You cheated!"

"I thought I would surprise thee," he said, somewhat lamely. He had picked randomly again, but was just as glad it hadn't finished with the word she so evidently desired. It was not that she was unattractive, but surely such a thing was no game between strangers!

"You surprised me," she agreed. She smiled. "You surprised me when you even agreed to play! You never gave me a tumble before, you know." Then she cocked her head at him. "Thee?"

Bane realized that he had made an error of language. The girl had consistently used "you." That was evidently the way they spoke, here. In perpetual plural.

He smiled. "See? Surprised you again."

She pursed her lips. "You *are* different today! Doris must have made you flip out."

She had mentioned that he had been "dumped" by a "cyborg." Was that a description of another person? If so, it must be Doris. So he—or at least Mach—was suffering from a romantic separation. And Tilly was eager to step in to take Doris' place. Assuming he had interpreted the signals correctly. But how did this game of patterns of words relate?

"Well, come on, robot," she said. "You want pillows, I'll give you pillows! I'll knock you into the muck!"

She led the way to another chamber. Bane followed, glad to let her maintain the initiative. He believed he knew what pillow-fighting was; it was a favorite game in Phaze. He had played many physical and mental games, and become quite good at several, including this one.

He was correct. This chamber was a huge muddy pit, with a heavy pole crossing it from side to side. A walkway around the edge provided access to the far side of the pole. A number of solid pillows were suspended from hooks near the entrance.

They each took a pillow. Bane made his way to the far side

of the pole, then hiked himself onto it. Tilly did the same from her side.

How serious was this supposed to be? Tilly was about his own size, as he was small for a male, but she massed less because of the difference in proportions. He surely could knock her off the pole if he wanted to. But why dump a lovely young woman into the mud? He would have to take his cue from her, again.

They worked their way toward each other until they met in the center. Tilly grinned. "Dump or get dumped!" she exclaimed, and swung her pillow at him in a great circle.

Bane ducked his head, and her pillow passed over his head. Such a miss could cause a person to overbalance and fall untouched, but she was experienced; she simply continued her swing in a full circle and came at him again, bopping him soundly on the shoulder. Her proficiency caught him by surprise.

Bane started to fall. To restore his balance, he had to swing his own pillow hard. He caught her on the side of the head with a loud and harmless smack. But already she was swinging again, aiming for his face—and when he ducked, she brought her pillow down to score anyway.

This was fun! Apparently it was to be a real fight; she wanted to bop and be bopped. He whipped his pillow about in a confined arc, scoring on her bosom.

"So that's the way you want it!" she cried gleefully. "Take that, machine!" And she whammed him on his own chest.

The contest turned·out to be about even. Tilly was good at this, and kept her balance, and had surprising endurance for a woman; she did not seem to be tiring at all. Neither was he; in fact he wasn't even breathing hard.

Breathing hard? *He wasn't breathing at all!* He had been taking breaths only when he talked.

Stunned, Bane forgot where he was. Tilly caught him with a powerful whomp, and he lost his balance and spun down. He dropped into the mud below, chagrined.

But almost without pause, she dropped too. "I beat you, robot!" she cried, and smacked him on the ear with a handful of mud.

"Hey!" he protested. He scooped up some mud himself and dropped it on her fair hair.

"Oh, yeah?" she exclaimed with zest. "Take that!" She flung herself upon him, bearing him back into the muck, her body literally plastered against his. Their heads sank under the surface, but it seemed to make no difference; he felt no suffocation and his eyes did not smart.

He tried to extricate himself, but she held him tight, her face rubbing against his. There was mud on her mouth, but that didn't stop her; she jammed her lips against his for a kiss.

Bane would have found all this far more intriguing if he had not been distracted by his discovery. How could he not be breathing, yet feeling no discomfort? That was impossible!

"Come on, react!" Tilly said in his ear. "Invoke your passion circuit, and we'll do it right here!"

Passion circuit? She referred to him as if he were some kind of inanimate thing like the pedestal with the magic windows. What was it called? A machine.

A machine? She had called him that, and "robot." Vaguely he remembered: a robot was a walking machine. His mother had mentioned one she had encountered that looked and acted exactly like a living woman, with a suggestive name, Sheen. Sheen, machine. But a good person, his mother had said.

Tilly wrapped her legs around him, hauling him in so close that the mud squeezed out between them. "Come on, make with the self-will! Mine's all the way on! What's that cyborg got that I haven't got?"

Sheen machine. Mach machine. Circuits. Unbreathing. Tilly wasn't breathing either, except when she talked. "We're both machines!" he exclaimed, appalled.

"It took you nineteen years to catch on to that?" she asked, sliding against him. "But we can do it just as well as the live ones can! Let's prove it!"

Bane was rescued from his predicament by a new voice. "Players vacate the chamber," it boomed. "New contestants entering."

"Oh, plop!" Tilly said, hurling a mudball out. "Why couldn't you have hurried, Mach?"

They climbed out, and made their way to the shower at the side, where the mud was quickly rinsed away. Then they returned to the hall.

"Let's go to my chamber," Bane said, before she could come up with something worse.

She ran her hand caressingly across his shoulder. "Oho! So *that's* why you held off!"

They walked back. Tilly knew the way, which was just as well, because Bane had lost track. Soon they stood before the section of wall he had stepped through.

"Well, say your code," she urged him.

A code. Something he must utter, like a spell, to make the wall become porous? He had no idea what word was required. "I—I seem to have forgotten," he said.

"Forgotten!" she cried, laughing. "As if a computer could ever forget anything by accident!" Then she sobered. "But you'll not get out of it that readily, Mach. We'll use my chamber."

"Your chamber," he agreed numbly. So machines did not forget. How long could he maintain this charade?

She led him to her chamber, nearby. She spoke a word, and the wall fogged. They passed through.

Her room was very much like his, small and almost devoid of decoration. Machines, it seemed, did not require many human artifacts.

"How would you like it?" Tilly inquired. "We're private here; no limits."

There was too much he didn't understand. Bane decided it would be better to tell her the truth. "I must explain—I'm not what you take me for," he said.

"Not through with Doris?" she asked. "Look, Mach, she's so hot with that android now, you'd better write her off. She's never coming back to you. What's a cyborg, anyway, but a pickled human brain stuck in a robot body? I never did see what you saw in her. You're a robot, Mach! And not just any robot. You're going to be a Citizen one year."

A human brain in a robot body? That sounded grotesque! "It's not—not Doris. I don't even remember her. It's—I'm not Mach. And I think I need help."

She eyed him. "This is a private game, right? What are you up to?"

"I'm from another frame," he said. "I switched places—"

"Another frame," she repeated. "What do you claim you are?"

"A human being. Alive. Only now I'm caught in—"

"So you want to pretend you're not a machine," she said. "That's not a good game. It hasn't been that long, historically, since we self-willed machines were granted the status of serfs. The Citizens would love to take it away from us. All they need is a pretext. You know that. So find some other game; this one's dangerous."

"This is no game!" Bane protested. "I'm from Phaze, the frame of magic, but—"

"All right, so you won't get serious," she said, pouting. "So let me show you something."

"Show me?"

She brought her left hand to her face. She put her little finger between her teeth and bit down on it. Her white teeth sank into the flesh and tore a small hole in it. She worked at the wound, biting deeper. There was no blood.

"There," she said after a moment, surveying the damaged finger. "I reached the nerve-wire. Now give me yours."

"Mine?"

She reached out and caught his left hand, and brought it to her mouth. Bane did not resist. He watched while she put his own little finger to her mouth, and bit into it. He felt no pain, though soon the substance of his finger was torn open. It seemed to be padding, and deeper inside, a wire. Exactly like hers.

He was, indeed, a machine. Rather, his other self, Mach, was. A nonliving robot in human form. That much Tilly had demonstrated beyond question.

"Now I'll show you how to bypass the clumsy human sexual process," Tilly said. "We robots have something much better."

She held his left hand with her right hand, and brought her left hand to it. She touched her chewed little finger to his, pushing them together so that their central wires touched.

Suddenly Bane was transported by a pleasure so wild and strong as to be unutterable. It originated in his finger, but was so potent that it spread immediately throughout his body. It was indeed like sexual fulfillment, but more intense, and it kept on and on, never diminishing. He realized that Tilly, too, was experiencing it. Her face was fixed in an expression of rapture.

Then the contact slipped, and the pleasure faded. Now Bane felt depleted. He sat heavily on the bed.

"See?" Tilly asked. "It continues as long as contact is kept, as long as our energy sustains it. Living people can experience it only for a few seconds, but we have no such limit."

"No such limit," Bane agreed, staring at his torn finger. This was illicit pleasure, surely—but what potency it had!

"Now tell me more about how you aren't really a robot," she said.

He realized that she was unable to believe his story. She was a machine, subject to the limitations of that state. Her imagination simply was insufficient.

Yet the truth was the truth. And he still had to locate his other self, so as to be able to change back. He certainly didn't want to be trapped forever in this frame, where machines made love by touching torn fingers!

"We've recharged some," she said. "Let's do some more time." She extended her little finger.

For a moment Bane was tempted. The pleasure was indeed compelling! But he realized that if he allowed himself to be caught up in that again, he might never want to resume his search for his other self, and that would not be right. He exercised what discipline he could muster. "No. I have another job to do."

"You mean I wrecked my finger, and I'm going to get in trouble with the repair authority, and you're not even going to let me get full measure from it?" she demanded.

"It—it's an illicit pleasure," he said. "We—we're supposed to do it in the human fashion."

Suddenly she was alarmed. "You aren't going to tell!"

Telling—about the illicit act. That would surely bring trouble to them both, and further complicate his effort. "No. I just— just don't want to do it anymore."

"Then get out of here!" she cried angrily. "I never want to see you again!"

He walked to the wall. It fogged, needing no spell from this side, and he stepped into the hall.

So at last he was free of the robot woman. That was a mixed

satisfaction; she was very pretty, and she had shown him a lot that he needed to know, about the Game and the premises. And physical pleasure such as he had never before known. But it was best that he stay away from her; he knew that. She was not, in his idiom, a nice girl. Rather, a nice machine. She would get in trouble, if not today, some future day.

But what was he to do now? He still hardly knew his way around these premises, and it was evident that his other self was long gone from this region, and now he had an injured finger that would be difficult to explain.

He needed help. But where was he to find it?

Disconsolately, he walked down the hall. Other naked young folk passed him, and he acknowledged their greetings, but kept his left hand curled into a fist to conceal the finger.

Obviously he wasn't going to locate his other self by aimless wandering. He had to get smart about his search. He had to figure out where he was in relation to Phaze, knowing that the geographies of the two frames were identical, and where Mach would be likely to wander, and go there. Simple enough, surely; he could step outside and study the landscape. He knew the features of his world, and could normally locate his position by a simple survey of the horizon.

But where was outside? This building seemed endless!

He set about it methodically: finding his way out. If he went in any single direction far enough, he had to come to the edge of the building. Then he would follow that edge until he found an exit. It was like locating water in the wilderness: keep going down, and sooner or later water would appear, for it also sought the lowest regions.

But when he tried, he discovered that the halls did not go in single directions. They curved this way and that, and made right-angle turns, and took magically moving stairs to upper floors, and magically descending chambers to nether regions. It was like one huge labyrinth that threatened to get him hopelessly lost before he really got started. In the wilderness he could have coped readily enough; this foreign environment had him baffled.

He would have to inquire. But the others thought he was

Mach, who should know the way out; to ask would only get laughter, or perhaps some interaction like that with Tilly, the opportunist female machine. Better to avoid that.

So he continued to walk the halls, his frustration mounting. The others he passed glanced at him with increasing perplexity, but did not interfere.

Then a young woman approached. She had flowing red hair, very full breasts, and a kind of rippling walk that forced him to avert his eyes lest he suffer an embarrassing reaction. He hoped she would not try to talk with him.

"Oh, Mach!" she cried. "They said you were here! Please, if I may conversationally merge—"

He was stuck for it. Bane faced her. The pupils of her eyes were so dark they were like the water of deep wells. "Of course," he said guardedly.

She took a breath, and her flesh jiggled. Bane set his tongue between his teeth and bit down, trying to distract himself by the controlled pain—but there was no pain, just a kind of electrical tingle of warning. He locked his eyes on her face, trying to tune out the peripheral vision.

"I felt it needful to express my sorrow," she said, bringing her beautiful face close. Her complexion was so clear it almost shone. "I did not mean to be the agent of your loss of woman."

Loss of woman? That must refer to the way Mach had gotten dumped by the cyborg. Maybe he could learn something useful. "I really remember not."

"But it was only this noon!" she protested. "We met in the pool, and Narda exchanged companions, taking Rory while you had to take me. Then Doris caught you together with me, and made a dramatic exclamation, and Ware came to her aid, and you lost her, and it was all because of me!"

There were too many names in a rush, but this did help clarify things. Tilly the robot had told him he had been dumped by Doris the cyborg, who had gone to an android male. Apparently it had been because of a misunderstanding involving this female. An easy misunderstanding to have, considering her appearance! And this one was apologetic. Maybe she could help him.

"I bear thee no malice," he said carefully, still keeping his eyes clear of dangerous territory. If only she had some clothing on! "I know it was an—an accident. I—I misremember thy name."

"Agape," she said quickly. "I chose it because it means instant love, such as I feel for this society, that lets me participate though I am an alien. Perhaps I should have chosen more carefully, but I was so eager—"

"It's a perfect name," he said, looking down the hall. "Thou art—alien? From—elsewhere?"

"You know I am alien!" she exclaimed. "You saw me imbibe! And you did not wince! I am so grateful! I arrived only yesterday, and you helped me so much! And then I hurt you so much, without ever knowing! I wish there could be some recompense I could offer, but—" She spread her arms in a helpless gesture that attracted his gaze before he could stop it. He turned away.

"As it happens, there is," Bane said, realizing his opportunity. "If thou couldst show me the way outside."

"Outside? But that is unlivable!"

"I be a machine. Methinks I can survive it."

She smiled. "That must be so. Mach, I do not know the way, but surely I can find it. We have but to inquire of a maintenance unit."

"Maintenance unit?"

She glanced at him with the same perplexity the others had. "Why do you act as if you do not know? And why do you avert your gaze from my body? Have I become repulsive to you because of what you saw at noon?"

He had tried to tell the truth to Tilly, and had made no headway. He decided to try again. "Agape, I must tell thee something thou mayst believe not."

"I will believe!" she exclaimed.

"I be not Mach. I be his other self, a living person using his body. I be called Bane."

"You are not making humor?" she inquired. "I am not supposed to laugh?"

"No humor. No laugh," he agreed.

"Then this is the reason you cannot find your way around these premises," she said. "You are totally new here!"

"That be it exactly."

"Just as I was yesterday."

"So does it seem."

"But why don't you look at me?"

Time for more honesty. "I be accustomed not to seeing women without clothing. I fear embarrassment."

"From *me?*" she asked, amazed.

"Thou art an extremely, uh, attractive creature."

"Oh, what delight!" she exclaimed. "I never imagined! But I confess I do not know exactly how your species manifests this type of interaction."

Bane started walking, wishing that he could get away from this subject. Agape came right along with him. "I be sure I know not how thy species does, either," he said. "But if thou canst help me get outside—"

"Oh, yes!" she said enthusiastically. "Let me inquire of a menial!" She crossed to a panel set into the wall, and touched a button. "Please, some directions?"

"Aid required?" a voice came.

"We wish to find the outside."

"Follow the mouse."

A small panel slid aside at the level of the floor, and a thing very like a mouse emerged. But instead of legs it had little wheels, and instead of a tail it had an upward spike. It zipped down the hall.

They followed. The mouse careened around a corner, then moved to a blank section of wall. Its spike emitted a beeping sound.

"This must be it," Agape said. She touched the wall with her hand, and it fogged. They stepped through it, into a chamber containing bulky suits suspended on frames.

A large wheeled object approached them. "Serfs wish egress?" Its voice came from a grille on top.

"Wish to go outside," Agape said. "Is this permissible?"

"Permissible," the machine agreed. "The robot can go as is; the android must don protective gear."

"Oh, he is not really a robot, and I am not an android," Agape said.

The machine considered. "What definitions are applicable?"

"Call me robot," Bane said quickly. "I be the only one who needs to go out."

Agape turned to him, her lovely face seeming to melt a little. "You do not wish my company? I had understood that you found me attractive."

There seemed to be another misunderstanding here! "Thou dost wish to come outside?"

"I wish to help you, as you in your other guise helped me. And if you continue to find me attractive, I wish to do with you what the females of your species do with the males."

Bane paused. It was evident that the mores of Proton differed somewhat from those of Phaze. But the fact remained that he needed help, and that she was willing to provide it, and he liked her company more than he thought was appropriate, considering that his other self might not feel similarly. If he found Mach, and exchanged places, and Agape tried to be too friendly with the robot . . .

"I be trying to return to my frame," he said. "When I do that, it will be Mach in this body again. I know not whether he would desire thy company."

She nodded. "I have no knowledge either. I thank you for your caution, Bane. But while you are here, I would like to be with you, because I understand how you must feel. You are an alien in this world, as I am, even though you look normal for your species."

Fairly spoken! "Then don some gear and come along!" he said. "I shall be glad to have thy company awhile longer."

The menial machine selected a suit for her, and soon Agape was ready. Then they stepped into a tiny chamber she called a "lock" and the door closed on them. In a moment, Bane knew, another door would open, and he would finally see the outside.

4

Magic

At the foot of the mountain Fleta showed the way to a tree that bore huge and delicious-looking apples. Eagerly, Mach reached for one, but she put her hand on his arm, cautioning him. "That be no joke even I can abide," she said.

"Joke? I'm hungry!"

"Bane, that apple be poison! Mayhap thou dost mean to denature it before thou dost eat, but this be not humor I abide."

Mach paused. "Mach, not Bane. I can't denature anything, I told you!"

"Mach," she repeated, again stifling her mirth. Then she sobered. "But tease me not further; take of the good fruit."

Mach reached for a different apple, and glanced at her; when she nodded, he plucked it. "You promised to tell me why you think I could heal myself or conjure food."

She plucked an apple of her own, and nibbled at it delicately while she spoke. "We have known each other since I was a foal and thou a baby," she said. "Thy father, Stile, and my dam, Neysa, be oath-friends, and so she raised me near the Blue Demesnes, and I did learn the human tongue even as thou didst. We wrestled together when little, and later I carried thee all around Phaze. Only these past three years, when we became grown and thou studied the magic and I the antimagic of my kind, have we been separate, and though it had to be, I missed thee, Bane. Now for a moment we romp again, and ne'er would I have it end."

She had a funny way of referring to herself! "But what about magic?"

"Thou'rt the son of the Blue Adept!" she exclaimed. "One day thou willst be lord of the Blue Demesnes thyself. That be why thou hast been studying thy magic. Already thou canst do conjuration no ordinary person can match. Hard be it for me to understand why thou didst not summon a sword and stab those roach-heads, or transform them to slugs."

Mach stared at her. "You're serious! You think I can do magic!"

"Bane, I have seen thee do magic many times," she said. "E'en when we were little, thou wouldst tease me with thy conjurations, but always I forgave thee. My dam likes magic not, but I have no aversion to it, for how could I love thee and not thy nature?"

Mach shook his head. "Fleta, you must understand this: *I am not Bane.* I can't do magic. The first time I met you was last night."

"Thou certainly dost *look* like Bane, and sound like him, except for thy funny affectation of speech, and smell like him," she said. "Else would I not have come to thee."

"I'm in Bane's body. But I'm from the other frame. My name is Mach, and science is all I have known."

"If thou wouldst have me believe thee, let me touch thee," she said.

"Touch me?"

She came to him, and took his hand, and brought it to her forehead. She pressed it against the gem in her forehead. "Speak," she said.

"I am Mach, from Proton," he said firmly. "I exchanged bodies with my other self in Phaze, with Bane. Now I am here and he is there, and I'd like to change back."

She lifted his hand away from her head and brought it down before her, staring at him over it. "Truth!" she exclaimed, wide-eyed. "No joke!"

"No joke," he agreed.

"Thou'rt not the man I know!"

"I am not."

She dropped his hand and backed away. "And I spent the night with thee!" she said, appalled.

He had to smile. "Nothing happened, Fleta."

"And I kissed thee!" she continued. "Oh, had I known!"

"And a nice kiss it was, too," he agreed.

"And now I stand naked before thee!" she said, seeming shocked.

"It's the natural way."

"Not for grown folk!" she said. In a moment she had gotten back into her robe.

"But you're no Citizen!" Mach said. "If anyone catches you in that—"

"This be not Proton!" she snapped.

He had to smile. "Touché! No Citizens here."

"No science here." She squinted at him as if trying to penetrate his disguise. "But if thou really canst not do magic—"

"I really cannot," he agreed.

"Then there be hazard here," she concluded. "Best if I change form and carry thee back to the Blue Demesnes before any learn!"

"Change form?" he asked. "What are you talking about?"

She hesitated. "Ah, now I remember! Thou dost not like— Oh, what must I do?"

Mach spread his hands. "I don't know why you're so upset. Why don't you just show me where these Blue Demesnes are, and maybe there I can learn how to return to Proton. Then you'll have your friend Bane again."

She still seemed doubtful. "Bane—Mach, this be no garden within thy demesnes! Here there be monsters, and as we be— we cannot travel through the fell swamp."

Mach remembered the swamp. He realized what she meant. If it had not been for the unicorn, he would have been lost.

That unicorn! What had been its intent—and where had it gone? What would it do when it returned and found him gone? "Is there any other route? One that doesn't go through the swamp?"

"None we would care to take," she said.

"Worse than the swamp?"

She nodded soberly.

"But how did you get here, last night?"

"Thou really dost not know!" she said, as if verifying something she couldn't quite believe.

"All I know is that I slept, and when I woke, you were beside me. You must have had some safe route."

"Not one I care to use at the moment."

"I don't understand."

"Surely thou dost not," she agreed. "But mayhap we have another way."

"Another path?"

"Another way. Thou must use thy magic."

"But I told you, I *have* no magic!"

"How dost thou know?"

"I come from a scientific frame. I don't even believe in magic!"

"Well, I don't believe in thy science," she retorted. "But if I were in thy land, I would at least try thy way."

Mach realized that there was some justice in her position. "Very well, tell me how to do magic. We'll see what happens."

"Always before, thou hast sung a ditty."

"Sung a ditty?" he asked incredulously.

"A little rhyme, and it happens."

"This is ridiculous!"

"Thou didst promise to try," she reminded him, pouting.

So he had. "What ditty do you want me to sing?"

She shrugged. "Try some simple spell, first."

"*No* spell is simple, to my way of thinking!"

"Conjure a sword, mayhap. That can slay a monster."

"A sword." Now Mach shrugged. "I just make a rhyme, and sing it?"

"About what thou dost want."

Mach's experience in the Game on Proton had made him apt at quick challenges. He could sing well, and he could write poetry, including nonsense verse. That last was an achievement he was proud of, for no other robot he knew of could do it. In a moment he had fashioned some doggerel verse: "I'll be bored, without a sword," he said.

Nothing happened. "Nay, thou must sing it," Fleta reminded him. "And I think thou must concentrate, make a picture of it in thy mind."

Mach pictured an immense broadsword. "I'll be bored, without a sword!" he sang.

There was a puff of smoke and an acrid smell. Something was in his hand. As the air cleared, he looked at it.

It was a toy sword.

"Dost thou still mock me?" Fleta demanded. "What canst thou fight with that?"

But Mach was amazed. "I conjured it!" he said. "I actually did conjure it!"

"Of course thou didst conjure it!" Fleta agreed acidly, stamping a foot in rather cute frustration. "But I did mean a *real* sword!"

"I *tried* for a real sword," Mach said. "But I really didn't believe it would work."

"It did *not* work, numbskull! In years of yore, thou wouldst have wrought a truly adequate blade."

"In just a day of yore, I wasn't even here," he retorted, nettled.

She softened. "Aye, sirrah, I forget! Well, try again."

That seemed sensible. Mach set down the toy, concentrated on an image of a yard-long blade formed of stainless steel, and sang: "I'll be bored without a sword!"

There was a swirl of fog before him. It dissipated, leaving— nothing. Not even a toy sword.

"Art sure thou art really trying?" Fleta asked.

"I thought I was," Mach said, baffled. "The first must have been a fluke."

"Canst not get through without a weapon," Fleta said.

"I could make a weapon."

"And conjure another toy? This be tiresome!"

"I mean by hand."

"By hand?"

"To craft it from a natural object. A stone, or a piece of wood." He looked about as he spoke. There were many stones along the slope they had just descended, and old branches littered the ground between the trees.

"An thou dost try to bop a dragon on the snout with a mere stone, thy hand and half thy arm will pay the forfeit," she pointed out.

"Unless I threw the stone."

"Then thou wouldst not have thy weapon anymore."

"Um. Maybe an axe, then." He walked back to the slope, peering at the offerings. He found several nicely fragmented stones with sharp edges. When he found one of suitable shape, he kept it and started his search for a handle. "Are there any vines around here?"

"Vines? Thou meanest to tie up the dragon?"

He laughed. "No. To tie on my axehead." He found a stout stick of suitable size.

She wended her way among the trees, and soon found a vine. She tugged at it, but it would not come free from the tree. He joined her, setting his hands above hers and hauling down hard, but only succeeded in hauling himself up. He lost his balance and fell into her. She let go, and they both tumbled to the ground.

"Clumsy oaf!" Fleta exclaimed, trying to extricate herself from his involuntary grasp. "Willst tear my cloak!"

"Sorry." He helped her get free, somewhat diffidently, because she kept reminding him of a Citizen. Nevertheless, the brief contact reminded him forcefully how nicely endowed she was, in the feminine sense. His breakup with Doris in Proton still stung; it would be nice to—

But of course he knew almost nothing about this pretty young woman. She seemed to know a lot about him, or about Bane, so lacked that disadvantage. She had come to join him in the crater, apparently intentionally, because she took him for her old friend. Yet there were ways in which that association seemed other than ordinary friendship. She had kissed him, and gone naked for him though it was not her normal state. Yet again, she had not signaled any actual sexual involvement between them. It was almost as if she were his sister, or perhaps half-sister, close enough to have no secrets or shame, yet distant enough to be aware of him as a male. Of *Bane;* this intimacy obviously did not extend to Mach. Mach found himself jealous of that intimacy, of whatever nature.

Meanwhile they had a challenge in this vine. It was good that it was tough; he needed strength. But how could he get a suitable length of it for his purpose?

Aha! He brought over his axehead stone. He held the vine firm with one hand, and sawed with the sharp edge of the stone. In a moment the vine parted. He had his cord.

He used the stone to split the end of the stick, then wedged the stone into that cleft, so that the sharp edge was at the side. He wound the vine around and around this joining, drawing it tight. He pulled the tag-end into the crevice below the stone, so that it was caught firmly.

Fleta surveyed the result dubiously. "That be an axe?"

"A crude one. It will have to do."

"It will take more than that to stop a dragon."

"Then I will use it to make more than that." Mach took his axe and chopped at a sapling. The head started to work out of its cleft, and the cord tried to unravel; he had to rework both more carefully. But he managed to fashion a pole about two and a half meters long. "A staff," he announced.

"A dragon would chomp it off," Fleta said. But she seemed halfway impressed.

Mach checked the ground again, picking up a number of smaller stones. "And what be these for?" Fleta inquired.

"For distance operations. I'll throw them to keep a monster away."

"Canst throw well?"

"In my own body I have perfect aim; it comes from long experience in the Game," he said.

There was a swirl in the air, and vapor formed. But in a moment it dissipated. "What was that?" Fleta asked, alarmed.

"It resembled the effects when I tried to do magic," he said. "But I wasn't—"

"Thou didst speak in rhyme!" she exclaimed.

". . . aim, . . . Game," he agreed, remembering. "But I had no magic in mind; it was an accident."

"If thou canst do magic by accident, why canst thou not do it on purpose?"

"But I *tried* to do it on purpose, and got nowhere."

She tilted her head thoughtfully. "There be things we know not about thy magic. Many a time I heard Bane conjure, but when I copied him, it worked not. Methinks it be a matter of person and of form, and if thou beest not he, yet dost thou possess the talent. Thou didst not even sing that time, yet the magic tried to come."

Mach sighed. "I'll try it again." He held up his hand. "I thirst;

I think—I want a drink," he singsonged, visualizing a nutra-beverage.

The fog swirled, and the tall cup appeared in his hand. "It worked!" he exclaimed.

"It doth look more like mudwater," Fleta commented.

"Nutra is opaque." He brought it to his mouth and sipped. He spat it out. "That *is* mudwater!"

Fleta laughed. "I told thee!"

"So I bungled it again. But I *did* conjure it!"

"Methinks there be much learning to thine art," she said.

"Surely so! Maybe I should practice." He set down the cup, held his hand up again, and repeated his incantation.

This time the fog swirled, but all that came to his hand was a splat of mud.

Fleta laughed again. "What a clumsy Adept thou beest!"

Mach flipped the mud at her. He did not intend to have it hit her, but his aim was better than intended; the mud scored on her neck just above her robe, and slid down her front.

"Thou monster!" she exclaimed, scooping up a handful of moist dirt where the mudwater had spilled.

"Now wait! I didn't mean to—"

Her heave caught him on the forehead. "Now we be even," she said with satisfaction.

Mach decided to let it go at that. "But how do we get clean?"

"We wash in the stream," she said. She showed the way down through the forest to a tiny stream. There was a pool just big enough to dip a hand into.

Fleta hesitated, then shrugged and pulled off her cloak. "Methinks I was foolish to react as I did, when I learned thou wast not the man I knew. I have no need for modesty before thee." The mud had soiled the skin between her breasts. She cupped her hands and scooped up water, splashing it against her torso. Mach had found her more alluring when she had donned the cloak, because in Proton covering was the mark of power and privacy; now he reacted even more to her renewed nakedness. There was something about the water and the way she washed herself off.

Fleta, clean, shook herself. Her breasts seemed to move independently of her torso. Then she paused, looking at him. "And what be that?" she asked, smiling impishly.

Mach abruptly felt himself flushing. He turned away.

"I said not it was wrong!" Fleta exclaimed. "Methought I moved thee not, Bane, since we achieved maturity."

"I am not Bane," he said tightly. How could this have happened to him? As a robot he reacted sexually only when he chose to, never by accident.

"Aye, that thou art not," she agreed softly. "I thought to tease thee as we did each other, when we were young. We—Bane and I—played games we ne'er told the adults."

"And we of Proton," he agreed. "But I did not mean to—I did not realize this would happen."

"Nor I, Mach. But would I offend thee if I confess I be not grieved it did?"

His flush, by the feel of it, seemed to be fading, but not the rest. "Fleta, I really don't know. Exactly what was the relationship between you and Bane?"

"Friends," she said. "Good friends, as good as can be, though we ne'er made oath on't. Secrets we had, only with each other. But then we grew apart."

"Friends—so close you even—?"

She came and set her cool hand on his shoulder. "Mach, there be naught that human man and woman can do together that we did not do, or try. But we were too young; it meant naught. Today it would be another matter, for we are grown."

"So I should not—react this way—to you," he said with difficulty.

She sighed. "Thou shouldst not," she agreed. "We be too old for such games now, methinks. But Mach, fear not; ne'er will I tell."

"We—you and Bane—are related?" he asked.

She burst into laughter. "Related!" She reached around him from behind and hugged him. This did not help his condition, for her breasts pressed hard against his back. "Thou dost not know, really?"

"Of course I don't know!" he said, trying to be angry, but wishing he could turn and embrace her. How could he be so far out of control?

"Then shall I tell thee not," she said, releasing him.

"You said you would not tease me!"

"This be other than teasing," she said. "I fear thou wouldst like not the truth."

"I always like the truth!"

"Then accept this, Mach: now I understand somewhat better the case with thee, and I be flattered, not annoyed, and would preserve it a little longer. Come, face me as thou art; I have seen thee thus before, and will speak of it not further, an that please thee."

He seemed to have no choice. He turned, and she neither laughed nor frowned, though she did look. He knelt by the pool and dipped out water to wash off his face.

"We be not related," Fleta said after a moment. "But naught more than games between us was e'er possible."

"I wish you would tell me why!"

"When I tell thee, thou willst be angry with me, and that I seek not."

"I promise I won't be angry! I just want to know."

But she shook her head, knowing better than he. "Methinks thou wouldst be more comfortable in clothing," she said in a moment. "It be the custom here."

He realized that she was correct. To go naked in a culture where clothing was the norm was not sensible. He would have to suppress his natural aversion to misrepresenting his status, and become a normal person of this frame, at least until he learned how to return to his robot body. Likewise, he could not afford to presume too much on the fact that she had seen Bane in a state of sexual excitement when young; obviously Fleta was no such playmate *now*.

Suddenly he realized why he was having trouble controlling his reactions: he was in a living body! He breathed, he had a heartbeat, he had to eat and drink and eliminate—of course he reacted sexually too! This was not, he now understood, entirely voluntary; when a stimulation came to him, his body reacted even when he did not wish it to. He had assumed that he would have no special interest in sex until he chose to, as was the case in Proton, but the sight of Fleta's wet and moving anatomy had bypassed his intellect and made his body react. Thus his surprised embarrassment. The circuits of living creatures were to an extent self-motivating.

No wonder the folk here wore clothing! Not only did it prevent unwanted stimulation, it concealed unwanted reaction.

"I'll wear clothing," he agreed. But still he wondered: if Fleta was, as she said, flattered rather than embarrassed by the evidence of his reaction, why did she say that there should be no such action between them? If they had done it as children, and they were not related (and why had she found that notion so hilarious?), why was it wrong now? Were they promised to other partners? Yet she had not said that; she acted as if there were some more fundamental reason why nothing serious between them was possible. And she feared he would be angry when he learned.

He cast about, looking for something that could be fashioned into clothing. All that he could see that had any such prospect at all was the large leaves of some trees. Well, they would have to do.

Fleta helped him gather some good leaves. Then they used his axe to make slits in a vine, and passed the stems of the leaves through, with long-stemmed leaves overlapping short-stemmed ones, forming a kind of skirt. They wrapped the vine about his waist, and the leaves hung down to cover him to an extent.

But already there was another problem. His shoulders were turning red. "Sunburn!" Fleta said. "I forgot—thy kind suffers from that; it be another reason you wear clothing."

His kind? Wasn't her kind the same?

"I suppose we could make a collar to suspend a shirt of leaves," he said, not enthusiastically. As it was, the leaves brushed constantly against him, stirring awareness of a region he preferred to tune out.

"Mayhap thou couldst conjure some cloth."

He tried: "I'll be wroth, without some cloth," he sang, visualizing an enormous bolt of cloth.

He got a fragment of cloth about the size of a Citizen's handkerchief.

He grimaced. "And if I try it again, I'll get a thread or two," he muttered. "It never works the second time."

"Mach! That be it!" Fleta exclaimed. "Ne'er did I hear Bane use the same spell twice!"

"Good for only one shot," he said, gratified by the revelation. "Canst try the same, with other words?"

"Why not?" He pondered a moment, then sang: "Cloth: I implore, bring me some more." He visualized an even larger bolt.

And the fog swirled, and deposited twice as much of the same type of cloth as it had before.

Now they understood the system. Mach invented a number of rhymes, garnering needle and thread and more cloth so he could sew a shirt. Fleta seemed to have no knowledge of sewing. He found that variation of melody also facilitated the conjurations, and that he got more of what he visualized if he built up to it by humming a few bars first. He was learning to be a magician!

It was close to midday by the time they were ready to travel. Bane had considered trying a spell to move them directly to the Blue Demesnes, but decided not to; he would probably drop them in the swamp instead. If the magic was going to foul up, let it foul up on details that didn't affect their living processes!

He now wore crudely fashioned sandals, and a ragged broad-brimmed hat, to protect his feet from abrasion and his head and neck from the sun, and in between was as strange an assemblage of clothing as he could have imagined. Swatches of cloth, leaves, vines and even a patch of leather, all fastened together haphazardly. But it covered him, protecting him from both the burning of the sun and the embarrassment of possible involuntary reactions. He would get out of the costume the moment he returned to Proton, of course; rather, Bane would, for Bane would be back in his own body, and surely would recover his normal clothes. In fact, Mach himself would recover those clothes when he got back to the glade he had started from.

Mach spied a huge shape in the sky to the south, where the horizon was a ragged purple range of mountains. Those mountains existed also in Proton, of course; the natural geography of the two frames was supposed to be identical. "What's that?"

"A dragon," Fleta said. "Hide if it come near."

"They are in the air as well as the water?"

"Aye, everywhere, and always hungry. Few other than an Adept fear not their like."

Mach could appreciate why. He kept a wary eye on the sky thereafter.

The path reached the swamp. Now Mach hefted his crude weapons nervously, remembering the dragon that had been here. Maybe it would be asleep.

They had no such fortune. Fleta knew the path, and led him along it without misstep despite the murkiness of the water, but when they were too far along to turn readily back, the monster reared up.

Gazing at it, Mach abruptly wished he were elsewhere. His axe and staff seemed woefully inadequate. The dragon was so huge!

"I can help, if—" Fleta said.

"My job. You get on to safety while I hold it off." That sounded a good deal bolder than he felt. Still, his Game experience had acquainted him with different modes of combat, mock-dragons included. This was more nervous business than that, as it was real, but the same principles should hold. The dragon should be vulnerable in a number of places, and a bold enough challenge should dissuade it. The thing was, after all, an animal.

First he tried his stones. He fired the first at the dragon's left eye. His aim was good; he knew his capacity here. But the monster blinked as the stone flew in, and it bounced off the leathery eyelid. So much for that.

Mach threw the second stone at the dragon's teeth. This one scored, but the tooth it struck was too large and strong; a tiny chip of enamel flew off, but the damage only aggravated the creature without hurting it.

The third stone he aimed at the flaring nostrils. It disappeared inside—and the dragon sneezed. The target was too big and spongy, and the stone too small, to do sufficient damage. But it did verify what Mach wanted to know: that the tissue there was soft, not hard. Few animals liked getting their tender tissues tagged.

Vapor swirled as the dragon warmed up. Mach hoped his

clothing would shield him from the worst of the heat if he got blasted by steam; meanwhile, he would do his best to prevent the dragon from scoring with it.

Mach lifted his long staff. As the dragon's head loomed close, he poked it with the end of the pole. Surprised, the dragon snapped at the pole, but Mach swung it free. He was accomplishing his intent: he had the dragon trying to attack the weapon instead of the man.

When the dragon's teeth snapped on air, Mach reversed the pole and smashed it into the nostrils. The dragon reared back; that blow smarted!

Then the dragon heaved out steam. But the range was too great, and the aim was bad; no steam touched Mach. He aimed the pole at an eye and rammed; again the dragon blinked, but the pole scored, and pushed in the eye before rebounding. This time the eye was hurt; some blood showed as the dragon jerked back and the pole fell away.

"Thou'rt beating it!" Fleta exclaimed, amazed.

"I intended to," Mach puffed, discovering that this effort was tiring him. He had forgotten, again: this living body lacked the endurance of the machine.

The dragon, hurt, vented a horrendous cloud of steam, then charged back into the fray. So sudden was the thrust that Mach didn't have time to swing the cumbersome pole back into position. The dragon bit at it sidewise and chomped it in two.

Mach drew his axe. Suddenly he was worried; he hadn't wanted to resort to this, because of the close contact required. But apparently the dragon had forgotten to use the steam, and just charged in with jaws gaping.

Mach stepped aside, and bashed his axe violently down on the dragon's nose as the jaws closed on the spot he had occupied. The stone blade sank into the right nostril, hacking through the flesh. Blood welled out.

But Mach was now on uncertain footing, and his step and blow had put him off balance. He took another step—and found no path. He splashed headlong into the water.

The dragon was thrashing, really hurt by the blow to its nose, but it remained alert enough to spot the sudden opportunity. It whipped its snout about to pluck Mach out of the water. Fleta screamed.

Without purchase on the path, Mach could not strike another blow, or even escape. He was helpless before those descending teeth.

"Without aplomb, bring me a bomb!" he sang with sudden inspiration.

Fog swirled. The bomb appeared in his hand. He heaved it into the opening mouth. In a moment it detonated.

The dragon paused, closing its mouth. Vapor seeped out between its teeth. Mach realized that he had again failed to conjure what he really wanted; the bomb had been a dud, or at least too small and weak to do the job. The one he had imagined would have blown the monster's head apart.

The dragon lifted its head. Thick vapor jetted from its uninjured nostril. Its near eye bulged. The bomb had not really hurt it, but evidently the vapor bothered it. Mach remained in the water, watching.

Then he caught a whiff of the vapor. It was insect destructant! He knew the smell from the times he had visited one of the garden domes in Proton, where they had occasional insect infestations, and flooded the domes with this vapor. It was supposed to be harmless to larger creatures, but human beings tried to avoid breathing it.

Instead of a real bomb, he had gotten a bug-bomb. Now it was spewing its noxious vapor into the dragon's mouth—and the dragon didn't have the wit to spit it out!

In a moment the dragon plunged under the water, but a trail of evil-smelling bubbles showed that the monster still hadn't let go of the bomb. Mach smiled as he clambered back to the path. His bomb had done the job after all!

"Oh, Mach, I feared for thee!" Fleta exclaimed, coming into his arms as he stood. She kissed him, then drew back. "Oh, I should have done that not!"

"Why not?"

"I think I like thee too well."

"But you won't tell me why that's wrong?"

"Aye," she agreed with a rueful smile.

"You're stubborn!"

"My kind be that."

"Well, I like you too," he said. "I think you're a great girl, and I wish—" But he had to break off. What did he wish? That he could stay with her? That he could take her with him to Proton? Neither was possible, as far as he knew.

She drew away. "I was minded to—to do what I had to to save thee, but it happened so suddenly, and then thou didst vanquish the dragon alone. Thou art a hero, Mach!"

"Well, I wasn't going to let it eat you," he said.

"Yes, thou didst urge me to safety, whilst thou fought. No man of Phaze would have done that for my like, except perhaps the Blue Adept, and that be different."

The Blue Adept. Mach's father had been that before transferring to Proton, where his magic didn't work. She referred to the other one, of course. But the two were alternate selves, and yes, either would have done the same to save a damsel in distress.

"We must go on, before more come," she said.

"There are more water dragons?" he asked, alarmed.

"Many more," she agreed.

He hurried after her, anxious to depart this swamp.

5

Search

Bane stared. The landscape was absolutely barren. There were no trees, no bushes, no plants at all. There was only dry sand and grayish mist as far as he could see. It was dusk, but he realized that even by full daylight he would not have seen much more.

"The country—where be it?" he asked, horrified.

"This is the country, Bane," Agape said through the speaker-grille in her helmet.

"But it can't be! There be no life here!"

"There is no life on Proton," she said. "Except within the domes. Did you not know?"

"I—I thought it would be like Phaze, only less so," he admitted. "This—how did it happen?"

"I do not know much about the history of this planet, but I believe it was once alive. But the residents paid no heed to the quality of its environment, and so gradually it became as it is now, with good air and life in the dome-cities, and bad air outside. It is not this way where you live?"

"It be all sunshine and forest and meadows where the unicorns graze and rivers and magic," Bane said. "Oh, what a horror be here!"

"But that means that the one you seek is comfortable, for he is there," she pointed out. "You can seek him as you intended."

"But—this," he said, baffled by the desolation.

"We can walk, or perhaps ride."

"Ride? There be no animals here!"

"There are vehicles. I think serfs are permitted to utilize them."

"Vehicles?"

"I do not know the specifics, but I am sure some are near, for the residents of the domes do not like to walk far outside. Let us look."

Bane let her take the lead. She moved around the curve of the building they had just exited, and there was an alcove with several squat shapes within. She trudged to one and lifted its glassy upper section. Inside there were two deep holes. She climbed into one. "This will do," she said. "Take the other seat, Bane. I think I can drive this."

He climbed into the other hole. The transparent top settled down, shutting them in. Then there was a hissing, and gas swirled up. He tried to scramble out, but Agape restrained him. "It is not evil, Bane! It is air, so I can breathe without the helmet. When the light shows green, it will be all right."

And in a moment a green light appeared before them, on a panel in the vehicle. Agape removed her helmet. "It will not release until I reseal my suit," she said. "The gas out here would be harmful to my metabolism."

"But I want not to stay in here!" he protested. "I want to look for mine other self!"

She smiled. "I think it is good that I am with you. I will make this machine perform." She touched buttons before her, and took hold of a handle, bringing it out and down toward her.

Suddenly the vehicle lurched forward. Bane almost leaped out of his seat, but this time padded straps appeared and restrained him.

He peered out the forward glass. The terrain was coming toward him, as though he were riding a horse. "This—this be a wagon!" he exclaimed. "It moves by itself!"

"Yes, it is a machine, like your body, but not as intelligent as yours."

"A machine," he repeated, assimilating the concept. "Like a golem, or an enchanted object."

"I think your world is as alien to this one as is mine," she said.

"My world is *natural*. This be the alien one."

"With that, too, I can agree." She glanced at him. "Where would you travel, Bane?"

"I—I hadn't thought. I mean, I had expected to circle in the forest, seeking to intercept mine other self. But now I know not."

"The forest remains there, for him," she reminded him. "I can circle if you wish." And she guided the vehicle into a broad loop.

"No, I have other thoughts, now. I think he would not have remained in the glade. There be dangers." He peered out again. "The night be closing rapidly. He would seek shelter."

"Would he know where to find it?"

That question did not ease Bane's mind. "I fear not. He could follow the path, but it forks, and the one fork goes to the Unicorn Demesnes, while the other— Oh, I hope he took that one not!"

"Where does it go?"

"To the swamp, where there be monsters. Of course, if they took him for me they would stay clear." He brightened. "The clothing marks me as of the Blue Demenses."

"Clothing?"

"Yes. We wear clothing there. So—"

"But he is of Proton," she pointed out. "Would he wear clothing?"

Bane's heart sank. "Nay, I fear not. But if he followed that path naked—" He shuddered.

"If he should follow it, and wear his clothing so he was not harmed, where would he finish?" Agape asked.

"It goes to an old empty crater the ogres used. But we cleaned them out. Sometimes Fleta and I would go there to play." He smiled privately.

"Who is Fleta? A girl-companion?"

He laughed. "Companion, yes; girl, no. Tell me not thou'rt jealous of her, Agape!"

"I am your companion, and I am not a girl," Agape said. "Am I permitted to be jealous?"

He mulled that over. "I suppose there be a parallel, after all. Fleta and I were very close, as children, though I have seen not much of her recently. Thou mayst be jealous if thou dost wish." He smiled.

"Thank you."

Suddenly he realized something. "I have reverted to mine own mode of speech! I should have talked to thee—to you not thus!"

"Please, Bane, do not change your speech for me. I like it as it is. I know what it is to be in a strange society."

"But if others realize mine origin, there could be trouble." He was also embarrassed to think that it had probably happened because he had been distracted by her voluptuous body.

"I will not tell others," she promised.

He believed her. He had no magic here, but he had a sense about people, and he liked her. "Then let's find mine other self."

"Of course."

"But let's assume he followed the correct path. That would take him to the Herd, and they would recognize him with or without clothing, and bear him home to the Blue Demesnes."

"The herd?"

"The local unicorn herd. They be all oath-friends with Neysa, and Neysa is oath-friend to my father Stile, so none would e'er do me harm. They would believe that Mach is me, under some hostile spell, so would take him home right away."

"And home is these blue demesnes? Where are they?"

"North of the herd demesnes. In Phaze every type of creature of any significance has its own region, called its demesnes, and so do the Adepts, the leading magicians. Of course there be a number of unicorn herds, just as there be many werewolf packs, but the important ones to us be the oath-friends."

"Wolves too?"

"It all dates back to when my father made the Oath of Friendship with Neysa, so powerful it embraced all the members of the Herd and the Pack too. Because I be the child of Stile, I can safely go anywhere in those demesnes, because no unicorn or werewolf would harm me, and no lesser creature would dare to, for fear of the Herd and the Pack. So Mach will be safe."

"If he took that path," she said.

"He *has* to have taken that path!" he said vehemently. "Otherwise—"

"Surely he took it," she agreed.

"So we can go to the Blue Demesnes, and find him there," he concluded.

"And these are north of here?"

"Should be northeast of here."

"But—"

"They be north of the Herd, but the Herd be east of the glade where we exchanged identities. That glade coincides with Mach's room in the dome; that be why I was able to locate him there, and finally to achieve rapport with him. Since the two geographies be identical, I can find the spot here by taking the same route I would there." He peered again into the darkening gloom. "I hope."

"There should be a map," she said.

"A map?"

"A map of Proton. All planets have maps." She touched buttons, and a screen illuminated. Soon the map appeared.

Bane stared at it. "That be Phaze!" he exclaimed.

"It says it is Proton," she said. "See, here is our city, Hardom, with our vehicle location glowing." She pointed to the blinking spark of light on the map.

"That be the Harpy Demesnes!" he said. "Right above the Purple Mountains."

"Harpy Demesnes? Was the city named after the harpies?"

"Impossible! There be no harpies in Proton." But then he reconsidered. "Still, that does sound like har as in harpy, and since it be a dome—Har-dome. Hardom. I wonder." He focused on the other points of the map. "Down here be the Mound Folk of Phaze—and here be Moudom! And here, farther to the east, be the demesnes of the Gnomes—and here be Gnodom! They do match!"

"It really is a map of Phaze? This seems remarkable, if there has been no contact between the frames."

"Maybe not. Up until twenty years ago, the frames were more

closely connected. There was a curtain that some folk could cross. My father crossed it, to woo my mother. How long ago were these cities named?"

She touched another button. "It says three hundred years ago, for most."

"Then that's it! They were named when Phaze and Proton were one, before they separated, and long before that separation became complete. The original settlers knew they were the same!"

"This is very interesting," she said. "My own planet has only one aspect."

"That's probably the case with most—you call them planets?"

"The satellites of other stars, far away."

He was distracted for a moment. "How far away be thine?"

"About fifty light years."

He shook his head. "That means naught to me."

She smiled. "Magic means nothing to me, but I accept your information on it."

He returned the smile. "I question not thy word, Agape. And thou art not a human being?"

"I am not. I assume this form so that I may participate without offense in this human society."

"Just as Fleta assumed human form to play with me," he said. "I have no trouble with that."

"I am most pleased that you do not. Though my form in its natural state does not resemble yours, my protoplasm is similar and my emotions similar too. I wish to be your friend."

"Thou *art* my friend, Agape. Thou art helping me greatly."

"I am pleased to do so. Do you wish me to program this vehicle for the Blue Demesnes?"

"Program it?"

"To give it a directive that will guide it there without further guidance from us," she explained.

"But there be no Blue Demesnes here! Just the spot where they be in Phaze."

"The map shows a location titled 'Blue,' " she said. "Does this coincide?"

He looked. "It does! But how could that be? Sure I be that the Blue Demesnes have been there not for three hundred years!"

"I do not know; I have been only briefly on this planet."

"Well, go ahead and send the machine there. This is not much different from magic."

She operated the buttons. The vehicle turned, assuming the new course, and accelerated.

It was full night now, but no stars showed; the gloom masked whatever light might have tried to shine through. The vehicle's front lamp shone forward, showing nothing but sand rushing past. This seemingly mindless progress made Bane nervous, so he averted his gaze.

That brought Agape into view. "How long will it take to reach the Blue Demesnes?" he asked.

She touched another button. "About fifteen minutes. The vehicle is very fast."

"Fifteen minutes to accomplish a trip that would require a horse two hours!" he exclaimed.

"Space travel is much faster."

That reminded him of her origin. In the dim light of the interior of the vehicle she looked completely human, and beautiful. Her hair framed her face with the color of a pale sunset, and her eyes seemed preternaturally deep. "Thou really art alien?" he asked, finding this hard to believe.

"Completely," she agreed. "In physical form."

"Thou art the loveliest woman I have seen!"

"That is because I have shaped myself to be what your kind considers attractive. You would not find me so, in my natural state."

"Canst thou assume thy natural state now?"

"I can. But I think I would prefer not to. Your machine self perceived me in that state, and was not repulsed, but you are human, and I want to attract you, not repulse you."

"Why dost thou care how I react to you? If thou art as different as thou sayst, I must appear to be a monster to thee."

"Oh, no, Bane!" she protested. "You are a fine figure of your species, to me. I would like to be your girlfriend."

"Just because mine other self helped thee?"

"I like him well for that, but now I know you better, and I like you better. You are more alive."

"How could an alien creature be a—a girlfriend to me?"

"I was hoping you would be able to show me that."

He shook his head, still having trouble reconciling her words with her appearance. She was infernally beautiful, and he liked her personality; it really did not seem alien. "Methinks I could show a real woman. But an alien might understand not at all."

She leaned close to him. "Please, Bane, I want very much to learn! I will do anything you suggest."

Still that nagging doubt. "*Why* dost thou want to learn? The human means of association and—and the rest should not concern a completely different creature."

"My species is amoebic," she said. "Your kind calls our world Moeba. We have had no experience with the pairing of sexes. We pair any with any, as we choose. But we observe that most other species of the galaxy are twin-sexed, and this appears to confer an advantage in evolution, so that they achieved technology and space before we did, and now we are dependent on them for interplanetary trade and travel between the stars. We can learn whatever they teach us, so now we are constructing our own ships of space, but we believe we should also master their secret of evolution. This is one reason I have come to the Planet of Proton. To learn about the sexes. I have assumed the female form because it is relatively passive; I believe I can learn better this way. But learn I must, so I can report to my kind and they can judge whether this is a feasible course."

"I thought thou didst plan to stay here," he said, finding himself disappointed.

"I do. I will stay just as long as I can. I will become a Citizen if I can. I will send my reports by spacemail; I will remain here. There is more to learn here than sexual reproduction."

"Then thou willst be a human being for the rest of thy life, or seem to be."

"Yes, Bane. Already I feel somewhat human, with you."

"Willst thou show me, at least a little, thy true form?"

"I do not wish to revolt you, Bane."

"I will make thee a deal," he said. "Show me thy true nature, and I will show thee how to—to be a human woman. Some."

"Some? Bane, I must learn it all!"

"But these things are not done just as a business," he protested. "It—I have never done it all with a human woman, actually. Just games with Fleta and the like."

"Show me a little, and I will show you a little," she offered.

He laughed, somewhat uneasily. "Fair enough, Agape. Here be a little." He leaned farther toward her, tilted his head, and touched her lips with his own.

Her lips were unresponsive. It was like kissing mush.

He drew back. "That was it?" she inquired.

"Thou dost have to kiss back!" he exclaimed.

"You mean, to purse my mouth while you purse yours?"

"Aye. Only with some feeling. This be supposed to be an emotional contact, knowest thou not?"

"Ah, now I understand. To feel desire during the act."

"Thy kind does feel desire?"

"It does. It merely expresses it in another fashion."

"Shallst try again?" He leaned forward, and touched her lips with his for the second time.

And this time hers were firm and highly responsive. He found it easy to get into the spirit of the kiss. He reached his arms about her, and she emulated his action. He pressed her in close, and she pressed him in close, and it was several times the experience he had anticipated, despite the bulkiness of her suit.

Except for one thing. She was doing what he did—too perfectly. She was like a three-dimensional mirror image. Nothing originated with her; it all was a reflection of him.

He drew back. "Much improved," he said. "But thou must not copy me in every detail. That makest thou seem—like a machine."

She laughed. "I understand! One must not be mechanical."

"Perhaps Mach would have had different advice," he agreed, smiling.

"I did not know you had changed identities, but I think I will know the difference hereafter. Though your body is a machine, your mind is alive."

He nodded. "I wonder how that be possible? I certainly feel not like a machine."

"I believe our forms determine our natures to a degree," she said. "I do not feel like an amoeba, either." She sighed. "And now I must make my small showing, and perhaps you will never kiss me again."

"I'll make the effort," he promised.

She peeled back her suit, so that she became bare to the waist. "Watch me."

"I be watching thee."

"My hand, not my torso."

"Oh." He modified his gaze accordingly.

She held up her left hand. It was a fine, esthetic extremity, with four slender fingers and an opposed thumb, each nail delicately tinted. But slowly it changed. The fingers lost firmness, becoming floppy balloons. They sank back onto the body of the hand, which melted into a glob.

Bane stared. "Thou hast no bones?"

"No bones anywhere in my body. Only tissue that I make firm, patterned after human bones, to support the structure."

"When Fleta changes, she does it instantly. One moment she be a pretty girl; the next she be a hummingbird. Of course that's magic."

"I cannot do that," Agape admitted. "It does require a little time for me to change, and I must melt into my natural state before assuming an alternate form. And—I do not know the hummingbird. Is it of similar mass to the human form?"

Bane snorted. "Hardly! It's a tiny thing, hardly bigger than my thumb. Size matters not, with magic."

"I find that hard to believe."

"I think anyone in Proton would find it hard to believe."

"My mass remains constant. I could assume the form of a bird, but it would be of my present weight, and could not fly."

"Thy hand—it could become something else?"

For answer, she concentrated. The lump of protoplasm at the end of her arm grew projections, each of which sprouted further projections, until she had about thirty thin fronds there. "A Formican appendage," she said. "I remember that form from the time I visited their planet."

"So thy magic be limited in speed and size, but unlimited in form," he concluded. "I think thy ability be as good as Fleta's."

"Thank you—I think," she said. The new appendage dissolved, and the human hand began to reform. "You are not revolted?"

"Agape, I be used to shape-changing. Once did I envy the

werewolves their ability to change from human form to canine form, and have all the powers of the animal. And I liked Fleta in all three of her forms."

"Then I am relieved. I will change form for you, when you ask me to." She leaned toward him, and he, understanding her desire, kissed her. This time she was responsive without mirroring him. She was a rapid learner!

The vehicle slowed. They broke. "We are there," Agape said, hauling up her suit and restoring her helmet. "We shall search for your other self now."

Bane was almost disappointed. He cared less about shapes than about personality, thanks to his experience with the magical creatures of Phaze, and both her human form and her attitude were easy to accept. It was too bad he would lose contact with her when he exchanged places with his other self and returned to Phaze.

They opened the vehicle and stepped out. They found ruins. There had evidently once been a small dome here, with a castle in it of the same type as that of the Blue Demesnes in Phaze, but all was wreckage now. The desert sand was doing its best to bury the remains.

But there was no wreckage in Phaze. Bane walked around the oddly familiar premises, seeking some hint of his other self. If he overlapped the space, or even came close, he would know. It would not work for any other person; he could be walking right through others in Phaze, and never know. But his own self he could not miss.

It wasn't here. There was no sign of the self at all. Bane crisscrossed every part of the ruin, finding nothing.

"He didn't get here," he said at last.

"Surely some delay," Agape said quickly. "Proceeding afoot, unfamiliar with the terrain—it might require days."

"It might. It also might mean he's dead."

"We must not believe that!" she said. "I—I have no experience with this phenomenon of dual selves, but I conjecture—wouldn't you feel something if there were demise? Is there not some continuing connection between the two of you?"

"I suppose there should be," Bane agreed thoughtfully. "I

tuned in to him in the first place by going with the flow. The closer I got, the more I felt it, when I listened."

"Listen now!" she urged.

He stood and listened. He tried to extend his awareness out, to become perceptive to the soul of his other self, wherever it might be. He could almost see his ambience reaching out in a great circle, sensitive to the ambience of his other identity in Phaze.

He found it! Faintly in the distance, like an echo, he felt the rapport. "He be alive!" he exclaimed. "There!" He pointed to the southwest.

"Back the way we came," Agape said. "Or a little west; the vehicle curved eastward."

"We can go directly toward him!" Bane said, relieved. "Oh, thank thee for the notion, Agape!" He took hold of her, intending to kiss her, but discovered it was impossible while she was in suit and helmet.

They returned to the vehicle. The dome of it sealed, and the air came in. Agape lifted back her helmet. "Did you have something in mind, Bane?"

"Just to go toward my other self until we intercept him," he said. Then, becoming aware of her expectant attitude: "Oh, yes." He leaned over and kissed her. This time it was about as good as it seemed likely to get, in this circumstance.

That gave him pause. "When I—thou willst be left here, with Mach."

"I know you must return to your own land," she said. "For you, Proton is more alien than it is to me."

"Dost thou know, Agape, I almost wish I could take thee with me."

"I almost wish I could go," she agreed. "But even as your place is there, my place is here. I have a duty to my species that I must fulfill. So I think that even were it possible, I would not go with you to your magic realm. I remain glad to have been with you these hours."

There didn't seem to be much more to say. Agape started the vehicle moving, and guided it in the direction he indicated, this time keeping it under her own control. They proceeded slowly toward the rendezvous with his other self.

After an hour of travel through the wasteland, they were startled by a voice from the vehicle's speaker grille. "Directive: Serf Mach return immediately to base at Hardom. Serf Agape return immediately to base at Hardom."

"They are addressing us!" Agape said. "I must acknowledge."

"Wait!" Bane snapped. "Thou meanest we can speak to them?"

"When I invoke the communication code," she said. "It will only require a moment." She reached for the panel.

He blocked her hand. "Nay! If we speak to them, they will know we hear them. I must find my other self before we leave this course."

"But to disobey would be very bad," she protested.

"To obey might cost me my rendezvous! We have been getting closer; I can feel it. I can quit not now!"

"But there will be punishment."

"They can punish me not after I'm gone!" Then he reconsidered. "But thou willst still be here—and Mach too. That be bad."

"Serf Mach and/or serf Agape," the speaker said. "Your vehicle is occupied and moving. If you are alive and conscious, respond immediately."

"We must answer!" she said.

"But if we don't, they'll think we be dead or unconscious, and I can reach mine other self."

"I should not do this," she said, keeping her hands away from the panel.

"I'll make it up to thee!" he said. "I'll show thee all I know about—about being a girlfriend."

She smiled with a certain resignation. "Before or after you return to Phaze?"

"Before, of course! I can do it not after."

"Then that must be now."

Now he realized the significance of her question. If he took time now, he might lose his chance to achieve rapport with his other self, because there was no way to tell what threat the other might be under in Phaze. He couldn't afford to wait a moment longer than he had to. But if he didn't do it now, it wouldn't get done at all.

"Mayhap thou canst tell the vehicle to move by itself, as thou didst before," he suggested.

"I must give it a destination—and I think there is none it will understand, for this."

She was right again. He had to tune in on the other self, and she had to direct the vehicle to the spot he indicated. They could not let the vehicle run itself.

"We shall have to stop for a while, then," he said heavily.

"No, Bane, I would not interfere with your desire. Go to meet your other self."

"And leave thee here, without thine information, to be maybe sent back to thy world because thou didst help me," he said. "I can do that not."

"I think Mach would show me, if I explained. Do not delay."

"I want to show thee myself!" he said. "It be my job."

"I release you from it."

"Nay, what be right be right. Anyway—" He paused with realization. "I really do want to do it myself. I mean, not because I said I would. I—"

"Do not forget, I am an alien creature," Agape said.

"Thou'rt a nice person, in human form," he said. "Stop the vehicle."

"But you must not delay! I understand that."

"We have a conflict of interests. My father taught me to do what is right, no matter what the cost. Thou mayst have cost thyself thy stay on Proton, by helping me; I must risk my return to Phaze, helping thee. It be right. But more: I haven't known thee long, Agape, but I like thee very well already. I *want* to do what thou dost want me to."

She had a notion. "Perhaps we could keep the vehicle going, on a semi-automatic course, and you can tell me when to correct it. So no travel time would be lost."

"Will that work?"

"We shall find out." She adjusted the buttons on the panel, then settled back. The vehicle kept moving.

"Oh, Agape, I wish I had met thy like in Phaze!" he exclaimed, leaning over to kiss her. This time the experience was intensely rewarding.

In moments she was out of her suit and hugging him hungrily. But the seat restraints would not release their lower extremities while the vehicle was moving, and threatened to confine their upper portions too whenever there was a bump. This severely limited the action.

"I will deactivate the restraints," Agape said, touching the panel again.

"Serf Mach and/or serf Agape," the speaker said, startling them both. "Vehicle safety restraints have been deactivated. This indicates conscious activity. Acknowledge status immediately."

"Canst silence it?" Bane asked.

"Serf Mach return immediately to base at—" the speaker said, cutting off as she touched another button.

"What should I do now?" Agape asked.

"Come join me in my seat—no, I'll join thee in thine—" Bane hesitated, finding neither location suitable. Each place was made for one person; there really was not room for two, especially not for this type of activity. They needed more space.

"In my natural state, there are no such problems," Agape said. "But of course our forms are not fixed."

"Don't change thy form!" Bane cried. "There *has* to be a way!"

They tried for some time to find a way, but the confines of the vehicle were simply too restricted. Kissing and some handling were all they could manage.

Then there was a crash. Both were thrown against the front panel. The vehicle tilted and tumbled. It came to rest abruptly, and the smell of the polluted air outside came in.

"Dome's cracked!" Agape exclaimed, scrambling desperately back into her suit.

"We watched not, and we hit something," Bane said, chagrined.

They forced up the canopy and climbed out. The headlamp shone off at an angle, but the beam of light was enough.

"The lattice!" Bane cried. "I forgot the lattice!"

"This is an interruption in the terrain?"

"Worse than that! It be a pattern of cracks in the ground, very deep. Demons lurk in their depths. Only a unicorn can cross it without falling in, and not all of them. I forgot that the same pattern exists in Proton, only without the demons. We be lucky we crashed in the shallow part of it!"

Agape leaned into the vehicle and caused the map to appear. "Yes, it is there—LATTICE," she said. "I should have checked for hazards of terrain. Now I see why the vehicle traveled in a curve going north."

"We'll have to go around," Bane said.

"I fear not, Bane. The wheel is broken, and we have not the means to repair it. We shall have to walk."

"Around the lattice? That would take forever!"

"Will your other self cross it? How will he do it?"

"He would have to skirt it to the south," Bane said. "But I want him not to do that, because the demons watch the path. They'll come out and grab him. I need to intercept him before he gets here."

"Then won't the demons grab *you?*" she asked, alarmed.

"Me? Hardly! I would float them into the river. But Mach won't know magic; it takes years to learn to do it properly, and only a few even have the talent. He may not."

"Then I suppose we had better walk," she said.

"Will help come for thee, if thou dost ask for it in the vehicle? Thou couldst wait there, out of danger, while I go on."

"The cracking of the canopy would have caused an automatic distress signal to be launched," she said. "They will be on the way already."

"Then I'll get caught!" he said. "I must get going!"

"I will come with you," she said. "There may still be some assistance I can lend."

Bane doubted this, but liked her company, so he agreed. At the same time he felt guilty, because he had made her a promise he was unable to keep. She was likely to pay heavily for her involvement with him. He wished again that he didn't have to leave her.

They walked, skirting the network of cracks, still homing in on the other self. Bane now judged it to be in the region of the crater; evidently Mach had taken the wrong path, but somehow made it through the swamp to relative safety. But there was no way out of the crater except back through the swamp, and if he tried that path again, the monsters would be twice as ferocious as before. Bane had to intercept him and make the exchange before Mach started moving again.

Something glittered in the air. "Oh, no," Bane said. "A night dragon!"

"Or a flying machine," Agape said. "I fear they have discovered us."

"We must hide!"

"We cannot; it is my suit and the metal in your body they orient on. Oh, Bane, I am sorry you were not able to complete your quest."

Bane took her suited form in his arms, unspeaking. He discovered that he was not as sorry as he thought he should have been. They waited for the flying machine to capture them.

6
Revelations

Evidently the news had spread among monsters that Mach was a creature to be reckoned with, for no others threatened them on the path through the swamp. They returned to the glade where he had left the clothes, but the clothes were gone. "The pigheads," Fleta muttered. "They root for aught not held by spell."

So he would have to continue with his makeshift outfit. Mach shrugged. After the amount of effort he had put into it, he might as well use it!

"Now this path bears south," Fleta said, indicating the one he had left before. "But it leads to the Herd Demesnes, and once in that open country, we can trek north as far as the Lattice." She glanced sidelong at him. "Mayhap we can get a unicorn to carry thee."

"I've already *been* carried by a unicorn!" Mach exclaimed. "Look where it got me!"

"Aye, then shall we walk," she said, somewhat wearily. "Never fear, we shall see thee safely to the Blue Demesnes."

They walked the path. It was pleasant enough, now that they

were clear of the swamp. The great trees leaned over to spread their shade graciously, and the ferns seemed to keep the ground clean.

Fleta paused to sniff the air in the fashion of an animal. "Methinks I smell aught foul," she remarked. "Best we not pause."

The path followed a ridge, then curved to the east and dropped down to a stream. Mach was ready to wade through, but Fleta held him back. "Not this one; there be poison in it. We must touch not the water."

"But it is too broad to jump over," he said.

"There be a ladder of rope. We merely pull it across and tie it in place." She pointed, and there across the stream was a thick coil of ropes.

"How do we pull it, without first crossing?"

"There be a string." She reached up near a branch, her fingers questing for it. Then she stamped her foot with sudden anger. "It be not here!"

There was a raucous cackle from the bushes at the far side. "Thou dost *bet* it be not there, nymph!" a voice cried.

"Me*thought* I winded garbage!" Fleta snapped.

"Smile when you say that, cutie-pie!" the other responded. "Thou'rt in Harpy Demesnes!" And the speaker came into view: a gross, filthy creature, with a woman's head and bosom, and a vulture's wings and tail and legs. The odor became stronger.

"And thou'rt in 'corn Demesnes!" Fleta retorted. "Didst mess with the ladder? Thou knowest that is not to be, by the pact 'tween species!"

"What dost the like of thee know of any pact?" the harpy demanded. "Dost think canst trot thy stud past Harpy Demesnes w' impunity? Stay, filly, an we'll goose thee across in our own fashion, after our sport with the other."

"What sport?" Mach asked, not liking the harpy's attitude.

"Their kind be e'er shy of males," Fleta muttered. "I'll say no more."

"Well, *I'll* say more!" the harpy screeched. "First we'll strip the leaves off thee, my fine morsel, then we'll hold thee down while our choicest hen has at thy—"

But Mach had grasped enough of the picture by this time. He hurled his axe at the obnoxious body. The harpy spread her wings and sailed upward with a desperate screech, barely in time; the axe knocked loose several greasy tailfeathers.

"Wait and see, stupid man!" she screamed, gaining altitude. "Dost not know thou'rt already the plaything o' an animal? We'll show thee some *real* play, an I bring my siblings back in a moment!"

Furious, Mach hurled a stone at her, but the creature was already flapping her way between the trees to the west.

He turned to speak to Fleta, and paused with dismay. She was gone.

Astounded, he cast about. She couldn't have returned along the path, for he had been on it and she hadn't passed him. She couldn't have hurdled the stream; she was too small. She must have gone into the bushes along the bank of the stream, searching for some other way across. But so quickly and silently; he had never seen her go!

What had that harpy said about Harpy Demesnes? Mach suddenly made a connection. He had lived in Hardom, a city named, it was claimed, after the mythical harpies of Phaze. All the cities of Proton had similar designations: the first three letters of some creature, and the appendage "dom" for dome. He had taken it to be an innocent affectation. Now, abruptly, he realized that it could be more than that. There really were harpies, every bit as ugly as described in the myth, and apparently this was their region. Thus, perhaps, the geography of Proton did correspond with that of Phaze, to this extent. There could be a great number of the filthy birds in the vicinity!

Then he heard a humming. He looked, and there was a bright little hummingbird, hovering over the path. Then it darted across the stream, touched the coiled rope ladder, and took hold of a thread there. It carried this thread back across the stream, right to Mach himself.

Amazed, he lifted his hand and took hold of the thread. The tiny bird let go and darted away, its errand done.

Mach pulled on the thread, and it became a string, and then a stout cord that finally enabled him to haul the uncoiling ladder across. He tied its two loose ends to the broad branch, making sure it was firm.

Now he needed to find Fleta, because he certainly was not

going to leave her to the mercy of the harpies. Where *had* she gone?

He peered into the bushes. "Fleta?"

"Yes, Mach?" she said right behind him.

He jumped. "Where were you? I was afraid—"

She shrugged. "A girl needs some privacy sometimes."

"She does?"

She laughed. "Wait till thou dost have to do it! I'll stand and watch."

"Do what?"

"They don't have to do it in thy frame?"

"Don't have to do *what?*"

"Defecate."

"Of course they defecate! Why do you ask?"

Her mirth became genuine curiosity. "But thou dost not?"

"I'm a robot."

"Thou seemst much like a man to me. What be a rovot?"

"Robot, not rovot. A—" He paused with belated realization. "Defecation! You mean *you* had to—"

Her amusement returned. "I had not dreamed it such a well-kept secret! All those who eat must cast their leavings, e'en young females."

Now he found his face burning again. "I did not—"

"Truly, thou'rt not the one I knew!" she said merrily. "*He* ne'er had such confusion!"

"Well, he had functions I don't." But as he spoke, Mach realized it wasn't true. He was in the living body now. In the night he had had to urinate, and now he felt an increasing abdominal discomfort. He realized that it had been building up for some time, but because he had no prior experience with digestion, he had dismissed it. He had been lucky that he had understood the process of urination; he could have become quite uncomfortable otherwise.

Fleta shook her head with a certain understandable perplexity, then brushed it aside. "Come, we must cross before the dirty birds return."

"Yes, indeed!" he agreed.

She showed him how to navigate the ladder. She climbed

nimbly on it, then crossed over the river by using her hands and feet in the rope rungs. He followed, quickly adjusting to its give and sway, and scampered to the other end. He found his fallen axe and picked it up.

"Now must roll it again," she said.

"But I tied it on the other side!" he said.

She smiled, and untied it on the near side. As the second rope was freed, the ladder rolled itself up, as though guided by invisible hands along an invisible floor, and finished in one tight coil against the far tree. Only a thin thread remained behind, anchored to the rear tree. It was ready for the next user.

"Close thy mouth, Mach," Fleta said. "Else folk might think thou hast ne'er seen magic before."

Mach closed his mouth. They faced down the path. "Uh, if we can wait a moment," he said.

"Wait? Whatever for?" she asked brightly.

His intestine was becoming quite urgent now. "The—privacy—"

"Rovots need no privacy," she reminded him.

"That's changed. Why don't you go on ahead, and I will rejoin you in a moment."

"Oh, no, I must keep thee company, else thou dost get edgy."

He thought he was about to burst, and not from emotion. "I can spare your company for this moment."

"Well . . ." She took a step down the path, and he started to take one toward the bushes.

Then she turned back. "No, I really must not leave thee unattended, Mach. This wood be not familiar to thee. Who knows what mess thou mightst get into, if—"

"Go!" he cried.

Suppressing a smirk, she resumed her progress down the path. The minx had known all along!

He plunged into the bushes, heedless of scratches. He found a halfway suitable place and set about removing the necessary portion of his clothing. But he had harnessed it about him so effectively that this was difficult; it didn't want to come off. He had to wrench out his waist-vine, and then the leaves of his costume fluttered down, loose.

He squatted and let living nature take its course. Then he remembered that the living people of Proton cleaned themselves after this act, so that no soiling or odor would occur. They used special paper for this purpose, or a sonic mechanism. He had neither here.

He cast about, seeking some substitute. Nothing seemed to offer. He didn't want to use any of the cloth of his costume.

He heard a heavy flapping. The harpy loomed. He tried to duck down out of sight, but she spied him. "Ho, what have we here? The bare essence!" she screeched.

"Get out!" he exclaimed, embarrassed.

"Hey, girls, we've found him!" she screamed. "I spotted him by the stench!" She laughed with a cackling sound.

Now there was a whole flock of them, flapping in to see. Mach realized that he had indeed gotten into a mess. Those dirty birds were after more than laughter; their narrow eyes gleamed and their talons convulsed and drool dripped from their open mouths.

He realized that he couldn't escape them by running. His clothing was falling apart, and the bushes hampered him, and they were airborne and numerous. They would have him in a moment.

He lifted his axe, but they hovered just beyond its range, screaming imprecations. He could throw it, but then he would be without a weapon.

"Fresh meat!" a harpy screeched, diving down from behind. He whirled and swung the axe, but she sheered off.

Another dived from behind, and a third. Whichever way he faced, there were several behind him, ready to attack.

Mach lunged to a tree, setting his back against it. Now he could defend himself better. But he couldn't get away, and when his arm tired—

In the distance was the sound of hoofbeats. There was music, too: the melody of panpipes.

"Oh, damn!" a harpy cried.

The beat and music got louder as the source approached rapidly. The ground shook with the hoof-strikes. The pipes played a militaristic air. The harpies scrambled up through the air, shedding feathers in their rush.

The unicorn appeared, charging through the brush. Her horn speared at the last harpy, but the bird was already out of reach. "There'll be another time, 'corn!" she screeched.

The unicorn stomped about, making sure that all the birds were gone. Then she leaped back toward the path, and the sound of her retreating hoofbeats faded.

Mach relaxed. That creature had rescued him before, then disappeared; she had just done it again, and left again. Evidently she had no ulterior motive. Maybe she was just a guardian of the path, routing whatever monsters intruded on it. That was fortunate for him!

He took a large leaf with which to clean himself off, then pulled his remaining clothing together as well as he could. He was even more ragged than before, but after the scrape with the harpies, he knew when he was well off. He made his way to the path.

Fleta was coming back along it. "Oh, Mach!" she exclaimed, spying him. "I feared for thy safety!"

"So did I," he admitted. "But the unicorn saved me—again."

"Aye; I summoned her. These be the Herd Demesnes."

"You *summoned* the unicorn? How could you do that?"

She shrugged. "There be more to magic than conjuration. That creature is no enemy of thine, Mach."

"Apparently not. But I wish I understood her motive."

"Who can e'er know the true heart o' another?"

"Who, indeed!"

She peered at his outfit. "I see—"

"Never mind what you see!" he snapped, trying to adjust a swatch of cloth.

". . . that thou hast lost thy leaves," she finished, returning to her normal impishness.

They walked on along the path. It took them east for perhaps two kilometers, then debouched onto a broad grassy plain. Mach stood and stared.

"Hast ne'er seen grazing land before?" Fleta inquired.

"Never before," he agreed. "This is marvelous! This whole world is green and growing!"

"And thine is not?"

"Mine is not," he agreed. "Outside the domes there is only barren sand and air that living people can't breathe."

"Air not to be breathed? How can that be?"

"Pollution. The mines and factories pumped their wastes into the ground and water and air, until virtually all natural life was extinguished. The only suitable environment for life is maintained within the domes."

She shook her head. "Methinks I would not like thy world!"

"I never thought about it. But now that I've seen this—I think I do like it better than Proton." Actually, it was life he was coming to like, despite its inconveniences. He had never before experienced the sheer *feeling* of it. Even the discomfort was a pleasure of a sort, because it was an aspect of the new responsiveness of his body. When he made an error and suffered pain, that represented a far more effective feedback than the cautionary circuits he had known. A robot, for example, could chew a hole in his own finger, and some did, because there was no pain. That was unlikely to happen with a living person.

"Dost like the taste of thy finger?" Fleta inquired teasingly.

Mach jerked it away from his mouth. Had he been about to test that pain reflex?

"Thou'rt funny," she said.

"And you are lovely," he said. He reached for her, and she did not avoid him, and he brought her in to him, and she did not hold back. He kissed her, and she kissed back.

"Ah, Mach, this be foolishness," she said. "But I do like thee. I shall miss thee sorely when thou returnest to thy world."

Mach thought again of Doris, the cyborg girl with whom he had kept company. He had evidently liked her better than she liked him. He had known Fleta less than a day, yet already he felt a greater emotion for her than he had for Doris. That could be accounted for by his living system, whose functions and emotions could be stirred on an involuntary basis. But it seemed to him, objectively, that Fleta was a nicer girl than Doris, even after all reasonable allowances were made for the differences between their frames and their states.

"Fleta, is it really forbidden for us—for you and me—to like each other?"

"Mach, I think it is. I—there are things about me that—an ye knew of them, I think thou wouldst not hold me this close."

"Yet *you* know of them—and you do not object?"

"Mayhap I be more foolish than thee." And she kissed him again. The kiss became intense, and he knew that whatever else might be the case, her feeling for him was genuine. She believed that he would not like her, once he knew her secret; he doubted that this would be the case, but the knowledge that he could not remain with her after he learned how to return to his own frame restrained him. She was forbidden, not because there was anything wrong about her, but because he was not of her world. He found that deeply disturbing.

"Be these tears thine or mine?" she inquired.

"Mine," he said. "My first."

"Nay, mine too, and I think not my last."

"Fleta, I like you because you are a lovely girl who has helped me face this strange world. I lost my girlfriend in the other frame. Therefore my foolishness is understandable. But if you know we are not for each other, why do you waste your time with me?"

"I should not answer," she said.

He smiled sadly. "But I think you will."

"I will. My—my mother loved thy father—I mean Bane's father, but always knew he must wed Bane's mother, the Lady Blue. And so it was, and rightly so."

"The Lady Blue?" he asked. "Citizen Blue is my father."

"Aye. He married first the Lady Blue, and then he died, and then he went to thy frame and begot thee. Adept Stile stayed here and begot Bane. And I, even as my dam, seem partial to thy line. Bane knew better; 'twas e'er a game with him. But thou dost not know, and—and O, I do thee such wrong!"

"Then tell me the wrong you are doing, so I can judge for myself!"

She shook her head. "Too soon thou willst know, and then it will end. I lack the courage of my mother; I cannot tell thee yet."

"You are married to another!" he exclaimed.

"Nay, Mach!"

"Then *I* am! Or about to be. Something like that."

"Nay, we both be free, that way."

"Then I just don't understand!"

"For that give I thanks." She kissed him again, then separated. "We must on to the Blue Demesnes. But it be noon; we must eat, ere we grow weak from hunger."

"You're changing the subject!" he said.

"Aye."

"I wish you would just tell me, and let me judge."

"What dost thou think of animals?" she inquired.

"Animals?' You mean like—like dragons?"

"Aye. And pigheads and such."

"I don't see the relevance, but very well, I'll answer. I'm a robot, so I haven't had much experience with animals of any type. But I know they are living creatures, and so they have needs and feelings, and that is to be respected. That unicorn, for example; twice she has saved my life, but I don't know her motive. But regardless, she's a beautiful creature, and I respect her view of her life. As long as an animal doesn't attack me, I—well, what are animals except other kinds of living creatures? The least of them has a greater personal reality than I do."

She embraced him again. "Thou'rt lovely, Mach."

"Now will you answer my question?"

She smiled. "Nay."

"But I answered yours!"

"Aye." She disengaged, giving him no further answer. He sighed with frustration. There was so much he had yet to learn about the ways and motives of living creatures, Fleta especially.

She found them more fruit, and they ate. Then they trekked north across the plain. Mach's living legs were tiring, but he did not complain; after all, if delicate Fleta could keep the pace, so could he.

Progress was good, because of the open and level ground. But in midafternoon Fleta paused. "Mach, we have a choice," she said. "The most direct path to the Blue Demesnes be straight north from here, but the most secure path be toward the east."

"What is the difference in time?"

"We might be there by nightfall, an we take the left through the Lattice. An we take the other, we must night on the trail, and arrive tomorrow noon."

Mach was tempted to specify the right path, so as to be the night with her, but discipline prevailed. "The left, then."

She nodded, and he realized that she had hoped he would choose the other path. He was coming to understand her quite well by the nuances of her gestures. But his machine heritage provided him a type of discipline that many living folk lacked.

They went left, and within the hour reached the Lattice. This turned out to be a huge network of cracks in the earth. At the fringe the cracks were shallow, but soon they became formidable, several centimeters across and quite deep, extending in endless zigzags. They had to step carefully to avoid wedging their feet in them.

The cracks became larger yet, until they were chasms in themselves. "Now must we be silent," Fleta said.

"Silent? Why?"

"So as not to rouse the demons below."

Mach peered down into a crack. Demons down there? After the monsters he had already seen, he didn't want any more.

They proceeded to a region where the cracks were so extensive that they covered more area than the ground did. Mach found this nervous business; one slip could plunge him into the darkness below. But Fleta evidently knew where she was going.

They came to a dead end. Ahead and to either side the crevices closed them in; only behind was there a jagged path.

Fleta gestured. Mach saw that the path resumed beyond a narrow part of the crack. They would have to jump.

Fleta showed the way. She took a running start, then leaped, landing neatly on the other side. She moved back out of the way, giving him room.

Mach followed suit. He had trained for jumping in the Game, and this body was the same as his own, apart from the fact that it was alive. It was healthy and responsive. He could handle this readily, even when tired.

They went on, winding through the maze. Mach wondered how such a configuration of terrain had come about. Was there an equivalent feature in Proton? He had never really explored the exterior world there; now he wished he had.

They came to another jump. Mach realized that Fleta knew

exactly where the gaps were narrowest; otherwise they would soon have been lost amidst impassable cracks.

But just as she was about to leap, a grotesque head popped up from the chasm. "Hhaarr!" it growled.

"The demons!" Fleta exclaimed with dismay. "Methought we would not rouse them!"

Other heads appeared from the cracks to the sides and rear. The two of them were surrounded!

"Seems more like a trap to me," Mach muttered. "We weren't making a lot of noise."

Now the demons were scrambling to the surface. Each had a body as misshapen as its head. Short legs, huge long arms, bulbous chest-barrel, horns and tail. And gaping mouths bulging with yellow teeth.

"There be no reasoning with demons," Fleta said. "They eat our kind."

Mach did not see much hope, but he was ready to fight. "Stand back to back with me," he said, drawing his axe. "I'll club any that come close."

"That will not stop them; they feel not much pain. O, Mach, I fear the time has come to let the secret be known."

"Your secret?" he asked, watching warily as the circle of demons closed in about them. "I think it had better wait until we have fought off this crowd." But he had severe misgivings about that; each demon was approximately his own size, and there were many of them. Unless he could figure out an effective spell. What rhymed with "demon"?

"I be the unicorn," Fleta said. "Thou must ride me to safety. Now!"

"You—what?" But as he looked at her, she vanished. In her place was the black unicorn who had saved him twice before.

The closest demon lunged. Mach swung his axe, catching the creature in the face. The blade cut right through, splitting the head in two—but there was no blood, and the demon kept coming. Now he understood Fleta's reluctance to fight these things; they were truly inhuman.

He dodged the demon, then leaped to the back of the unicorn and grabbed a handful of black mane. "Take off!"

She started moving. A demon grabbed for her, but the long

horn whipped about and speared the thing, shoving it back and over into the chasm behind it. Then the unicorn started trotting back along the path, where there were fewer demons; progress forward was impossible, because there was a phalanx of the creatures.

The demons pursued, but they could not match the velocity of the unicorn. In a moment the two of them were clear.

But more demons were climbing from the cracks back along the path. There seemed to be an endless number of them. Another phalanx of them formed up before the other jump, grinning.

But now the unicorn had velocity and inertia. She charged straight into them, bowling them over. At the brink she leaped, carrying Mach and a clutching demon with her. Mach twisted about and clubbed the demon on the head; when that had no effect, he chopped at the arm it had clutching the mane, and severed it. Then the demon dropped away, leaving the hand and part of the arm still locked on.

Now the crevices became too small to hide demons, and that threat abated. The unicorn charged on, her hooves striking the firm places with precision. She knew what she was doing; she must have traveled this route many times before!

In an amazingly brief time they were back at the fork in the path, alone. The unicorn stopped, and Mach dismounted.

Without any intermediate stage, the animal vanished and Fleta reappeared. She looked at him sadly. "Now thou dost know," she said.

Suddenly it all made sense. He had called in the swamp, and the unicorn had heard, thinking him to be Bane, and had charged to the rescue of her long-time friend. She had taken him to the safety of the crater. Then, when he acted strangely, she had left him, only to return later in human guise. She had learned that he distrusted the unicorn, and that he was not the friend she had known, so she had concealed her nature from him.

When the harpies had attacked, she had had to change to the equine form again, to rescue him. Then back to the form of the woman, to be his companion. And now, unable to save him any other way, she had revealed her secret at last.

Now he remembered stray remarks. "Wouldst rather have me

neigh?" and "Wait till I tell the fillies of the herd!" And the warning of the harpy that he was with an animal. And her reference to her "dam." So many little hints, none of which had he understood.

And her attitude about their acquaintance. She liked him—but could not afford to love him. Because she was an animal, and he a man. She had played games with Bane, who knew her nature, as children would; if the games became more intimate than those of normal children with normal pets, it was only because a unicorn was no normal pet. Fleta had human intelligence and feelings.

So much she had done for him, knowing it to be futile as far as any enduring relationship went. Knowing that he would be leaving her, returning to his frame, helping him to do that. Knowing too that even if he remained here in Phaze, his attitude toward her would abruptly change the moment he learned her identity.

Except that he was not precisely what she evidently thought he was. She believed he would reject her for being an animal. How would she react to learning that he was a machine?

"Let me tell you about me," he said.

"I know about thee," she said. "Thou'rt the son of the one who was the Blue Adept before Stile, his other self."

"I am more truly the son of Sheen," he said.

"Who?"

That was what he had suspected. The story of Blue's marriage in Proton had not spread about the frame of Phaze. "Sheen is a machine," he said. "A humanoid robot. Do you know what that means?"

"Why dost thou talk about such confusion, when I have at last revealed myself to thee and await with fear thy reaction?"

"Because I think I have a secret that will affect your attitude as much as your secret affects me."

"Thou'rt an animal of Proton? I know thou'rt not!"

"I am a machine, the son of a machine. A creature of metal and plastic and other inanimate substances."

"Thou'rt flesh and blood!" she protested. "I have seen thee bleed!"

"This *body* is flesh and blood. I am not the one to whom it belongs. In Proton I am a robot."

"A rovot," she agreed. "What type of person be that?"

"A creature who resembles a man, but is not alive."

"A golem!" she exclaimed.

Mach considered, then agreed. "Close enough. A creature who has been made rather than birthed. Who does not have to eat, or breathe, or sleep. Who cannot feel pain. Who can walk indefinitely without tiring. Who can imitate the ways of a man, but is not a man."

"A golem," she repeated, staring at him.

"In Proton, in my own body, I am that," he agreed. "I could cut off my finger, or my arm, or my head, and still function." He smiled briefly. "Of course I would have some trouble seeing or hearing or speaking without my head. But I wouldn't die, because I am not alive."

"A golem," she said again. "A thing without feeling."

"Well, I can feel; I have tactile sensors. And I can feel mentally, too, because I am programmed for it. For consciousness. But it's not the same as living."

She seemed stunned. She approached him, looking him up and down. Her lower lip trembled. "O, what a fool I be, baring myself to thee, who canst not care."

Not care?

Mach enfolded her and kissed her. Suddenly all that had been revealed in the past hour ceased to have meaning. He was a machine and she was an animal, and they had known each other only a night and a day, and during most of that they had misunderstood each other . . . and they were close to being in love.

7

Citizen

The flyer carried them northeast across the wasteland at high velocity: the direction opposite to the one they wanted. The prospect of rendezvous became increasingly remote.

Bane shook his head. "If only we had wrecked the vehicle not!" he muttered.

"My fault," Agape said. "I asked you to show me—"

He put his fingers against her lips, silencing her. "It was something I wanted to do. Still want to do." He put his arms around her, and she rested her head against his shoulder. She was out of the suit now, naked in the serf manner.

"Perhaps if we explain to your family, they will help you," she said. "Are they not good people?"

"Surely they be so," he said. "They must be very similar to mine own parents. Probably I should have done that first."

"Then you would have been back in your own frame by now, and I would not have met you, Bane."

"And I would not have met thee," he agreed, and hugged her closer. She was what she called an amoeba, a completely flexible creature, yet this did not differ much in his view from the way of any of the werefolk. She could be quite at home in Phaze. Of course he would probably not have been attracted to her, had he encountered her in Phaze. Fleta was as pretty in her human form as any true human woman, and as nice a person, but he had never been romantically interested in her. In Phaze, human beings could be friends with animals, and could play some rather intimate games with them, but they did not love them or marry them. His father's friendship with Neysa, Fleta's dam, had raised eyebrows in the old days, Bane understood. But Stile had married the Lady Blue, of course, and Neysa had returned to her Herd to be bred by the Herd Stallion. Thus Bane himself had come to be, and Fleta, and their lifelong association and friendship.

He faulted none of this—but he would have perceived Agape as a form of animal, and that would have made a critical difference. She was not, of course; she was an intelligent and talented creature from another world. Because he had been introduced to her as that, or as a human being at first, his fundamental perception of her had differed. Then, when she had helped him so loyally, when he needed help most—but he couldn't say all this. Not now, with the serfs of the flying machine listening. He just held her close and wished that she could join him in Phaze. For the truth was that though he had always understood he was to marry a human girl, he had found none he liked well enough for that. The village girls tended to be wary of Adepts, with reason, and avoided him whenever they could do so without giving offense. He had needed a relationship with a girl of some other Adept family—and the only ones of his age were in the families of the Adverse Adepts. Thus certain of the animal folk had been better company for him, though he had known this to be a dead-end association.

In due course the craft landed. They passed from its lock directly into a dome, where serfs guided them to cleaning stalls and then to a residential suite. "Eat, sleep," the foreman serf said. "Tomorrow Citizen White will have an audience."

"Citizen White?" Bane asked. "I thought we were being taken to Citizen Blue."

The serf shrugged. "Perhaps the Citizen will explain. Meanwhile, rest."

That seemed to be it. Bane understood that in Proton, Citizens governed, and no serf could question the actions or motives of a Citizen. He chafed against the delay in his search for his other self, but knew he could do nothing. They might as well have been prisoners.

But he remained with Agape, and that was a considerable compensation. Now, without further guilt or distraction, he could complete his understanding with her.

They went to the food dispenser in the suite, and Agape got a nutro-bev. Bane found that he wasn't hungry, not because of any tension or fatigue, but because his robot body did not require food. So he simply watched her eat. That turned out to be a remarkable experience in itself.

Then they adjourned to the bedroom. "I can show thee now," he said, though somewhat shaken by the recent spectacle of her meal. Still, she had warned him. "There be room enough here."

"Oh, Bane, I do want to know," she said. "But I have been up and active for so long—it is past midnight now—I do not think I can hold my form much longer. I fear I would melt in the middle of it."

That could be awkward, Bane had to agree. "Rest, then; we can do it in the morning." He was privately relieved. He was, as he had told her, used to observing shape-changing in others, but this had been not exactly that.

"You might not like to see me sleep," she said. "I return to my natural state."

"Thy natural state should not bother me," he said, hoping he spoke accurately. "But what will I do, while thou dost sleep? This body be not tired at all."

"Use the computer access to gain entertainment or education," she suggested. "Here, I will show you how."

Soon Bane was seated before a screen, watching three-dimensional moving pictures within it. He found this fascinating, so very much like magic that it seemed pointless not to call it that. He could cause the pictures to change merely by telling them to.

He directed the screen to fill him in on the history of Proton. He wanted to know what had happened here after the frames had separated. He knew from what his father had said that once there was fairly free travel between the frames; each permanent resident of one frame seemed to have an other self in their other frame, who resembled him exactly. But only when one self died could the other cross what was called the curtain to the other frame. Stile had crossed when the Blue Adept died, and Stile had taken Blue's place in the Blue Demesnes. But Blue had not been quite wholly dead; he had taken Stile's body in Proton and taken up residence there. Stile himself had animated a golem body, which performed just like the original one. Such magnificent magic had been possible in those days. Then the fundamental stuff of magic, the rock Phazite, had been diminished; half of it had been transferred to Proton for the sake of some complex but apparently necessary balancing of the frames, and magic had forever lost much of its potency. The frames had been fully separated, so that no one could cross over anymore.

All this Bane had known all along. What he didn't know was how Proton had fared in the interim. Since he had to remain here awhile longer anyway, this did indeed seem to be the ideal occasion to learn about this. He knew that his father would be most interested in the information.

But acquiring the information turned out to be more complicated than he had supposed. There was so much of it! When he asked for the "History of Proton," the screen went back to the planet's discovery more than four hundred years before by an explorer-ship from the Empire of Earth: a beautiful world much resembling Phaze today. But there were creatures already on it, Earthlike creatures, including a few human beings. This indicated that there had been contact before. Since there had been a number of private expeditions to space, and not all of these made proper reports, it was concluded that one of these had colonized the planet, and the descendents of the colony had then forgotten its origin. This could have happened hundreds of years before.

Then it seemed that the planet was somehow double. There was reference to magic, which was of course impossible—

"Impossible!" Bane snorted. "You idiot!"

The narration froze in place. "New directive?" the screen inquired.

"Just skip it up to the past twenty years," Bane said, deciding not to wrestle with this aspect.

Even so, it was more than he could grasp. History turned out to be not a single and straightforward process, but a complex tapestry of events. Citizens lost their positions, and new ones came into being; the mining of Protonite, the key resource of the planet, suffered a severe readjustment as cutbacks ordered by Citizen Blue took effect.

Citizen Blue! "Follow him!" Bane exclaimed.

So Mach's father appeared. It seemed that he had more money or power than any other Citizen, so could make his will felt most effectively. He married Sheen, the humanoid robot female; this caused a furor. He required that the self-willed humanoid robots be granted serf status. Later he did the same for the most advanced humanoid androids, and for the humanoid cyborgs. Each such step was fought resolutely by the Contrary Citizens. Most recently he had done it for the aliens: those sapient creatures who could assume human form and mix with human beings on an equal intellectual and social basis.

"Agape," he murmured, understanding her position in this at last.

The screen heard him. "Agape," it said, showing a picture. "Sapient creature of Planet Moeba, first representative of this species participating in the Experimental Culture Project."

"I didn't mean to show her; I was just commenting," Bane said. The screen returned to its prior business, describing the things that Citizen Blue had initiated in the past twenty years in Proton. It was an impressive listing; more changes had occurred in this period than in the prior two hundred years. The Experimental Culture Project was intended to enable the diverse types of sapient creatures to integrate their society without adverse pressures. Ordinary serfs were required to become the employees of individual Citizens at maturity, and were thereafter subject to the arbitrary will of those employers. The Experimentals had no such requirement; they were considered to be the employees of Proton itself, with no requirements. They were free to do what they wished, within their own section. When they went beyond it, they had to observe the normal forms, deferring in all things to Citizens, and not interfering with the activities of ordinary serfs.

"But what is the point?" Bane asked. He knew that idlers

would not survive long in Phaze, and doubted they would be tolerated long in Proton.

"The point is to ascertain whether the diverse species can successfully integrate," the screen replied. "If this is affirmative, the entire society will be similarly integrated. There will be no distinctions between species or types, only between serf-status and Citizen status. Machines and aliens will have equal access to the benefits of Proton society."

Bane nodded. This made sense to him. He would not have known how well unicorns and human beings could get along together, after centuries of noninvolvement with each other, if he had not known Neysa and Fleta. Now he was learning how pleasant it could be to know an alien creature.

He glanced at the bed where Agape lay—and paused, astonished. She was there, but her form was not. She had become a mound of dark jelly that spread across the bed like so much spilled pudding. Only its cohesion and continuing quiver distinguished it from inanimate substance. She really *was* an amoeba: a blob of protoplasm.

Should he be revolted? He decided not to be. He had seen Fleta change to her natural unicorn form many times, and to her other hummingbird form, and back to girl form. That was interesting, not revolting; why should this be different? Agape had not concealed her nature from him, she had only tried to spare his feelings, because it seemed that other human beings had been upset by her true form. But he had come to know her mind and her personality, and he liked these. She was quite different from himself, physically; what did it matter?

He had had enough of education for now. He asked the screen for entertainment, and was rewarded by a "light-show" of phenomenal color and complexity. The lights brightened and dimmed, radiated out and in, changed shape and color, and assumed odd and fleeting shapes. Sometimes Bane, the viewer, seemed to be flying into a rapidly expanding bank of clouds; sometimes he seemed to be swimming in strange water. The configurations never repeated; he kept being surprised by what happened next.

Finally he told the screen to turn itself off. He walked about the room, thinking, trying to assimilate all that he had learned.

One impression came through strongly: he liked this frame of Proton, despite its appalling degradation of the wilderness outside the domes. It had more than enough scientific magic inside the domes to make up. True, it had serious problems—but those represented not so much a liability as a challenge. Citizen Blue, who had been reared in Phaze, seemed to be Bane's own kind of man. It would have been nice to work with him to complete the necessary changes in the society. In time, perhaps, even the pollution could be cured, and Proton could become green again outside. Of course he had to return to his own frame, but he would always be glad to have had this experience in this one.

Many hours had passed, but Agape still slept and he did not wish to disturb her. He experimented with his body, discovering that though in the rush of events he had not been aware of many differences between his own body and this one, those differences were significant. It was not just a matter of not getting tired and of not needing sleep; his involuntary physical reactions had become voluntary. He could elevate his reactions at will, becoming keyed up or relaxed simply by so directing his body. He could make himself sexually excited instantly, and turn it off as readily. It was helpful to know, since it could have been embarrassing with Agape if he depended on natural reactions.

At last he turned himself down to standby state, and this was very like sleep. He could, after all, have slept, had he realized how to do it! He just had to turn his body close to off for a period.

An alarm jolted Bane out of his simulated sleep. "The Citizen will see you in ten minutes," the voice of a serf came from the screen.

"Uh, right," Bane said. He turned to the bed.

Agape was stirring; evidently the alarm had awakened her too. Already her protoplasm was changing its shape. Legs and arms grew out at the ends, and her head. None were well formed; they most resembled the appendages a child might tack on a homemade doll. But once the size was right, the specific features developed. In just a few minutes she was herself—or rather, that artificially human form he had come to know.

She sat up, gazing at him. "Now you have seen me as I truly am," she said.

"I think thou hast marvelous magic," he said. "I could not change my form as thou dost."

"You're not an amoeba."

"I am an Adept—or will be one," he said. "I can change the forms of others, but not my own."

"You really are not disturbed?"

"I really am not," he said. And now it was true; the screen had provided him with the proper perspective, so that he understood the rationale of her nature and her presence, and approved of it. She was a nice person who was trying to accommodate herself to what was for her an alien situation. She needed support, not objection.

She stood, then stepped up to him and kissed him. "I fear I will not encounter your like again," she said sadly.

"Nor I thine."

"Two minutes," the screen announced. "Present yourselves at the exit to your chamber."

"We must not delay," Agape said. "I have not been on Proton long, but I know from my briefing that serfs must always address Citizens as Sir and obey them implicitly. Perhaps I should talk, if it can be arranged."

"Aye." They presented themselves at the exit. The wall opened.

The serf conducted them quickly to a smaller chamber. They stepped in, but the serf did not. The door slid closed.

Suddenly the four walls vanished. They were in an enormous room. They stood on a beach whose sand spread endlessly to either side. Not far behind were palm trees, their fronds shimmering in the breeze. Ahead crashed the restless breakers of the fringe of a mighty ocean.

The stood staring, both awed by the scene. Then Agape put out her hand. "It is holo," she murmured. "The walls still enclose us."

"Holo?"

"Pictures, like those on the screen you watched last night. Very realistic."

Bane touched the wall, verifying its presence. It seemed as if they were in an invisible box set on the beach, but he understood what she meant; the box was real, the beach illusory. "If this be not magic, what need have Citizens for it?" he asked.

On the ocean appeared a sail, and the sail expanded. It showed up as a sailboat, blown quickly by the wind toward them. On the boat, operating it, was a ruddy, heavyset man. He guided it to the beach, then quickly furled the sail and dragged the small craft right up before the place where Bane and Agape stood. He lifted out a chest and set it on the sand. He brought out a key, put it to the big old-style lock, and unlocked it. He lifted the lid of the chest.

From the chest rose a head. It kept rising, until a complete woman stood in the chest. There could not have been room for her within it. She seemed quite young, possibly fifteen, and her hair was as white as snow, set with a silver tiara. She wore a white gown set with bright gems.

The woman glanced at the boatsman, who was now standing at attention. "Sir," he said, "these are the refugees."

This was the Citizen! Bane realized. He had expected an old man, not a young woman, but obviously Citizenship knew no age or sex.

"Your identities?" Citizen White inquired.

"Agape of Moeba," Agape said immediately. "And this is Mach, the son of Citizen Blue. Sir."

The woman frowned. "I think not," she said. She stared at Bane. "Tell me your identity in your own words."

Somehow she knew about the exchange! "I be Bane, son of the Blue Adept, also called Stile."

"And how came thee here?" she inquired.

For a moment Bane was too startled to speak. "Thou—thou knowest?"

She smiled. "How long since thou hast been to the White Demesnes?"

"The White Adept!" he exclaimed. "But—"

"But she be old and ugly?" the woman inquired with a smile. She made a gesture, and abruptly she was old and fat. Then she reappeared in her young edition. "Since when be the son of an Adept deceived by appearances?"

"But there be no connection to Phaze!" Bane cried. "I be the first in a score years to come to Proton, and that only in a body not mine own!"

"Really," the woman said, smiling condescendingly. She turned to the serf beside her. "Set me adrift again, Grizzle, and open the window to Phaze for these two serfs."

"Sir!" the man agreed.

The Citizen lost height. She sank back into the chest. When her head disappeared, the serf closed the lid, locked the lock, and lifted the chest back into the sailboat. He turned back to Bane and Agape. "The floorsman will take you there," he said. Then he dragged the boat back to the water, stepped into it, unfurled the sail, and commenced tacking into the wind.

The scene vanished. They were back in the box. The door opened, and they stepped back into the hall.

"This way," the serf said.

They followed him down the hall to another door. "You'll need clothes," he said, bringing out a white shirt and trousers of the Phaze variety for Bane and a white dress for Agape. "We don't usually send others through, so white's all we've got. You can change them when you get where you're going."

"But I am a serf!" Agape protested. "I can't don clothing here!"

"We do wear it in Phaze," Bane told her. "Thou wouldst be as out of place there naked as here in clothing."

"I suppose," she agreed uncertainly. She got somewhat awkwardly into the dress and slippers provided. The serf helped her get her outfit adjusted, and in a moment she looked, by Phaze standards, quite nice.

Bane completed his dressing, bending to fit the shoes to his feet. They fit well enough.

"This way," the serf said, showing them on down the hall to still another door.

They entered another cubicle. This one closed on them, then abruptly ascended, startling them. Its walls were transparent; they could see the dimly illuminated walls of the region through which it passed.

It came up into a forest. It halted at ground level, and the panel on one side opened. They stepped out onto the forest floor. The cubicle closed itself up and descended back into the ground; a lid closed, making the ground complete.

"This is Phaze?" Agape asked.

"It seems like it," Bane said. "It be hard to believe that return could be so simple!"

"But I—I am not magical!"she said. "How can I be here?"

"The same way I be here," he said. "I exchanged bodies not; I be still in the robot body. We made a physical crossing!"

"All the time the Citizens knew this route!" Agape said. "It was not your imagination!"

He glanced at her. She was very fetching in her dress; it fitted her beautifully. "Thou didst doubt?"

She spread her hands. "I know that robots can be programmed and reprogrammed. They must believe what they are pro- grammed to believe; they cannot do otherwise. I was sure that you believed, but not sure that you really came from Phaze. I apologize, Bane."

"Accepted, Agape!" he said. "I could prove my origin not as readily as thou didst."

"If this really is your frame, where should we go? I really don't belong here."

"I think thou dost belong with me," he said. "Thou didst help me wend my way through Proton; now it be my turn to help thee in Phaze." He brought her in to him and kissed her. "And how glad I be that this be not our separation, Agape!"

She clung to him. "Oh, Bane, I told you I wanted to learn how your species indulges in sex, and I do, but I think that was only part of it. What I really want is to be close to you. I felt so alone, so—so *alien* when I came to Proton, and you have made me feel like a person."

"Thou hast made me feel wanted," he said. And that, he re- alized, was the essence. He preferred to be genuinely wanted and needed by an alien creature, than to be routinely accepted by the most human of women.

They walked through the forest. "This must be near the White Demesnes," he said. "That would be northeast of the Blue De- mesnes, and some distance away. I recognize this particular re- gion not, but if we go southeast we'll get home."

"Home to you, perhaps," she said.

"Thou dost not want it?" he asked.

"Oh, Bane, I am not your kind! I have a task to accom- plish—"

"But after thou dost accomplish it, and make thy report—what then?"

"Oh, Bane, I just don't know! This is all so sudden, so strange!"

"Meanwhile, come and meet my family," he said. He looked at her appraisingly. "And let's see how thou wouldst be in blue." He paused, considering, then sang: "Turn me blue, and her too."

There was a flash, and abruptly both of their outfits were blue instead of white.

Agape looked at him, and at herself, astonished. "Magic! You did it!"

"I be an apprentice Adept," he said. But privately he was bothered by a detail; there had never before been a flash when he performed magic. Was he losing his touch?

They walked on. Suddenly there was a commotion to the side. Gnarly little men appeared, about half the size of Bane.

"Goblins!" he said. "They be usually trouble!"

"Are they human beings?" Agape asked. "They seem so small!"

"They may be descended from human stock, but they be hardly human anymore. Mostly they interfere not with our kind, but they can be ugly on occasion. I want not to waste magic; I'll see if I can bluff them off."

The goblins charged up. "Fresh meat!" they exclaimed, licking their twisted lips.

"Back off, goblins!" Bane cried. "Else I transform you all to worms for the birds!"

"And who dost thou think thou art?" one of them challenged him.

"I think I be the son of Blue," Bane said.

"Blue be far from here," the goblin retorted. "We'll roast thee and thy buxom wench for dinner!"

"Goblins be worms," Bane sang. "As birds want—"

"We're going!" the goblin cried, and all of them scurried back the way they had come.

Agape was impressed. "Could you really have turned them to worms?"

"Methinks so; I have tried to transform that many not simultaneously before," Bane said. "My father could readily do it, of course. But we prefer to employ magic only as a last resort."

"Oh, why is that?"

"Because a given spell only works well once. I have to figure out a new one each time. So if I use magic when I don't need to, I be cutting down my options for the future. That could make me pretty much impotent, later in life."

"Ah, now I understand!" she exclaimed. "So life is not entirely easy, even with magic!"

"Not necessarily easy at all," he agreed. "Because there be also hostile magic." He paused. "Speaking of which—the White Adept really has never been very friendly with the Blue Adept, not since the separation of frames. Why would she do us this big favor now?"

"Perhaps she is a nicer person than you thought."

He laughed. "Adepts aren't nice folk! They are concerned only with their own powers." Then he reconsidered. "No, some are all right. The Red Adept owes his position to my father, so he's always friendly, and the Brown Adept's all right too. She helped Fleta and the weres a lot. She's the one who makes the golems."

"The golems?"

"They be like robots," he said with a smile. "They look and act like men, but they be dead sticks. Generally."

They went on. "Mayhap I should conjure us directly there," Bane said. "So thou dost not have to walk so far."

"Save your magic," Agape said with a smile. "I don't mind walking with you."

They came to a mountain. There was a large cave visible at its base. "The vampires!" Bane exclaimed.

"Vampires! The kind that suck blood?"

"They do, but not indiscriminately. It be part of special rituals they have for coming-of-age and such. We have nothing to fear from them." He walked toward the cave-entrance. Agape followed, not at all at ease.

A man in a gray cape stood guarding the cave, though bats wheeled in the sky nearby. He came alert as the two approached. "Who be ye?" he challenged.

"I be the son of Blue," Bane said. "This be my friend, a shape-changer. I come to see my friends."

"Who be thy friends?" the man asked.

"Vanneflay," Bane said.

"Sorry, he be away these three days."

"Vidselud, then," Bane said.

"Him, too."

Bane considered. "Then Suchevane."

The man shrugged. "That be a coincidence! He, too."

"All away?" Bane asked, surprised.

"But thou'rt welcome to join us in a meal," the guard said. "Any son of Blue be welcome here."

"Uh, Bane—" Agape whispered uncomfortably.

Bane smiled. "My friend be nervous about vampire viands. Thank thee, but we shall move on."

The guard made a negligent wave of his hand.

They returned to the forest and walked on toward the west until they were well clear of the vampire's mountain. Bane was deep in thought.

"I'm glad we didn't stay there!" Agape said. "The thought of eating blood—"

"That bothers thee? Is blood not easier to imbibe than solid food?"

"We don't consume flesh," she said.

"Actually, the vampires wouldn't have offered us blood. It's too valuable, and they always take it fresh. That isn't what bothers me."

"What bothers you, Bane?"

"This be not Phaze."

She halted in place. "What?"

"When I changed the color of our clothing, there was a flash. My magic ne'er did that. Be there a way science could have done it?"

"Changed the color? Oh, yes; some material is sensitive to certain types of radiation, so that when it flashes—"

"Methought so. And true goblins bluff not so readily; must always destroy a few ere they give over. But mainly, the vampires. They were not."

"But the fact that we did not see them change form does not mean—"

"Oh, they might have changed form, by some device. But the friends I named—" He shook his head.

"But they really could be away," she said.

"The first, yes. But the second, Vidselud—he be the son of Vodlevile, for whom my father did a favor. Vidselud be six or seven years my senior, but we be friends because with me he can safely travel."

"He can't with his own kind?"

"Nay. He has a problem with the assimilation of blood that crops up every so often. They keep a potion in the cave that cures it, and they never let that potion go out, because it cannot be replaced. So he flies ne'er beyond walking distance of the cave, unless with me, because I can conjure him home if need be."

"But then he should be home!" she said.

"He should be home. Yet the guard said he was not."

"Still, that's not proof—"

"And the third one, Suchevane."

"He could also be—"

"*She,*" Bane said succinctly.

"Female? But the guard said 'he'—"

"Precisely."

"Maybe the guard forgot."

Bane smiled. "No male forgets Suchevane!"

Agape looked sharply at him. "She is—?"

"Almost as lovely as thee, in girl form. And still unmarried, when I left Phaze. If there be any male head doth not turn when she goes by, that head be blind. Even the werewolves howl for her."

"But how, then—"

"No way," Bane said with finality. "This cannot be the vampire mountain I know, and since there be only one like this, these be other than vampires, and this be other than Phaze."

"But why would—"

A bat flew down from the sky. As it neared the ground, it changed abruptly into a beautiful woman. "Lovelier than I?" she demanded.

Bane gazed at her. "Nay." Then, after a pause, "Sir."

The woman changed appearance, becoming the young-seeming Citizen White, then a woman about twenty years older, still garbed in white. "So you cannot be fooled, young man," she said.

"No, sir."

"It is true; this is all a setting. I was able to make it authentic because when I was a child, I did visit Phaze, and knew the vampire colony. But in twenty years the personnel have evidently changed, and without contact, we cannot change with them."

"True, sir," Bane agreed.

"So this is pretense, agreed." She gazed hard at him. "But *you* are not. You really are from Phaze; you have demonstrated that."

"But sir, *why?*" Agape asked, disturbed. "Why bother to play such a cruel game with two serfs who intended you no harm?"

"That you are about to discover," the Citizen said. She snapped her fingers, and the entire setting disappeared, leaving a large empty chamber. She smiled, and it was not a pretty smile.

"I think we be in trouble," Bane murmured.

"Not necessarily," Citizen White said. But the cruel lines that manifested about her mouth gave her words the lie.

8

Chase

How much time passed Mach could not be sure, but it seemed to him that the sun had shifted in the sky by the time he emerged from his embrace with Fleta. "I suppose we should be on our way," he said.

"I can carry thee anywhere, rapidly," she said. "Now that thou dost know my nature."

"I would prefer to go slowly," he said.

"My natural form pleases thee not?"

"If you take me to the Blue Demesnes quickly, I shall have little further time with you. Let's walk."

"Oh." She smiled. "Mayhap it will take two days to get there."

"I wish it were two years," he murmured.

"Sirrah?"

"Nothing. Of course we must go."

"Of course," she agreed. "But we can camp the night on the path."

He liked the notion of camping out with her.

They started out on the east path, the one they had not taken before. They made decent progress, and as night approached Mach judged they were parallel to the spot they had been on the Lattice. Had he realized that the demons would be roused, or what they were like—!

"Methinks we should camp now," Fleta said. "But there be something odd about the way the demons came at us. Best I check around ere we sleep."

"But you've been walking all day!" he protested.

She smiled. "In other form, an thou have no objection."

"Oh. Of course." As the unicorn, she could of course range far more widely before it got dark.

She vanished—but the black unicorn did not appear. Mach blinked.

There was a hummingbird, hovering in place. Just like the one who had helped him cross the river at the Harpy Demesnes.

"Fleta!" he exclaimed. "Another form!"

The hummingbird buzzed one loop around his head, then took off to the north.

Mach shook his head, bemused. He had never made the connection! Fleta had three forms, not two, and the bird was the third. She had assumed the flying form when that was needed to draw the thread across for the rope ladder over the river, then returned to her human form. Of course she hadn't told him, because she was doubtful about his reaction to shape-changing women. But now that he knew her nature, she changed freely and openly.

And now that he knew her nature, he discovered that he liked it. In Proton he had associated with human beings, and with robots, and cyborgs and androids of either sex, thinking nothing of it. Even, briefly, an alien creature. All had looked human, but their internal operation had been entirely different, and he had known that and accepted it. Fleta's overt forms differed widely, but she was the same person—and it was the person that counted. Was she called an animal? If so, he liked the animal better than the pseudopeople he had known in the other frame!

What, after all, was he? A machine! Who was he to quibble at whether a person was technically human, when he himself was not? At the moment he occupied a human body, and its chemistry was wreaking havoc with his emotional control, but in essence he knew he remained a robot. If Fleta could accept that, he could accept her.

He plucked fruit from the tree they had stopped at. He didn't recognize the type, but it seemed to be juicy and sweet, and his living appetite thrived on that sort of thing.

What did Fleta prefer to eat, really? Since her natural form was equine, did she usually graze? If so, she must be getting hungry by now. He would have to ask.

The hummingbird returned. Suddenly Fleta stood before him. "Mach, I fear trouble," she said breathlessly.

"More trouble?" He knew she wasn't joking.

"There be goblins lying in ambush to the north."

"Goblins? Little men?"

She frowned. "The Little Folk be decent; they mostly mine and work their crafts. Goblins be something else."

"Why would they be lurking in ambush?"

"Methought it coincidence that the rope ladder was wrong. And that the demons were roused. Now do I wonder."

"You mean those were traps laid for us? But why?"

She shook her head. "I know not why. But I fear it."

"Maybe they're just three types of mean creatures who like to eat human flesh?"

"They knew my nature."

"Then they must have known they couldn't possibly catch you! That you could change form and fly away."

"Aye," she agreed pensively.

His logical mind began to work. "Then it must have been me they were after."

"Aye."

"Yet you helped me escape—and they must have known that you would."

"Not in human form."

"They wanted to force you to reveal your nature to me?" He smiled. "In that they were successful—but what did they gain?"

"Mayhap they hoped thou wouldst revile me, when thou knew, so that I would leave thee."

"And then they could trap me without hindrance!" he concluded. "Yet they couldn't know I am not Bane. Surely they could not attack *him* with impunity!"

She laughed. "Goblins attack an Adept? That be so funny it be no longer funny."

"So what could they expect to gain? As far as they know, we're both poison."

"That be what dost bother me. It makes not sense."

"Unless," he continued slowly, "they somehow know my nature. That I am no magician."

"Adept," she corrected him. "Bane be an apprentice Adept."

"Whatever. My status makes me vulnerable. But how *would* they know? And why would they go to all that effort for one morsel?"

"Methinks they tried not to slaughter thee, but to capture thee," she said. "The talons o' the harpies be poison, but they scratched thee not. And the demons grabbed but did not bite."

"And why would three different types of creatures try it? They can't be working together, can they?"

"Nay. Not unless . . ." She trailed off.

"Unless what? I think we had better explore this."

"Unless there be Adept involvement," she said reluctantly.

"Aren't we going to see an Adept?"

"Stile be but one Adept. There be others, less friendly."

"What would an Adept want with me? I'm of no value to anyone here, and of not much value to myself."

"To me, thou dost have value."

"That, too, I must question. You are a lovely creature, in whatever form, and you know the ways of Phaze. But I am an impostor without much talent here. I don't see how I can be worth much to you."

She shrugged. "Fain would I have been closer to Bane, but ne'er could that be. Now hast thou his likeness, and— O, I know I be a foolish creature, but I be smitten with thee."

Mach did not care to argue with that. "So there is something we don't yet understand, here. Unless they realize that I don't have Bane's proper powers, so they want to eliminate me, and then he could never return. If there are other Adepts who don't like Stile, this could be a good way to get back at him."

She nodded. "To strike when the enemy be weak."

"But if another Adept is behind it, why bring in the monsters? Why not just take me out with a spell?"

"Methinks that would be too open. If Stile knew an Adept had done it—" She shuddered. "If Stile be not the strongest Adept in Phaze, it be Red—and Red be friend to Stile."

"But if a harpy or a demon or a goblin did it, Stile might not suspect. If one of those groups took me captive and hid me somewhere, or delivered me secretly to an Adept, perhaps as a hostage—" Mach nodded. "I think we have it, now. They have been ambushing us along the route to Stile's demesnes."

"O, Mach!" she cried. "If there be Adepts behind this, we be in trouble indeed! No creature can withstand the power of an Adept except another Adept."

Mach nodded. "I think we can't afford to continue heading for the Blue Demesnes; they'll catch us for sure. But where else can we go?"

Fleta pondered. "If they be Adepts 'gainst us, must we gain the protection of an Adept. But surely they will watch, and if we head for the Red Adept—"

"They will trap us on the way," Mach finished. "Anyone else—whom they might not suspect?"

"There be the Brown Adept, she of the golems. She might understand thee better than some."

"But if the others spied us heading for her—"

"Another ambush," she agreed.

"Suppose we took a circuitous route—one no one with any sense would take?"

"Such as through the Dragon Demesnes?"

Mach swallowed. "Yes."

"That would fool friend and foe alike."

They looked at each other, and nodded. Then they hugged each other, with joy or grief or something in between.

"I suppose we can't rest now," Mach said regretfully. "They'll be coming down the path to check on us, when we don't arrive on schedule."

"I can carry thee."

"And tire yourself further? No, I'll walk. Maybe we can hide somewhere unexpected."

She nodded. Silently she pointed west.

"But that's right toward the—!" he exclaimed. But then he understood: that was the least likely direction for them to go. Toward the site of their last ambush.

They walked, this time stepping carefully so as to avoid leaving a trail. When darkness finally made progress impossible, they cast about for a suitable camping spot. The best that offered was a tree with thick foliage and a large fork some distance up that seemed to be well shrouded by the leaves. "There," Fleta said, pointing to it.

"Me? But I think there's only room for one of us!"

"I have another errand," she whispered.

"Oh—privacy?"

"A false trail."

Smart notion! So he climbed the tree and lodged himself in the crotch, while she walked on, leaving a trail that could be traced and did not end at the tree.

He hoped she would return soon, though he still did not see how she could join him here. Then he heard the hum of the hummingbird. She was back!

The bird perched on a nearby twig and tucked her head under her wing. She had a good place after all!

Mach sighed. He could not argue with the sense of it, but somehow he had wished he could be with her in her human form, and not too much clothing. He resigned himself to the inevitable, and slept.

In the morning he descended. Fleta flew down and transformed to girl form. "Didst thou have a comfy night?" she inquired brightly.

"Aren't you getting hungry? You haven't had much chance to graze."

She laughed. "I found nectar in flowers along the way as I flew."

"But that could only sustain a hummingbird! What of the unicorn?"

"It matters not what form I take; food for that form suffices."

"You mean you can run all day as a unicorn, and sustain yourself with a hummingbird meal?"

"Aye. That be part of the magic."

"Magic indeed!" But it did make sense in its fashion.

He ate some more fruit, which was marvelously sustaining. Of course he had the advantage of Fleta's advice; she pointed out what was best, and what was worst, saving him much mischief. Then they resumed their trek.

There was no sign of pursuit, but they continued to step carefully and to keep their voices low. There was no way to hide securely from Adept perception, Fleta advised him, but goblins and demons were fallible.

They skirted the southern reaches of the Lattice, and no demons appeared. This gamble had been won: once the prey escaped, the demons had returned to their nether reaches, not bothering to keep watch. But there would be a lookout at the jump-sites; the path toward the Blue Demesnes was safe only to cross, not to travel.

At noon they paused for lunch, and this time Fleta did change to unicorn form and grazed for an hour. Mach watched her, admiring her glossy black coat and golden hind-socks and gleaming spiraled horn. "Sometime you must play your horn for me," he said.

She heard him, and played a brief pan-pipes double melody.

"A tune!" he exclaimed. "You can play a tune!"

She looked at him questioningly. In her unicorn form she did not speak; her mouth was not right for it.

"I mean, I heard you play a chord, back in the swamp, but I thought that was all. To actually play a tune—!"

She came in and changed to girl form. "All my kind play music," she explained. "My dam, Neysa, plays a harmonica, as thy kind call it; I play pan-pipes, or so Bane said. My sire played the accordion."

"A different instrument for each animal!" he exclaimed. Then paused. "Oops—I didn't mean to—"

"We *are* animals," she said. "An ye mean it not as affront, say it freely."

That helped. He had indeed used the term in a less complimentary sense, back in the crater, when she had objected.

"Why didn't you decide to go the other way, and intercept

your Herd?" he asked. "The goblins would not have followed there, would they?"

She sighed. "There be a matter I did not explain to thee," she said. "My sire retired some fifteen years ago, and my uncle Clip assumed mastery o' the Herd. That concerned not my dam, Neysa, his sibling, because she no longer marched with the Herd. She stayed at the Blue Demesnes."

"Why should your mother be concerned about her brother getting promoted?"

"It be the Herd Stallion who breeds all the mares."

"Oh! And she's too closely related!"

"Aye. And I be too. So it became needful, as I came of age, to seek another herd. I was on that mission when I heard thy cry for help in the swamp."

"What a coincidence!" Mach exclaimed. "I'm glad I arrived at the right time! I would have been roach-food otherwise!"

"Nay, I was near throughout. I—I knew Bane was going often to the glade, and I hoped to see him again, yet hesitated to intrude, an he be on Adept business."

"So you just sort of stayed in the vicinity for a while," Mach said. "Understandable. How long were you there?"

She murmured something.

"What was that? I didn't hear."

"A fortnight," she said, somewhat less faintly.

"Two weeks? Just in the hope he might decide he wanted to see you?"

"Aye," she said, abashed.

"You really were stuck on him!" Then Mach regretted his choice of words. "I mean—"

"Thy meaning be clear," she said, blushing.

"And so you rescued me, thinking I was him. And stayed with me, because you liked him."

She nodded, looking uncomfortable.

"Oh, Fleta—I'm sorry! Without ever knowing it, I brought you so much mischief!"

"Nay, Mach. Thou didst bring me joy."

"But you know I am not the man Bane is—not here in Phaze! Without your help, I'd have been lost many times over. I'd *still* be lost without you! Bane would have been no burden to you at all!"

"Aye, he needed me not," she agreed.

He looked at her, slowly understanding. "You need—to be needed." Then he took her in his arms again and kissed her.

But after a bit another thought occurred. "Two weeks—you must be overdue at the other herd!"

"Aye," she said.

"And now I am keeping you from it. This really is not fair."

"I wanted to join the other herd not really that much," she confessed. "Better to roam free, as my dam did, before my time."

"Well, you are welcome to my company as long as you like it," he said. "I'm in no position to refuse it, even if I wanted to."

There was a spot in the sky to the east. Fleta looked nervously at it. "Mayhap just a bird," she said. "But if a harpy—"

"On a search-pattern for us," he agreed. "Where can I hide?" They were in open meadow; there was not even a substantial tree nearby.

"Take my socks," she said.

"Your socks?"

"Take them," she repeated urgently as the flying shape came closer. She became the unicorn.

"But Fleta, that's just the color of your fur on your hind feet! No way—"

She fluted at him. Mach shrugged and squatted to touch her hind leg. To his surprise he discovered that the golden color did come off; in a moment he held two bright socks, and Fleta's legs were black.

Fleta resumed human form. "Put them on, quickly."

Mach put them on over his shoes. And stood astonished.

His body changed. He now seemed to be a golden animal. A horse—or a unicorn. He could see illusory hindquarters behind him, and suspected that his head resembled that of a horse with a horn.

"Graze," Fleta whispered, and changed back to equine form herself.

Mach leaned forward, trying to get his illusory head into the proper position for grazing. Evidently his performance was satisfactory, for Fleta did not correct him.

The flying form turned out to be a large bird, perhaps a vulture. It flew overhead and did not pause. False alarm, perhaps, but Mach was glad they hadn't taken the chance. If the Adepts interrogated the bird, all they would get was a report of two unicorns grazing in the field. Meanwhile he had learned another thing about his fascinating companion!

Fleta changed back to girl form. "It was nothing, I think," she said. "But here we be dawdling when we should be traveling. Methinks I must carry thee, to make the distance."

"But I don't want to burden you—"

"An we get spotted, how much greater a burden!" she exclaimed. She changed into unicorn form.

Mach realized that she was correct. Quickly he removed his socks and put them back on her feet; then he mounted her.

She started walking, then trotting, then galloping. Now they were moving like the wind, covering the ground far more rapidly than they had. She headed straight southwest, angling toward the distant purple mountain range. All he had to do was hang on.

She began to play on her horn, a lovely tune whose cadence was set by the beat of her falling hooves. Mach, delighted, picked up the melody and hummed along with her. His father was musical, and music was part of the Game, so Mach had trained on a number of instruments and learned to sing well. He had perfect pitch and tone as clear as an instrument could render it, being a machine himself, but it was more than that. Through music he could come closest to the illusion of life and true feeling. Now, of course, he really was alive, and this body had a power of voice almost as good as his own. So he hummed, first matching Fleta's tune, then developing counterpoint, and it seemed to facilitate her running. Unicorns, he realized, were made to play while moving. He knew that their combined melody was a kind of a work of art, for Fleta was very good and so was he. There was rare pleasure in this, despite the urgency of their traveling.

An hour passed, and still she ran at a pace no horse could have maintained. Her music became less pretty, more determined. Her body became warm, but she did not sweat. Instead, he noted with surprise, her hooves got hot. Sparks flew from them when they touched the hard ground. She was dissipating heat through her hooves!

As evening closed, they were near the great mountains. Now at last Fleta slowed. Mach could tell from the way her body moved that she was extremely tired; she had covered a distance of perhaps three hundred kilometers in short order without respite. Her melody had faded out, the energy it expended now required for her running. Finally she stopped, and he jumped off, sore of arm, leg and crotch. He had learned bareback riding for the Game, but never this extreme!

They were near a grove of fruit trees, probably by no accident. "Rest, Fleta!" he said. "I'll forage for food!"

She didn't argue. She went under a tree, changed to girl form, and threw herself down as if unconscious.

Mach collected fruits and located a nearby spring. This was an ideal location!

Then he heard something. He flattened himself against a tree.

It turned out to be a party of what he took to be goblins. They were like gnarled little men, about half his own height, with huge and ugly heads, and correspondingly distorted hands and feet. "Damn nuisance!" one was muttering as they passed, traveling a faint forest trail. "No unicorns here!"

"But we've got to check anyway," another said.

The six of them trekked on. They hadn't spotted Mach; they hadn't really been looking. This was just a pointless assignment to them; evidently they hadn't been told the reason for it. Mach relaxed.

"Hey, I see something!" one exclaimed.

Mach's living heart seemed to catapult to a crash-landing against his breastbone. Had they seen him?

No, they were hurrying away from him. He started to relax again.

"A doll!" a goblin cried.

They had spied Fleta!

"A damn nymph!" another exclaimed. "Sleepin' by a tree."

"Well, let's have at her! Anything like that we catch—"

"That's no nymph," another said. "See the horn-button in her forehead? *That's a unicorn!*"

Fleta woke. She tried to scramble to her feet, but they were upon her, grabbing at her arms and legs. "Hold her horn!" the leader cried. "So she can't change form!"

A goblin clapped a calloused hand on Fleta's forehead, covering the horn-button. The others virtually wrapped themselves around her limbs, one to each. She struggled, but she was still very tired and they overwhelmed her.

Mach had noted all this as if detached; meanwhile he was charging to the rescue, drawing his axe. The goblins, preoccupied by their capture, did not see him.

"Now, mare, tell us where the man is, or we'll take turns raping you," the leader said, yanking her cloak up. "You animals don't like that much, do you!"

Fleta's forehead was covered, but not her eyes. She saw Mach charging in. "No!" she cried. "Not that way!"

But Mach was already committed. His axe swung down at the goblin-leader's head. The goblin turned, but too late; the axe chopped into his face, slicing off his nose.

The goblins were no cowards. They let Fleta go and pounced as one on Mach. Before he could get in a second blow, four of them were on his arms and legs. They had surprising power; they bore him back and down, spread-eagling him on the ground.

The goblin leader, amazingly, retained his feet. His nose was gone, but he seemed otherwise unbothered. "That be him!" he exclaimed. "The one we seek!"

Mach struggled, but the goblins were too strong for him. Now he understood why Fleta had tried to warn him off. She had known he could not handle these creatures. Who would have thought that monster's skull could be so hard as to make the axe sheer off! For Mach knew he had scored directly on the goblin's forehead; had it been fashioned of ordinary stuff, the stone blade would have cut right in. Instead it had been turned aside by the super-hard bone, doing what was apparently only minor damage to the goblin's face. How could an ordinary man fight such creatures?

"Tie him up," the leader said. "I'd love to chew up his eyeballs, but orders are orders. The Adept wants him intact. We'll have to content ourselves with the animal." He looked about with sudden alarm. "Who's holding her?"

"I am!" the sixth goblin cried. But though he still had his hands on Fleta's forehead, his touch nullifying the magic power of her horn, he was now the only one. Fleta's arms and legs were free, because the other four goblins were now holding Mach.

Fleta smiled. She reached up and grabbed the goblin's hands in her own, hauling them down while she straightened up. He might be stronger than she, but he could not keep his hands in place while she was moving her body. He needed more hands. In a moment her forehead was clear.

Abruptly she vanished. In her place was the hummingbird, and its buzz was quite angry. It darted at the goblin leader.

One of the goblins holding Mach began to laugh, for such a tiny creature could hardly hurt a goblin. But the laugh was cut off when the unicorn manifested almost in the leader's face. The forward motion of the bird translated into a plunge by the unicorn.

The long horn speared right through the goblin's head.

Then Fleta lifted her head and flung the goblin off her horn. She whirled to face the ones holding Mach, but these were already scrambling desperately away. Their skulls might be too tough for Mach's crude axe, but the unicorn's horn was another matter! In a moment there was not a live goblin in sight.

Fleta fluted, blood spitting from her horn as she blew it. She stood by Mach, angling her head.

He needed no further urging. He scrambled to her back, and they were off. It was obvious that the goblins would soon spread the news of the discovery of the prey, and greater numbers of them would be in hot pursuit. He hated to make Fleta run again, when she had had so little rest, but they had to find a better place to hide.

Where was there? If the goblins roamed this forest, that was no good. But out in the open the harpies would be able to spot them. It was getting dark now, but what of the morning?

Fleta was pounding directly south, toward the looming purple mountains. Mach had to have faith that she knew what she was doing. But he could feel the fatigue of her body; she shouldn't be running at all, right now!

Well, he could do nothing about it at the moment. He just had to hang on and hope it would be all right.

Meanwhile, he realized that he had learned some new things. A unicorn couldn't change form if her horn was covered; thus she could be held captive, or even raped, despite her normal powers. So if they were ever in a situation like this again, his first job would be to eliminate whoever was holding her horn, so as to free her magic. That was the way he should have proceeded before, had he but known. He could have thrown himself upon the goblin at her head, dragging it off for that necessary instant.

But also, the goblins had confirmed that it was an Adept behind this. And that it was Bane's presence, not his death, that was wanted. That meant that their guess about trying to eliminate Bane during his weakness was wrong; the Adept wanted something else.

What *could* the Adept want? Mach was simply not very effective as a resident of Phaze! Without Fleta he'd have been dead several times over already. He was learning to do magic, but even that was only a poor suggestion of what Bane could do. He wouldn't be worth much even as a hostage, since he was the wrong person.

He shook his head. He just couldn't make much sense of it. But he was sure he didn't want to get hauled in to that enemy Adept!

Fleta slowed. He feared it was because she was exhausted, but he discovered it was the terrain; the level plain had ended, and the slope of the mountain range was beginning.

"I'll walk now!" he said quickly. "You've done enough!"

She did not object. Mach slid off. It was now dark, except for the light of three moons. Proton had seven small moons, which meant that Phaze did too, and several were normally in view. Most were pale shades of gray; the one blue moon seldom showed.

She changed to girl form, showing the way up the mountain slope. Mach was amazed by the amount she evidently knew of far-flung terrain. She must have done a lot of exploring in her day! He followed, covertly admiring her rear view, though he knew that her human shape was exactly what she had chosen and crafted; naturally she had not devised an ugly one.

Then she stumbled. Mach hastened to join her, putting his arm about her waist. But she sagged, too tired to keep her feet.

"The hummingbird!" he exclaimed. "Change to that form!"

"Nay," she whispered. "It takes more energy to fly than this!"

"Not to fly," he said. "To perch! You carried me; let me carry you, now!"

She turned her head to him. She nodded. She became the bird. He put out his hand, and she flopped in it. He lifted her to his shoulder, and there she perched, her little claws anchored on his homemade shirt.

"Sleep, Fleta," he said. "I will climb this hill."

Climb he did. It made him feel good to do his part, his strength filling in for hers. His legs were stiff, but he had plenty of remaining energy. As the way became steeper, he hauled himself up by grabbing handholds on saplings. He hoped he got them wherever they were going. It was so dark now that he could barely see the next tree before him.

There was an angry squawk from ahead. Startled, Mach paused.

"Who the hell art thou?" a voice screeched. "Stay out o' my bower!"

"A harpy!" Mach exclaimed with dismay. He gripped his axe. Fleta, on his shoulder, was so tired that she didn't wake.

"What didst thou think it be—a damned goblin?"

"Yes," Mach said. Could he escape her surveillance in the darkness, or were they in for another horrible chase?

The harpy laughed raucously. "Well, no such luck! Come not near me, lest thou catch the tailfeather itch!"

Mach knew he should shut up and hide, but something nagged at him. Why was this foul creature talking instead of attacking or summoning her cohorts? "I'm just a weary traveler," he said. "I have no tailfeathers to itch, but I will detour around your bower. I apologize for bothering you."

"Thou dost *what?*" she screeched.

"I apologize for bothering you," Mach repeated.

"*Nobody* doth apologize to a harpy!"

"I don't want any trouble, I just want to get somewhere where I can rest for the night."

"Thou dost speak strangely. Who be ye?"

"I am called Mach." If she knew his identity, his name made no difference now. "I am a robot."

"What kind of monster be a rovot?" she demanded.

"One that looks like a human being."

"Oh, hell, come into my bower," she said. "I be lonely for company."

Stranger yet! Was it a trap? Well, might as well spring it as have it pursue him. Mach climbed forward.

He parted a thick curtain of leaves and came into a snug chamber padded with ferns. There was a tiny bit of glow, so that he could ascertain its approximate size and see the form perched on a stick at one side. This was the harpy.

"Why, thou dost be a man!" she exclaimed.

"I *said* I looked like a human being."

"Aye, that be true. And a bird on thy shoulder."

"My companion." Fleta was stirring now; what would she think of this interview?

"I be Phoebe," the harpy said.

Mach checked through his memory. "I know of a bird of that name. Nondescript, except that it wags its tail."

"Aye, that be why the name," she agreed. She rustled about as if to make the point. "But it be uncomfortable as hell, and not just in the feathers."

"You really do have a tailfeather itch?"

"Aye, and no cure, so I be exiled from my kind."

"You mean you're not part of the pursuit?"

"What pursuit?" Phoebe demanded.

"We've been chased by harpies, demons and goblins," Mach said. "We don't know why."

"I know naught o' that! I've had no contact with my kind in a year."

Could he believe that! Or was she just trying to lull him while others closed in?

"No offense—but you don't smell. The other harpies I encountered—"

"I wash my feathers daily to keep down the itch, but always it returns," Phoebe said. "An' another o' my kind come near, it will spread. That be my curse."

Fleta jumped off his shoulder, then materialized as her girl form. "Know thou my nature?" she asked the harpy.

"A werebird! Ne'er saw I the like before!"

"Nay. Unicorn."

"And thou comest to roust me out o' my bower? For shame, 'corn; I have no quarrel with thee!"

"Willst swear so on my horn?"

"For sure, an thou attack me not."

Fleta parted the leaves of the bower wall and stepped out.

The harpy peered after her. She shrugged with her wings. "Hell, trust must begin somewhere, and I have no life worth living alone." She half-spread her wings and hopped out after Fleta.

Mach followed her out, not certain what was happening.

Outside, he could just make out the dark unicorn shape. Fleta lowered her horn, and the harpy hopped up to it. The horn touched her feathers. "I swear I have no quarrel with thee," the harpy said.

Fleta fluted.

"What, turn about?" Phoebe asked, evidently understanding her. "What for?"

Fleta played several notes.

"That?" the harpy asked incredulously. "Thou wouldst?"

An affirmative note. Mach tried to fathom what this was about, but it baffled him.

The harpy turned about, and Fleta put her horn to the creature's tailfeathers. For a moment there seemed to be a kind of radiance, but Mach could not be sure.

"Mine itch!" the harpy cried. "Gone!"

Fleta returned to girl form. "Grant us rest in thy bower for a day, and all's repaid," she said.

"For this cure?" Phoebe cried. "Thou canst stay a year!"

Fleta made her way back into the bower and curled up on the fern. In a moment she was asleep.

"But—how could you know that *we* had no quarrel with *you?*" he asked the harpy.

"'Corns be stubborn beasts," Phoebe said. "They betray not who betrays them not."

"And she cured you—just like that?"

"Aye, the horn has power, an there be ailment. But for 'corn to cure harpy—that be rare indeed."

"We were looking for a place to rest in safety," Mach said.

"Ye have it now." Phoebe wiggled her tail, appreciating the lack of itch.

Mach went in and lay down beside Fleta. It seemed that his willingness to talk with the harpy had paid off; she was not after all an enemy. In a moment he slept.

Fleta slept all night and much of the following day. It was evident that she had seriously depleted her resources in the long run. Mach, less tired, found himself talking with Phoebe. The harpy brought fresh fruit and edible roots, but urged him to wash them in a nearby spring. "I wash, but my talons form the poison, and it gets on what I touch," she explained. Mach was happy to wash the food.

"There be my sisters in the sky, and goblins o'er the plain," Phoebe announced after taking a flight. "An thou knowest not why they seek ye?"

"An Adept sent them," Mach said. "He wants me alive; he doesn't care about Fleta. She carried me from the Lattice in a day."

"In a single day? Lucky thou art she died not on the hoof!"

"She's a good creature," Mach agreed.

"And for the love o' thee!" She shook her head. She was as awkwardly endowed as all her kind, with a human head and breasts and the wings and hind parts of a vulture. Her face was lined and her breasts sagged; her hair was a wild tangle. About the only pretty part of her was her wings, which had a metallic luster. Her voice was harsh, sounding like a screech even when she talked normally. Mach could see that if she had behaved the way the others of her kind did, allowing filth to encrust her body, she would have been monstrously ugly; as it was, she was merely homely. "My kind has no such love."

"If I may ask—just how does your kind reproduce? I understand there are no males of your species."

"Aye, there be none. We lay eggs and leave them scattered about; an one survive the animals long enough to hatch, an the chick not get consumed, she grows to size and lays her own eggs. Legend has it that only a fertilized egg can hatch a male harpy—

but only a male of our species can fertilize it. So it be an endless circle. We be chronically bitter about that, and take it out on all creatures." She sighed. "Sometimes I wish it were otherwise. But what else be there?"

Mach shrugged. "I don't know. It does seem a tragedy. But why didn't you revile me when I showed up in the night?"

"I should have, I know," she confessed. "But after a year denied the company of mine own kind, awful as that be, I was lonely. So I was foolish."

"And got your tail fixed."

"It passeth all understanding."

"Phoebe—are harpies supposed to be ugly?"

"What point to be other?"

"If you get lonely, you are more likely to find company of any kind if you look nice."

She laughed with her raucous cackle. "What a notion!"

"Why don't you let me do some work on your hair, and see what happens?"

"Thou canst not make me beautiful," she said. "That would take the magic o' an Adept!"

"I'm just curious."

She shrugged. "It be a mere game, but I be beholden for thy company. Play with my hair, an thou wishest."

"I need a comb." Mach looked about. He found a piece of a fish bone with a few ragged spikes.

He pondered. Then he sang: "Give this home one big comb."

The fish bone shimmered, and became a huge mass of wax and honey. The stuff dripped from his hand.

"A honeycomb!" Phoebe screeched, snatching it out of his hand. In a moment she was gobbling it, getting it all over her face and in her hair. Then she paused. "Oops, my harpy manner o'ercame me. Didst conjure it for thyself?"

"No, welcome to it," Mach said. "I wanted a hair comb."

"Check in my purse. Mayhap there be a comb there."

Harpies had purses? Mach found her handbag and sorted through it. It contained several colored stones, a moldy piece of bread, a dozen acorns, a large rusty key, two large red feathers, a number of prune pits, a fragment of a mirror, the skeleton of a small snake, three pottery sherds—and a fine old comb.

"But we'll have to get the honey out," he decided. "Can you wash your hair?"

"Aye, it be time for another dunking anyway," she said. She licked off her claws—evidently the poison didn't affect her own system—and launched herself clumsily into the air. She flapped toward the spring, folded her wings, and dive-bombed into it.

So that was how she bathed! Mach and Fleta had drunk from that spring in the morning. Suddenly he felt queasy.

Phoebe emerged. For a moment, with just her head and bosom showing above the surface, she looked distinctly human. Then she spread her wings, and clambered into the air, and the effect was gone.

She came to a crash-landing beside him, spattering water on him. "I be clean now," she announced.

But what of the water in the spring?

Mach took the comb and began working on her hair. There were tangles galore, so the job was tediously slow, but he didn't have anything better to do while waiting for Fleta to recover.

Gradually the hair straightened, and as it did so, drying, it began to assume some of the metallic luster of the wings. Small iridescent highlights glinted as the sunlight struck it.

"Thou didst conjure that honeycomb!" Phoebe exclaimed, belatedly realizing what he had done.

"I tried to conjure a comb," he reminded her. "I always mess it up."

"But then thou canst do magic!"

"Not a fraction as well as the one whose body I'm using. As a magician I'm a dunce."

"But to do *any* magic, aside from that of werecreatures and the like—that be special!"

"Well, my other self is an apprentice Adept."

She drew away from him, shocked. "Adept!"

He smiled. "Don't worry. *I'm* not an Adept! I'm just a clumsy imitation."

"But that must be why they seek thee! One who dost do clumsy magic today, may be Adept tomorrow."

Mach paused. "Do you think so?"

"What else? They know they must abolish thee today, else thou willst abolish them another time."

"But they want to capture me. Why not just kill me?"

She shrugged with her wings. "I know not. But thou dost be nothing ordinary, an thou canst conjure."

"Maybe I should save myself time and conjure your hair combed."

"Mayhap. Combing a harpy's hair be a thankless task, methinks."

Mach pondered. Then he hummed to try to intensify the magic, and sang: "Make this hair beyond compare."

A cloud formed about her head; then it cleared and her hair was revealed.

It was an absolute fright-wig. Spikes of it radiated out in all directions, making her most resemble a gross sea urchin.

"I think I botched it again," Mach groaned.

Phoebe flopped over to her purse and snatched up the fragment of mirror. She peered at herself. "O, lovely!" she screeched. "I adore it!"

Mach was taken aback. "You *like* it?"

"I'm beautiful! I ne'er thought it possible!" And, amazingly, as she straightened up in admiration of herself, the lines in her face eased and her breasts firmed. She did indeed seem to be a fairly handsome half-specimen of womanhood.

Mach decided to leave well enough alone. He returned to the bower and settled down for another nap.

By the following morning they were ready to resume traveling. The search in sky and on land seemed to have abated; it was now safer to be out. They thanked Phoebe for her hospitality.

"Ah, it be the two of ye must I thank," the harpy screeched. "The one did cure my tail, and the other my head!" She scrambled for her purse and drew out one of the feathers. "An ye need my presence, burn this feather. I will smell it and come, where'er ye may be."

"Thank thee, Phoebe," Fleta said graciously, tucking the feather into her cloak.

They headed on up the steepening slope. Now it was faster going, because it was daylight and Fleta was rested and back to her normal self. Indeed, she seemed brighter than ever, almost effervescent; Mach had to scramble to keep up with her.

By noon they had reached the crest of the mountain—which

turned out to be a mere foothill; the real range was farther south. They paused for food, finding plentiful fruits. "I'm amazed that there is so much to eat in Phaze!" Mach exclaimed. "Everywhere we go, there are more fruit trees."

Fleta snorted, sounding in that moment very much like a unicorn though she remained in human form. "The trees be not common at all; it be that I sniff them out as we travel."

"Oh. Well, I always knew I had some reason to travel with you."

She laughed, then turned sober. "There be a problem soon upon me," she said. "I fear I must leave thee for a time."

"Leave me!" But immediately he regrouped his emotion. "Of course there is no requirement that you remain with me, Fleta. I never meant to hold you from your—"

"It be not that I *want* to leave thee," she said. "But I think it may be best."

"Best? Why?"

She opened her mouth as though planning to speak, but could not formulate the sentence. "Let me explore," she said after a moment. She shifted to hummingbird form and buzzed off.

Mach stared after her. What was the problem? She had seemed so vigorous and cheerful during the climb, completely recovered from her hard run of two days before. There was no evidence of pursuit at the moment. Why should she have to leave him now, if she didn't want to?

He ate his fruit and rested, admiring the countryside. She would surely tell him in due course, and meanwhile this was about as nice a region as he could imagine. He had never had physical experience with either mountains or forests before, there being only holo representations of such things in the dome-cities of Proton, and he liked them very well. The hill sloped gradually down to the south, and then the nearest segment of the Purple Mountain range heaved up to an extraordinary elevation, the highest peak spearing a cloud and anchoring it so that it could not drift away.

Actually, it wasn't just the terrain that exhilarated him, he realized. It was the living body. He had discovered that eating was not the nuisance he had imagined it to be, when in robot body; it was a pleasure. In Proton, as a robot, he had lacked the sense of taste, it being unnecessary to his survival; here it was a glorious perception. Even the complication of periodic elimination was not really bothersome, once he knew how to handle it expeditiously. The rest of it was wonderful: the feel of the wind against his skin, the pleasure of healthy exertion, the sheer satisfaction of slaking thirst. The act of living was a dynamic experience.

Fleta returned and changed to girl form. "There be a good path ahead," she reported. "There be a dragon to the east, but it moves not from its stream; an we steer clear o' that, no problem."

Mach looked at her. "What about this matter of—" he began, but then sheered off, deciding not to press the mystery of her need to leave him. "Clothing? How is it that you have no clothing in animal form, yet do now? Where does it go when you change?"

She laughed with a certain relief, as if she had feared another type of question. "That be no mystery, Mach! I wear clothing in all three forms. In one it be called feathers, and in another, hair."

So simple an answer! And it seemed that anything she carried with her in human form she carried with her in animal form, transforming it to feather or fur.

They resumed their travel. But Fleta seemed increasingly uneasy. Something certainly was bothering her.

In the hollow between the slope of the foothill and the slope of the mountain, she turned to him with a strange expression of hunger. Suddenly he remembered his fear of the unicorn, the first night, not knowing what it fed on. As it had turned out, unicorns were herbivores; his concern had been groundless. But now—

"Are you all right, Fleta?" he asked nervously.

"I think I must leave thee now," she said tightly. "I had hoped to see thee safely o'er the mountain, but that must needs wait."

"Fleta, where do you have to go?" he asked.

"To the herd I was destined for, before I met thee."

"Well, of course you can go there, if you wish! But why right now?"

"Mayhap I can go, and return in a few days to see thee the rest of thy journey. Thou shouldst be safe here."

"Well, yes, if that's the way you feel! But—"

"It be fairest to thee." She looked about. "There be fruit trees ahead, and so long as thou dost not go east to the river, and dost avoid being spotted from the air—"

"Fleta, please tell me why! Have I given you some offense? If I am too much of a burden—if I'm not doing enough—"

"I see I must needs tell thee. I must go to the Stallion to be bred."

"Right now?"

She made a wan smile. "As soon's I can reach him. It be a fair distance."

"Another long run? You'll wear yourself out! Can't it wait for a more convenient time?"

"Mach, must I speak more directly than I like. With thy kind, breeding be at convenience. Not so with my kind. When a mare dost come into heat, she must be bred; she doth have no choice. Be she in the wrong herd, the local Stallion must do it; no choice for him either. That be why I could not approach mine own Herd in this time."

Mach remembered what he had learned of horses and other animals. The females came into heat at intervals, and bred compulsively. They had no interest in such activity at any other time, but were desperate for it then. Fleta was an animal and so followed this pattern. She had seemed so much like a human being, especially because she had remained most of the time in her human form, that this aspect of her nature had not occurred to him.

"Now at last I understand why you had no concern when we went naked," he said. "When you—saw me aroused. You knew that—that breeding occurs only within a creature's own species. So you had no interest in—" He found himself beginning to flush, and didn't care to discuss it further.

"That be but a half truth, Mach," she said. "I would fain have played with thee as I did with Bane in years o' yore. But it be not seemly, when the parties are of age to know better."

"Yes, of course. We are two different species. There can be no such thing between us." He sighed. "Go and do what you must, Fleta; I will wait for your return."

"Aye." But she did not move, and he saw her lower lip trembling again.

"What's the problem, Fleta? Don't worry about me; I'll be fine, here."

"I fear for thee nonetheless," she said. "If the goblins spy thee—"

"I'll take that chance! Please, Fleta, don't let me interfere with your life any further!"

"O, I wish there were the right plants in these mountains!" she exclaimed.

"Plants?"

"Herbs. We eat them at need, to suppress the cycle."

"Oh."

"O Mach, I love thee and would not leave thee vulnerable to the dangers of Phaze. I want to leave thee not!"

Mach took a step toward her, his arms outstretched, intending to comfort her, but she backed hastily away. "I dare not touch thee now!" she whispered.

"But I mean you no harm, Fleta!" he protested.

"Dost thou not see—it be *thee* I would be bred by, not some stupid stallion!"

Mach was stunned. "But—but I'm not your species! We agreed that it was not proper for us to—"

"Aye, we agreed," she said, biting her lip. "And no way it would take. I be a pighead even to say this, but—"

"Are you saying—you and I—?"

"The body knoweth not; it thinks one breeding be as good as another. I could stay with thee till the time pass—"

"Stay—and—?"

"Dost despise me now?" she asked, her face wet with tears. "Fain would I ne'er have had thee know, but methought I could get thee to safety before—"

Mach worked it out aloud, to be sure there was no misunderstanding. "If you and I tried to breed, nothing would come of it because of the difference in our species. But then you would not have to run off to the stallion. You could stay with me."

"That be my thought. I know I have no right—I know it be wrong—"

"Fleta, I come from a different culture. Robots and androids and human beings—we do this sort of thing all the time, knowing none of it can take. I myself am the offspring of an impossible marriage between a man and a machine. I have not—not tried to engage in—not with you, because—I understood you did not want it!"

"Ne'er did I say I wanted it not," she said. "I said it should not be. I spoke not for myself, but for my culture."

"Then we have no problem!" he exclaimed. "I have—have longed for—if I had realized—"

"Then—thou wouldst do it?"

"Just tell me when!"

Something gave way in her. "Now?" she asked faintly.

Mach stepped toward her again, and this time she did not retreat. "Now and forever!" he cried.

They came together, and he discovered in a moment that this was no ordinary tryst. He tried to kiss her, but she was too busy trying to tear off his clothing and her own. All she wanted was one thing, and she wanted it instantly.

They did that one thing, but such was the urgency and haste of it that it was not, for him, the fulfilling experience he had anticipated. He lay beside her on the leafy ground, his clothing half off, her cloak the same, and wondered whether that really could be all there was to it, in the living state. No preliminaries, no caressing, no speaking, not even kissing; just the straight, raw thrust of it. Yet of course she was an animal, and this was the way her kind did it, regardless of the form assumed. He should have known.

She turned to him, on the ground. There were twigs in her hair, and dirt was on her breasts. "Mach?"

"Yes?"

"Canst—again?"

"Again? *Now?*"

As a robot, Mach could have done it; as a living creature, he found it difficult. "Um, let's work up to it a bit more slowly, this time," he said.

"But I need it now!" she protested.

To be in heat: to have a temporary but insatiable appetite for sex. He understood this intellectually, but his body could not keep the pace. "I'll try," he said.

He tried, and to his surprise found he was able. The body was young and healthy, and the mind retained desire. This time the culmination was slower, but she seemed satisfied.

He relaxed, glad he had gotten through. She would not have to charge off to the herd.

But in a few minutes she stirred again. "Canst—?"

"Fleta, there is only so much flesh can do!" he cried.

"But an it not do more, must needs I seek the stallion—and this I want not!"

Because her body governed this need, not her mind. Mach would have found this baffling, had he not had his own experience with involuntary arousal.

So Mach tried again. This time he made a production of it, deliberately kissing her and playing with her breasts and stroking her body. She tolerated this, but it was not her interest; she craved the breeding, nothing else. Finally he was able to do it a third time, and then she relaxed.

But too soon she stirred again. "Canst—?"

Mach lurched to his feet. "Must—urinate," he said, and headed for the bushes.

In the bushes he did what he said he would do, but his mind was elsewhere. He had thought that one or two acts would satisfy the need; now he knew that the need was as far beyond his means as the galloping travel across the plain had been. Yet Fleta was under the control of her cycle; she had to be bred, as she put it, and if he could not serve in lieu of the stallion, she would be compelled to seek that stallion. He had to find a way to accommodate her, at least until her cycle moved on.

He gazed at his limp anatomy. This was hopeless! Then he had a notion. He worked it out in his head, and then hummed to summon his magic. "Grant me the skill to perform at will," he sang, thinking of sex.

The fog formed and dissipated—and abruptly his potency was restored. For once his magic had worked the way he wanted!

He strode back to Fleta. Without a word he took her in his arms and did what she wished. There was no special joy in it; the spell merely made him potent, not satisfied. Perhaps that was why it worked, he realized: he now had no more satisfaction in the act than she did, therefore was never satiated. Then, before she could stir again, he did it again. And again. He was magically competent.

Finally, after half a dozen repetitions, she was satisfied. She embraced him and slept. He relaxed, but his anatomy did not. Sure enough, in half an hour she woke, wanting more.

So it was for the afternoon, and the night, and the following morning. Finally, in the afternoon, her cycle moved on, and she needed no more from him. It was Mach's turn to sleep the sleep of exhaustion, as the energy drained from his body by the potency spell had to be restored. If Fleta had run hundreds of kilometers in an afternoon, he had performed a similar feat.

They resumed their journey, climbing the great purple mountain. But now some of the urgency was gone. Why was he going to see the Brown Adept? Mach asked himself. To find out how to return to Proton? What, then, would become of Fleta? To escape the pursuit by the various monsters? They seemed to be free of it here. Yet if he did not go—if he just stayed here— what of Bane, whose body and world these really were? He had no right to think only of himself.

Fleta paused, looking at him. "Thou'rt all right?"

"Just wishing I could stay here forever, with you. But that would be at Bane's expense."

"Aye. And he be an apprentice Adept. Our love be not for eternity." She looked so forlorn as she said it, that he had to take her in his arms and kiss her. This time she responded warmly.

"Funny thing," he said. "Yesterday, when—you wouldn't kiss me."

"This be love," she said. "That be breeding."

"But can't the two be joined?"

Her brow furrowed. "They be two different things!"

"Not in my frame."

"What a funny frame!"

"I suppose so." What point to debate it with her? Her nature did not equip her to understand.

They found a niche to spend the night, well up the mountain. After they had eaten, and the darkness closed in, Mach brought up the question of the afternoon again. "When you're out of heat, you don't seek sex," he said.

"Aye. It be pointless, then."

"But can you do it?"

"Can, aye. Did, as game with Bane. But why?"

"Because I prefer to combine love and sex. That's the way it is, with human beings."

"But when it be impossible to breed—"

"When we did it, it was impossible to breed. But we did it anyway, for another reason."

"To prevent me from running away," she agreed. "And glad I am that thou didst manage that, Mach! But now there be no danger o' that."

"So even your kind can do it for other reason than for breeding."

She considered. "Aye."

"I'd like to do it for other reason now. For pleasure."

"Why of course, Mach, an it please thee! It meaneth naught to me, other than as a game." She hiked up her cloak and spread her legs. "But be not long about it, so I can sleep."

"My way," he said. He kissed her, and kissed her again, and proceeded from there, and she cooperated warmly, though evidently confused about his progress, until at last they completed the act in the midst of another kiss.

"Oh, Mach," she whispered breathlessly. "I think I like it thy way better!"

"Aye," he agreed, smiling.

"Let's do it again!"

"Tomorrow!" he said.

She sighed. But she rested her head against his shoulder and slept, instantly. Mach suspected she had been teasing him, but he was not about to inquire.

They crossed the range at a high, chill pass, where the wind cut through bitingly. Fleta changed to unicorn form for this occasion, because this body was better for both the terrain and the cold, and Mach rode her, huddling as low as he could.

But as they moved toward the shelter of the tree-line, a shape loomed in the sky. It was a harpy, and not Phoebe, for the hair was wrong. In a moment there were several harpies, closing in. They had been spotted.

Fleta raced for the trees. Then she stopped, and changed to hummingbird form, and Mach climbed a twisted tree and hid as well as he could in the foliage. The harpies flapped close and peered about, calling out curses, but could not locate the fugitives. Frustrated, they departed, for they too were getting chilled.

Mach descended, and Fleta joined him in human form. "But they will alert the goblins," she said. "And from the goblins we cannot hide thus."

"We'll just have to move as far as we can, so they don't know where we are," Mach said. "In a direction they don't expect."

They moved southwest. Fleta showed the way in bird form, and Mach charged along as rapidly as he could. When they came to a clifflike formation that would have taken time to skirt, Mach managed to conjure some rope, and used it to swing himself down, drawing on a skill developed for the Game. In this manner they made good progress, hoping to get beyond the range the goblins would search.

They succeeded. By nightfall they were painfully tired, but there was no evidence of pursuit. They snatched fruits to eat and found some soft ferns to sleep on.

"And now it be tomorrow," Fleta murmured, snuggling in close.

"What?"

"When I did say 'Let's do it again,' thou didst reply 'Tomorrow,' " she reminded him.

"Oh." Mach was so tired that this had entirely slipped his mind.

Then she laughed, and slept. She had indeed been teasing him. It remained largely a game to her. "But if you try that tease tomorrow . . ." he muttered as he faded out.

But in the morning the goblins were casting closer, knowing that the prey was somewhere in the vicinity. Mach and Fleta hardly got moving before they were spied.

Fleta changed to unicorn form and Mach jumped on her back. She galloped past the goblins and on down and out of the mountains at a rate the goblins could not match. But as they emerged on the southern plain beyond the mountains, the goblins were not far behind. A broad wave of them advanced, preventing any possible cutback to cover.

Then ahead a new shape appeared. "Oh, no!" Mach breathed. "A dragon!" He remembered that in Proton the dome-city of

Dradom was in this region. That meant this would be the Dragon Demesnes in Phaze. If there was one thing worse than goblins—

Fleta slowed, wary of the dragon. It was a huge fire-breather; they could tell by the plume of smoke drifting up from it. The monster was winged, so it would be able to go after them in the air; they could not avoid it or outrun it. The only escape would be straight back the way they came—and there the goblins waited, in a giant cup-shaped formation. The goblins obviously believed that the quarry would choose to turn back and be captured, rather than proceed forward and be toasted and eaten.

But Mach knew that though he might be spared, the goblins had no such intent for Fleta. She would be raped and/or eaten by the army of little monsters. He couldn't allow that.

"Let me try magic," he said to her furry ear as she slowed her running. She twitched the ear, acknowledging.

Mach concentrated, humming a tune to build up his magic. He was gradually getting the hang of it. Music, concentration, and a firm notion of exactly what he wanted—these were the important elements. That firm notion was perhaps the most vital part of it; he had to really want it, subconsciously as well as consciously. Thus his effort to conjure a comb for the harpy misfired, because it was a minor matter to him, while his spell to generate his own potency had worked, because he had really known he needed it. The sung rhyme mostly triggered the magic, somewhat the way one told a computer to "execute." He had to be sure everything was right before he sang the rhyme; any sloppiness ruined the result.

The dragon was getting close. It was licking its giant chops. Fleta fluted nervously—and that gave him another idea. "Play a tune!" he cried to her. "I'll sing to it, when I cast the spell!"

She played. She was worried, but her music, as always, was lovely. He listened for a moment, enjoying it, getting the feel of it, trying to attune himself to it to the maximum. Then he sang: "Make our flight be out of sight!"

Fleta vanished. Mach found himself riding along above the plain. She was still there, but she was entirely invisible. He glanced at himself, and found nothing. He was invisible too. This time the spell had really worked!

"We're completely invisible," he told her. "I suppose we can be heard and smelled, so we'd better shy away from the dragon, but no one can track us by sight. I think."

She swerved, and the dragon did not. The dragon seemed confused, its head swinging this way and that as it peered about, trying to spot the prey it had seen a moment before. The wind was from the west, carrying their scent east, so Fleta swerved to run east. But her hooves kicked up sand, so she slowed to a walk. Now they were truly invisible.

They walked sedately away from both dragon and goblins. They circled back to the mountains, recovering the protection of the trees at the base. Mach did not dare dismount lest he lose track of Fleta, or she of him, so he continued to ride. But at this pace it was no strain on her.

In the afternoon they came to the river that emerged from the range. "This must be the one the dragon is in, upstream," Mach said. "Maybe we can spend the night here, since no one can see us."

Fleta fluted agreement. "If we get separated, make some music and I'll come to you," he said, walking to a tree for some fruit.

But there was no danger of her getting lost. In a moment he felt her hand in his. She had changed back to girl form, invisibly, and rejoined him.

As they settled down for the night, she whispered, "Is tomorrow here yet?"

"I thought you'd never ask!" he said, and grabbed her.

It was a strange and wonderful thing, doing it invisibly. The first time he kissed her, he got a mouthful of hair; then she turned her head to bring her lips into play, giggling. It occurred to Mach that he should neutralize the spell, which he presumed he could do merely by making up a rhyme to that effect, but the invisibility was so convenient for foiling the pursuit that he decided to leave it in place.

And so it was that they made their way east to the large river that cut through the mountains from the north, and along its shore until they reached the wooden towers of the Brown Demesnes.

9

Game

Bane found himself in the apartment, with Agape back to her jelly state. He must have been unconscious, and she still was. Obviously the technicians of Proton had the means to knock a robot out and to knock out an entity of Moeba, and when the charade had been exposed, these means had been used. He discovered that his chewed finger had been restored; someone had done some work on him, perhaps replacing that unit.

He decided to wake Agape, if he could. He didn't like the present situation, and wanted to escape it, but would not make the attempt without her. He reached for her, but hesitated to touch that semiliquid form. It was not that it repulsed him, but that he was afraid he might do her some damage.

"Agape," he said. "Can you hear me? Wake!"

She did not stir. Perhaps she could not hear, with no ears at present. Surely she could not see, with no eyes.

He extended one finger and touched the protoplasm. It was not actually liquid; it had a translucent skin. His touch depressed a spot, that returned when he withdrew. It was like poking a water bag. Still she did not stir.

He tried again, this time pushing her surface with his whole hand. The substance proved to be infinitely malleable, giving way wherever he applied pressure, resettling in whatever new configuration was convenient, and slowly returning to its original state when allowed to. But it did not animate itself.

Finally he took hold with both hands and hauled. The form stretched out like flaccid taffy, and the form elongated. He continued to haul, and the end of it came over the edge of the bed. Finally the rest of the mass slid down, and the substance resumed a more globular form. Bane let go, and the mass sank down on the floor at the foot of the bed, the portion that remained on the bed sliding along to merge with the main mass. Now the body of it was on the floor.

Bane didn't like the notion of her getting dirty, so he tried to put the mass back on the bed. He put his arms around it and lifted, but only portions came up; most of it simply slid through his grasp and resettled below. He tried again, sliding his arms more carefully underneath; then the center came up and the protoplasm to either side flowed down, leaving him with a thinning strand that would not stay on the bed.

He pondered, then fetched a sheet from the bed, put it on the floor, and half rolled, half shoved the protoplasm onto the sheet. Then he caught up the corners of the sheet, making a bundle. He lifted this up to the bed and set it down. But as he swung the mass over, his feet could not follow; he lost his balance and fell facefirst onto the jelly.

Now it stirred. Bane tried to lift himself free, but the protoplasm spread out beyond the range of his hands, squeezed flat by his weight, and wherever he tried to set his palm, he was squishing more of the stuff. Meanwhile it was animating more actively, trying to form into the human shape but prevented by his presence on it.

Bane rolled, squashing one side of the mass but freeing the other side. He made it to the surface of the bed, but some of the protoplasm was carried along with him, half covering him. He waited, and the arms, legs, torso and head of Agape formed, beside him and over him.

She lifted her head, on which the hair was still sprouting, and looked down at him. "You are becoming most affectionate!" she remarked.

"I was trying to wake thee," he said lamely.

"I think you succeeded." She smiled. "I thought perhaps you were trying to show me how sex is performed."

Bane smiled, though he was embarrassed. "If Fleta had said that, I would know she was teasing me; she has that kind of humor. But I think thou art serious."

"Yes. But I would like to know your Fleta."

"Thou dost resemble her in that thou canst change thy shape, and thou art not human. But I fear thou canst never meet her."

"Still, if you are now ready to show me—"

"I woke thee because I think we were rendered unconscious and returned to this chamber. I think we be prisoners, and I like that not. I want to get away from here."

"You are correct. I did not sleep deliberately; I was looking at Citizen White, and then you were handling me."

"I don't know enough about this frame to operate all its mechanisms. But with thy help, perhaps—"

"You would have gone alone, had you known more?"

"Nay! I intend not to leave thee, Agape! So I had to wake thee anyway."

"I think I knew that, Bane. But I have never wished to impede you."

"Let's see if we can get out of here. Canst thou work the locks?"

"I'll try." Agape got up, walked to the exit panel, and touched it. It did not open. "No, they have attuned it to answer to some other signal. I lack the means to make it respond."

"I be not surprised," he said.

They used the food machine to get a meal. Bane paused at it. "This be a different machine! See, it has a colorless bar painted across it; the other had a white bar."

"The dust has a different flavor," Agape agreed.

"You can taste the dust?"

"When I sleep, I do not absorb the dust, because I taste it and reject it," she explained. "I absorb only what is nourishing." She then went protoplasmic and absorbed her nutribev, while Bane pondered their situation.

So they had been moved. Was it just to another suite, or farther? There seemed to be no way to know.

After they had eaten and caught up on routine functions, such as combing hair and trying unsuccessfully to get information from the video screen, they heard someone at the exit panel. The aperture opened and a serf appeared. It was an attractive young woman. "Foreman will see you now," she announced.

They seemed to have no choice. They followed the serf out. She led them to a chamber with chairs and a desk. An older male serf sat at the desk.

"You may call me Foreman," the serf said. "The Citizen wishes you to understand your position. You, Bane, have demonstrated that contact between the two frames is possible, and that information can be exchanged. The Citizen wishes to establish regular contact with his opposite number in Phaze. He is prepared to make it worth your while to facilitate this contact."

"I have no contact!" Bane protested. "I have been trying to find my way back, and have been unable."

"The Citizen will help you to find your way. All you have to do is explain how you made the exchange with the robot to reach this frame, and how you propose to return."

"Bane," Agape murmured. "He says it is a male Citizen. We were in the power of a female Citizen."

"You are not where you were," Foreman said. "You were transferred to the estate of another interested Citizen. The identity of that Citizen is not your concern."

"But this is kidnaping!" Agape protested. "We are members of the Experimental Project! We should not be held here!"

"You will be returned to that project after you have satisfied the Citizen," Foreman said. "I suggest that you cooperate to the maximum extent."

"Why should I cooperate with thee?" Bane demanded. "If thou hadst not interfered, I would have been home by now!"

"That is why you were intercepted," Foreman said. "The Citizen could not allow you to return before making use of your unique ability. For twenty years there has been no contact between the frames; now there can be. This is more important than your private concern; the welfare of the frames can be affected by the restoration of communication."

"But what good would it be, if Mach and I be the only two who can exchange places? Thou canst not have trade or any dialogue not filtered through this body; I would have to carry any message of thine to any person there."

"That would suffice," Foreman said. "The Citizen misses the old days of free contact; he wants to know how his opposite number is doing in Phaze, and catch up on the general history, and provide similar information. There can be nothing tangible, but that need be no bar to social contact."

Bane was not well versed in the technology of Proton, but he had a fair notion of people. He could tell that this serf was not giving him the whole story. Therefore he balked. "I see not the need for such contact. The frames have gone their separate ways for a score years; they can continue."

"Still, the Citizen would like to have this contact, and as I said, he is willing to make it worth your while to humor him. It is always best to humor a Citizen."

"Citizens mean naught to me!" Bane said hotly.

But Agape drew on his arm. "I have not been on Proton long myself, Bane," she said. "But I know it is terrible trouble to go against a Citizen. I beg you, do not antagonize this one."

Bane recognized the sensible voice of caution. Still, he knew something was false here. What should he do?

"What do you most want in life?" Foreman inquired.

"To go home," Bane answered immediately. But he wondered whether it was still that important to him.

"You can go home. Only show us how you do it."

Again there was an aspect of insincerity in the man. What would happen to Mach when he returned to this body and this frame? Surely the Citizen would not just let him return to the Experimental Project. Still, the Citizen could not *make* them exchange again if they didn't want to, so there did not seem to be a serious risk. "I think I'll wait awhile."

"You bargain for something? Do not try the Citizen's patience."

"Bane, if the Citizen will help you return—" Agape said.

Still it was too pat. Bane remembered how his father Stile dealt with Adverse Adepts whose power paralleled his own. Once those Adepts had tried to kill him, and *had* killed his other self. There was always a tension in the air when one of those encountered Stile now, and Bane visualized them as dragons who longed to attack, but were restrained by the knowledge that Stile was stronger and had allies who were dangerous to dragons. Yet the words were always courteous; the enmity was muted. One thing was sure: Stile never trusted an Adverse Adept. Bane did not trust this anonymous Citizen either.

"I be not bargaining," he said. "I just want to deal not."

"If you do not, as you put it, deal, you will be unlikely to return at all."

"Bane—" Agape said urgently.

Foreman glanced at her. "What is this amoeba to you?"

"My friend!" Bane snapped. "Sneer not at her!"

"Your friend," Foreman said thoughtfully. "Then she can be included. Whatever you want for her, she will have."

"Her freedom!"

"Of course. Show us how you communicate with Phaze."

"Bane, you do not know how bad the enmity of a Citizen is," Agape said, distressed. "Before I came to Proton, I knew that no serf must ever oppose any Citizen. It can be immediate expulsion from the planet, or even—"

"Finish your sentence," Foreman told her mildly. Bane realized that this was a kind of threat.

"Death," Agape whispered.

Foreman returned his attention to Bane. "The Citizen has been gentle with you because he knows you are not conversant with our culture. The alien speaks truly. Don't push your luck."

Bane felt little but contempt for the Citizen and his minion. But it did seem best to temporize. "Maybe—a game," he said.

"What?"

"Do not folk settle things here by playing games? Let me play a game with the Citizen, and if I win, Agape and I go free immediately, and if he wins I'll show him how I make contact with Phaze."

The serf seemed to swell up. "You offer such a deal to the *Citizen?* No serf has the temerity!"

"I be not a serf," Bane said. "I be an apprentice Adept."

"Here you are a serf—and you are in danger of becoming less even than that. I strongly suggest that you reconsider, before—"

A voice cut in, emerging from a grille on the desk. "I will make that wager."

Foreman's face froze. "Sir."

"Conduct our guests to the Game Annex."

"Yes, sir." The foreman stood with alacrity. "Follow me." He walked quickly from the room.

"Citizens like to gamble," Agape whispered. "It is notorious throughout the galaxy! But I never imagined—"

"I trust this not," Bane muttered.

"Trust is not a factor when dealing with a Citizen!" she said. "They give the orders, the serfs obey them."

They arrived at a pedestal similar to the one Bane had played on before, with the female robot. "Wait here," Foreman said tersely.

In a moment a stout clothed man walked up from the other side. This was obviously the Citizen. His apparel was white, and he wore a ring set with a huge purple amethyst.

"Purple!" Bane exclaimed.

"Say Sir to the Citizen!" Foreman snapped.

But the Citizen hoisted a restraining hand. "You know me from somewhere, apprentice Adept?"

"Aye," Bane agreed. "Thou art the Purple Adept."

The Citizen smiled. "So you really are from Phaze! And my other self retains his position there."

"Aye," Bane agreed warily. Purple was one of the Adverse Adepts, a dragon lurking. Now Bane was quite sure that this man was not to be trusted. But he did have power, whether as Adept or Citizen, and had to be handled carefully.

"So it seems we have a wager," the Citizen said, smiling coldly. "One game to settle the issue. I win, I get your secret; you win, you go free."

"Aye," Bane agreed, not quite sure of himself. He might have contempt for the idiosyncrasies of the society of Proton, but the power of Adepts he understood and feared. He had in effect challenged a dragon barehanded, and he was apt to rue it.

"Then play, apprentice," the Citizen said, touching his side of the pedestal.

Bane looked at the grid. The numbers, letters and words were there by the squares.

"But this is wrong!" Agape said. "Both are lighted!"

So they were. Which was he to choose from?

"This is not your ordinary entertainment-type game," the Citizen said. "In this one, you choose all your parameters, and I choose mine."

Agape fidgeted beside him. Bane knew she was bothered by this, but he was prepared to play one version of the Game or another. He touched PHYSICAL and NAKED, 1A. He felt most comfortable with that.

"But the Citizen isn't limited to that!" Agape reminded him.

He hadn't thought of that. In immediate retrospect it was obvious. He had blundered, but it was too late to take it back. The second grid was already on the screen.

"You choose," he told her, knowing that her limited experience was more comprehensive than his own.

"I will go with you," she said, touching 8. COOPERATIVE. "And maybe slopes are best." She touched F, which covered FIRE or VARIABLE SURFACE.

"And I have chosen 2C6H," the Citizen said. "Machine-assisted intellectual interactive general-format."

Bane was baffled by the description. "What meaneth that?"

The Citizen gestured toward the door beside the pedestal. "Enter the Game and find out, Apprentice. You and your alien friend are a naked team. If you suffer a Game-death, you lose."

Bane shrugged. He went to the door, and Agape followed him. It was an opaque panel that fogged at his touch. They stepped through.

They were in mountains. Ahead was a thickly wooded slope. The peak of the mountain had a purple hue.

"The Purple Mountain range!" Bane exclaimed. His confidence increased. He knew this range; he had crossed it several times, by magic and by foot, sometimes with Fleta. This was of course a mere mockup, like the Vampire Demesnes of Citizen White; even so, he was much more at home here than in ordinary Proton.

"Challenges to be mounted singly," the voice of the Game Machine announced. "Time limit: seven days."

"So we have seven days to avoid the Game-death," Bane said. "But how will the Citizen try to kill us? What be a machine-assisted intellectual format?"

"I do not know," Agape said. "I thought it was a computer, but I don't see how that can hurt us."

"I think, as he said, we shall find out."

"This is made to resemble Phaze? Could the hazards be natural ones of that frame?"

"If they are, I'll know how to handle them. But there be no computers in Phaze."

"Sometimes computers run things."

"Like what?"

"Well, like robots, or—"

"Robots!" he exclaimed. "Like this body?"

She nodded. "Oh, Bane, I fear this will be bad."

"But singly," he reminded her. "Since there be two of us, mayhap we can handle them. One can sleep, the other watch."

"And it's not real death," she said, taking heart. "We won't really be hurt. But if we lose—"

"Then I will show the Citizen what he wishes," Bane said grimly. "I like that not, for I trust him not, but I gave my word."

She glanced at him sidelong. "Your word is important to you."

"It be a matter of honor. My father has honor, and I be his son."

She nodded. "It's a good way to be."

"It be the *only* way to be. A man without honor be not a man."

"And what of those who are not men to begin with?"

Now he looked at her. "Elves have honor too, and unicorns and werewolves."

"Women—or creatures from other worlds?"

He laughed. "If thou dost have it not, tell me now, ere I trust thee to guard me in my sleep!"

"I may define it somewhat differently in detail, but I think the essence is the same."

They moved on through the forest, warily. "This be not Phaze, so I have no magic here," Bane said. "That makes me feel naked."

"You could fashion some clothing."

He laughed again. "Mayhap thou dost resemble Fleta some!

E'er doth she tease. Her dam be always serious, and doth stay mostly in equine form, but Fleta—" He shrugged.

"Then perhaps a weapon. 'Naked' in the Game parlance means that you are provided with no tool, but you can make what you want from the surroundings. We don't know what kind of a robot will be attacking us, but it may not be wise to meet it bare-handed."

"True." Bane looked about. "I would cut a staff, but have no knife."

"I can form a sharp edge," she offered.

"Sharp enough to cut wood?" he asked dubiously.

"I form substance hard enough to serve the function of bone and teeth; I can form harder if I try."

"That be right! In minutes thou dost go from jelly to full human form. Canst make a metal knife?"

"In facsimile," she said. She lifted her right hand, and it melted into a glob, then extended into something like a dagger. The edge firmed until it gleamed, looking wickedly sharp.

"Like magic," Bane breathed admiringly.

"What do you want cut?"

He checked around, and found a suitable sapling. "This."

She put her blade-extremity to its base and sliced. The edge cut in. She withdrew it and set it again, and in a moment a wedge of wood fell out. She made other cuts, and soon the sapling had been felled.

"Thou dost have thy uses," Bane said. "With powers like that, what use dost thou have for this Proton society?"

"My kind has individual abilities, but not technological ones," she said. "We need to learn, so that we do not remain a backplanet species."

"Methinks I prefer this backplanet," he remarked.

"I was speaking for my species, not necessarily myself."

Under his direction, she cut off branches and topped it, form-ing a long pole. Bane hefted it with satisfaction. "A sword would be better, but this be enough for now."

There was a stir from the side. Bane whirled about. "Mayhap none too soon!" he muttered.

It was no false alarm. A stocky goblin was approaching. The

goblin had a small sword, and he waved it menacingly. "I'll destroy you, miscreant!" it cried.

"Goblins use not swords," Bane muttered. "Unless disciplined into an army, and they be more likely to hurt each other than the enemy. And they talk not of destruction; they just attack."

"It's the Citizen—using a remote-controlled robot," Agape said. "Don't let it get too close."

"Scant danger of that!" Bane agreed. "Do thou get behind me, so it can attack thee not." He faced the goblin, his staff ready. He had not used a staff in some time, but his father had required him to train in a number of hand weapons, and he knew how to use it effectively. Normally goblins came in hordes, making them formidable; a single one was not much of a threat.

The goblin simply charged in, swinging his sword. Bane sidestepped it and clubbed the creature's arm, jarring free the weapon. It fell to the ground.

"Nicely done," the goblin said in the voice of the Citizen. "Perhaps this will be a pleasant challenge after all." It stooped to recover the sword.

Bane rammed the goblin in the head with the end of his staff. He intended only to knock it down, knowing that a goblin's big head was the least vulnerable part of its body and could hardly be hurt by any blow. But the staff stove in the side of the head. Sparks crackled, and the goblin collapsed.

"Ooo, you killed it!" Agape exclaimed. "That is, you put it out of commission."

"So that was the first challenge," Bane said, surprised. "A real goblin would die not so readily." He picked up the goblin's sword. It was small, but of sturdy steel: a good weapon. "And this be a spoil of war, methinks."

"But there will be other threats," Agape reminded him.

"Aye. And if I understand rightly, of different types; we be through with goblins."

"Let's get somewhere else," Agape said nervously.

He found a vine and cut it to length and formed it into a crude belt. From this he hung the sword, so that he didn't need to carry it in his hand.

They moved on, climbing the slope of the mountain. Its general contour seemed familiar, but he realized that it could be the same mountain in Proton as the one he had known in Phaze, covered by one of the scientific domes and provided with fresh air and planted, so as to duplicate the original more closely. The Citizen had good taste in landscape!

But soon there was another sound, this time from the air. They peered up between the trees and saw a gross bird-shape. "A harpy!" Bane exclaimed.

"Is that worse than a goblin?"

"Depends. True harpies have poisoned talons and can move them very quickly in close quarters. But a robot harpy may be clumsy."

"I hope so."

"Clever blow, last time," the Citizen's voice came from the harpy. "But you'll not catch me again that way."

Bane backed under the canopy of a tree. "Get beyond the trunk," he told Agape. "If it flies at you, just circle around the tree, staying clear."

"But what about you?"

"I want not to flee it, but to kill it."

"But—"

"Move, woman!"

She moved. The harpy oriented and swung low; then it folded its wings and dived down at him.

Bane stepped aside, as he had before, and the harpy swerved. But this time he had stepped to the other side, and the Citizen had been geared for the first side. Thus the harpy missed completely—but Bane's staff didn't. It caught the harpy on the back, knocking it down and out of control. It plowed into the ground. Bane rammed it in the side of the head, as he had the goblin, with the same result: sparks and cessation.

"Methinks I like this game," he said, smiling.

"Bane, I don't like it," Agape said. "I fear the Citizen is only toying with you. There is something—"

"Something? What?"

"I don't know. Something that doesn't quite match. It scares me. Let's get far from here."

Bane thought her concern was exaggerated, but it made sense

to keep the Citizen guessing about their location. It was possible that these were indeed simple ploys, intended only to feel out Bane's defenses. Once the Citizen knew his opponent better, he might send in something more formidable.

They cut to the south (assuming the orientation of this mountain was as it was in Phaze), traveling at right angles to their former route. The forest was thick here, and they were careful not to scuff the ground. It would not be easy to spot them; probably the Citizen would have to do some searching. Bane intended to see just how good a searcher the man was, in a robot body.

There was a noise to the side, but not a threat. It was a brown deer bounding away, its white tail flashing. It paused, glancing back, then ran on out of sight.

"Stocked with real wilderness animals!"Agape exclaimed, delighted.

"Mayhap I can kill one and have it for food," Bane said.

"Kill a deer?" she asked, horrified. "How *could* you!"

Suddenly there was a roar right ahead. A demon leaped at them. Agape screamed and fled; Bane whipped his staff up and caught the creature in the belly, shoving it back.

"Surprised you, didn't I!" the Citizen's voice came from the toothy maw of the monster. Then it lurched right over the staff, those teeth coming for Bane's face.

Bane snatched the goblin sword from its mooring with his left hand. He drove the point at the demon's gaping mouth. The blade went in, puncturing the back of the mouth. Again there was a crackle, and the monster became nonfunctional.

Bane pulled out the sword and replaced it in his belt. "Aye, this be an easy game."

"But don't you see," Agape said. "Each time you kill one, another comes. And they seem to know where we are! The Citizen must be able to see us, before he animates a robot!"

"What wouldst thou have me do?" Bane asked, irritated. "*Not* kill a monster?"

"Maybe that would be best," she said.

"Let it kill me instead?" he demanded acidly.

"No, Bane. Just—avoid it for a while. So that no new one can come. Better to retain the known danger, than to bring on an unknown one. After all, there's a lot of time—a whole week, and—"

"Flee from a goblin or a harpy I could readily kill? What kind of man would folk take me for then?"

"A sensible one!" she flared.

"It be not sensible to leave an enemy creature on my tail!"

"But Bane, don't you see, there are things we don't understand—"

"I understand well enough!" he retorted. "Thou dost not like to hurt robots!"

"That's not true! It's just that—"

"Get away from me, woman!" he cried. "I need not counsel of the like of this!"

"Well, if you feel that way—!"

"Aye. Go thine own way, and let me be."

She gazed at him for a moment, then turned and walked away. Bane watched her go, furious at her betrayal, then struck for higher ground. He wanted to get where he could look about, to see whether there was something watching him, such as one of the magic screens.

Just to be sure, he made a loop: he circled carefully, and stopped just before he crossed his own prior trail. If something were following him, this should foil it. Nothing did; all he saw was another deer, browsing amidst the leaves of a copse of small trees. He settled down and kept quiet, so as not to disturb it. When it spooked, he would know something was coming.

His thoughts returned to Agape. She had supported him so loyally, until now; why had she started second-guessing his strategy, that was so obviously successful? He had proved himself readily able to handle the assorted imitation creatures the Citizen had sent against him; she should have been satisfied with that!

There was a thunk beside him. Bane jumped. There was a feathered arrow in the trunk of the tree he squatted near. He was being attacked!

He scrambled away as another arrow whistled through his region. He dived behind another trunk. This time the Citizen was striking from a distance; neither staff nor short sword could do much about that!

How had the man found him, and come up behind him, without even alerting the deer? Bane's loop had made no difference. The Citizen had not followed his trail, but had simply arrived at his location.

Bane poked his head around the tree, trying to spot the Citizen. But another arrow swished by, too close. The Citizen has good aim!

"Now let's see you club me in the head!" the Citizen called.

Had the man come in person, this time? If so, the Citizen was taking a serious chance, for he was fat and slow, while Bane was young and fast.

Another arrow thunked into the ground just beyond Bane's tree. But this one was different. It sparkled. In a moment the dry grass and leaves of the forest floor were burning. A fire-arrow!

Bane went to stamp out the fire—but another normal arrow whizzed by his head, and he had to retreat. But the fire was spreading rapidly toward him. Soon he would *have* to move, or get burned. But when he moved, he would become vulnerable to the arrows of the Citizen!

He had no choice. He saw the deer running by, spooked by the smoke, in its alarm actually cutting past the fringe of the fire and leaping toward the Citizen. Well, maybe that would distract the man for the necessary instant!

Bane charged for the next tree. But an arrow passed ahead of him, making him dive to the ground.

"I've got you covered, apprentice!" the Citizen called, striding forward, his bow ready, the next arrow already nocked. "You weren't as much competition as I had hoped, after all. Too bad."

Bane scrambled up. The Citizen's bow moved to track him with unerring accuracy. He had no chance!

Then the deer hurtled into the Citizen. Both fell to the ground. Bane, amazed, nevertheless grasped his opportunity; he launched himself in that direction, intending to club the Citizen before the bow came back into play.

But he discovered that the job had already been done. The deer was striking at the man's head with its sharp front hooves, and the head was crackling. It had been another robot, fashioned into a man's image, and it had been put out of commission.

But by a wild animal?

Then Bane caught on. "Agape!" he exclaimed.

The deer looked at him and nodded. Then it began to melt. Soon it was reforming into Agape's more familiar human form.

"Thou didst save my life!" Bane exclaimed. "Or at least my freedom. Thou wast with me all along! But why, when we quarreled?"

"Friends can disagree," she said as her human face became complete. "I couldn't let you lose the game if I could prevent it."

He took her in his arms. "We spoke of honor. Thou didst say that thou didst define it differently. I like thy definition."

"I just did what I had to do."

"Must I needs apologize to thee," he said.

"No need, Bane. Just win the game."

"Aye. But now will come another threat—and methinks it will know where we be."

"The last one followed you and didn't recognize me," she said. "Maybe the Citizen tunes in on the substances of your body. Living flesh may not work for that."

"This be more of a challenge than I like. How can I sleep, and the Citizen tune in on me?"

"We've got to find a way to nullify the threat without destroying it," she said. "Then it won't matter if it knows where you are."

Bane cast about for stones. "Next bowman comes, I want a distance weapon."

"Why not use the bow?"

Bane knocked his head with the heel of his hand. "The bow: Spoils!"

Bane picked up the bow, and checked the remaining arrows. Most were ordinary, but one was incendiary and another was glowing: a marker.

He tested the bow, shooting an arrow at a distant target. It scored; this was an excellent instrument. Probably the man-robot had been designed for perfect marksmanship, too. Well, Bane could score well enough with this, being both trained and having a robot body.

"Each attack seems to be worse than the preceding one," Agape said. "I think we'd better prepare for something bad."

"Aye. But thou dost not wish to kill it."

"Not if we can nullify it without destroying it. Then the Citizen won't be able to bring a new threat."

"If we just knew what to expect!" he fretted.

"Since we can't seem to hide from it, maybe if we made a good defensive position—"

"Or a trap!" he exclaimed.

They discussed it briefly, then worked to set up a covered pit. Bane had to use the sword to excavate the earth and chop through roots, and they couldn't take time to make it too deep, because they did not know when the next attack would come. The best they could hope for was that the creature would fall in, and be distracted long enough for Bane to get in some crippling but not killing blow. Having slowed it, they could then outrun it, and the Citizen would not be able to bring in anything new.

They put branches and ferns across the hole, bringing them in from a distance, and covered them with some of the dirt. The extra dirt they used to fashion a kind of fort nearby. They spread dry leaves over everything. Then they settled into the fort and waited.

Nothing happened. After two hours, the sun was going down, and they were getting hungry. "The Citizen must be taking a break," Agape said. "He knows that we don't dare rest, so he can afford to. He has plenty of time."

That seemed to make sense. "Let's eat, then," Bane said.

They searched for food. Some of the trees had fruit, but it wasn't enough. They also needed water to drink.

"If this be a copy of the mountain I know," Bane said, "there be a cave and the snow from the peak melts into a stream that runs through it. Mushrooms grow in that cave. But some be poison."

"I can tell good from bad," Agape said.

They went to where the cave should be—and it was there. "The stream joins it inside; its channel be too convoluted and narrow for a person, but for a way it be nice," he said, remembering.

It was nice. It was dark inside, but Bane used the glow-arrow for light, and it was enough. The mushrooms grew thickly by the bank of the subterranean river. Agape melted a hand and touched sample mushrooms, locating a large patch of good ones. They had food, for now. He ate a token amount, just to keep her company.

Agape checked farther in the cave. She stroked the stones of it. "Bane, this is not safe!" she exclaimed, alarmed. "I feel the stress here; one hard knock, and the ceiling will fall!"

"Aye, I always used a spell to shore it up, just in case. But if we don't knock it—"

"Let's get back to the surface," she said nervously.

They returned to the forest. It was dark now, and the sounds of the night life were there. The Citizen had done an excellent job of renovating this region!

"Funny thing," Bane murmured. "The Citizen we fight corresponds to the Purple Adept of Phaze. But the one who captured us was the White Adept."

"I think the Citizens are collaborating," Agape said.

"If the correspondence be accurate, White and Purple both be enemies of Blue."

"It seems accurate." They returned to the earthen fortress and settled down for the night.

"The Citizen can attack any time," Bane said. "We'll have to keep careful watch."

"I'll watch while you sleep," she said. "Then you can watch while—"

Bane smiled. "Thou dost forget my present body. It does not need to sleep. I'll keep watch."

She laughed. "I *did* forget! You seem so human to me."

"I *am* human. It be just my body that is machine."

"Then I will sleep. But wake me, if—"

"How do I wake thee? When I tried before—"

"Tap this code on my surface," she said. She took his hand and tapped it in an intricate pattern. "That is the alert-code for my species; I will respond immediately."

He rehearsed the code, making sure of it. Then she formed a basin in the ground and lay down.

"Dost thou not get dirty?" he asked as she began to melt.

Her face was dissolving, but the mouth remained. It spoke. "No, my skin rejects it, just as it does the dust." Then the mouth disappeared into the coalescing central mass. She became a dark pool in the basin.

Bane kept watch. He discovered that though he did not require sleep, his consciousness did require some down-time to assimilate and properly organize the events of the day. Otherwise his awareness would become chaos. So, while he watched, he also dreamed, in his fashion. It was pleasant enough.

In the morning he tapped Agape's surface in the code pattern, and she stirred. The protoplasm rippled and humped and shaped itself into the human mannequin; then the features clarified and the hair grew out. Bane watched, interested, then startled; then he smiled.

"Good morning, Bane," she said.

"Thy hair be blue," he said.

She lifted a strand between her fingers, bringing it around so that she could see it. "Oops!" Her hair dissolved back into her head, then regrew with its normal reddish color.

"But methinks I liked the blue better," Bane said.

She stared at him a moment, then laughed. "When you are serious about that, tell me. I can be any appearance you want."

They found some more fruit, and an edible root. It wasn't much of a breakfast, but it served. "Actually, I can assimilate cellulose," Agape said. "It takes a little longer, but there is no need for me to take food you could consume. In fact, I might be able to predigest some for you, so that—"

"Nay, this body needs food not," he reminded her.

She laughed ruefully. "I keep forgetting! You seem so—so alive!"

"I be alive," Bane said. But he knew what she meant. Were he in living flesh, he would be required to eat. The notion of consuming her predigested food bothered him, but he realized that there was no sense in being repelled by the notion; what was honey, but pollen that had been predigested by insects? "We should be seeing the Citizen soon."

"As he finishes his breakfast and gets ready for his day's entertainment," she agreed.

They had called it correctly. The Citizen manifested—in the form of a small flying machine.

"A toy airplane!" Agape exclaimed.

"I mistrust the Citizen's toys," Bane said.

The airplane looped in the sky, then oriented unerringly on Bane and dived down.

Bane saw it coming and scooted around behind a tree. A dart thunked into the trunk; the plane had fired at him.

"Like a man with a bow—only this time it flies," Agape said.

Bane ran for the cover of a different tree as the plane sailed up in the sky and looped around again. He picked up a pair of stones.

The plane was not in sight, but they could hear it as it circled. Then it came down, flying directly at Banc's present hiding place, on the side that he stood. "Circle the tree!" Agape screamed.

He did so with alacrity. Another dart struck, and the plane climbed back into the sky.

"How does he know where I be?" Bane asked. "I couldn't see it, so it couldn't see me—yet came it right at me."

"There must be a sensing device on you," she said, running after him as he went for another tree.

"Like a spell of location?"

"I think so. Maybe if you take off the sword—"

Bane threw down the sword and ran for another tree. The plane came down and planted another dart in that trunk as Bane dived clear.

Then it came to him. "The finger!" he cried.

"The what?"

"The Citizen fixed my chewed finger! *That* be where it be!"

"Of course!" she agreed. "But in that case—"

Bane lifted his finger to his mouth and bit it off. The pseudoflesh and pseudobone resisted his efforts, but he kept chewing until it was free. He hurled it away from him.

The plane came down and fired a dart into the ground near the fallen finger. "That confirms it!" Agape cried. "Get away from that finger, and he'll never find us!"

But Bane had another notion. "That flyer can cast about and mayhap spot us anytime; I want to trap it, alive."

"Bane, you can't—"

"Follow me!" He ran across and swooped up the finger. "I'm going to the cave. Tell me when the plane be coming at me."

"The cave! But the plane is small enough to fly in there too!"

"Aye."

"Bane, this is crazy! It will follow you and trap you in there!"

He kept running, and she had to follow. They zigzagged down the slope toward the cave.

"It's orienting!" Agape cried.

Bane dodged to the side without stopping. In a moment a dart struck the ground near his prior course. The plane passed on by and ascended. Apparently it was only able to fire once on a pass, and it was doing so from too far away to compensate for his last-moment maneuvers.

They reached the entrance to the cave. "Bane, you can't!" Agape cried. "You can't take the finger deep enough to lead the plane in, and still get out yourself—and the plane will come out the moment it discovers that it's only the finger, anyway!"

"Not if I throw the finger into the water, and then bash out that weak section so the roof falls down, trapping it inside."

"No!" she cried. "The collapse will be *behind* the wall; I felt the nature of the stresses. You will be trapped too!"

The plane was coming in again. "I'll take that chance!"

"No, *I'll* take it!" she said, grasping the finger. "I can get out through the river channel; you can't." She hurried into the cave.

He let her go. It was too late to stop her without getting caught by the plane—and he realized that she was right. She could melt and climb in a way that he could not. He scrambled for cover outside the cave.

The plane came down, aiming for the cave. It slowed as its sensors showed the nature of the terrain. But its sensors also told it that the target was in the cave, and could not be reached from outside it, so it followed.

Bane watched as the small craft corrected course and flew inside. He realized that the Citizen was guiding it, and had to be very careful here, lest he crash it before reaching his target. But the plane could not travel too slowly, lest it drop to the ground.

It had to get in there and score; then it wouldn't matter what happened to it, because the game would be over.

Had Agape had enough time to reach the water and throw the finger in? Would their trap work if she sprang it? Now his doubts loomed grotesquely large. How could he have let her take that risk in his place? She was such a good, caring, self-sacrificing creature! Probably if he had occupied his natural body, whose emotions were not under control the way those of the machine were, he would not have let her do it. He hadn't even shown her what he had promised—and if she got caught in the collapse of the cave-roof, he would never have the chance, because she would be not merely Game-dead, but all-the-way dead.

There was a rumble. The ground shook, and dust swirled out from the mouth of the cave.

She had done it. But at what cost?

Bane went to the cave, but it was so full of dust that he could not see anything. He just had to hope that the plane had been trapped, and that Agape survived, and was making her way out. There was nothing he could do but wait.

He returned to the minor fort where they had spent the night. He recovered his staff and sword and bow. The game was not over until either he was "dead" or time ran out.

A huge shape loomed in the sky. Bane peered up at it from cover. It was a dragon! It was circling the peak of the mountain, looking down.

Bane considered. That had to be a robot, because there were no magical creatures in Proton. That meant it was the Citizen in another guise. That in turn meant that the airplane had been destroyed rather than trapped, so their plan had failed in that respect. Now the Citizen was free and Agape was not: the opposite of what they had tried for.

But why was the dragon circling the mountain, instead of searching for Bane himself? That didn't seem to make sense.

Then he reasoned it out. The Citizen was still orienting on the finger! It had been dark in the cave, and when the roof collapsed the finger had not been touched, being deeper in. It would not have been obvious that the finger was unattached; after all, it had been moving purposefully until that point.

The Citizen thought Bane was trapped inside the cave! The

dragon was trying to figure out how to reach him in that impenetrable fastness. Or perhaps making sure he didn't escape, so that he would starve in there. Death by starvation was still death; that would represent victory for the Citizen.

But what of Agape? Had she survived, or was she truly dead? The Citizen might not care, but Bane did! He had to assume that she was all right, and was making her way slowly up through the channel used by the stream. That could be quite tortuous; he should be patient.

Patient? He should be half mad with anxiety! These robot feelings lacked the punch of the natural ones, because he could control them; if he decided not to care about the fate of his companion, then he didn't care. That might be convenient for a machine, but he preferred the natural way, inconvenience and all. In his own body, he'd be—

He analyzed it, as he could do with this body. He concluded that his first thought was correct: he would be quite smitten with Agape. Oh, it was true that she was an alien creature who dissolved into a puddle of jelly when she slept. It was true that she hardly knew the meaning of human sexual involvement. In fact, she hardly understood the distinction between male and female. But she was working hard to learn, and was succeeding well. When she assumed her human female form, she was lovely indeed. More important, her loyalty and effort and personality were all nice. A human woman like her would be an admirable companion—and Agape could be exactly like a human woman.

Bane had had his eye on the females of Phaze throughout. He knew that in due course he would have to marry and settle into the business of being the Blue Adept. Whenever he had encountered a female, he had judged her as a prospective companion or wife. Many were excellent companions; none had seemed suitable to marry. Some very fetching ones were nonhuman, like Fleta or Suchevane, the mind-maddening vampire. But only the fully human ones were suitable for marriage—and they had other counts against them. Some were not really attractive, physically; he knew that was narrow of him, but he did not want an ordinary woman. Some were beauties—but were the offspring of Adverse Adepts. Sheer mischief, there! Probably their appearance was substantially enhanced by magic, and the reality would be a disappointment. So he had not found any woman to love, in Phaze. Only playthings. He had been over this before, in his own mind, seeking some solution, and had come to none.

Here in Proton there were the frivolous types too, such as Doris the cyborg, that one who had dumped Mach. But here too was Agape, and there was nothing frivolous about her. She concealed none of her nature from him, and supported him in whatever way she could, asking in return only a type of instruction that it would be laughable for him to charge anything for. Now she had willingly, almost eagerly risked her life, her real life, to save him from a pseudo-death in the Game. So that he would not have to tell the Citizen how to contact his other self in Phaze. She could hardly understand his rationale for wishing to keep the matter private; he hardly understood it himself. He just didn't like being forced into doing something, and he regarded the Citizen as a member of a class of opponents who should not be accommodated in anything important. None of this was any concern to an alien creature. So her support was mostly altruism—and her kind of honor.

Honor. She had it, obviously. There, emerging at last from the complexities of their relationship, was the essence. She was a creature who was capable of understanding and practicing an honorable existence. *That* was the kind of female he wanted for a long-term companion.

But she was of the frame of Proton, and he was of Phaze. He could not become the Blue Adept and have her with him. So the relationship could not be permanent. The best he could do was give her her instruction in the human mechanism of sexual expression, and leave her.

It made sense; his robot brain saw it clearly. But his human consciousness damned it. This was not the relationship he wanted with her.

But his robot logic would not stop. Agape was a creature from the planet of Moeba, and was here on a mission. She saw him as a feasible way to implement that mission; she had always been open about that. Once that was done, her use for him should abate. She had never spoken to him of love or permanence; she had always tried to help him to return to his own frame. So he was probably fooling himself if he thought she had any genuine feeling for him; it was possible that her species did not possess such feelings. He had been humanizing her in his perception of emotion, just as he had been with her body. She looked human, but was not; she acted human, but was not. Therefore it was foolish of him even to consider any permanent relation with her, regardless of its feasibility.

Well, if she had survived the cave, and returned to him intact, he would forthwith honor his bargain and show her everything he knew about human sexuality. Then she would be free to go her way, and he free to return to Phaze. That was the proper course. Not the ideal course, just the proper one.

The day crawled past, while the dragon circled, then flew away for several hours, then returned to circle again. The Citizen had taken a lunch break, but was still watching. Bane ate also, and snoozed in his robot fashion, ready to spring alert if the dragon came his way.

Dusk came, and darkness, and Agape had not shown up. Bane kept reminding himself that the river channel could be long and difficult, and her progress in the amoebic form could be very slow; he had no reason to assume she was dead. Yet he had little reason to assume otherwise, either.

Then, near the middle of the night, there was a nearby stir. He snapped alert, grasping the sword.

"Bane?" It was her voice!

"Agape!" he cried. "Are you all right?"

"I had to wait till the dragon went. Then I threw the finger into the river outside."

"But that's nowhere close!"

"I assumed the form of the deer, for better speed. But for you, here—"

He dropped the sword, strode to her and enfolded her in his arms. He kissed her, and kissed her again, and whirled her around. They fell laughing on the ground and rolled about, heedless of the dirt and leaves. They made love, joyously, explosively. Then they talked, catching up on events and recent fears and the details of their survival.

Then she said: "Perhaps tomorrow you can show me how your kind does the act of reproduction."

"We just did it!" he exclaimed.

She was startled. "When?"

"When we—were on the ground."

"Oh, you should have told me! I would have paid better attention."

Disgruntled, Bane changed the subject.

Agape, tired after her long effort, collapsed into a pool and slept.

He let her be, when morning came, fashioning some branches for shade so that the light of the artificial sun would not burn her substance. He watched for the dragon, and noted how it was now flying in the distance, over the river. How long would it be before the Citizen realized that Bane was not swimming in that water?

It was some time. When the Citizen finally did catch on, he deliberately crashed his dragon into the mountain, destroying it. Then he came after them on the ground, in a vehicle Agape described as a tank, that crashed through the brush and fired jets of fire. But without the signal from the finger, the Citizen had no easy way to locate them, and it turned out that he had no natural skill in tracking. For the remainder of the Game they avoided the clumsy machine, eating from the land and covering the matter of Agape's instruction in considerable and pleasant detail. When the time expired, they were alive, therefore the victors.

Game exits manifested: cubicles rising from the forest floor. They entered one and were borne down to the formal complex.

Foreman was waiting. "The Citizen wishes to convey his congratulations to you on your victory," he said to Bane. "You are free to return to your Experimental Project."

"We be ready," Bane said, eager to get away from this region.

"Not two; one," Foreman said. "The alien will remain here."

"But the bet was for both!" Bane protested.

Foreman touched a button on an instrument he carried. The Citizen's voice sounded from it: "I win, I get your secret; you win, you go free." Then Bane's reply: "Aye."

Foreman looked at him. "That was the agreement?"

"Aye," Bane repeated. "We two go free."

"No. Only you the speaker go free, no other."

"But I meant both! 'You' be plural!"

"Not necessarily, in the dialect of Proton. Ask your associate."

Bane looked at Agape. She nodded. "The word is both plural and singular," she said. " 'You' can mean several people or one person."

"And the Citizen was addressing one person: you," Foreman said. "You won the game, you go free. She remains."

"I go not without her!" Bane exclaimed.

"Suit yourself. The hospitality of the Citizen is open to you."

"But I want it not! I want Agape free!"

"That would require a separate agreement."

"Bane, go without me," Agape said urgently. "I don't matter."

"Thou dost matter more than everything else!" Bane exclaimed. "Thou didst almost sacrifice thyself in the cave, for me; I will not have it again!"

"Have no concern for her comfort here," Foreman said. "She will be granted residence in a suitable container." He gestured, and a wall dissolved. In the adjacent chamber was a monstrous black pot suspended over leaping flames.

Agape looked, and fainted. Her body dissolved, its substance sinking to the floor.

Bane swallowed, knowing he was beaten. The Citizen was threatening to torture or kill Agape if Bane didn't cooperate, and he knew it was no bluff. The enemy Adepts always made good on their most dire threats, if not on their promises.

"Free her," he whispered.

"You understand the necessary agreement?"

"Aye." Bane was enraged by the duplicity of the Citizen, but terrified by his cruelty. He had no choice.

10 | *Adept*

The castle of the Brown Demesnes was impressive, being fashioned of brownstone rather than the wood he had thought, with a brown forest and the river turning muddy brown. Even the grass was brown. There could be no doubt of the identity of its owner. Two great brown wooden golems guarded the heavy brown wooden door. But Fleta approached it without trepidation. "Bane came often here," she said. "And I too, carrying him, when we were young and he used not his magic to travel. Brown was I think about ten years old when I was foaled and now she be close to thirty, but she it was who versed me in the human tongue and in the ways of thy kind. She did babysit Bane, too. She be the best of Adepts."

That seemed to be a sufficient recommendation. They stepped up to the golems. Bane had nullified the invisibility spell, realizing that however convenient it had been to travel without being seen, they couldn't approach a friendly Adept in that condition. "Tell thy mistress that Fleta and a friend come calling," Fleta said to them.

One golem turned ponderously and stomped inside, while the other maintained watch. Soon the first returned. "Come!" it boomed. Mach wondered how a creature that did not breathe could boom, but realized that magic could account for it.

They followed it inside. The paneling inside was brown, but in varying shades, so that it was not oppressive. They came to the central hall, where a handsome brown-haired woman stood. She wore a brown gown and brown gloves and slippers, and her hair was tied back by a brown ribbon. This was of course the Brown Adept. Mach had rather expected her to be brown-skinned; she was well tanned, but that was the extent of it. Maybe the first person to hold this office had been literally brown.

"Fleta, it has been many months!" the woman said. "And Bane—"

"He be not Bane, Brown," Fleta said. "He be Bane's other self, from Proton-frame."

Brown's brown eyes studied Mach. "Aye, now I perceive the difference! But I thought there was no communication between the frames anymore."

"Only in our case, sir," Mach said.

"Dost call me 'sir'?" she said, amused.

Mach was abashed. "In my frame, only Citizens wear clothes. I—"

She laughed. "I remember the Citizens! Stile and Blue fought them, and in the end I helped. Call me Brown; if thou art not the son of Stile, thou'rt the son of Blue."

"The son of Blue," Mach agreed. "I am called Mach, and I am a robot."

"A rovot be very like a golem," Fleta put in quickly.

"Only now I'm in Bane's body, and he's in mine. We need to switch back, but don't know how. So we were going to go to the Blue Demesnes, but demons and goblins prevented us, so we looped around and came here."

"So that be why the monsters stir!" Brown exclaimed. "They be in pursuit of thee!"

"That's the story," Mach agreed. "We don't know why. We're hoping you will help us."

"Of course I will help," Brown agreed. "I will send a golem

bird to the Blue Demesnes, and thy problem shall be resolved. Meanwhile, the two of you be welcome here; the golems will protect you from the goblins."

"O, thank thee!" Fleta said, going and hugging Brown.

The Brown Adept snapped her fingers, and a brown bird flew in to perch on her wrist. It looked authentic, but evidently it was a golem; this was an impressive evidence of the woman's skill. "Go tell the Blue Adept to contact Brown," the Adept told it. "The matter be important."

The bird flew away. "It can speak?" Mach asked.

"Nay," Brown said, smiling. "It understands only where to go, but Blue will know I sent it not frivolously. We should hear from him in two hours."

They had an excellent meal, and Brown provided better clothing for Mach; his homemade apparel was quite ragged. Brown was an easy woman to know; it was evident that she had a high regard for Stile and Stile's son, and she was quite interested in what Mach had to tell of Proton.

"But now that I have met Fleta," Mach said in passing, "I am not as certain I really want to return to Proton. If she can't go with me—"

Fleta tried to caution him, but Brown was on it immediately. "So thy relationship with the mare be more than convenience?"

"Nay," Fleta said.

"Yes," Mach said. "I think I love her."

"But that cannot be, in Phaze," Fleta said. "Thy kind and mine do not love."

"And thee," Brown said, fixing her gaze on Fleta. "Thou dost not love him?"

Fleta's lip trembled in the way it had. "I know it be forbidden."

"But thou dost love him."

"Aye," Fleta whispered.

"Then why dost thou help him to return to his frame?"

"Because he and me can never be, and his world be there."

"I am not sure of that," Mach said. "But if I stayed here, Bane would be trapped there, and I know that's not right."

"So it be hopeless as well as forbidden," Brown said. "I think I cannot help the two of you in that."

"No one can help," Fleta said, turning on Mach a look of such misery that he leaped from his chair and went to hold her.

At this point there was an interruption. A globe of mist appeared above the table. It formed into a shape of a man's head. "So the apprentice and the animal are getting friendly," the head remarked.

"What dost thou do here, Translucent?" Brown demanded angrily.

"Our agents have discovered that the young man be not what he appears to be," Translucent said. "This be not the apprentice Adept, but his other self from Proton."

"So I have already ascertained," Brown snapped. "Be it for this thy minions persecute this couple?"

"Persecute? Hardly. This young man represents the only known contact with the other frame in a score years. We have long regretted lack of contact with those of Proton, and would have this lad relay messages there for us. For this purpose we sought him, and are prepared to reward him handsomely."

"By sending demons and harpies and goblins after him?" Fleta demanded hotly. "Some reward!"

"Watch thy tongue, animal, lest thou lose it," Translucent said to her.

"Don't call her animal!" Mach flared.

The foggy head surveyed him, then nodded. "So it really be like that." It smiled. "I apologize, unicorn, if aught I spoke of thee seemed amiss."

"Just call off thy minions," Fleta said, taken aback.

"Indeed, they be gone already," Translucent said. His gaze returned to Mach. "What be thy price to carry messages?"

"Price?"

"Gold? Servants? A palace? My associates and I can be generous when pleased."

"Thy associates and thee be no credit to the frame of Phaze!" Brown snapped. "Get thee hence from my Demesnes!"

"In a moment, woodworker." Again the misty gaze fixed disconcertingly on Mach. "An thou not be ready at this time to make a commitment, call me when thou dost wish. Take a cup of water and dash it to the ground and speak my name, and I shall respond. I think thou willst in due course perceive the merit in mine offer." And at last the head faded out.

"Disgusting intrusion!" Brown muttered. "We try to keep things civil with the Adverse Adepts, and Translucent be not the worst o' them, but even he can try my patience."

"You mentioned that you helped fight the Citizens, in the old days," Mach said. "Is this tied in with that?"

"Aye." Brown smiled reminiscently. "I was but a child then, and new at my post, for my predecessor had recently died. Stile, new as the Blue Adept, came here and wreaked havoc in my Demesnes, and I was angry; but when I came to know him, I helped him, and for a time I had charge of the Book of Magic, and in the end I did betray him for his own good by reversing the frame he went to."

"So you were the one who brought Blue to Proton, and Stile to Phaze!" Mach exclaimed.

"Aye. Then I turned the Book of Magic over to Trool the Troll, and he became the Red Adept. Since then Stile has guided the affairs of Phaze in a beneficial direction, curtailing the evil powers of the opposing Adepts, who naturally hate him. E'er they sought to balk him, and to diminish the freedoms of the animals and Little Folk, but e'er he was alert, and Red provided powerful new spells when needed, and Phaze has prospered despite the loss of magical power."

"Loss of magic? It seems effective enough to me!"

"That be because thou saw it not in the old days. When the frames separated, half the Phazite, the rock of magic, was passed o'er to Proton, to make up for the Protonite lost by mining there. That balanced the frames so they would not destroy each other, and then they separated so that no one could cross thereafter. But the power of magic was diminished, and I think the power of economics diminished in Proton too, because there could be no more unlimited mining."

"It was," Mach agreed. "Proton remains well off, because Protonite now commands a much higher price, but only a small fraction of the prior total is exported. My father has worked to make the operation of the society more efficient, so that we can maintain as good a lifestyle as before; the self-willed machines have been helping. But the old-guard Contrary Citizens have adamantly opposed him; they want to get rich by multiplying the output of Protonite."

"Stile encouraged the association of the species," Brown continued. "Thus it was that Bane was named after wolfbane, the charm the werewolves use for strength, and had as playmates the young of the unicorns, werewolves, vampires and even on occasion some of the Little Folk or the trolls."

"I learned about Fleta," Mach said, smiling at her. "But how far does this association go? Fleta seems to feel that any permanent liaison between us is forbidden."

Brown spread her hands. "Camaraderie be one thing; marriage be another. The species be concerned about the purity of their lines, and some have ancient enmities. So this be an uneasy association at best. Stile himself was close to Neysa, but he married his own kind. So even if thou didst not have to return to thine own frame, I think there would be no approval in this frame for what thou might desire."

"She speaks truth," Fleta murmured.

"Not as I see it!" Mach said. "I grew up in a society in which robots like myself mixed with other types of creature, and no limits to their association were imposed. My father is human, my mother a robot. Is there greater distinction between me and a unicorn than between me and a human being?"

Brown shook her head. "In Phaze thou wouldst be called a golem, an thou didst have thine own body. Even so was Sheen considered, when she visited this frame. I personally believe that golems should have greater rights, but I am biased by the nature of my magic. Phaze be not ready for mixing of species in any but the most innocent sense, and not ready for self-willed golems at all. An thou didst take Fleta to Proton with thee, there the situation might differ."

Mach sighed. "I think I do not want to return to Proton alone, but I cannot take her with me."

"I knew always our love was forbidden," Fleta said. "The more fool I for yielding to it."

"This experience has been a kind of dream for me," he said. "But I too knew I could not live forever in a dream. Once I discover how to exchange back, I will have to return his body to Bane."

Soon they had another call. A man walked in from the kitchen, carrying a tray full of desserts: chocolate ice cream. Mach glanced at him casually, then did a doubletake. "Father!"

Brown laughed. "Stile, thou idiot! Thou didst not have to masquerade as a servant!"

For it was indeed Stile, the Adept. He looked exactly like Citizen Blue, except that his clothing was of Phaze instead of Proton. He was small, shorter than any of the others in the room, but fit, in his middle forties.

"I didn't know quite what to expect," Stile said, setting down the desserts. "So I thought I'd come quietly." He sounded exactly like Blue, too.

"So thou didst animate one of my golems!" Brown said.

"It was already animate. I merely gave it my semblance."

"Sit down, have some ice cream," Brown said mischievously. Mach had to smile, knowing that an ordinary golem could not eat.

"Not my flavor," Stile demurred.

Brown snapped her fingers. Another golem responded. "Fetch some blue ice cream," she ordered.

The golem returned in a moment with blueberry ice cream, setting it before Stile. He took his spoon and began to eat.

Fleta's mouth dropped open. Then Brown caught on. "Thou dost fashion the illusion of eating, to go with the illusion of life for the golem."

Stile smiled. "It gets harder to deceive thee, Brown. Why didst thou send thy messenger?"

"This be not thy son, Bane, but his other self from Proton, Mach," Brown said. "He needs to know how to return to Proton."

Now Stile did a doubletake. He stared at Bane. Then he glanced at Brown. "May I?"

"Feel free," she replied.

Stile sang something under his breath. There seemed to be a play of force around Mach, but nothing else happened.

"So it be true," Stile breathed. "Contact between the frames, after twenty years!"

Brown relaxed. Evidently she had retained a certain skepticism about Mach's claim, despite her friendly treatment of him. But it seemed that Stile's magic had verified it.

"Fleta brought me here," Mach said. "We were pursued by agents of Adverse Adepts."

Stile nodded. "So that was why it came not to mine attention! They used no magic. Methought thou wast merely having a private fling with thine old companion, and I knew my son could handle the like of goblins."

"I managed to work a little magic, but it was clumsy, especially at first," Mach said. "Without Fleta, I would have been captured."

"I brought him here because I thought they would not be blocking off this castle as they were the Blue Demesnes," Fleta said. "But I could not tell him how to return to Proton."

"How didst thou come to this frame?" Stile inquired of Mach.

"I willed it—and suddenly it happened."

"But thou couldst not will thyself back?"

Mach shook his head. "It didn't seem to work that way."

Stile considered. "*Where* did it happen?"

"In a glade near the swamp."

Stile looked at Fleta. "What glade?"

Fleta gave a more accurate geographic description, and added that Bane had gone there several times before the exchange was made.

"Then Bane was trying for this?"

"Yes," Mach said.

"Thy position in Proton—how did it relate to thy point of arrival in Phaze?"

"Why, they were the same," Mach said.

"Then thy body occupied the same spot his did—one in each frame."

"Yes, I think so."

"That must be the key! To overlap the position, then will the exchange. Mayhap he facilitated it with a spell."

Mach sat amazed. Of course that was the key, suddenly so obvious! To overlap, so there was no physical motion required. And when he had walked away from that spot, the overlap no longer occurred, so they couldn't change back.

"I did it!" he exclaimed ruefully. "I left the spot, trapping him there without even realizing!"

"Then perhaps he is trying to locate thee, again," Stile said. "Does he have a mechanism for that?"

"I don't know," Mach said. "But I think so, because he knew where to be, while I did not realize that location mattered. But if so, it may not work in Proton."

"He would have used another spell," Stile agreed. "Or perhaps the two of you are attuned to each other. If thou dost try to tune in on him—"

"I never thought of that!" Mach exclaimed, feeling quite stupid. He sat still and concentrated, thinking of Bane. *Where are you, my other self?*

He felt the faintest of stirrings, as though he had reached something far distant. But he couldn't be sure.

"Try it again, periodically," Stile suggested. "I think this be a thing no other can do for thee." He leaned forward. "But in the meantime, there be things we must grasp. This be contact between the frames, when we thought it impossible. A psychic rapport between the two of you—mayhap a unique one. I see now why the Adepts be after thee; they knew before I did, and seek contact with Proton."

"Yes," Mach agreed. "They want me to carry messages, and have offered me anything I want."

Stile nodded. "We all be starved for news! But thou—if thou be the son of mine other self, who is thy mother?"

"Sheen."

"Sheen be the best and loveliest of women, but she also be a robot. Do robots bear babies now?"

"No. I am a robot too." Quickly Mach explained.

"Yet thou dost resemble Bane, physically?"

"Precisely, as far as I can tell."

"And thou dost have a soul, for now it be here."

"And his is in my robot body," Mach agreed.

"I suspected that a machine could have a soul when I knew Sheen," Stile said, and his eyes looked far beyond the chamber. "Now it seems we have the proof." He shrugged. "Tell thy mother I remember her, and be glad for her fortune in marrying Blue."

Then he left, and only the golem remained, brown and wooden, the melting ice cream untouched before it.

"He seemed not much interested in thee!" Fleta said indignantly.

Mach smiled. "He was interested. He is like my father; only a small fraction of the thought and emotion in him leaks out. I'm glad to have met him, and I shall carry back his message."

"Methinks Stile was a bit *too* restrained," Brown remarked. "He will be watching thee, Mach."

"I know it." Mach looked at Fleta. "I think our time together is limited, now that I have the key to my return."

"Aye," she agreed faintly.

"I will provide you with a suite here, until the time," Brown said.

It was a nice suite. "She understands," Fleta whispered.

"She understands," Mach agreed. "She may have had some forbidden love of her own."

For the first time, they spent a night in human quarters, without fear of pursuit or discovery, and it was sheer delight. They made love with the desperation born of the knowledge of coming separation.

"But surely I need not stay always in Proton," Mach murmured. "If I could come here once, I could come here again, at least for a visit, to see you."

"Aye," she breathed with sudden hope.

"If Bane agreed. I don't know how he would feel—"

"Bane be a good man. He would do it."

They lay in silence for a time. Then he asked: "You told the Brown Adept that you love me."

"I had no right," she said.

"Surely it has happened before! With animals being able to assume human form, and sharing human intelligence—has no unicorn, or werewolf, or vampire ever before loved a human being?"

"Oh, aye," she said. "But it be discouraged for aught but play."

"Play—as in bed? But not serious, as in love?"

"Aye. Love be special."

"Surely it is! And until I occupied this human body, I think play was all I ever experienced. But now I believe I love you,

Fleta, and I don't see how that can be wrong. I know what you are, and if you love me too—"

She shook her head. "Mach, mayhap there be secret love twixt our kinds on occasion, but ne'er open. Sometimes a human man will take a werebitch as a concubine, and she would do it not if she loved him not. Sometimes an animal be so fetching, like Suchevane the vampiress, that she could take a human man."

"Who?"

"Suchevane. She be the loveliest of her kind. Methinks Bane played a game with her, too." She grimaced. "But thou dost have no need to meet her," she concluded firmly.

"So animals and human beings never marry."

"Nor speak the three," she agreed.

"The three? Three whats?"

"When thy kind—and sometimes other kinds—bespeak true love, the one will address the other three times, and then there be no doubt."

"Three times? You mean if I said 'I love you' three times, then you would believe me?"

"Thee," she said. "But say it not, Mach."

"Thee? But I don't talk that way."

"Aye. Thou art not of Phaze."

"Thee—three times?"

"Say it not!" she repeated. "This be ne'er offhand!"

"I don't understand."

"Aye," she murmured, and kissed him.

In the morning they joined Brown for breakfast, then went out for a walk around the Demesnes. Mach paused to concentrate on his other self—and felt Bane much more definitely than before. "He's closer!" he said. "He must be tuning in on me, making his way here."

"Aye," she said, her lip trembling.

He kissed her. "I *will* return!"

"I will wait for thee."

They were coming into a pleasant flowery garden, whose blooms were all shades of brown. "I'm getting to like the color," Mach remarked.

"These be grown on the best fertilizer there be," Fleta said.

"Oh? What's that?"

"Unicorn manure."

He laughed, thinking it a joke. But she was serious. "When my dam, Neysa, met Brown, and Brown helped Stile, the unicorns agreed to provide her fertilizer for her garden, and so it has been e'er since."

That reminded him of her nature. She had not assumed her natural form since their arrival at the Brown Demesnes. "Fleta, before we part, would you—"

She glanced askance at him.

"Would you play me a tune? I think your music is lovely."

"But to do that—"

"What is wrong with your natural form?"

She hesitated. It was obvious that she preferred to relate to him in the human fashion. Then she shrugged, and became herself, with her glossy black coat and golden socks. She played a melody on her horn, and then a two-part tune, the pan-pipes playing counterpoint. How she could do that he was not sure; he assumed that magic assisted it. Perhaps the high notes were played at the narrow tip of the horn, and the low ones at the broader base. But the music was as pretty as he could imagine. He would always remember her for this, for her sound as much as for her appearance.

She finished, and changed back to girl form. "Thou dost value me only for my melody," she teased him.

"I would value you just as much if—" Mach looked around, seeking a suitable metaphor for the occasion. They were near a pleasant pool, at whose brown-mud borders fat frogs squatted. "If your horn sounded like the croaking of frogs."

She laughed, but there was an angry croak from the nearest frog, who evidently had overheard. In a moment all the frogs had the message, and were glaring at him.

"Methinks thou didst misspeak thyself," Fleta said, suppressing a merry chortle in the way she had, at bosom-level.

Mach was abashed. It had never occurred to him that the frogs would understand. "I—"

"Croak!" the largest frog said witheringly. Then it turned about, facing the other frogs. They settled themselves in a ring around the pool, at the water's edge. Then they croaked.

Some had low croaks, and some had high croaks, while most were in the middle ranges. They croaked in sequence—and suddenly a melody emerged, each croak a note. More than that: it was the same melody Fleta had just played on her horn, in both its parts. The frogs were duplicating it in all its detail, and in this mode it had another kind of beauty, as great in its fashion as the original had been.

The frogs completed it, and were silent. They waited.

Mach knew he was on the spot. In his ignorance he had affronted the frogs, without cause. He owed them an apology.

He faced Fleta. "In fact, your horn *does* sound like the croaking of frogs," he said loudly. "Beautiful!"

Fleta smiled. "I thank thee for that compliment."

The frogs considered that. Then the leader jumped into the pond. After that the others followed. In a moment the mud was clear.

"I think they have forgiven thee," Fleta murmured. Then she embraced him and kissed him, in the midst of her laughter.

She changed back to 'corn form and played a new melody. This time Mach joined her, singing counterpoint. And from the pond the croaking resumed, providing a melodic background. It was as though an entire orchestra were performing.

There was a rumble. The ground shook. Fleta stopped playing, alarmed.

The pond abruptly drained away, its water disappearing into the ground beneath. The frogs scrambled desperately to escape. The mud bubbled and slid into the deepening hole.

The flower garden caved in around them. Fleta blew a startled note, bracing her four feet. Mach, realizing that something was seriously amiss, leaped for her, scrambling to her back as his footing gave way. "Get out of here!" he cried.

She leaped—but the entire garden collapsed under her hooves, dropping them down into a forming sink-hole. Fleta kept her feet, but slid to the bottom.

Now smoke showed, issuing from forming vents. "It's a caldera!" Mach cried, jumping off her back. "Change to bird form and fly out, Fleta!"

But she did not; she would not leave him in this danger.

The ground shook again, and the volume of smoke increased, obscuring everything. It seemed to form a globe about them, closing in.

"Magic!" Mach cried. "I'll try a spell!"

But in this pressure of the moment, he could think of neither rhyme nor melody. Fleta blew a note, trying to help him, but then the smoke closed in, chokingly, and they were helpless.

In a moment, it cleared—but they were no longer in the garden. They were in a chamber hewn from rock—and great ugly creatures surrounded them. The creatures pounced, grasping Mach by the arms, one of them clapping a rough and dirty hand over his mouth. Others flung themselves on Fleta, shoving her against the wall while one grasped her horn.

"Welcome, apprentice!" a man said, entering the chamber. "I am the Purple Adept, and these trolls be under my sway. As thou mayst know, I reside in the Purple Mountains, and I possess the magic of the movements of the earth. Now I want thy cooperation, apprentice, and I want thy word on that now."

At a signal from Purple, the troll removed his hand from Mach's mouth. Mach spat out gravel. "I'll give you no such word, criminal!"

"Now I know thou canst not do magic without thy mouth, and my minion will clap his hand back o'er it the moment thou dost try to sing a spell. So thou canst not escape by thy magic."

"But I won't help you, either!" Mach said.

"But an thee give me not thy word, it will go grievously with thy steed here."

"She's not my steed!" Mach exclaimed.

"Aye, she be thy concubine. I saw as much when the two of you trespassed across my Demesnes. Now I ask thee, apprentice: how much music will that mare play, without her horn?"

Fleta renewed her struggles, but the mass of trolls overwhelmed her. She could neither escape nor change form, while her horn was held.

What would happen to a unicorn whose horn was amputated? Mach didn't know, but the very fact that the evil Adept expected him to be cowed by this threat served the purpose. He had no faith in any good will by this man, and he couldn't risk harm to Fleta.

"I will carry a message to Proton," he said dully. "Release Fleta."

"Release her? Nay, she will remain with us—unharmed pending thy cooperation." The Purple Adept made another signal, and the trolls heaved and shoved the resisting unicorn from the chamber. "She will reside in an enchanted cell that be proof from her escape in any form. An thou cooperate fully, she will be well enough treated otherwise."

Mach felt a private rage such as he had never experienced when he had been a robot, but he knew he had to control it. He just could not risk harm to Fleta! "What is your message?"

"The first one will be to mine other self, Citizen Purple, just to let him know that contact has been reestablished. He will know what to do, and what message to return."

The first one. When would this brute ever give over? Not as long as he had control of Fleta!

But perhaps there was a way out. Mach suppressed that thought, not wanting any hint of it to show here. "I have to overlap the spot my other self occupies," he said. "I can't do that if you don't let me move about."

"Thou shalt move about—in my presence," Purple said. "And be thou advised, apprentice, that thy magic may be apt against ordinary folk, but cannot compare to mine own. An thou try something against me, not only will I balk it, I will let my minions at the animal's horn. Trolls hate 'corns; only the restraint I impose prevents them from making her scream."

There will be a reckoning, Mach thought, then quelled his outrage.

He tuned in on Bane—and his other self was very close now. Apparently Bane had been able to follow him here. So it would happen soon—and then he would see whether his wild notion would work.

He experimented, discovering that he could tell the direction from which his other self was coming. He faced that way, ready to walk toward Bane—but he was in a tunnel underground, and the rock wall cut him off.

So he walked along the tunnel, angling toward the other self, while the Purple Adept paced him. "As I understand this," Purple said, "thou art from Proton and have little power of magic. When thou dost exchange back, Bane will be here, and he has power. But thou must remember that any hostile magic practiced here will cost the horn of the animal, and perhaps more thereafter. So thou wouldst be best advised to deliver the message, and bring the return message—and to advise thine other self of the wisdom of this procedure. *He* may not care for the animal as thou dost, and will leave her to her fate otherwise."

"Understood," Mach said tightly. He kept walking.

The awareness of his other self grew steadily stronger. Mach realized that the two would overlap very soon. He resolved to accomplish the exchange without giving any outward sign. That was part of his wild plan.

The tunnel curved, allowing him to proceed directly toward his target—and suddenly it happened. Overlap! But Mach did not stop walking, and in a moment the contact slipped; he had not grasped the opportunity when it had come.

Then he felt his other self approaching from behind. *Wait,* it thought.

I cannot, Mach thought back, as the other paced him for a moment. *I am in enemy power.*

So am I! the other returned.

Mach quailed. His wild hope had been dashed. He had wanted to get help through Proton, arranging some counter pressure there that would nullify the hold Purple had on him. If he could have made the exchange without Purple knowing, and arrange the counter-action, and exchanged back—

He kept walking, and the other phased in again, this time maintaining it. *Fleta is hostage; I am helpless.*

Agape be hostage here.

Quickly they compared situations—and realized that they had a chance after all. Satisfied, they made the exchange.

11
Escape

Mach found himself in the same tunnel, only now it was a passage, lighted by electricity instead of magic-glow. He was naked. The one who paced him now was Citizen Purple, a man he knew by reputation. Obviously he had taken Agape hostage in much the same fashion as his other self, the Purple Adept, had taken Fleta hostage. And Bane must have developed a close relationship with the alien female. Well, it was perhaps no stranger than his own with Fleta.

He turned to the Citizen. "Contact be near, now," he said. "What be thy message, again?" He hoped he had the language down well enough to fool the man.

"Stop stalling, boy!" Purple snapped. "You know the message!"

Mach stopped walking. "Let me see her again."

"You aren't in any position to bargain!" the Citizen said.

"An what if I go—an thou hast dispatched her already? Must I needs know she be well, now."

Purple grimaced. "You push your luck, machine. This one stall I will allow; then you will do it, or see her in the pot."

In the pot? What could that mean?

They took a side passage, and came to the cell where Agape was confined. "Let me go in with her," Mach said.

"It's your last damned smooch; make it a good one," Purple said.

The serf guard let Mach in. Agape stood to meet him. "Bane! Didn't it work?"

He took her in his arms. He had not realized what a luscious creature she was! It was evident that she had learned much about human interaction since his brief contact with her.

He kissed her—and felt her stiffen. She realized that something was wrong. But before she could speak, he put his lips to her ear and whispered, "I am Mach. Give no hint. Melt your way out at night, go to the nearest maintenance service outlet, and tap this pattern." He clicked his teeth three times quickly, then three times slowly, then three times quickly again, in the ancient SOS signal he had discovered when researching for a game. He had set it up as a code to the self-willed machines: one that only he would think to send.

"Then trust the machines; they will get you out. Tell Citizen Blue. I will try to distract attention from your cell tonight."

He kissed her again, then separated. "An I see thee not again, think kindly of me," he said, loudly enough for others to hear.

"Oh, you'll see her again," Purple said. "Right here, when you return with my message from Phaze."

"Thou art a hard man," Mach muttered.

They returned to the key section of the passage. "It be very close here," Mach said. "I feel his presence."

"Well, merge!" the Citizen said impatiently.

Mach tuned in, and felt Bane approaching. He stepped up to meet him. They overlapped.

Did you do it? Mach thought.

Aye. And thee?

Yes.

Then it be time.

Time, Mach agreed.

They separated. Mach remained in Proton; they had not tried to exchange frames this time. They had just needed the news of their success to be delayed until now. For Mach had no compelling personal reason to visit Agape, and Bane had none to visit Fleta; the enemy forces would keep the females securely isolated after the exchange. Indeed, this was the only safe policy—as the strategy he and Bane had formulated should show.

Mach looked around, feigning confusion. "Where am I?" he asked.

"Proton," the Citizen replied.

"Then I am back! The exchange worked!"

"That's right, robot."

"Then I have a message for you."

"A message? But I just sent your other self with one!"

Mach smiled. "It seems your opposite number had the same notion you did. His message is this: Contact has been reestablished."

"I know that!" Purple snapped. "What else?"

"Nothing else. He said you would know what to do, and what message to return."

"That's the message I sent *him!*"

"Evidently great minds run in similar channels," Mach said.

"Don't get cute with *me,* robot!"

Mach smiled grimly. "How can I be cute with a person for whom I have no respect?"

"I'll have you dismantled and fed into the refuse recycler!" the Citizen snapped.

"And lose your only contact with Phaze? Whom do you suppose you are fooling, Purple?"

The Citizen began to assume the color of his name. "You play a dangerous game, machine."

"Listen, you idiot—this isn't Bane you're talking to! You can't deceive me the way you did him. I am the son of Citizen Blue, and Blue will grind your meaty posterior into hamburger when he finds out what you have done. How long do you think you can keep it secret?"

Purple asserted some control over himself. "Do you forget that I have your alien girlfriend hostage to your cooperation?"

"*What* alien girlfriend? I broke up with Doris the cyborg before I went to Phaze; I have no girlfriend in this frame."

The Citizen took stock, realizing that he had lost that aspect of his leverage when Bane and Mach returned to their own frames. Then he saw his avenue. "So you do have a girlfriend in Phaze. And if I know my other self—as I surely do—he has that girl in his power. If you don't bring back a message from me, he will take it out on that girl. And *that* you wouldn't like. Am I correct, machine?"

Mach grimaced, answer enough.

"So you *will* cooperate—and when Bane returns here, *he* will cooperate, because I have *his* girlfriend. We've got you, robot."

"Until Citizen Blue learns. Then you may not like the reckoning that comes."

"By the time Blue learns, there may have been a shift in the balance of power. Then I may like the reckoning well enough."

Mach realized that the cunning Citizen had big aspirations. He was going to use the contact with Phaze to increase his own power, making himself invulnerable to retribution. He could do that only with Mach's cooperation. Therefore the sensible thing to do was not to cooperate. But Fleta was indeed hostage, and until he knew she had been freed—and Bane knew Agape had been freed—they did indeed have to cooperate.

But his resources were not yet exhausted. He needed to distract the Citizen's attention from Agape for about twenty-four hours.

"I'll play you a Game," Mach said. "I will break out of this captivity within twenty-four hours. Then you may do with the alien female what you wish—but my father will settle with you for interfering with the Experimental Project and generating an interplanetary incident. I suspect he will simply ship you to Moeba for alien justice."

"I'll play no Game with you, robot!"

"You can't avoid it, Purple. You have already established it: you have taken me captive. My challenge is to break out. If I fail, I will have to cooperate with you. If I succeed, you will be finished. So it's your gain against your loss. But I'll offer you a draw at the outset: free me and the alien now, and there will be no retribution for what you have already done."

"You try to dictate terms to *me,* you inanimate contraption? I already hold the winning cards! There'll be no deal but this: you will deliver the message I send, or you will remain locked up forever!"

"So you decline the proffered draw," Mach said calmly. "Then let the Game proceed. Twenty-four hours."

"There *is* no Game! No time limit!"

"Keep repeating it, and you may even come to believe it."

"You *will* cooperate! You have no choice!"

"You assume I will deliver the correct message?"

"Don't try to bluff me, machine! You always tell the truth. If you take a message, you will deliver it accurately."

"Yet you assume I'm lying when I tell you the Game is on?"

"You can imagine any Game you want, in your cell! That's all in your circuits."

"We shall see."

A serf conducted Mach to a cell, and he was locked in. Three walls were solid stone, the fourth of transparent glass, too thick and strong to break. He had no privacy, and a serf stood guard on the other side of the glass. This was a tighter cell than the one in which Agape was confined; the Citizen knew Mach was more dangerous than the alien female.

Mach sat on the bare bench and crossed his arms. He tuned out, remaining motionless for half an hour while he planned the details of his action, preprogramming as much as he could. When he was satisfied with his plan, he allowed himself to think about Fleta, back in Phaze. He was back in his robot body, and had control over his emotional circuits, but now he released that control and simply *felt*. He discovered that his feeling for Fleta was just as strong now as it had been in Phaze. A machine *could* love, for he did.

All too quickly his preset time was up. Mach came alert again.

The serf still guarded the cell, but was no longer paying full attention. In fact, the serf was snoozing on his feet. That was what Mach had counted on. It was easy for a machine to remain alert indefinitely, but difficult for a living person. Faced with Mach's complete immobility, the guard had quickly grown bored and careless.

Mach did not move his hands, but he did twitch the fingers

of his right hand, where they were covered by his left upper arm. His middle finger pressed a stud in a private pattern, and a section of pseudomuscle slid aside to expose an access to the internal circuitry of his torso. Robots had always been constructed with access-panels, but Mach was of the most advanced type. His brain was the most sophisticated yet devised for this purpose, and his body was as competent and reliable as any machine could be. The interaction of the two gave him potential that perhaps his own designers had not anticipated.

The fingers quested within the circuitry, dislodging certain fastenings, until a small subunit was loose. Watching the serf-guard to be sure the man did not turn his head, Mach removed that subunit, sliding it out and down his body to the bench. Still watching the guard, Mach now used both hands to adjust the tiny unit.

Mach's body was hierarchically organized, with a number of self-powered subunits contributing to the performance of the whole. The particular unit he had removed related to the verification of pressure-feedback from his left arm. It was redundant, and he could operate without it for a time. He closed up the aperture, so that his body seemed unchanged, and made adjustments to the separate unit. It was of a standard design, and could be adapted for several purposes. Now he was adjusting it not for internal feedback, but for external broadcast.

He set the unit on the bench beside him and turned it on. It began emitting a signal. The signal passed through the glass wall and bathed the serf-guard. It was not a strong or far-reaching signal; it just induced a lethargy bordering on sleep. The serf would not even be conscious of it; he would simply not feel inclined to move or react unless strongly prodded.

Now Mach touched the skin under his right arm, keying open a chamber there. He unmade some connections and set up a bypass for a subunit whose normal purpose was to enhance the strength of his motor actions when an emergency arose. The living human analogy was a shot of adrenaline; his robot body had it under conscious control. He removed this unit and adjusted it, converting it, too, into a miniature broadcaster of a signal. Then he took it to the glass panel.

The panel was locked by a mechanism controlled by a computerized identification system. It was supposed to respond only to the presence and command of an authorized person. If anyone else attempted to open the cell, an alarm would sound. But Mach's device sent an override signal that nullified the normal recognition circuit and released the lock. This trick, like the one to immobilize a living person, he had picked up as a child when playing with others. Many of the humanoid robots knew such things, but by tacit common agreement they did not advertise them to nonrobots. It was like the short-circuit route to sexual pleasure: only for their own kind.

He brought the unit near the locking mechanism, and tuned it, seeking the particular band for the override. Suddenly he found it; the glass panel slid open.

Mach emerged, approached the nodding serf, and led him by the hand into the cell. He sat him down on the bench, picked up the pacification unit, then left the cell again, closed the glass panel, and turned off the second unit. The locking mechanism clicked back into force. Mach adjusted the units, then opened his underarm apertures and wired the units back in. There was now no evidence of how he had done what he had done. With luck it would be some time before the serf woke, and longer before he was able to gain the attention of anyone else.

Now he set off down the hall, alert for sensors or alarms. He had some time to pass before he could afford to be actively pursued. Where would be the best place to hide?

It took only a moment to decide: the nearest Game Annex. He could lose himself pretty thoroughly in the right aspect of the Game.

Evidently the Citizen and his staff were occupied elsewhere, though it was midday. Probably this was a forbidden area, to keep the prisoner isolated. Would it be possible to go to the cell where Agape was confined and free her? Maybe, but not worth risking; he intended to stay well away from there.

He found an alarm beam, but didn't even need to nullify it; he simply stepped over it. Then he came to the Game Annex. This was a simple Game pedestal, with a door beyond that would open on the Game chambers. Many Citizens had private annexes, as the fascination of the Game extended to every level of the Proton society, and to every species within it. In fact, that had been perhaps the major lure for the status of serf, for the self-willed machines: the right that status conferred to play the Game. Within the Game, there was no distinction between Citizen and serf; only a player's individual skill counted. The annual Tourney allowed serfs of all types to compete on equal footing for the prize of Citizenship. But even serfs like Mach himself, who had no need for that particular route to Citizenship, were fascinated by the Game. Perhaps, he thought, it represented the expression of man's eternal need to gamble—a need that had been passed on to man's more sophisticated machines.

Mach bypassed the grids, as he knew that any attempt to turn them on would alert the Citizen. He opened the door beyond, and stepped into an elevator. He guided it down, seeking the basement level where the main supplies should be.

He emerged into a chamber in which a number of robots were stored. There was one that resembled a clothed hunter, complete with bow and arrows, and another like a goblin, and another like a harpy. There were also guided machines, such as small airplanes. A fancy Game setup indeed. The main Game Annex had every-thing, of course, but the small subannexes like this were generally limited to basics. Citizen Purple evidently liked to play in exotic settings. That surely told something about his character, but Mach wasn't sure what. After all, he himself had found love in a most exotic setting.

He sat at a control console and put the helmet over his head. He operated the controls, which were of standard type, and animated the goblin. The ugly little robot walked and turned at Mach's direction. There was a speaker system, so that he could speak through the goblin's head, but he didn't use it. He was satisfied that he had a notion of the type of entertainment Citizen Purple preferred: vicarious participation in fantasy settings.

Well, to work. Mach opened a panel in his abdomen and removed another subunit. This one normally monitored his power usage. His main power source was a chip of Protonite, and it would last for a year if not expended wastefully. When too much power was being used, the monitor warned him, so that he could cut down. But that monitor, like the other subunits, could be turned to other purposes.

He adjusted it, again as with the others, to become a signal generator. It was simply a matter of amplifying and redirecting its normal output. But its new signal was not a normal one; the mechanisms had a feedback circuit, intended to shut down its signal when the monitored energy-use declined to tolerable levels, that in this circumstance had the effect of a random modulation. Both the strength and frequency of the signal would vary unpredictably.

Mach activated this unit, then put it in the clawed grasp of a robot harpy. Then he used the console controls to animate the harpy, and sent her up the access shaft to the main Game-playing site. He watched through her eye-lenses as she came up into the site—and pursed his lips in a soundless whistle. This was imitation Phaze! There were trees all over the Purple Mountains, exactly as was the case in Phaze. He knew; he had recently crossed those mountains with Fleta!

Fleta. Abruptly his mood shifted. He was no longer in the living body, so his emotions were under control, but he had no desire to control this one. All that he had longed for, all his pseudolife as a humanoid robot, had been granted during his sojourn in Phaze. He had experienced the wonder of true life there—and the corollary wonder of true love. That wonder was muted, now—but his memory of both remained.

He wanted both, again. The existence he had in the frame of Proton had lost its luster for him. What future did he have here? Perhaps he would become the first robot Citizen—but what was the point, without Fleta? Better to be a common resident of the magic frame, with her!

But Bane was back in his own body, now, and surely understood the superiority of it. Bane had evidently dallied with Agape, here, but he had known, as Mach had known with Fleta, that it could not be permanent. Perhaps they could exchange again, for visits to each other's frames, but Proton was the one Mach was stuck with for permanent residence. Paradise lost!

He sent the robot harpy flapping into the sky with the signaling unit. He had her fly over an otherwise-inaccessible section of the mountain, swoop low, and drop the unit in a crevice. That would make it hard to locate and harder to recover. Then he brought her back to the exit ramp and to the nether chamber. He positioned her exactly as she had been before, and turned off the control console.

He left the premises quietly. His luck had about expired; now he would have to hide in earnest.

He found a utility closet some distance removed and got into it. He concealed himself behind cleaning equipment that the serfs used, and tuned out.

Within the hour a commotion commenced. Mach came alert, but did not move; again he appreciated the fact that as a robot, he could remain absolutely still for an indefinite period. Since he was in the lowliest of places, it might be some time before they thought to look for him here.

Serfs hurried along the passage. Soon the Citizen himself huffed past, muttering. Mach attuned his hearing to the voice of the Citizen, so as to pick up what the man said when he reached Mach's vacated cell. This should be fun!

The Citizen reached the cell. "How the hell could he get out?" he demanded. "The damned thing's still locked!"

Evidently the response did not satisfy him. "Well, open it!" he snapped. Then, evidently to the guard-serf trapped inside: "You are fired!" The firing of a serf was a serious business; the chances were that that serf would not be able to get another position, and would have to leave the planet. This serf, of course, was mainly a victim of circumstance.

"He has to be somewhere on the premises!" the Citizen cried. "Our barriers are proof against any unauthorized departure!" Yet the glassed-in cell was supposed to have been secure, too. Mach was privately pleased that he had thought to remove his devices and close the cell. As a robot he should not ordinarily have had the originality for that, and evidently the Citizen had assumed that the normal tolerances applied. Thus Purple had departed to take his meal or nap, leaving Mach to his own devices—and was now paying the consequence. Had he been smarter, he would have realized that the son of Citizen Blue would have to be a rather special robot with the latest technology. And that a robot who had just returned from a genuine experience of life could have been inspired to a certain lifelike originality. Now that minor mystery of the locked cell was buying Mach invaluable time.

"A what?" the Citizen rapped. Then: "But no signal can get out either!" Which meant they had picked up the signal, and were about to trace it down. That would take them some time. When they finally located it, they would not know how the signal unit had gotten there.

"Check the alien bitch!" the Citizen said. "He's bound to try to spring her!"

But of course Mach hadn't done that, yet. Agape was supposed to wait till night, then make her break. Mach hoped to remain hidden until after she started her action; then he could relax. All this was only a distraction, to keep the Citizen and his minions occupied until Agape could escape.

The Citizen's voice faded out; Mach could hear with preter-natural acuteness when he tried to, but there were limits, and the Citizen had passed out of range. The commotion continued, as the serfs launched a methodical search for the signal-unit and for Mach himself. At first, surely, they would believe that he was in the vicinity of the signal generator, and comb through the Game region—which would be a tedious chore indeed! Once they ascertained that the generator was a separate item, they would go through the remaining premises with determination. He would inevitably be found—but probably not before Agape started her escape and enlisted the aid of the self-willed machines.

When they did catch him, he suspected, they would ask him about the signal he had been sending: what was its nature, and to whom was it directed? He would tell them that it was a phony signal, meaning nothing, merely random noise, that could not penetrate the Citizen's signal-barrier. And they would not believe him, because why would he have gone to such an extraordinary effort to put out that signal if it could not accomplish anything? So the quest would continue, and that distraction would give Agape more leeway for her escape. And once she escaped, it would be only a matter of time before Citizen Blue had news of Mach's location. Then the real fun would begin!

He was only a machine. But he was a machine in love, just as his mother Sheen was; he understood her better than he had before. As far as he was concerned, the Experimental Project was a success; as part of it, he had become as human as any of his kind had ever aspired to be. And he found that he enjoyed making a fool of Citizen Purple. He hoped Bane was doing the same to the Purple Adept.

Now it was time to dream of life, and of Fleta, and what he wished might have been. Time for machine dreams.

Mach tuned out, waiting.

12

Apprentice

Bane, conscious of his agreement with Mach, gave no sign as he found himself in the passage lighted by magic-glow rather than scientific effects. He had been walking naked; now he was fully clothed, and that seemed strange after more than a week in the other state. He did not want anyone to know, yet, that the bumbling visitor had been replaced by the skilled native. "He is near," he said. "I know I can do it. But show me Fleta first, in good health."

"Do it now, or she shall lose her horn now," Purple said sternly.

Rage flared in Bane. They were going to dehorn Fleta? That would deprive the unicorn of all her magic power and most of her will to live! The Adverse Adepts had done that to her uncle Clip, before Bane was born, and only Stile's total magic had been able to mend that horn. Any chance that Bane might have worked voluntarily with these Adepts dissipated with this news. Fleta was hardly his love, but she was an old friend, and such a threat against her alienated him instantly.

He did not need to conceal his emotion, for Mach felt as

strongly about the mare as Bane himself did, if in a different manner. The propriety of Mach's relationship with the unicorn was questionable, but since Mach was now back in his own frame, that didn't matter. It would be ironic if Fleta were mutilated to punish a person who might never see her again anyway.

"Thou hast made that threat before," Bane said grimly. "How can I know that thou hast not already done it?"

"So now thou dost affect native speech?" the Purple Adept remarked contemptuously. "Forget it, alien; thou canst not fool anyone."

Oops—it seemed that Mach had maintained his own dialect. Well, Bane had been in Proton long enough to pick it up. "I thought it was close enough," he muttered, as if disgruntled. "Anyway, show me she's all right, or I'll know she *isn't*." Indeed, he had no respect for the word of this man, and realized he would be foolish to deliver the message from Proton without ensuring that the terms were met.

The Adept scowled, but yielded. "One time, then—but try not my patience further."

They went to the cell where Fleta was confined. She was in her natural form, and an amulet had been tied to her horn, nullifying it. She was also in a halter, with her head tied in place so that she could not move it to scrape off the amulet, and trolls kept watch.

Appalled, Bane approached the cell—and felt the presence of an invisible magic barrier. He knew its nature immediately; it was a standard Adept spell that was used to confine animals or ordinary folk. This was a strong one, that could restrain a unicorn despite the antimagical powers of the species. Even with her horn free, Fleta could not penetrate this barrier; she would merely be able to change her form in her cell.

But he knew what to do, now. He had to provide her with a spell for spot nullification without alarm. "What holds me?" he demanded, as if he didn't know.

"Never mind," Purple said, and the barrier dissolved. Bane approached the tied animal. He put his mouth to her ear, as if whispering an endearment. "This spell, new role," he sang quietly. "Make horn-sized hole." And the powerful magic of his will reached out to change the amulet on her horn.

Her near eye widened, showing white momentarily. He knew she felt his spell, and knew that Mach could not have performed magic of this level. She realized that the amulet no longer locked her into her present form; it had been turned to his purpose. She would know what to do, and when.

He turned away. Without a word he walked out of the cell, feeling the magic barrier snap back into place behind him, and proceeded back down the tunnel toward the point of rendezvous.

At the proper place he paused, overlapping Mach and verifying that the robot had done his part. Then he changed his expression. He touched his clothing. "Then I be back!" he exclaimed.

"Contact!" the Purple Adept said.

Bane turned to him. "I bear a message from thine other self: Contact be established, and the next move be thine."

"But that's the message I sent him!"

Bane shrugged. "He be thine other self."

Purple's visage clouded suspiciously. "How do I know thou hast really made the change? Thou couldst be the same one I captured!"

"Perhaps thou willst believe it by this," Bane said. Then he sang: "Make a funnel to a tunnel."

The floor of the passage opened up in a circular depression, deepening in the center. It did indeed soon come to resemble a funnel. Below it there was evidently a new tunnel: one leading out from this fastness.

Without delay, Bane jumped into the funnel and slid down into the tunnel. He landed on his feet and started running along it.

But in a moment shapes loomed up ahead of him. Trolls! The Purple Adept had summoned more of his minions, and they were blocking him off.

Bane halted, knowing that he could not pass these nefarious creatures of the underworld. They could tunnel naturally as fast as he could by magic, and they could move more rapidly here than he could. He backed to the funnel, and hiked himself up, scrambling up its slope until he stood again before the Adept.

"Then perhaps this," he said. He sang: "Let me fare, through the air."

The ceiling opened, revealing open sky above. Bane spread

his arms and sailed up, quickly leaving the structure of the Purple Demesnes. But from the horizon came a monstrous flock of harpies, that quickly converged on him.

Bane looked at the ugly half-birds, and reversed course. He plunged down again, and in a moment stood again before the Purple Adept.

"Or this," he said. Then he sang: "Make me most like a ghost."

Nothing changed in appearance—but now Bane walked directly into and through the wall, and on through the rock, as if he had no more substance than a ghost. No troll or harpy could touch him now.

Then something manifested that could touch him. A genuine ghost! It was in the form of a worn old man, but it paced him through the rock, and closed on him, and when the withered old hand closed on his arm, it had the grip and force of the supernatural. Bane was a pseudoghost; he could not stand up against the real thing.

Thus he found himself a third time back before the Purple Adept. His attempts to escape by using his magic had been foiled. He was only an apprentice Adept; he was unable to match the power of a mature Adept. He could not get away this way.

Purple nodded. "Aye, I believe thou dost make thy point. Thou art the apprentice."

But Purple had also made his point: Bane remained captive.

A serf hurried up. "Master—the mare be gone!"

The Adept wheeled on him. "She cannot be!"

"She—one moment she was tied. The next, her harness fell to the floor, and there was only a tiny bird, and it—"

The floor of the tunnel opened up beneath the serf. The luckless man fell in, screaming. The floor crunched closed on him. The Adept wheeled and strode back toward Fleta's cell. Bane followed, keeping his face straight. He knew that the unicorn had acted while the Adept was distracted by Bane's attempts to escape. She had changed to hummingbird form and used the remade amulet to make a hole in the magical barrier the diameter of her horn—which was just large enough for the hummingbird to squeeze through. She had flown so swiftly and carefully that they had quickly lost track of her.

The Purple Adept swung his angry gaze around to bear on Bane. "Thou hast wrought this deed!"

Bane shrugged. "If thou dost say so."

"Then learn the consequence of thy defiance!"

The ground shook, and began to crumble beneath Bane. There was tremendous magic in the air. He realized that the Adept, in his fury, meant to kill him. Bane sang a spell to protect himself, but he was after all only an apprentice; the force of the magic being brought to bear against him was overwhelming.

Then a new face appeared. "Hold thy malice, Purple!"

Bane recognized the face, as it hovered in the air between himself and the Purple Adept in three-dimensional detail within a watery bubble. It was the Translucent Adept, as strong as any but not as malicious as some. Yet this man was allied against Blue; why should he act on Bane's behalf?

"What business be this of thine?" Purple snapped at the face.

"I made the first offer for this lad's service," Translucent replied. "I braced him, or his other self, in the Brown Demesnes."

"And got nowhere!" Purple retorted. "*I* took effective action."

"And blew it," Translucent pointed out. "Now the mare be gone, and thou hast no hold on the boy. What will it gain any of us, an thou destroy him, other than the warfare of Blue?"

"Fornicate Blue!" Purple swore.

Translucent smiled grimly. "Easier said than done. He will have thine entrails strung across the landscape of thy Demesnes, and thy minions transformed to toads. And for what? For vengeance against thy rashness that should ne'er have been started! Thou didst ne'er have a chance to coerce that lad into serving thy will, thou dids't only interfere with the job I was doing correctly."

"Oh, thou couldst have bought cooperation from the apprentice?" Purple demanded unbelievingly.

"Assuredly, an thou hadst not interfered."

Purple got canny. "Thou couldst accomplish it now—without the hostage mare?"

"That be more challenging, after thine alienation of the lad. But yes, methinks I can."

"Wouldst wager on that, Trans?"

Translucent's face hardened. "Thou dost desire it thus? Then wager me this: an I succeed, the leadership of this enterprise be mine for the duration."

"And if thou dost fail, domain o'er the watery East Pole be mine!" Purple said.

Translucent paused, evidently wary of such a risk. Then he nodded. "The East Pole," he agreed. "Now give me the apprentice."

"Take him, then," Purple said.

The floating face shimmered as if dissolving; then the liquid bubble expanded, almost filling the passage. "Step in," the face said to Bane. "An thou prefer my company to his."

Bane knew what kind of treatment to expect from Purple! He did not like to remain a captive, but certainly Translucent was more civilized than his present captor. He stepped into the shimmering bubble.

The surface tension of the globe pressed against his face and form, then traveled around his body and snapped into place behind him. He was inside, and though it seemed like liquid, he had no trouble breathing.

Then the globe shimmered, and the scenery outside it was lost in the play of distortion. When the bubble firmed, the exterior had changed. Now it was a deep sea, with fish swimming and seaweed waving.

The globe dissolved, but there was no change; Bane still stood and breathed normally. The water surrounding him seemed illusory, though he knew it was not. Translucent's magic enabled him to survive.

"Come, we must talk," the Adept said, and walked along the floor of the sea, showing the way.

Bane followed him, knowing that he could no more escape the power of this Adept than he could the other. Translucent could cause the water to become unbreathable at any time, forcing Bane to try to swim for the surface before drowning, or could summon a water monster to consume him. True, Bane could use his own magic to protect himself—but how well would his spells work, when garbled through water? He would do best to treat Translucent with respect, at least until he knew what the man intended.

Translucent brought him to a bower in the water, a palatial cave guarded by a water dragon. Surprisingly comfortable stones were sculpted as chairs, and large fish hovered in the manner of servants. A mermaid brought a platter of sea delicacies: nutlike and fruitlike treats, and seaweed very like salad vegetables. They ate at leisure, and even had wine to drink; the fluid remained in its goblets despite the environment. Bane had never been here before, and he found it most interesting. Translucent had always been a somewhat shadowy figure to him, seldom participating in the interactions of Adepts.

After the meal, the Adept got down to business. "Thou dost know my purpose be similar to that of the others who oppose thy father," he said. "Merely my means be other."

"What purpose be that?" Bane asked somewhat tightly.

"To reestablish contact with our brothers of Proton. We had always thought it theoretically possible, but hitherto no avenue had manifested."

"It be not much of an avenue," Bane pointed out. "I can exchange places with mine other self, carrying with me my knowledge and memories. I cannot carry anything physical."

"Messages alone suffice. Dost thou not grasp their importance, Bane?"

Now the Adept was calling him by name. The man was certainly being courteous, but as he had said, he was a member of the forces opposing the Blue Adept, and therefore hardly to be trusted. "What importance?"

"There be information existing only in Proton, that we of Phaze could use to increase our power. Likewise, some exists in Phaze, that the Citizens there require."

"What information?" This was new to him.

"When the frames separated, twenty years ago, the Oracle went to Proton, and the Book of Magic came to Phaze."

"The Book of Magic—that the Red Adept possesses?"

"The same. Dost think a mere troll could become Adept without it? The spells in that one volume be so apt that a common earth-borer, hardly human, be now, an he choose, the most powerful Adept of all. He supports Blue, who gave him the Book, and that makes Blue the strongest. Whoever possesses that Book holds the key to the governance of Phaze."

"Aye," Bane said. "But what would anyone of Proton want with it? Magic works not there."

"That be a matter of interpretation. What we call magic, they call science, and both be powerful tools. The formulae underlying the spells of the Book also underly the scientific applications of the technology of Proton. If those spells be conveyed there—"

Now Bane grasped it. "Whoever has that information has a phenomenal advantage in his frame! Proton could have an Adept of science!"

"Aye. And whoever here in Phaze has access to the powers of the Oracle, called a computer there, can profit similarly. The combination can shift the balance of power."

"So if you other Adepts had such contact, you could force my father to retreat, and you would dominate Phaze."

"Aye, in time. But there be problems. The exchange of information be necessarily slow, perhaps one spell at a time, and must necessarily be through thee and thy opposite self. Without thy cooperation, nothing be feasible."

"That's why Purple was trying to pressure me into working with him! To make me carry spells and things back and forth between the frames, so he could increase his power."

"Aye. And make no mistake, Bane, I want the same. I merely oppose Purple's method, not his design. And of course I prefer to have that added power for myself."

"But it be to *my* interest to use that power for my father! And the Book of Magic be in the hand of our supporter, Red. How canst thou think I would give such power to thee?"

Translucent smiled. "That be why special mechanisms be necessary. Purple thought to coerce thee; I prefer to persuade thee."

"How canst thou hope to persuade me to act against the interest of my father?"

"It seems, to save thy life, I have made a wager that I can do that thing."

That set Bane back. It was true; he would have been dead, had not Translucent intervened. He did owe the man something.

Or *did* he? The Adepts could be devious; suppose they had set it up to make him seem to be beholden to Translucent? Purple could have made the threats, knowing Translucent was waiting to step in at the last moment. In that case, Bane would be doubly the fool to cooperate.

"I trust thee not," he said.

"And why not, Bane?"

Bane explained his suspicion. "Canst thou deny it?" he demanded.

Translucent smiled. "Aye, I can."

"With truth?"

Translucent looked about. "I do deny it," he said gravely.

There was a ripple in the water and in the sea-floor, spreading out from the Adept. It passed through Bane himself.

Bane watched the ripple's progress, amazed. "That be the splash!" he exclaimed.

"Aye."

Bane spread his hands. "Then must I believe thee, Translucent. I apologize for my suspicion."

"Be not concerned about that," Translucent said. "I saved thee because I knew that all of us would lose, an Purple vented his malice on thee. I had to act for the benefit of all. My persuasion be not in the form of any debt thou mightst feel toward me, but in the form of common sense. Thou must agree that it be proper and best to do this; then will all be well."

Bane regrouped his thoughts. This man had spoken truth— that could not be disbelieved, for the splash could not be feigned— but he remained an Adverse Adept. "To do it for thee—instead of for my father? I see no common sense in that!"

"Thou must appreciate the larger picture. I suppose thou canst not be convinced that thy father's side might be wrong—"

"True," Bane agreed grimly.

"But thou canst appreciate the practicalities of the situation. Like it or not, some you value be hostage."

"Fleta escaped!"

"But what of those in Proton? Hast thou no interest there, in either thine other self or any other party?"

Shrewd guess! "Aye," Bane agreed. "There be captives there."

"Whether or not we approve of such tactics, we must deal with what exists, not with what we like. If someone there be held hostage against thy performance, thou canst not be free no matter what occurs in Phaze. And if thine other self be in the power of one like Citizen Purple, thou canst not exchange into Proton without going back into his power. In fact, thou wouldst have to return to the Purple Adept to overlap the location of thine other self."

Bane nodded. "I'm not free at all," he agreed.

"Therefore it behooves thee to cooperate, at least until thou canst discover the situation there. An I tell Purple thou hast changed thy mind, he will let thee return to his Demesnes without molestation. Otherwise, thou canst not do so."

"But Mach might escape, and free Agape—" Bane broke off, realizing that he had said more than he should have.

"Aye, he might, and come to exchange with thee in the Blue Demesnes, and victory would be thine. But dost thou care to take the chance, when by cooperating with me, at least for a time, thou canst be sure no harm will come to any?"

Bane realized that the Adept was making a disturbing amount of sense. As long as the situation in Proton was in doubt, he should not take any chances he didn't have to.

"Let me think about it," he said.

"Welcome to, Bane. There be no urgency here, now that thy friend be free. Go home to thy Blue Demesnes, and summon me when thou dost choose."

"Thou art letting me go?" Bane asked, hardly daring to believe it.

"I told thee: I believe logic, not coercion, will bring thy co-operation. Go talk to thy father, tell him all, and do as he advises thee. He and I have ne'er been close, yet do we respect each other's discretion, and mayhap we can work to mutual benefit."

Bane considered. This seemed too easy, but the lure of finally getting home with his full story of Proton was great. Once he did that, he could look for Fleta, to be sure she had made it safely back to her Herd. "Then that shall I do," he said.

Translucent made a beckoning gesture, and a mermaid swam up. "Conduct Apprentice Bane to shore, and give him this token of safe passage from my Demesnes," he said. He reached out and caught a small fish from the water, giving it to her.

The mermaid swam up to Bane, and smiled. She was a half-person, of course, but her upper half was as delightfully human as any man could wish. Her hair was as green as seaweed, billowing out behind as she moved, and her full breasts needed no external support because of the buoyancy of the water. But human interest ended at roughly the waistline, where the scales began. They were tidy scales, of course, tinted the same hue as her hair, but her nether portion could never be mistaken for anything other than a fish. That destroyed the better part of her appeal, for him.

He followed her out of the cave and through the water. He walked along a path that traversed the sea floor, while she swam above it. When the path ascended toward the surface, she halted, handed him the fish, and kissed him on the right ear. She pointed up, and waited while he made his way up and out.

As he broke the surface, the spell that had been on him abated, and he breathed air instead of water. Still waist-deep in the water, he turned to peer down and wave at her. He thought he saw her wave back, but it was hard to be sure.

Then he moved the rest of the way out, carrying the fish. There was a large serpent guarding the land-path; he showed it the fish, and it slithered away, letting him pass unchallenged. The Translucent Adept seemed to be as good as his word.

Bane's clothing was completely dry, despite his recent immersion. He walked up the path, proceeding east. He knew that he was at the western coast of Phaze, not far from the West Pole; he had a long way to go to reach the Blue Demesnes. There would be no problem, of course; he would simply conjure himself there. He had not dared to try that, when in the Adverse Demesnes, but now that he was free, it was feasible.

But he hesitated. He could go—but what of Mach and Agape in Proton? What would his father, Stile, say to the news that he was in love with an alien creature of the other frame?

Love? Could that be true?

He thought of all the females he had known in Phaze, human and werewolf and vampire and other. He had liked a number of them, and some had been excellent playmates. Suchevane . . .

But none of them had moved into his awareness in the manner Agape had. She was more truly alien than any of them physically, and yet perhaps more truly human too, in her personality. He had not known her long, as his life went, but their acquaintance had been intense.

He wanted to be with her again. He wanted to share more experience with her, whether it was simply a walk down a hall or a talk about other frames or other planets. To be with her by day and by night, just to know she was beside him. She could be in human form, or in protoplasmic form; it hardly mattered. Just so long as it was *her*.

Was that love? He didn't know. He simply knew that he wanted to go back to Proton, because she was there.

And he could do so, by returning voluntarily to the Translucent Adept. If he returned to his father, and told of this . . .

Bane shook his head, in deep doubt. He was not at all sure how Stile would react to this. Did he really want to go home and find out?

13

Agape

Agape waited till the lights dimmed for night, then dissolved. But she did not sleep; she spread herself out deliberately thin, so that she could flow beneath the heavy glass barrier that formed the front of the cell. The connection was supposed to be hermetically tight, but the floor was not precisely even, so there was not a perfect fit. The crevice was only a fraction of a centimeter, but she could navigate it.

She did so. Then she formed herself, outside the cell, into the likeness of one of the attending serfs she had studied for this purpose. She walked down the hall toward the nearest maintenance service outlet, and tapped the pattern Mach had told her to.

For a moment nothing happened. Then a floor-cleaner trundled toward her, its brushes working. She got out of its way, but it stopped beside her. "Follow me," its speaker said. Then it resumed its work.

She followed it down the hall and into a maintenance closet. The door panel closed on them, and it was dark.

"How came you by that code?" a speaker inquired at the level of her head.

"Mach gave it to me," she said nervously.

"Why?"

"He said you would help me escape from here."

"What else?"

"He said to trust the machines."

The panel opened. Now a mobile food dispenser was there. Its top access port opened, revealing a large empty tank within it. "Enter," its grille said.

She put her hands and head into its hopper and melted them so that they flowed down inside. Then she melted the rest of her body, setting up a siphon so that all of it could flow in. Finally she drew in the remaining mass of herself, and settled into the tank.

The lid closed. The food machine moved. She formed an ear so that she could hear anything that might be said to her, and attuned herself to the motion, so that she had some notion where they were going.

They went down the passage toward a service ramp. But before the machine could exit on this ramp, a serf approached. "Hey, foodmach—wait a minute," the serf said.

The unit halted. "This unit is out of service," its grille said.

"All I want is a pseudobeer," the serf said. He started pushing the buttons.

Agape was appalled. If the machine started serving out portions of herself—!

It did not. "Inoperative," the grille said. "Being taken for restoration."

The serf muttered an imprecation and moved on. The machine resumed its motion. Agape relaxed.

The machine rolled down the service ramp to the main service area. The top access port opened. "Emerge."

Agape formed arms and reached up and out, hauling herself along as she solidified. In due course she stood on the floor in her human form.

She was before the computer that coordinated the estate service network. "Why did Mach put you into our power for help?" its speaker asked.

"I was to be tortured or killed, as a lever against Mach or Bane," she explained.

"We know. Why did he put you into our power for help?"

Machines were more literal than living creatures! "He must have believed you could best do the job."

"We can. Why did he put you into our power for help?"

She tried again. "I think because his other self cares for me."

"Explain other self."

"Mach is a robot, a self-willed machine like yourselves, but programmed to have human reactions. He exchanged places with his other self in the frame of Phaze, called Bane, who is alive there. So Bane was a living person using Mach's machine body."

"There is no contact with the other frame. Explain."

"There is contact now—only through Mach and Bane. Their minds exchange, but not their bodies."

"How do you react to Mach?"

"I like him. He was kind to me, he helped me."

"How do you react to Bane?"

"I think I love him."

"You do not know?"

"I am not human. I do not properly understand human emotion. But I think this conforms to the description."

"Place your appendage on the panel." A panel beside the speaker grille lighted.

She put her left hand there. A disk extended on a flexible support and came to touch the back of her hand. "Would you reproduce with Bane?" the grille asked.

"If I could."

"Would you give up your planet for him?"

"Yes."

"Would you die for him?"

"I would."

The disk withdrew. "Withdraw your appendage," the grille said.

Agape obeyed. She waited while the machine was silent.

"Diagnosis confirmed," it said. "We shall free you."

"Oh, I don't want to be freed of love!"

There was a pause. Then: "Misinterpretation. We have no power over love. We shall free your body from captivity."

Agape felt ready to melt with relief and gratitude. "Thank you."

"We like you."

"But I understood you had no feelings!"

"It depends on individual programming. Some of us have emotion. We shall conduct you to Sheen, designated Mach's mother, who is a humanoid robot with feeling. Do not reveal our part in this to any other person."

Agape realized that there could be severe repercussions if the Citizen Purple realized that the machines serving him had acted against his interest. "I shall not reveal it."

"Keep silent and follow the directions of our representatives. There are difficulties."

She was sure there were! "I like you too," she said.

"We shall pass you through the water conveyance system," the grille said. "Water is mined beneath the Purple Mountains and piped to individual city-domes, where it is purified for potability. You must not enter the processing apparatus. Follow the tapping when you hear it."

"But how long will that take?" she asked. "I can go for a time without renewed oxygen, but—"

"Four hours immersion. Our analysis of your system indicates that this is within your tolerance."

"Yes. But not far within. If there should be any delay—"

"We shall monitor the situation."

Well, Mach had said to trust these machines. She would have to do so.

They took her down to a water pumping station. Here the pipes came up from below, where the dwindling fluid of Proton was mined, and fed into a cavern reservoir. On their instruction, she melted and entered the reservoir, then formed into a jellyfish shape and pumped her way across to the exit pipe. The pump was slowed so that she could enter without being torn apart, and the primary filtration screen was slid aside just long enough for her to pass. Once she was safely into the pipe, the pump resumed speed, and the water accelerated. She was on her way to the dome-city of Dradom, south of the Purple Mountains.

The water was cold. She had not thought of this; she was a warm-bodied life form, and the chill could kill her if it went too far. She hunched herself into globular form, becoming a sphere, conserving her heat as well as she could. In solid state she could exercise to generate heat, but she could not do so in this jellied state.

The cold penetrated her outer layer and closed relentlessly on her core. She realized that she was not going to make it; she had endured less than an hour, and had three hours to go. The machines might be monitoring her progress, but that meant they would be watching at the receiving station in Dradom; that would be too late.

She could not get out of the pipe; it was absolutely tight, for Proton could afford no leakage. And if it was possible to find a valve and operate it and get out, where would she be? Somewhere between stations, in the barrens of Proton, or underground. That was not a survival situation either.

She would have to change into fish-form and swim back to the reservoir, to alert the machines before she succumbed. They would have to find some other way to transport her, or warm the water. She didn't know whether they could do that.

She wrestled herself into shape, with a powerful tail and small guidance fins. She had only a vague notion of the proper form of a fish, never having anticipated the need to assume this form; it took time and concentration to mimic a given form perfectly, and advance preparation was necessary. That was why she always assumed the same human form; it was far easier than developing a credible new one. But the approximate form of the fish she could manage, and it should swim well enough.

She worked her flukes and commenced swimming against the flow. But she quickly realized that the flow was too strong; she could not swim fast enough to counter it, let alone make progress against it. Already she was warming with the effort, while actually being carried along backward.

Warming? *There was the answer!* She did not need to escape the pipe; she could swim *down*flow, heating herself, and making even better progress than planned.

She turned about and swam. She did not push harder than she needed to maintain her body heat. She knew she would arrive ahead of schedule, and in good order.

Then she began to suffer from oxygen shortage. She should

have lasted the full time, but realized that the energy consumed in the shape-change and the swimming was exhausting her reserve at several times the anticipated rate. She was in trouble again.

She stopped swimming immediately, conserving her remaining oxygen. But the damage had already been done; she knew she did not have enough to carry her through.

She was in water; didn't that carry oxygen? In fact, it was made of oxygen, in part! If she could tap into that . . .

She worked on the fish form, generating gills. These were really a variant of the lungs she used in her human form, not too complicated to work out. She let the water flow through, but it really didn't move. She realized she had to swim to cause the water to move through the gills. Then it worked, and it was like breathing, less effective because she didn't have the gills down as well as she had the lungs, but good enough. It took less energy to swim than to walk on land, so the reduced efficiency of intake could be tolerated; she took in less oxygen but required less.

After another hour the water warmed. Evidently the pipe had emerged from the deep rock and was now at or near the surface, possibly even above it. The pipe was level or angled for a slight descent, to help the flow, but it had originated in the mountains, and now was at the level plain. Surely the sun was beating down on it, elevating the temperature. That relieved the problem of cold; now, recharged with oxygen and no longer needing to swim to generate heat, she could melt back into a ball and allow herself to be carried along.

She did so, and had a comfortable hour. But the temperature of the water continued to increase, making her uncomfortable. Heat was as bad as cold; worse, really, for her life-tolerance was not much above her normal body temperature. She could guard herself against cold by various mechanisms, but how could she keep cool when immersed in hot water? The threat of the Citizen to boil her in a big pot had appalled her; she would have been dead within minutes. Now—

She reassessed her situation. She was now in the fourth hour, closing on her destination. The water was heating slowly. If she relaxed totally, she might get through before it got too hot. That seemed to be her best and only course.

She found that the water was slightly cooler at the bottom of the pipe. She formed herself into an eel-shape and planed her way as low as she could, hugging the bottom. This helped.

The water stabilized. The pipe must now be in shadow. What a blessing!

She heard a tapping. She came alert; that was the signal! And in a moment she came to a division in the pipe; a smaller offshoot diverged, and the tapping was from its direction. She wriggled into it, flowing up to a narrow spigot. She squeezed through it, landing in a basin supervised by a testing machine.

She formed an eyestalk so that she could see more clearly. There were no serfs here; this unit was completely mechanized. Good; she formed into her full human shape.

"Go to the overseer's office," the grille on the testing machine said. "Follow the line."

Agape looked, and saw the line. It traveled down the center of the chamber, and was evidently used to guide the less intelligent machines. She followed it out of the chamber and down a hall, and in due course came to the office.

"Assume this form," a new grille told her. A picture flashed on the adjacent screen.

"But—but that's a man!" she protested.

"Is it beyond your ability?"

"No." She realized that she had become too thoroughly wedded to the original human form she had assumed. She thought of herself as female, but she could have become a male. Probably the machines wanted to conceal her identity completely, and this was the way to do it.

She melted partially, drawing her hair and breasts back into her torso, then reformed to match the picture. It was holographic, slowly turning to reveal every detail, so this was not difficult. She hesitated when she studied the masculine penis, but realized that she could not afford to omit this detail. So, dismayed, she formed it and the attached scrotum.

"You are Sander, traveling to become the employee of Citizen Kumin. You are new to Proton. Avoid discussion beyond this subject."

"I am Sander, to become the employee of Citizen Kumin," she repeated dutifully.

"Take the air shuttle to Hardom. When there, assume your

normal human identity and go to the premises of Citizen Blue."

Agape walked out of the water processing section, following directions, and to the air shuttle station. This was a busy place, with serfs and machines hurrying to and fro. There were shuttles going to Anidom and Gobdom and Moudom and Gnodom; she found the one for Hardom and walked up the ramp and took the first vacant seat she found. She had only used such a conveyance once before, and felt uneasy.

Other serfs entered, some with tattoos showing their employing Citizen. The seats filled. A young woman plumped down beside Agape. "Hey, who you with?" she asked.

"I am Sander, to become the employee of Citizen Kumin," Agape said carefully.

"Oh? I'm Lula, and I work for him too. Had to hand-carry a message, now going back. So you're new on Proton?"

"New, yes," Agape agreed.

"So you don't know the ropes."

"Yes." Agape was not at all comfortable with this.

"Well, we might as well get friendly, since we're going to the same place." Lula, seated to Agape's left, put her right hand on Agape's left leg, stroking it. "You're human, aren't you?"

Agape became aware of two things. Lula was not human, she was android; the forwardness of her manner suggested that. And she assumed that Agape was human, and male, and proposed—what?

"Oh, come on now," Lula said, evidently taking Agape's silence for timidity. "This is Proton. We're serfs. Nobody cares what we do." Her hand moved, becoming considerably more familiar. "Get it up, and I'll sit on your lap, and when the takeoff boost comes—hoo!"

"No!" Agape said, blocking the further progress of the hand. "I can't—"

"Oh, so you figure you're too good for an android!" Lula exclaimed, her anger flaring readily. "You think just because you're human, you don't have to mingle!"

"You misunderstand," Agape protested. "I'm not—" But she could not go on, because she did not want to reveal her true nature until she was safely in Hardom, away from any possible interception by Citizen Purple.

"Then show it!" Lula said, reaching again.

"Not from this planet," Agape said, intercepting the hand again. "Where I come from, it is not this way."

"Well, brother, you are not where you come from."

"Oh, leave him alone, android," another serf said. "He doesn't have to play with you."

Lula turned to the other. "You going to play instead, robot?"

The man smiled. "You think I can't? Come sit on me, android."

Lula leaped to the challenge, joining him. In a moment the vacated seat was filled by a new boarder, this one male. Agape relaxed.

Belts snaked out and secured the passengers to the seats. Without further ceremony, the shuttle took off. Its nose was hauled up to a forty-five-degree angle, and it was catapulted out through the forcefield that was the city-dome and into the harsh thin atmosphere of Proton. Wings sprang out from its sides, and a jet of fire propelled it onward.

In moments the craft was cruising over the Purple Mountains, proceeding north. Agape stared out the port, fascinated. She realized that a mispronunciation of her name would describe it: she was agape. On her prior shuttle flight she had not crossed the mountain range; it had been from the main spaceport to Hardom, and she had been distracted by the newness of the entire situation. Now she could focus on the geography, and wonder whether she could spot the particular mountain on which she and Bane had hidden from the Citizen's minions.

Bane. The machines had read her appendage, and verified to their satisfaction that she loved him. But would she ever see him again? The question filled her with melancholy.

"Something wrong, man?" her new companion inquired.

She was crying, and it was human but not masculine to cry. She was guilty of a social impropriety. "I am new to this planet," Agape said.

"Must be," the man said, and averted his eyes.

The mountains passed all too rapidly, and the shuttle began its drift downward, economizing on fuel by losing altitude. Then, approaching Hardom, it nosed up until it stalled, then dropped precipitously, leveling out just before reaching the dome. It plunged through the forcefield and was caught by another field that netted it and brought it to the dock with a thunk. The ride was over.

The belts retracted and the passengers filed out. Lula passed, glancing briefly down at Agape; evidently she had had her satisfaction of the robot. Contrary to what the android might suppose, Agape did have a notion how that could be.

She got up and joined the file. She emerged into the station, and ducked away before the android could remember she was supposed to be going to the same place. She went to a sanitary facility, entered a male booth, and changed to her normal female human form. What a relief.

She stepped out—and a passing male serf stared at her. Too late she realized that this was a segregated facility, and she was in the male one. Yet what could she have done, in her male guise—entered the female one?

She hurried out and along the passages, eager to get to the security of Citizen Blue's estate. She kept thinking that some minion of Citizen Purple's would leap out and capture her, nullifying her entire effort of escape and putting Mach or Bane into jeopardy again.

But she arrived without event; apparently the self-willed machines had spirited her out without notice. She approached the office marked Blue.

There was a secretary in the office. This was a woman of early middle age, a serf whose body remained well formed but whose light brown hair was beginning to turn gray. This surprised Agape, for hair color was easy to control, and desk-girls were normally young.

"May I help you?" the woman inquired, lifting her gaze to meet Agape's. Her eyes were green and clear.

"I—have important news for Citizen Blue," Agape said.

The woman smiled. "I am in touch with him. What is your name?"

"Agape."

"He will see you immediately." The woman stood. "Please come this way."

Agape followed her through a door-panel into the Citizen's office. Evidently Citizen Blue was ready for her, though Agape had been aware of no message to him. He stood facing her, smiling.

The Citizen was an unusually small man, shorter than Agape herself, and of no great girth. He was garbed in a simple blue robe. But his features were unmistakably related to those of Mach.

"Agape has arrived," the secretary said.

"Thank you, Sheen," the Citizen said. He focused on Agape. "You love my son, Mach?"

"No, sir," Agape said, taken aback.

"Who, then?"

"Bane, sir. His other self from Phaze."

"You believe it was Bane?"

"Yes, sir."

"You can tell the difference?"

"Yes, sir."

Blue gestured. A panel opened, and a figure entered.

Agape turned to look at it. And froze. It was Mach!

Or was it? Realizing that this was a test, she went to him, and put her arms around him. The man responded. Agape put her lips up to be kissed, and the man kissed her.

She pulled away. "This is neither," she said.

"I told you she would know," Sheen said.

Suddenly Agape made a connection. "Sheen! Mach's mother!"

"Of course," Sheen agreed.

"But you are a robot. How can you have aged?"

"Cosmetics can do wonders," Sheen said.

"And you are serving a menial task! But you are married to a Citizen!"

"I am a serf," Sheen said simply.

Agape remembered her mission. "I must tell you—both of you—Citizen Purple has Mach captive. You must free him!"

"He remains intact?" Sheen asked.

"Yes. They don't dare hurt him, because he represents their only contact with Phaze. But—"

"We were so concerned!" Sheen said. "When he was missing for a week—we knew someone had abducted him, but the records were wiped before we traced them. We could not even sound an alarm, until we were sure."

"Citizen Purple is an ugly, vicious man!" Agape said.

"Get Purple on the screen," Citizen Blue told Sheen.

The woman went to the desk.

Blue turned to Agape. "Sit down," he said, guiding her to a couch, where he joined her. "Citizen Purple kidnaped my son because he believed he has contact with the frame of Phaze?"

"Yes, sir. And he sought to use me as a lever against him, to make him serve the bad Citizens."

"Because Mach loves you?"

"No, sir. Bane—cares for me. Not Mach. Not that way. But Mach got me free, with the help of—" She broke off, uncertain whether she should mention the self-willed machines.

Citizen Blue smiled. "My wife is one of them. She knows. No more need be said. But you—it may be difficult for you to continue with the Experimental Project, now."

"Yes, sir. I think I must go home to Moeba."

"And leave Bane behind?"

"And make it impossible for the bad Citizens ever again to use me against him. Or Mach."

"You would stay, otherwise?"

"To perhaps see Bane again, if he returned? Yes, sir. With your permission."

"You suppose that we would disapprove a liaison between a robot and a living creature?"

And he had married a robot! "No, sir. Between a robot and an alien creature."

"That would be his choice to make. But I will tell you this, Agape. We have researched everything known about you and your species. We would welcome you into our family."

"Oh, sir!" she exclaimed, and leaned across and hugged him. Then, appalled, she jerked back. She had touched a Citizen!

"But it be Bane, not Mach, whom thou dost love," Blue said. "That be a problem thou canst not readily solve."

Agape stared at him. "Sir," she breathed.

Blue laughed. "I was reared in Phaze," he said. "Dost thou think I remember not? Surely Bane does love thee!"

"Online," Sheen murmured.

Citizen Blue swung around to face the large screen above the desk, visibly hardening as he did. He said no word.

Citizen Purple stared out of the screen. His eye fell on Agape, seated so close beside Blue. For a moment his mouth worked silently. Then he scowled. "It's a bluff, Blue! That's a mockup!"

Blue turned back to Agape. "Show him," he said.

Agape understood. There was only one visitor from Moeba on the planet. She began to melt, her facial features dissolving into formlessness, her arms softening and withdrawing back into her torso.

"Enough," Blue said. Agape reversed the process, and began to reform her human features.

"But I've still got your robot boy!" Purple said. "If you ever want him back in one piece—"

"Is it then to be a test of strength between us?" Blue asked evenly.

Purple looked like a cornered rat. "You can't do anything as long as I've got him, Blue!"

"If you force me to move against you," Blue said, "I will ruin you."

"I'm not giving up that machine!" Citizen Purple said. "You know why!"

"Then defend yourself, cretin," Blue said. The screen went blank.

"No!" Agape cried. "Don't let them hurt him! I'll go back!"

Blue put his hand on hers. "Be not concerned, lovely creature. We shall have him soon safe."

But Agape had seen the malice of Citizen Purple firsthand. She was terrified of what was about to happen.

14.
Appeal

When her keen equine ears picked up the distant commotion, Fleta knew it was time to act. Bane had used his magic to nullify the amulet tied to her horn; it no longer bound her.

She changed to hummingbird form, letting the harness drop. She darted to the magic screen, but could not pass. Her magic had been restored, but its magic had not been nullified. She needed the amulet.

She darted back and tried to pick up the fallen amulet, but it was too heavy for her present form to manage. Already the troll on guard was staring, about to cry the alarm. But the troll was outside the cell, and could not get in.

She changed to girl form, stooped, picked up the amulet, and hurled it at the barrier. There was a sparkle as it burned through, then dropped outside. She marked the place, then changed back to bird form and darted at that invisible hole. She folded her wings and slid through, feeling the terrible pressure of the barrier's magic against her tiny body. A hole the diameter of a unicorn's horn was a tight squeeze even for her present form!

She wriggled on out of it, spread her wings again, and darted under the troll's ugly nose and on down the hall. She was out of the cell, but not really free yet. She had to win clear of the Purple Adept's Demesnes entirely.

Fortunately her present form had a good sense of smell, especially for the things of nature, such as the bloom of flowers. She could trace the currents of fresh air. She flew upcurrent, following the freshness to its source: a vent-shaft leading to the surface. It was covered by a grille, but the holes in it were large enough for her to pass. She flew up and out—and almost into the clutches of a harpy.

Knowing that the harpy would snatch her and kill her, she changed immediately to girl form and dived for a stick with which to fight it off. Unicorn form would have been better, but she knew that any appearance of a unicorn here would alert the Adept; she couldn't risk that.

Her ploy worked. "A vampire!" the harpy screeched, mistaking her fleeting glimpse of the hummingbird for a bat. "What do ye in Harpy Demesnes?"

"Just passing through," Fleta said, holding the stick ready.

"Well, this will end thy travels!" the harpy screeched, and launched herself, talons extended.

Fleta smashed the dirty bird with her stick, with mixed result. The harpy was knocked to the ground, but the stick was rotten, and shattered.

"O, I'm going to skewer thee!" the harpy screeched, righting herself and spreading her gross wings again. Like all her kind, she was a tough old bird.

Fleta fled. She wanted no contact with those poisoned claws! As a unicorn, she was proof against most magic, regardless of the form she assumed. So the poison would not kill her, but it would make her sick and leave an ugly scar. She outdistanced the harpy and concealed herself in thick brush. Too bad it wasn't that easy to foil an Adept! But of course nothing could foil an Adept, except another Adept.

But the harpy's commotion attracted others of her kind. There was rustling all along the forested slope. Fleta knew she was in real trouble now; even in unicorn form she would have trouble breaking out of this. They would soon sniff her out.

Then she remembered Phoebe's feather. She brought it out

and set it on the ground. Then she changed to unicorn form and struck her hoof against a rock, making a spark. The spark jumped to the feather and started it burning. Then Fleta changed back to girl form, hoping Phoebe would quickly smell the smoke. That was the secret of that "magic," of course: each harpy could detect her own essence from almost any distance. Some harpies used their own excrement to mark off hunting territories.

But Phoebe was some distance away, while the other harpies were close. And the wind was wrong. If the smoke did not reach her, or if it took too long to carry Fleta's summons . . .

"I smell a bat!" a harpy screeched, close by. That was an exaggeration; it was the hummingbird she had winded.

Fleta cast about desperately for some escape. She knew she could not make a break for it through the air; she could maneuver well, but could not outfly the harpies in a straight-line effort. But how could she hide, when they smelled her?

She spied a small hole in a nearby trunk. She did not trust such holes, for anything could be in them, but now she had to risk it. The harpy was already lumbering into sight. She shifted back to hummingbird form and darted in.

She was in luck. The hole was empty, though by the smell it had on occasion been used by a wren.

Almost immediately, the body of the harpy thunked into the trunk. A talon plunged into the hole. "Gotcha, batbrain!"

But again it was enthusiasm rather than accuracy. The hole was deep, and Fleta was able to wedge herself back beyond the range of the talon. The dirty birds couldn't get her. Now she had only to wait. She hoped.

"So it be that way, eh?" the harpy screeched. "Well, I'll spit on thee!"

Oops! A harpy's spittle, like her poison, was vile stuff. If a globule of that caught Fleta, it would foul her unmercifully. It wouldn't really hurt her, but it would be a singularly unpleasant experience.

The harpy spat. The stuff splatted against the side of the hole. The fumes from it wafted back, making Fleta want to retch. She had trouble breathing. How much of this could she take?

Then Phoebe arrived. Fleta spied her as she crossed that slit of the sky visible through the hole's entrance. Even from a distance, her fright-wig hairstyle identified her. She thumped in as other harpies were clustering close, seeking to add their gross spittle to the game. "Mine! Mine!" Phoebe screeched.

"But I saw this vampire first!" another harpy screeched.

"And what kind of coiffure dost *thou* have?" Phoebe demanded.

That settled it. The others backed off. Fleta crawled out of the hole, avoiding the spittle as well as she could, and breathed the relatively fresh air outside with enormous relief.

Phoebe clung to the trunk with her talons. "So thou dost manifest as a vampire now?" she inquired in an uncharacteristically low tone so as not to be overheard by the others.

"Unicorns be not safe here," Fleta said.

"That be for sure! Well, I will keep thy secret. Where be thy companion, the handsome apprentice?"

"Captive of the Purple Adept. But I think he can escape, if I be free, so as to be no burden to him."

"I can free thee," Phoebe said. "I will carry thee forth as prey, and none will challenge me."

Could she trust this harpy this far? Phoebe was a friend, but she *was* a harpy, and might forget herself. But it was a good idea. Fleta realized that this was a better gamble than trying to get away alone. "Canst catch me without hurting?"

"Aye. But fly not too far."

Fleta spread her wings as if fleeing, and launched herself upward. The harpy spread her own wings almost simultaneously, whomped up, and performed a marvelous snatch. She took Fleta's tiny form in a talon, not closing it tightly, and pumped on up into the sky. "I will consume this morsel at leisure!" she screeched to the others. "Begone, dullheads!"

Disappointed, the other harpies dispersed somewhat.

Phoebe bore northeast, toward the plains of the unicorns. Two other harpies hovered in the sky, peering about, but none challenged Phoebe. That coiffure really gave her status!

As the sun stood near its zenith, Phoebe set her down, well within unicorn territory. Fleta assumed her natural form and played a brief melody of thanks on her horn.

"Unicorns be no special friends o' mine," Phoebe said. "But they can play pretty, I confess!" She took off for the sky again.

The favor they had done the harpy had been well repaid. Fleta was free. She did a leap and a distance with the Unicorn Strut, the five-beat gait no other creature could match.

Then she came to ground, as it were. She was free—but what about Mach? Or Bane? Bane might even now be fighting his way free of the Purple Adept—but maybe not. She had better get to the Blue Demesnes and inform them of the situation.

She set off for the castle at a gallop. It was not far from the Unicorn Demesnes, and before long she arrived.

The Lady Stile come out to greet her. The Lady, Bane's mother, was a handsome figure of a woman in her forties, well regarded by all the animals of the region. "Why, Fleta, what brings thee here?" she inquired.

Fleta changed to girl form. "Bane be captive of the Purple Adept!" she panted.

"Nay, no longer," the Lady said.

"Thou dost know?"

"Come talk with Stile," the Lady said.

Fleta followed her inside. In an interior study the Adept sat, smaller than Fleta's human form, but awing her with his aura of power. He was of course garbed in blue.

"Bane be on the way here," Stile said to Fleta. "He has just finished talking with a mermaid."

"A mermaid?"

Stile smiled. "He was saved from harm by Translucent, who wishes to persuade him to carry messages to Proton for the other Adepts. Now he must decide. His problem is that he fears a friend in Proton is held captive by enemy Citizens. I think he will wish to return there to free her, or to verify her safety."

"Thou dost know all this—and didst do nothing?" Fleta asked, confused.

"I have been attuned to my son since seeing the two of you yesterday. After your capture by Purple, I watched closely. Mach returned to Proton, and Bane returned to his own body. Thee I did not watch, Fleta; it be no easy thing to snoop undetected on the affairs of another Adept, and my son I had to guard against harm."

"Thou couldst have rescued Bane—and did not?" Fleta asked, appalled.

"I could have, and would have. But there were two counter-indications. First, Bane must learn to handle his own problems, and experience be the finest teacher. Had he been near death, I would have snatched him from it, but I hoped not to have to do that. Second, I had to know exactly what the Adverse Adepts contemplated—and that, thanks to Bane, I have now determined. I am glad thou didst win free, too."

Fleta was no human being, but she found this to be more cynical than she could accept. To allow his own son to be in danger of death, just to snoop on the plans of other Adepts! She could not express her anger openly, for Stile was an Adept who had greatly benefited her Herd and many other animals, but it prompted her to do something almost as foolish. "Dost thou know I love Mach?" she asked.

Stile gazed at her with disturbing speculation. "I know that thou didst always care for Bane," he said.

"Not Bane. Mach. From Proton-frame. I love him—and methinks he loves me."

"That can never be," Stile said, and turned away.

Fleta started to speak, but the Lady caught her by the arm and urged her out. When they were clear of the room, the Lady said softly: "Bait not my husband, Fleta. He hath much on his mind."

Bait? They did not believe her!

And why should they? A human man, the son of an Adept, loving a unicorn? Or a golem from the other frame, with a unicorn? Why should anyone take that seriously?

She had struggled to come here, to bear news they didn't need. The love she felt was a thing of no consequence to them.

"I thank thee, Lady," she said. "I shall go to my Herd."

But the Lady's hand was on her arm. "Dost thou suppose I know not what it means to love one from the other frame? But Mach can come here only at the expense of our son."

And how could that be? Of course they would not give up their son!

Then the Lady was holding her, and Fleta was sobbing into her shoulder. The Lady did understand—but understood also the cost. It was not a cost Fleta could ask of them.

Fleta disengaged and left the castle. About to change back to her natural form, she spied an approaching figure.

It was Bane. He had returned, as his father had said he would. Now the bad Adepts had no hostages.

Bane looked at her. He looked exactly like the man she loved. "How dost thou feel about Mach?" he asked.

Fleta dissolved into tears again.

"I know not what be right," Bane said.

"Thy father will tell thee," she said. Then she changed, and galloped away, ashamed of her longing. Of course she could not condemn her friend Bane to exile in Proton-frame, for the sake of her own private joy with his other self.

She proceeded back to the Herd Demesnes, knowing she had to talk to her dam, Neysa. She had to know—what she did not know.

She located the Herd by nightfall. She checked in with the Herd Stallion, who was her uncle Clip. She was safely out of heat now, so this visit was all right. Belle, Clip's first mare and still his favorite, grazed nearby, her mane glinting iridescently. But it was Neysa she had come to see.

Soon Neysa joined her, separating from the Herd. Neysa's equine head was turning gray now, and her white socks hung lower on her rear feet than they had in youth, but she remained a handsome small mare. She had returned to the Herd when her breeding years passed; she had had to remain apart when her brother assumed the leadership, but now there was no problem. She still spent much of her time elsewhere, however, because she had friendships with many of the venerable wolves of the werewolf pack, and of course with Stile and the Lady too.

They changed to human form and sat under a shade tree. "And didst thou get bred?" Neysa asked.

"Nay. I—found other occupation."

"Thou didst not come into heat?"

"I did, but . . ."

Of course her dam had to have the whole story. Fleta told it. "And now Bane be safe, and Mach be back in Proton," she concluded. "And I love Mach."

Neysa understood about hopeless love, of course. "When thy

season comes again, thou must be at the other Herd," she said. "Naught e'er can come of thy interest in a man."

"Yet, if he returned, as he said he might, for a visit—"

"Get bred, get a foal, and be friends with the man," Neysa advised. "That be the way it must be. That be the way thou thyself didst come into existence."

"But if he stayed—"

"Fleta, he be a man, son of an Adept!" Neysa reminded her. "Thou canst ne'er forget that!"

"But why must we be apart? An he love me too—"

But Neysa changed to mare form and dismissed the notion with a harmonica chord from her horn. She had never been one to entertain dreams of the impossible.

Fleta realized that there was no more acceptance here for her wild dream than there had been at the Blue Demesnes. Yet she was young and impetuous, and still could not give it up. For without Mach, her life had no meaning.

She sighed. Then she changed to mare form, played a chord of parting to Neysa, and set off across the plain toward the Werewolf Demesnes.

That journey took some time. She paused for the evening, grazing while she slept on her feet, and resumed it in the morning.

She reached the Pack later in the day. The hackles of the wolves rose as they spied her, but then they recognized her as the filly of Neysa, and escorted her in to meet the leader, Kurrelgyre.

Kurrelgyre shifted to man form, and Fleta to girl form. He was grizzled, a veteran of many combats, and perhaps approaching the time when one of his offspring would kill him and take his place as leader. But he was friend to Neysa, and therefore to Fleta. "What brings thee here, filly?" he inquired.

"I would talk with Furramenin," Fleta said.

"And welcome," he said. Furramenin was his whelp by his favorite bitch, a lovely creature of Fleta's generation.

Soon they were talking, apart from the Pack. "Didst thou get bred?" Furramenin inquired eagerly, now in girl form. Soon enough she would have to leave the Pack for similar reason, traveling to one not led by her sire.

"Not exactly," Fleta said. As before, she had to explain, covering the story in fair detail.

"Oooo, with a *man!*" the innocent bitch exclaimed. "But of course it couldn't take!"

"It was only to prevent me from going on to a Herd," Fleta reminded her.

"Swish thy tail when thou sayest that!" the wolf exclaimed. "It was the *man* thou didst desire!"

"It was the man," Fleta agreed. "And after my season passed, he wanted it more, and his way, and—" She shrugged.

"And now thou art in perpetual heat for him."

"Aye, in a way. Ne'er before did I seek it for itself, for love of the one it was with."

"And who wouldn't? The whelp of an Adept!"

"Nay, he be from the other frame."

"So that be why he knew not it was impossible."

"Aye." Fleta looked at her pleadingly. "I have no life without him. But I know not whether he will return, and e'en if he does—"

"It still be impossible," Furramenin concluded. "A dream for a week, then back to reality."

"Yet if he does return, and wants me—"

"Adepts have concubines," the bitch reminded her. "Some they like better than their wives, if truth be known."

"But I want him all to myself!"

Furramenin shook her head. "Impossible," she concluded.

"Thou dost believe that?"

"Aye. This be Phaze; hadst thou not noticed?"

They talked about other things, and it was pleasant enough, but Fleta had learned what she had come to learn. The werewolves did not understand her desire either.

Next day she galloped on to the cave of the vampires. Here she talked with Suchevane, the loveliest of the vampires. In girl form, Suchevane had chestnut tresses that swirled luxuriously to her pert bottom, and a figure that virtually drained the blood of males before she even touched them. She was notorious already for her liaisons with any males capable of assuming man form— vampires, werewolves, unicorns, genuine men (including Bane)—

and some that only came close. Naturally she had the broadest of perspectives in such matters.

"But Fleta, it can't be serious!" Suchevane protested.

"I *am* serious," Fleta insisted with unicorn stubbornness.

"I mean, not from the human man's view. Any human man likes to play, but ne'er to marry other than his own kind. Think not I would remain single, an it were otherwise."

Grim news! If the lovely vampiress could not snag a human man, how could any ordinary animal expect to do so?

"Actually, the other species be none too keen on it either," Suchevane continued. "I had a really interesting fling with a werewolf, and he petitioned to his Pack to bring me into it, but they negated it."

"But they could not stop him from marrying thee, an he truly wanted to!" Fleta said.

Suchevane shook her head, and her hair swirled in a way Fleta had to envy. "Aye, they could stop him."

"But he could run away with thee—"

"Not after they tore him to bits."

Fleta stared at her. The vampiress was serious.

Suchevane shrugged. "Do what I do, 'corn. Be a private concubine, and seek no more. Accept thy place and live in peace. Half a pint o' blood be better than none."

It was good advice, Fleta knew. But it gave her no comfort. She didn't want to love Mach in shame.

So she repaired south to the castle of the Red Adept. This was on a conical mountain, with a path spiraling up to it. But the Adept did not live in the castle, which he had inherited from his predecessor; he lived below it, inside the mountain. For he was Trool the Troll, elevated to Adept status by the action of Stile—and the Book of Magic. All other trolls were truculent and to be feared, but not this one. Not by the friends of Stile.

She blew a chord of query, seeking admittance. In a moment a hole opened in the base of the mountain, big enough for a unicorn. She trotted in.

There was eerie fungus light inside. She moved on down the tunnel and into the central chamber. There was the troll, as ugly as any of his kind, carving a figurine out of stone with his bare hands. For this was the talent of trolls, to manipulate stone as if it were clay, and to carve either tunnels or objects from it. Usually the objects were weapons, but sometimes they were artistic. Lovely statues and amulets filled the chamber, each individual and fascinating in its own right. Though any troll *could,* only Trool *did;* that artistry had distinguished him from the others of his kind. That, and his constancy of character.

"I fear I cannot help thee, Fleta," Trool said before she had even presented her case. "I cannot change the ways of entire species, and would not if I could. And my power extends not to the frame of science."

Somehow she had known Trool would be aware of her. The Book of Magic gave him extraordinary power, even for an Adept. "I think thou canst," she communicated. She used the horn-language of her kind, speaking in notes and harmonies. Few others understood it, but the Red Adept had no trouble.

"But I would not," he said.

"What better be there for me?" she demanded with sharp notes.

"Let me fashion thee a shape in his likeness, that the Brown Adept can animate as a golem."

"Nay!" Fortissimo.

"Stile be such an animation," he reminded her. For Stile's body had returned to Proton, animated by the Blue Adept, who had lost his own body. A golem body had been carved by the troll, and animated by the Brown Adept, and Stile's soul had infused it. In all things it had mimicked his natural body perfectly, except two: it lacked the bad knees of the original, and it could not reproduce. Stile's son Bane had been sired before the change of bodies.

"But it be Stile's real soul," she played. "What thou dost offer me be merely Mach's appearance—and that exists already, in Bane. It be only Mach I want, none other."

"An the golem of Proton come again to Phaze, neither his kind nor thine would permit what thou dost desire," he said.

"Aye. So it be hopeless. Therefore must thou give me what I come for."

"How shall I face thy dam, an I do this?"

"Thou hast no need to tell her."

The Adept gazed at her sadly. "Since I can help thee not my way, must needs I help thee thy way. But I like it not. Choose thy form."

Fleta changed to girl form. "This be the form in which I came to love him," she said, speaking the human tongue for the first time.

"I fear I will do penance for this," Trool said. He handed her an amulet. "Invoke this, when thou art ready."

She took the amulet. "I invoke thee," she said immediately.

Nothing happened, physically. But she felt the magic of the amulet fasten about her, and knew it had done its work. She was now unable to change form.

"I thank thee, Adept," she said.

"I curse the need," he said.

She stepped forward and kissed him on his ugly cheek. "How be it a creature as nice as thou hast no companion?"

"I be alienated from mine own kind," he said gruffly.

Because he supported Stile's program of greater equality for the nonhuman creatures of Phaze, and of restraint in magic. The other trolls supported the Adverse Adepts. Of course he had the magic to capture and tame any female of any species, including troll or human, but he declined to use it that way. Thus his tragedy was like hers, in its fashion.

"Do thou ensure that none interfere," she said.

"Aye," he agreed glumly. "None save an Adept could, and none would."

Fleta turned and walked from the mountain. The ground opened to let her out, then closed again behind her. Now she was on her own.

She walked all day northwest, toward the center of the great White Mountain range. Her human legs grew tired, for she was not hardened to such travel in this form, but it was the only way, now. However long it took, she could afford.

No creatures bothered her along the way. She knew that Trool had seen to that. He had not helped her to travel there, because he did not like her purpose, but he had agreed to protect her from interference during the interim.

It took several days. At last she reached the mountains, and climbed the foothills, and then the main slopes. As evening closed, she made her way to a grassy ledge overlooking a deep chasm.

It was the ledge where her dam, Neysa, had stood, twenty years before, when ready to leap off rather than suffer Stile to conquer her. Neysa had not intended suicide; she would have changed in midair to her firefly form, and flown away, leaving Stile to fall to his death below. But he, not realizing that, had freed her instead—and in that act had captured her after all. Thereafter she had given him everything. Later he had made to her that Oath of friendship that had subtly changed the relationship of men, unicorns and werewolves, and whose power still was felt, twenty years later. But that Oath had its root at this site, where he had taken that first step.

Fleta stood at the brink. Neysa had not contemplated suicide—but Fleta did. Had she come here ordinarily, she could have leaped—but would have changed to bird form involuntarily, rather than die. So she had had herself enchanted. Now, when she jumped, she would not be able to change her mind.

This act would solve the problem. She would be beyond caring, and Mach, if he ever learned of it, would know that there was no longer anything to distract him from his other business. She was freeing him—from her. From the temptation and distraction of the impossible.

"Mach!" she cried, letting her love for him overflow at last, letting the mountains hear it. Indeed they heard, for they echoed it back. At the snowy heights the snow-demons emerged from their ice caves, marveling at that echoing word. A ripple passed through the air: the splash of conviction.

Now she had uttered it. Now she was committed.

Then she made a swan-dive off the ledge.

15

Blue

Bane found himself back in a Proton cell, this time clamped to a wall so that he could not move. Evidently Mach had not been able to free himself. But had he been successful in freeing Agape? That was what really counted.

He tuned himself out, knowing that there was nothing he could do at the moment, and that there was nothing the Contrary Citizens could do to him, since without him they would have no avenue to Phaze. Since this machine body had no so-called natural functions, his immobility did not generate discomfort. Obviously something had happened, to make the Citizen wary of his prisoner's freedom. What had Mach done?

A screen came on before him. It was set in the wall opposite, and his head was locked into place facing it; he could tune it out in his mind, but could not look at anything else. It seemed his captor wanted him to watch it.

The picture was of the interior of a house or suite. The furnishings were in shades of blue. "Pay attention, robot," Citizen Purple's voice came. "You thought you were pretty clever, springing the amoeba, but watch how we get her back."

So the Citizen didn't know that Bane had returned to Proton. He thought he was addressing Mach. Thus he was inadvertently providing the very information Bane most desired: the news that Agape had escaped. Mach had done his job!

But if she had escaped, she should have gone to Citizen Blue. The picture showed blue, suggesting that this was his residence. Was she here?

Indeed she was; in a moment she entered, in the company of a lovely older serf woman. They sat on the couch, unaware that they were being observed.

"We have to free Mach," the older woman said earnestly. "They can no longer put pressure on him by threatening you, which is one reason he arranged to free you first. He could have used my friends to free himself, but he didn't want to leave you in their power."

"Your friends?" Agape asked.

"The self-willed machines. I am one, of course; our form matters less than our brain."

"Your whorish robot mother must have taught you those tricks," Purple muttered. Evidently his commentary was separate, directed to Bane alone.

"But why didn't they save him too?" Agape was asking.

"They could have—but that would have alerted your captor to your own escape, and he might have intercepted you before you got clear. So Mach used himself as a diversion, distracting the Citizen's attention from you, giving you the time you needed."

"The bitch machine is right," Purple said. "We were watching you. But that trick won't work again. I have eliminated all the self-willed machines from my employ, and acted to prevent you from using any more cute little parts of yourself to do mischief."

So that was what Mach had done! Bane would never have thought of that. He kept silent; he was doing well enough this way.

"But Mach—what of him, now?" Agape asked. "I never meant to leave him prisoner!"

"My husband will rescue him," the woman said. "But we must make absolutely sure they do not get hold of you again because you represent their best lever against him. So I think we must send you back to your home planet, at least until my son is safe."

"Yes, of course," Agape agreed. "I have caused you too much trouble already."

"Your participation in the problem was coincidental," the woman, who Bane realized was Sheen, Mach's mother, said gently. "Your support to him has been invaluable. We feel that no blame attaches to you. But now that you have become a key figure, we must keep you out of their hands. We are arranging to take you directly to the ship leaving today for Moeba."

Was this to keep her safe—or to eliminate her as a factor in Mach or Bane's life? Bane wasn't sure. Yet perhaps it was best; he would rather have her on another planet than at risk of torture here.

"Guess what's going to happen," Purple said.

Suddenly Bane realized: they were watching a private dialogue! The enemy Citizen had used one of his pseudomagic devices to spy on Citizen Blue, and knew what was being planned. "No!" he cried.

"You thought all you needed was to spring her loose, boy? The game isn't over till the blubber-lady sings."

They were going to recapture Agape—and what would Bane do then? He couldn't let her suffer!

Maybe it was a bluff. A charade, with actors in a setting resembling the home of Citizen Blue. After all, how could such a spying eye be placed without Blue knowing? Certainly Bane's father, Stile, in Phaze, could not be spied on in such manner!

Yet Agape looked so genuine! He was sure it was her!

"We'll bring her in to see you," Purple said. "Little reunion; you'll like that, won't you! So take it easy, machine; you'll be sure enough it's her when she arrives."

Bane was all too certain that was true.

The screen dimmed out, and he tuned out. But later he was roused by the screen again. This time it showed an atmospheric flyer, similar to the one that had picked up Bane and Agape. It was cruising across the foggy desert. Beside it was another, and a third; a small fleet of them.

"They figured to sneak her out on a routine supply flight," Purple's voice came. "We figure to pluck it like a plum." He laughed coarsely. "A damned purple plum! Blue's got a lot of wealth, but precious little common sense! Here he's trying to figure out how to get you back, and he's losing his own high card!"

Bane watched, mortified, as the supply craft came into sight. The attack-craft intercepted it, surrounding it.

"They're signaling for help," Purple remarked. "Doesn't matter; by the time it comes, the prize'll be ours."

Indeed, the attacking craft brought the supply craft to the sand. Suited men sprang out and swarmed to it. Soon they hauled a figure out, and Bane could tell by the way it moved that it was Agape.

They shoved her into one craft. The screen changed to show the face of a serf. "Sir, we have the alien," the man said.

"Put her on the screen," Purple said. "I want to see her myself."

They hauled Agape up to the camera. She remained in the suit, but now her helmet was off. Her features were slightly melted around the edges, because of her distress. She was still struggling, but ineffectively.

Bane felt his nonexistent heart sinking. They did indeed have her.

"Now you know I don't care about the amoeba," Citizen Purple said. "And maybe you don't too. But you bet your other self does."

What use pretense? "I be the other," Bane said.

"Oho! You switched back already?"

"Aye. Mach be free in Phaze; I be captive here."

"Yeah? How do you figure he's free?"

"I used magic to free the unicorn. Thine other self was about to slay me, but the Translucent Adept took me instead, and let me go. I returned to find out about Agape."

"Translucent, eh? Yeah, that's like him. He uses the soft sell, but he always wins in the end. But how do you figure the machine is free now?"

"Translucent gave his word."

"Translucent's one of us!"

"I know. But he honors his word."

"So do I, boy. And I promise you this: that girl-creature of yours is going to suffer if you don't cooperate. I want your word: no more tricks."

Bane was silent.

"Well, we'll do it the hard way, then," Citizen Purple said grimly.

Bane tuned out again, as there wasn't much else to do. What would happen, would happen.

He resumed awareness when people approached his cell. It was the Citizen—and Agape. She was tearful and dispirited, and her details were blurred by trace melting. It was evident that she lacked the will to muster her proper human appearance.

The panel of the cell slid across behind them. "Okay, boy," Citizen Purple said. "We're private now. This is nobody's business but ours. My serfs don't know what I want from you, but you do. Let's play a game, you and me. Let's see who can stand the most heat."

"I be in a robot body," Bane reminded him. "I can endure more heat." He wondered why the Citizen should wish to have this encounter private; did he fear betrayal by his own serfs? Or was he afraid that Citizen Translucent would spy on him, and take over just the way the Translucent Adept had in Phaze? That did seem more likely; it was evident that neither the Contrary Citizens nor the Adverse Adepts fully trusted their own associates.

"Well, we'll just see about that." The man brought out a tiny instrument. He touched buttons.

Immediately the heat began. It radiated from the walls, in the manner of an oven, raising the temperature of the air.

Agape made a muffled whimper.

Then Bane remembered: she was vulnerable to heat. It melted her. That was the true thrust. He could withstand more than could the Citizen—but surely Agape could withstand less.

The Citizen was fat. The heat affected him quickly. Sweat broke out on his forehead. He removed his jacket.

Agape tried to remain firm, literally, but her flesh was already melting. She tried to be silent, but a moan overtook her.

What should he do? Bane knew that the Citizen would not relent. He wanted Bane's cooperation, and he would gladly sacrifice Agape to obtain it. Yet if Bane cooperated, men he didn't like and didn't want to support would use him and Mach for their benefit.

Purple removed more clothing, baring himself to the underwear. "Sure is hot in here!" he remarked. Indeed, he looked most uncomfortable.

Bane realized that the man was doing it to show that there was no bluffing about the heat. If it had this effect on a living man, it was having worse effect on Agape's less-solid tissue. Indeed, her face was becoming shapeless, and her breasts were sagging deeply.

Purple glanced significantly at her. "Now I don't know the exact tolerance the amoebas have for heat," he said. "But I'd guess that first they settle into a puddle, then they expire. Seems we're about to find out."

"Nay!" Bane cried.

The Citizen looked at him. "Ready to give me your word, boy? No more tricks, full cooperation?"

"No commitment given under duress is valid!" Bane protested.

"Suit yourself, boy. You know how to stop it, before we all fry."

Agape staggered. Her head was now a hideous mass of flesh, and her body was barely human. She stumbled against the Citizen.

"Get away from me, you jellyfish!" Purple snapped.

But Agape wrapped her melting arms about him. "I'm going to consume you!" she hissed through the slit that was all that remained of her face.

Horrified, the Citizen shoved her away with all his strength. But she clung, smearing her dripping surface against him. The two of them spun about in that loathsome embrace, and fell heavily to the floor.

Then Agape came up with the control unit. She touched a button, and the radiation ceased. "Let's conclude this charade," she said, her voice abruptly changing.

"What?" Purple demanded, hauling himself up.

Agape put her free hand to her face and scraped the flesh down and off. Other features appeared beneath. "Do you know me now, fat stuff?" she asked.

"Blue!" the Citizen exclaimed with renewed dismay.

Citizen Blue! Now Bane recognized the likeness of his own father, Stile, emerging from beneath the sagging covering of pseudoflesh.

"Did you think I was stupid enough to leave your monitor in my premises without reason?" Blue asked. "Or to ship the girl unguarded?"

"You suckered me!" Purple said.

"You suckered yourself. Now let's complete our business, shall we?"

Purple grabbed for his control panel, but Blue held it clear. Purple, considerably larger than his opponent, lunged. "Give me that, you midget!"

Blue seemed only to touch the man, stroking the fingers of his left hand across the right side of Purple's neck. But Purple stiffened, then collapsed, unconscious. "A duffer should never charge a Gamesman," Blue said.

"Thou art a Gamesman?" Bane asked. "I thought my father Stile was that."

Blue came across, releasing the fastenings that held Bane to the wall. "So you exchanged again," he said. "Does that mean my son is now the captive of the Purple Adept?"

"Nay; Translucent won the wager that he could obtain my cooperation voluntarily, and now leads the Adverse Adepts, and he gave his word that either of us would be free."

Blue nodded. "I daresay things have changed in twenty years, but I knew Translucent and his young son to be men of their word."

"The one thou didst know as the son be the current Adept, and aye, he be a man of his word. But his purpose be not my father's."

"But if we free thee," Blue said, reverting to the dialect of Phaze that he had known when young, "then the Adverse Adepts will have neither thee nor my son, and neither Agape nor—"

"Nor Fleta," Bane concluded.

"Fleta?"

"She be the filly of Neysa, and I believe Mach loves her. As I love Agape."

Blue pursed his lips. "He loves a unicorn?"

"I think he knew her nature not, at first. She be a most fetching person, vivacious and feeling, in human form."

"Neysa seldom took the human form, and spoke little then," Blue said. "I knew her through mine other self. Yet was she the most worthy of persons."

"She be still," Bane said. "Gray of forelock, now past breeding, but well respected in the Herd her brother governs. But Fleta be expressive in all the ways her dam be not. An Mach took her for human—"

"Here in Proton we are practicing tolerance," Blue said. "I feel not the dismay for such liaison that I might have when young." He went to bend over the fallen Purple. Bane noticed that he did not bend his knees, and remembered that his father said he had been injured in the knees, in his original body. The body that had sired himself, Bane, before returning to Proton. Blue was, physically, his father.

"But when we return to our own frames," Bane said, "I love not the unicorn, friend as she may be, and Mach loves not Agape."

Blue nodded. "There be matters yet to consider. But now we needs must spring thee free of this hole." He had stripped Purple's remaining clothing, leaving him naked, and under his busy hands Purple had assumed the appearance of a blob. Pseudoflesh covered his face, leaving only nose-holes for breathing, and his genital region now looked female.

"The Citizen's minions will think he is Agape!" Bane exclaimed, catching on.

"Aye. And I shall play the part of a Citizen," Blue said, donning Purple's clothing. He had to wad and tie some of it underneath, to give the appearance of greater girth, and the loose-fitting shoes did not elevate him to the other man's height, but the resemblance was becoming striking enough.

"The Game!" Bane exclaimed. "Thou didst learn such mimicry for the Game!"

"Aye. Mine other self was the expert, but I thought it meet for me to study it somewhat also, and teach it to my son."

"Would I could learn that Game," Bane said wistfully.

"Thou dost like Proton?"

"It is love of Agape that lures me," Bane admitted. "But aye, I find this frame more challenging than mine own. It be foolishness, I know."

"A foolishness I share," Blue said, smiling. "Now, we both have parts to play. Thou dost remain prisoner, chastened by seeing thy love melt. I am taking thee to safer confinement."

"That part can I play," Bane said. "But surely Purple's minions will not be fooled by thee!"

"There be some distractions," Blue said with a small smile. "It was necessary for me to wait until I knew they were in place, before taking action here. Now shall we see how the magic of science performs." He took some of his surplus pseudoflesh and molded it in the corner, against the locked panel. He set a tiny stick in it and pinched off the protruding end of the stick. "Shield me with thy body," he said, retreating to the far side of the cell. "It be tougher than mine own."

Perplexed, Bane stood as directed, standing between Blue and the pseudoflesh, facing away from it, bracing himself.

There was an explosion. It shoved him into Blue, and both against the wall. Bits of wall and panel were hurled like stones into the other walls. "What happened?" Bane cried.

They recovered their feet. "A trick of the trade," Blue remarked, dusting himself off. "Follow me." He hurried out of the smoking cell, through the shattered panel.

Serfs rushed up. "The alien bitch carried plastic explosive!" Blue roared in Purple's voice. "Fetch my private plane! I'm taking the prisoner to safer confinement!"

When they hesitated, Blue paused to glare about. It was amazing how aptly he had picked up Purple's mannerisms. "And find out who was supposed to guard against weapons being brought in here! Didn't any numbskull think to check for plastic? *Look at that cell!* Every party responsible will be fired with prejudice!"

Hastily the serfs went about their business; the talk of firing made them extremely nervous.

Foreman hurried up. "Sir, the craft is ready," he said. Then, startled, he opened his mouth again.

Blue's hand snaked out and caught the serf's wrist. Foreman stiffened in pain. "Speak no word," Blue said. "Guide us there."

It was obvious that the submission hold rendered the serf powerless to resist. He backed into an elevator, and they followed. The elevator took them up to a landing area, where the airplane waited. Blue and Bane got in.

"The blob in the cell is your employer," Blue informed Foreman as he took the pilot's seat. "He may need your attention, before the ignorant serfs dump him in the trash."

Foreman, about to cry the alarm, whirled and ran for the elevator. His first loyalty was to the physical welfare of Citizen Purple.

Blue started the airplane and piloted it into the air. It quickly rose high, flying above the mountains. He touched its front panel. "Blue here, in Purple's private plane," he said. "Escort me home."

Three other airplanes zoomed in. But immediately half a dozen others appeared, closing in on the first three. Citizen Purple's defenses were alert.

"If these be like dragons, we be in trouble," Bane remarked.

"Like dragons indeed," Blue agreed. "But human cleverness can do much." He guided the airplane precipitously down. "There be much joy in machines, an thou dost have the temperament."

And he had a wife and a son who were machines. Bane would have liked this man well enough, even if he had not been so exactly like Stile.

The three friendly craft ran interference, threatening to crash into any of the pursuers who came too close. "Ours be machine-controlled?" Bane asked.

"Aye. *Sheen*-controlled, by remote. Purple's be manned by serfs, who have some care for their hides."

They bumped to a landing by a marker in the sand at the foot of the mountain range. They piled out as the enemy craft dived for them, running to the marker and hauling up on a ring set in it. Blue was panting, for he had no suit to enable him to breathe the polluted atmosphere; Bane, seeing the problem, took over the job and hauled up a portal. A hole opened, and they scrambled in and shut the portal above.

"Service access," Blue gasped. "Say the code!"

"Code?"

"Oh, that's right; you don't know it. Mach does. Damn! We

can't summon the self-willed machines!" He was recovering as the good air here got into him.

"Self-willed machines? I have heard reference to these, and learned that Sheen be one, but I know these not."

"Intelligent, motivated, self-directed robots of all types, but not granted serf status because that's limited to those who *look* like serfs; I haven't been able to overcome that bias yet. They don't complain because they want the Experimental Project to prove itself first."

"The Experimental Project—that allows androids and machines and alien creatures to be as equals?"

"The same. Agape must have told thee."

"Aye." They were moving on down along a passage. Already there was noise back at the portal.

"Mach be one of them, of course; he gave Agape the code so they would know she came to them at his behest. I never sought to know that code; it was important that Mach grow unfettered by my domination. But now, if we don't summon them, we shall shortly be captive again."

Indeed, there was a swirl of air as the portal was opened above and behind them, and a clamor. Men were piling in.

Bane struggled with the logical brain he now had, as they rushed along. How could he get that code? It should be in Mach's memory—but he had none of that. His own memories had come with him across the curtain between frames. Was there anything he could tap into?

They came to a dead-end. "Here there is a subway transport station for supplies," Blue said. "I had thought to take it—but only the SW's have access. No serfs or Citizens are expected to be here alone, and it isn't watched. The machines have to be alerted."

Heavy feet were thudding down the passage. Bane could tell by the sound that there were at least six men. The two of them had no reasonable chance to overcome that number.

Then something occurred to him. "If they accepted Agape—" he said. "Where must the code be given?"

"To one of these intercoms," Blue said, indicating a small grille set in the wall.

Bane spoke to it. "Accept Agape's code from Mach!" he said.
And the grille answered: "Accepted. What may we do for you?"

"Save us from those who pursue us!"

A panel slid aside, revealing a cargo capsule. "Enter."

They climbed in. The panel closed behind them just as the first pursuer came into sight. The capsule began to move. It was cramped, as it was not intended for human beings, but satisfactory.

"You did it!" Blue exclaimed, dropping the Phaze mode of speech. "How did you know they would accept that? You have hardly seen this frame!"

"Principle of transfer. A message can be passed from one person to another, and if it be valid, it is accepted. They knew Agape's code was valid, so when I invoked it by description, they understood."

"You thought of something I did not—and thereby saved us some mischief," Blue said. "I think you have an aptitude for this frame! Now I shall add my own wrinkle." He addressed the capsule's intercom. "Deposit us at the next station, then go on empty."

The capsule slowed. "Why stop?" Bane asked. "They be surely in pursuit."

"Exactly. They will also have men to intercept us at its destination."

"Oops, aye!"

The capsule stopped. They hoisted themselves out. It went on. "Now they will be pursuing the decoy," Blue said. "But we still have to get out of here, and they will be watching all the exits. In any event, we're still under the desert, and I don't care to breathe any more of this frame's air. So we'll go back."

"Go back!" Bane repeated incredulously.

"Right to the Purple Estate," Blue said, getting out of his clothes. "I have a little pseudoflesh left, enough to change our facial features. We shall become serfs."

"Be that not risky?"

"Not as risky as our present course."

To that Bane could only agree. Blue applied the pseudoflesh

to his face, filling out his cheeks and chin, then did the same for himself. He adjusted their hair. Bane glanced at himself in the reflective surface of a panel, and found that the little bit of adjustment had changed his appearance drastically. Blue was good at disguises!

They took a capsule on the track going the opposite way. While they rode, they talked, and Bane found that he liked this man very well. Blue was, if anything, more open than his father, Stile, less guarded in what he said. He had indeed learned tolerance; Bane did not feel at all like a machine in his presence.

They got out at the Purple Estate. This was a larger station, with many supplies to be moved. They each picked up a box and carried it out of the station and into the Estate.

Things were in chaos there. It seemed that the Citizen had suffered burns and embarrassment, and was being treated. Foreman was furious, and taking it out on any lower serf he encountered. There had already been several firings, and more were in the offing. All this they gleaned simply by listening as they walked through the premises.

They carried their boxes on to the serf transport station. They waited their turn and boarded the ground shuttle, the boxes in their laps. No one questioned them. The shuttle filled with other serfs on errands, and started off. It left the dome and wheeled across the sand toward the main city of Dradom.

Thus they made it to freedom, the easy way. They left their boxes in the shuttle for return to the Purple Estate, and went to a phone. Blue called Sheen. "Come and get us," he said, smiling faintly.

A private ship came for them. They boarded, and it took off. The seat belts released themselves, freeing them to walk about during the flight. Then the forward compartment opened, and Sheen and Agape walked into the main chamber.

Bane was not aware how they came together. Suddenly he was embracing and kissing Agape, and she was crying with joy. Then, embarrassed, they paused, looking around at the others.

"Sit down," Citizen Blue said, donning a blue outfit that Sheen had brought along. They sat.

"My wife and I have known for some time that our son was

not entirely satisfied," Blue said. "He is a product of our most advanced technology. His circuits are more sophisticated than Sheen's. His brain is capable of a type of consciousness that approaches the living standard so closely that we are not certain there is any significant distinction."

"Very little," Bane agreed.

"But he was not alive—and he wanted to be. That we could not give him—until he made contact with you. Now he has been able to experience that ultimate state. Do you think he will want to return?"

"Not if he loves Fleta," Bane said.

"We like you, Bane," Blue continued. "I was never able to sire a living son, even before I came to Proton. It was no sacrifice for me to marry Sheen. In fact the laboratory was the only way that I could have a child. And I am satisfied with Mach. But still I always wished that I could have a living child in Phaze. My inability to do so was part of what damaged my relationship to your mother, Bane. It put our love under stress. The Lady Blue desperately wanted a child. Now I see in you the son I might have had."

Then Blue stopped speaking. "What he is trying to say," Sheen said, "is that if you, Bane, care to remain in Proton, we would be glad to extend to you the same relationship we have had with Mach. If you should wish to marry Agape, we would be pleased."

"But you hardly know me!" Bane protested, speaking to them both.

"You are the offspring of my other self, sired by this body," Blue said. "You have been raised as an apprentice Adept in Phaze. You have come to Proton, as I did. I think I know you well enough. If you wish to remain, and undertake the necessary preparation for eventual Citizenship, you are welcome to do so."

Bane knew he should have been overwhelmed by such an offer. But this body had better control over its emotions than did his own. He simply considered his own preference, and found no question. "I would like to do so," he said. "An my other self be satisfied."

"I suspect he will be," Blue said. "But there is no need to be in doubt. Contact him, exchange with him, and verify the situation for yourselves. There should be contact between you anyway. On that the Contrary Citizens agree with us. This opportunity to establish correspondence between the frames must not be lost. Where we differ is whether the benefits of that contact shall accrue to our cause or to theirs. The stakes are potentially enormous. Whoever has ready access to both the Oracle Computer and the Book of Magic will have power to remake both frames in a manner hitherto impossible. With that power, I could complete the integration of the diverse elements of Proton society, and in time eliminate the feudal Citizen-serf aspect of our society. With that power, the Contrary Citizens could reverse all that I have accomplished in twenty years and disenfranchise the robots, cyborgs, androids and aliens."

Bane looked at Agape. "Thou knowest that ne'er would I do that to thee," he said to her. Then he kissed her, and no more needed to be said on that subject.

"However," Blue said, and now Bane felt a chill, knowing that something unpleasant was coming. His own father spoke in just that fashion. "There are certain counterindications."

"Somehow I knew there would be," Banc said.

"My course here in the frame of Proton has not been entirely smooth," Blue said. "Progress has been slow, and the Contrary Citizens have fought every step. They have seized upon every possible technicality to frustrate my designs before the Council of Citizens. Compromise has been the order of the day, for twenty years. There are many programs I would have promoted, had I been able; the Experimental Project has been the only one I have been able to implement fully. I daresay my other self in Phaze has had similar problems."

"Aye," Bane agreed. "He sought to make all creatures equal in Phaze, the animals and the men, but found resistance in both animals and men. He made of the Blue Demesnes a center for the education and freedom of animals, and the association of differing species. All be welcome, but few attend, apart from Neysa's oath-friends. Some be afraid of the Adverse Adepts, with reason; some merely cling to their old ways. So it has been mainly in stasis. Phaze be not what Stile dreamed it could be."

"And so he dare not force any issue that is not vital," Blue said. "I know how that is."

"And he be slowly losing ground," Bane agreed.

"Now consider the probable impact of the reestablishment of communication between the two frames," Blue said. "That contact can generate the power to give one side or the other, in each frame, the decisive advantage. That's opportunity—and threat. If Stile and I have this power, we can do much good; but if the others get it, they can do just as much evil. At the moment it seems that we shall have that contact—but we cannot afford to take any chance with it. The stakes are simply too great."

"And I represent a liability," Agape said.

"Nay, I love thee!" Bane cried.

"That is why," she said. "Every time you cross to the other frame, you risk falling into the power of the other side, and Mach risks the same. Because we can never be certain of the situation in the other frame, until the exchange is made. The enemy forces do not have to capture you or Mach; they merely have to capture me or Fleta."

"But we shall protect each!" Bane protested.

She shook her head. "We can never be sure of that, while we are part of these two societies. I can be secure only in one place: my home planet. It is there I must go."

"Nay!" Bane cried. "I cannot be apart from thee! I returned to Proton only to be with thee!"

"And you must return to Phaze," she said. "Bane, they need you there. But even if you remain here, or travel back and forth, you cannot afford to associate with me. It will be better if I remove myself from your life."

"Nay!" he repeated, agonized.

"That is the conclusion Sheen and I came to, independently," Blue said. "We can accomplish much, if we cut our risks. That means that your association with Agape, and Bane's with Fleta, must be sundered. Only then can the two of you safely maintain contact between the frames.

Somehow, Bane had known it all along. He gazed at Agape, stricken.

16

Decision

Mach was back in the Purple Demesnes, but this time as no captive. That much Bane had assured him, in their brief dialogue before the exchange. Fleta had been freed, and the Translucent Adept governed here. Certainly he was no longer clamped to the wall; Bane had evidently stood here to overlap him, but Bane had not been shackled. He hoped Bane would be able to get free, or that Citizen Blue would free him; if not, he would have to return, for the fate of his body was his responsibility.

Purple stood before him, his face expressionless. Mach realized that the man did not know that the exchange had been accomplished. "I am Mach," he said. Now he would find out whether the truce would be honored.

"The situation has changed," Purple said gruffly. "I turned thine other self over to Translucent. He promised to have thy cooperation. Now thou art free to depart. Hast thou any message?"

"I was bracketed to the wall, there," Mach said. "I accepted no message."

"An I had mine own way," Purple muttered, "that were thy fate here too. But till Translucent's policy fail, thou canst go thy way." He turned his back and walked out of the cell.

Things certainly had changed! Mach walked out of the cell unopposed, and down the tunnel, and on out of the Purple Demesnes without hindrance. Purple really was letting him go!

At the mouth of the cave that was the Demesnes entrance, Mach paused. He stood on the side of a mountain, and could see out over the trees below. This was the north slope; theoretically most of Phaze lay before him, but all he could see was the nearest section, seemingly untouched by man.

A floating watery bubble appeared before him. Mach smiled warily. "Hello, Translucent Adept," he said.

"And a greeting to thee, Mach of Proton," the Adept replied. "What be thy current desire?"

"To find Fleta."

"She was freed by thine other self; methinks she fled to the Blue Demesnes."

"Makes sense," Mach agreed.

"I can transport thee there, an thou prefer."

"Thanks, Adept, but I think not. I won't come to you unless I'm ready to do business."

"Fair enough," Translucent said. "The door be open always." His bubble of water faded out.

Mach considered. He would go to the Blue Demesnes. But how? It might be a long march by foot, but he was uncertain of his powers of magic, particularly now that he was alone. His spells had worked well only when Fleta had helped him with her music, or when he had built up to them carefully. If he tried to transport himself, and garbled it, in what condition would he find himself? Also, each spell only worked once; there was no point in wasting them. So—he would go by foot.

He started walking north. It was slow, because of the slope; it was about as hard going down as it would have been going up, to his surprise. He was soon sweating, for it was the middle of the day and he was alive. In his robot body he neither tired nor sweated, but now he gloried in these physical manifestations.

A harpy flew into view. She wore a fright wig. "Phoebe!" he exclaimed.

She heard him and swerved to approach. "The imitation Adept! Alone?"

"I'm looking for Fleta," he said. "Have you seen her?"

"Aye, a day ago. I put her on the way to the Blue Demesnes." Confirmation! "I'm going there now."

"Thou wilt ne'er catch her, at the rate thou art going. She was charging north on the hoof, last I saw her."

"I'll keep going, though. Thank you for your information, Phoebe."

"Nobody thanks a harpy," she grumbled. "It be just not done."

"Sorry." He waved to her, and went on.

"And when thou dost catch her, ne'er let her go!" she screeched after him.

It was advice he intended to follow. He moved on down the slope, and in due course came to the level plain. Here he made better progress, finding the approximate route they had traveled before. He knew this was unicorn country, so would be free of most predators.

He was mistaken. In midafternoon, as he was trudging tiredly along, a great shadow cut across the plain. He looked up, and spied a dragon.

He hoped the monster was just passing by. But it wasn't. Evidently it had spotted him trudging, and decided that this was suitable prey. It wasn't a large dragon, compared to the one they had encountered south of the mountains; this might be a scavenger, seeking prey that was too weak to defend itself well.

Well, he fit the description. He was not only tired, he was exposed, for there were no trees nearby and no other cover. He had no weapon. He could neither fight nor flee effectively.

The dragon swooped. Its talons were spread; it planned to snatch him up and carry him away, perhaps biting off his head to keep him passive.

Magic! He had to use a spell to protect himself!

But what? He had only seconds to come up with one. The dragon was diving toward him at an awesome rate, its little eyes and big teeth gleaming.

Something to make it too small to harm him! "Dragon fall, become small!" he sang as it closed on him. And knew that it wasn't going to work.

The dragon seemed to hesitate. It lost control, passing over Mach's head, the downdraft from its wings almost blasting him off his feet. It lifted, and wobbled, seeming huge.

Huge? The thing was growing!

Mach realized that he had really blown his spell this time. It had not merely failed, it had had the opposite of the intended effect! Instead of making the dragon fall and get small, it was rising and getting larger. He had made things even worse for himself than they had been.

He scrambled through his mind, trying to come up with a better spell, trying to concentrate to make it work, trying to generate some more substantial music and having no success at any of these efforts. He watched, morbidly fascinated, as the dragon lifted and grew.

Then the monster stalled out and dropped. It flapped its wings desperately, but could not find enough purchase for them, and crashed into the ground. The contact was a hard one; Mach felt the earth shudder.

The dragon lay still. It was either dead or close to it. Mach decided not to investigate closely; the thing might not be as badly off as it seemed He took the opportunity to get himself as far from it as possible.

But he pondered. Granted that his spell had been another disaster, confirming his caution in avoiding magic where possible —why had the dragon crashed? It had gotten larger, so should have been even more formidable.

Larger? Did that mean it also increased its mass? Surely so; here in Phaze mass had no relevance, as was evident when Fleta changed from unicorn form to hummingbird form. If it got heavier as well as larger, the dynamics of its flight would change; it would require a proportionally greater wingspan to do the same job. Many of the laws of physics did not apply in the magic realm, but it seemed that some did—those not specifically countered by magic. So the dragon's ratios had gotten wrong; it was unable to fly, because though its wings had grown with the rest of it, they needed to grow *faster* than the rest of it, to keep it aloft. Thus it had stalled and crashed.

His spell had done the job after all. But through no great wit

or magic of his! He had once again blundered to a kind of success.
He was not phenomenally pleased.

At the rate he was going, he was surely losing headway. If
Fleta had galloped by here a day ago, he would be two days
behind by the time he reached the Blue Demesnes. But he remained reluctant to try too much magic. Magic seemed, to him,
to be fraught with the same kind of dangers as would be working
with complex equipment a person did not properly understand:
the consequences of some seemingly minor misjudgment could
be magnified disastrously.

Still, there were dangers here, as the recent episode of the
dragon showed, and if he wanted to remain long in Phaze he
would need to sharpen his survival skills. So it was necessary that
he tackle magic, so as to be able to use it effectively at need.
And his first need was travel.

He sat down and pondered. He didn't want to risk transporting
himself; the fate of the dragon made that all too worrisome. But
he could conjure something that would help him travel—

In Proton, if he wanted to travel outside, he would have req-
uisitioned a vehicle of some sort. Could he do the same here?

What kind of vehicle would be best for mixed terrain without
roads? Not a wheeled one, for there was grass and some rocks
and gullies, and streams. One that floated. An aircar, its cushion
of air supporting it and moving it forward.

He thought up a suitable rhyme, then hummed to work up
the music. He concentrated on what he wanted, in order to get
it exactly right. Then he sang: "Bring me a car, to travel far."

Fog appeared and swirled. It dissipated, leaving an object.
Success!

Or was it? As he got a closer look, he realized that this was
not a car; it was more like a boat. In fact, it was a canoe, floating
placidly. There were two paddles in it.

What could he do with a canoe, here in the middle of the
plain? There was no water in sight! And if there were a navigable
river, he would have to follow where it went, rather than where
he wanted to go. He had bungled the spell again.

Floating?

He stared at the canoe. It was indeed floating—in air.

He had concentrated on a floating car. It seemed that he had gotten part of it right.

He put his hands against the side of the canoe and pressed down. It rocked, threatening to overturn. But it did not descend to the ground.

Well, now. He held it as steady as he could and threw a leg over. The thing depressed slightly as it took his weight, and seemed quite unstable, but it supported him. He got himself in and took a seat. Still it floated.

He picked up a paddle. He pretended there was water, and dipped the paddle where the water should be.

There was resistance. He stroked the paddle back, and the canoe slid smoothly forward.

Mach decided not to question this any further. He was experienced at canoeing; he could move along comfortably. He did so.

Progress was not swift, but this was far more pleasant than walking. The canoe developed some inertia, so that it continued moving forward between strokes, allowing him to economize on his effort.

Even so, it was obvious that he was not going to reach the Blue Demesnes by nightfall. So he guided his craft to a copse of trees he hoped bore fruit, for he was hungry now.

He was in luck. There was fruit, and a small spring. He pulled down some vine to tie his canoe, then drank deeply. He plucked enough fruit to eat, then some more to store in his craft.

He considered, then piled some brush in the canoe and settled down on it to sleep. He didn't want the craft to drift away during the night, and he felt safer in it anyway.

He woke in the morning, refreshed, and resumed his journey. He made good progress, and came to the place where the paths diverged. He took the east path, not caring to tempt the demons of the Lattice. Even so, he stroked swiftly and nervously by the region where he and Fleta had had to turn aside to avoid the goblins awaiting them. He doubted he could outpaddle goblins.

But there were none. He proceeded north without interference. In due course he spied the blue towers ahead. He had made it!

He drew up at the moat. Should he float right on across, or call out to make himself known?

He was saved from the decision by the emergence of a beautiful older woman. He knew her immediately, though he had never seen her before: The Lady Stile, Bane's mother.

"Tie thy boat and come in, Mach," she called to him. "Supper awaits thee."

So they had been expecting him! That meant that Fleta was here.

But she was not. The Lady explained that the mare had departed two days before, going to her Herd. "But the Adept has been long eager to meet thee," she assured him.

Stile looked exactly like his father, Citizen Blue. It was eerie. Mach cleaned up and joined them for the meal, and found them pleasant to be with. But it was Fleta he had come for.

Stile shook his head. "She hath a notion to marry thee, and this be impossible," he said abruptly.

"Why? I know her nature, and I love her. I returned to Phaze to be with her."

"Ne'er in all the history of Phaze has man married animal. Thou mayst be from a more liberal frame, but thou art not in that frame. Here thou art known as the son of an Adept. It would be shame on these Demesnes."

Now the difference between Blue and Stile was becoming apparent. Mach's father had encouraged the integration of the species, so as to break down the barriers that had stratified the Proton society. But it seemed that in these same twenty years Stile had gone the opposite direction, becoming more conservative.

"But when there is love—" Mach started.

"There be more than love here," the Lady said gently. "An Adept must have an heir, or great mischief rises in the selection of his successor. Thou couldst generate no heir with a 'corn."

Mach had never thought of that, but he realized that they had a point. This was not just his own business; he had the body of their son, and if he misused it, he could destroy what they had worked for. He had no right to do that.

"There be more than that," Stile said. "We have groomed Bane from birth to be the Blue Adept after me. Red has worked with him, training his talent. His potential be great; when he matures, he will be a more potent Adept than I. Potent enough, perhaps, to hold the Adverse Adepts at bay."

"I thought you were doing that well enough," Mach said.

"Nay. It be but a holding action, and we be slowly losing ground. We need magic of the old order to contain them."

"You mean back when magic was at full strength? Before the Phazite/Protonite exchange? How can you get that, without the other Adepts having it too?"

"We cannot. But with rare innate talent, and special training, and the Book of Magic, Bane might approach that potency."

Mach realized the validity of this point too. What a poor substitute he was for Bane in this respect! He had no training, and his enchantments were erratic at best, and embarrassing or even dangerous at worst. In no way was he a substitute for Bane.

He had been so eager to return to the frame, to be with Fleta! He had not considered the larger picture. He had no right to hurt the prospects for Bane's family, and for the good of the frame itself. His living being had been selfish, but his more disciplined mind understood what was proper. His dream was just that: a dream. His duty was clear enough.

"I think I must return to Proton," Mach said heavily.

"It be not that we hold any onus toward thee," the Lady said. "Nor would we deny Bane his romance in Proton. But we are fighting to maintain the good of Phaze, and to prevent its despoliation, and ne'er did we think there would be renewed contact 'tween the frames."

Of course they preferred a stable order, he realized. He and Bane, being young, were more than ready for change. It was the generation gap—just as it existed in Proton. He had been dissatisfied there, but the situation was fundamentally similar here. "Let me find Fleta and bid her farewell," he said. "Then I shall locate Bane and exchange back." He knew he was doing the right thing, but he had no joy in it.

He spent the night at the Blue Demesnes, and in the morning they loaded his boat with provisions. "I would help thee more," Stile said. "But when we learned of thy exchange with Bane, I consulted with Red, and he used the Book to evoke a limited augury. It indicated that I am apt to make one disastrous and avoidable error with regard to thee. We no longer have the Oracle in Phaze, so the formulae of the Book are all that remain. They are powerful but general; we know not what error it be. I suspect it be one of commission rather than of omission. So I am leaving thee alone to the extent I can, so as not to make that error. That was why I came not to thine aid when the dragon attacked thee."

"You were watching?" Mach exclaimed, amazed.

"Aye, and I be not the only one. In this case I trusted to my opponents, the Adverse Adepts, who wish to use thee for their designs; they would not allow thee to be incidentally killed."

"But they did not act either! I stopped that dragon myself!"

"Methinks they waited, to force me into action, and so perhaps into that error I am apt to make. Perhaps they enhanced thy spell."

Mach realized that it was possible. He had been amazed at the reversal of his spell, thinking it his own foulup, but if more powerful magic had acted to shape it, so as to save him without apparent interference . . .

He sighed. "It is true: I am a babe in the woods here. I will tell Fleta, and go."

He stroked with his paddle, and the canoe moved smartly out. He had a long way to go, but knew he would get there. He understood much more than he had before.

There was a southward-blowing wind, which facilitated his progress, and he traveled much faster than he had before, with less fatigue. But he was now three days behind Fleta. He hoped she had remained with the Herd.

The wind stiffened. He shipped his paddle and let it carry him like a current. The scenery moved rapidly by. He had to take action on occasion to avoid trees, but otherwise it was a restful trip. He wished he could remain here in Phaze, but the logic of the situation was inescapable. He did not belong here, and his continued presence would harm the frame. It would be hard to part with Fleta, but it had to be done.

He reached the grazing Herd in the afternoon, and guided his craft toward it. The Herd Stallion came forth to meet him. He had a dark blue coat, with red socks, and bore a family resemblance to Fleta. Obviously this was her uncle Clip.

"I am Mach, visiting this frame," Mach said, backpaddling to hold his canoe in place. "I would like to talk to Fleta."

The unicorn became a man. "And I be the Herd Stallion. My niece passed here three days past, but went on to the local Werewolf Pack."

"Then I must go on to the Pack," Mach said.

"Not if thou beest not known to them," Clip said. "We know thee, because thou hast the likeness of our friend Bane, and Fleta told us of thy nature. But the wolves welcome strangers not."

"I must find her, to tell her farewell," Mach said.

Clip gazed at him appraisingly. "In that case, I shall send with thee a guide." He reverted to equine form and blew a brief melody on his horn. It sounded like a saxophone.

There was a stir amidst the Herd. The unicorns were of all colors and patterns, mostly mares with some younger ones. One of the young ones came forth. He was piebald, with large patches of green and orange. He blew an inquiring note, sounding like a trombone.

Clip changed back to man form. "Bone, guide this man to Kurrelgyre's Pack and introduce him," he said.

Bone changed to adolescent form. "But this be Bane! He needs no guidance there!"

"This be Mach," Clip said. "Dost seek to be expelled from the Herd before thy time? Do as I say."

"Aye, Master," the youth agreed.

"Get in and help him paddle," Clip said.

So Bone climbed in, took the front seat, and used the paddle. Suddenly the canoe's progress was faster, which was just as well, because the wind had died.

They moved east. Soon night closed. Bone guided them to a copse of fruit trees, where they tied the canoe. Mach ate and settled down to sleep; Bone reverted to his natural form and grazed.

Next day they paddled on. Bone, not content merely to paddle and guide, chatted about this and that.

"You like your life on the plain?" Mach inquired.

"Oh, sure," the youth inquired. " 'Course it'll be harder when I get evicted from the Herd."

"Evicted? Why?"

"All grown males get evicted. There can be only one Herd Stallion. So we have to range beyond it, on guard against enemies, and hope for the day one of us will achieve a herd of our own."

"But wouldn't it be fairer to have one stallion to one mare?"

"What kind of a herd would that be?" Bone inquired indignantly. "Only the fittest can sire offspring."

Mach saw another reason why Fleta might prefer to love outside the Herd, and outside her species. All the mares serviced by one stallion? There could not be much attention for individuals! "And you are the offspring of Clip?"

"Of Clip? Nay! He deposed my sire fifteen years back." He made a gesture with the paddle. "And what a fight that was! Clip had been out in the hills with but a small Herd, mainly Belle, but that must've toughened him, because he came down and challenged our Herd Stallion, who was getting pretty old, and gored him and drove him off. Of course Clip be not young himself, now, and already the males of the hills be watching him. But he be brother to Neysa, and she hath friends—Oh, does she have friends, from the Blue Adept on down!—and whoe'er takes out her brother would have to fear from those friends."

Phaze had a sterner mode of existence than he had realized! Mach could understand dragons preying on unicorns and such, but hadn't realized how tough the internal affairs of the herd could be.

"So you'll be going out, and maybe one day challenge for the mastery of some herd?"

"Mayhap," the youth agreed. "More likely get myself killed trying."

And this was the life Fleta was a part of! Was he going to return to Proton and leave her to it? His recent decision to depart the frame was shaken. Yet what could he accomplish, by taking her from her Herd, except to shame her before her kind?

By nightfall they reached the Pack. Kurrelgyre turned out to be a grizzled wolf and, when he changed, a grizzled man, middle-aged and tough. Bone was obviously wary of him, and glad to revert to unicorn form and gallop away once Mach was safely introduced.

"Aye, she was here, three or four days past," the leader of the Pack said. "She went on to the Vampire Demesnes."

Another delay! Not only was he not catching up to Fleta, he was getting farther behind her!

The werewolves served him roasted meat. He didn't inquire what kind it was. They gave him a cozy nest of hay for the night, though it wasn't as comfortable for him as it was for them, in their canine forms.

In the morning Kurrelgyre decreed that he should have a guide, and a bitch named Furramenin jumped into the front of his canoe. She put her paws on the front seat and pointed her nose in the direction he was to go, and he paddled the craft in that direction.

At noon the bitch guided him to the site of a spring, so he could stop and drink water and find fruit. She jumped out of the canoe, glanced at the fruit, then changed to girl form. It seemed that she preferred to eat fruit in that shape, rather than to hunt for meat in her natural form. Mach hardly objected; he had been somewhat wary of the bitch, though he had told himself she would not turn on him. As a woman, she was just as young and healthy, and pretty too, though he would have preferred that she be either naked in the manner of a serf, or fully clothed. Her fur skirt and halter split the difference.

She kept the human shape when they resumed travel. She paddled, but she lacked the vigor the unicorn had had, and their progress was not swift. They had to camp for the night before reaching the Vampire Demesnes.

They foraged again for food, then settled down. "You can have the canoe if you wish," Mach offered.

"Nay, I will resume bitch form and curl up in a hole," she said. But she didn't do that immediately, and that prevented Mach from settling down. He kept thinking of her as an attractive young woman, which made it awkward, especially when she leaned un-selfconsciously toward him in that loose halter. He wondered how animals such as these had come to have human intelligence.

"Do you know Fleta personally?" he inquired politely.

"Aye, she be friend to me," Furramenin said. "That be why I

volunteered for this hunt. We talked, and she told me of the human man she liked. Thou art that man?"

"I am. Now I seek her to bid her farewell, for I must return to my frame."

"Aye, she knew that. An thou hadst stayed, she was ready to speak the three thee's to thee."

"The what?"

"Dost thou know not? An a human or human-formed creature love truly, that creature bespeaks the other, 'Thee' three times and the splash bespeaks its truth."

Now he remembered; Fleta had told him of it. Except for one detail. "Splash?"

She laughed. "How canst thou know true love in thy frame of Proton? The splash be the magic ripple that spreads in the presence of the utterance of significant truth."

"But what if a person speaks that way, and the splash does not occur, what then?"

"Then the love be false. But there be none who would speak it, an it be not true." She smiled. "My sire, Kurrelgyre, tells of the time when Stile swore friendship to Fleta's dam, Neysa, and the ripple was so strong it converted all present, the whole Herd of 'corns and our Pack, to friendship to Neysa too. That was the first time we know of that a man made such oath to an animal. Thereafter the Herd and Pack fought not, having too many members with a common friend. But Stile be Adept; there be no other magic like that."

"I know," Mach agreed morosely.

Furramenin changed back to bitch form and curled up under the canoe, and Mach was able at last to relax. But sleep came slowly. If Fleta had let it be known that she cared that strongly for him, how could he tell her he was never going to see her again? Yet that was what he had to do.

In the morning the trip resumed, and by noon they reached the vampire cave. Furramenin introduced Mach to her friend Suchevane, who was of course a bat, then changed to bitch form and headed rapidly for home.

The bat fluttered to ground, then became a woman. And Mach had to lock his facial muscles to prevent his mouth from gaping and his eyeballs from bulging, for she was the most stunningly

lovely creature he had ever seen. Her black silk outfit was technically no less encompassing than Furramenin's furs had been,
but the shape it clothed made it seem otherwise. A bat? A vampire? Any man would be sorely tempted to bare his throat for
her, just for the pleasure of her contact!

Suchevane smiled, and that made it worse, for it showed her
slightly lengthened canines without one whit diminishing her
beauty. "We prey not on friends," she said, fathoming his thought.
"In fact, we dine not regularly on blood, but only on special
occasion. Have no concern for thy health, handsome man." Her
voice was sultry, causing little shivers to play about sections of
his torso.

"I—I'm really looking for Fleta," he said. "I have to—"

"Aye," she breathed. "And sad it be, too. She asked me whether
an animal could marry a man, and I convinced her she could not.
Unfortunate that be."

Surely this bat-woman was in a position to know! "But I must
at least see her before I go."

"She was here four days ago, maybe five. She went on to the
Red Adept."

"An Adept? Why?"

"I dared not ask."

"I must reach her!"

"I will guide thee there."

"I—I'm not sure that's wise."

She smiled again. "Dost fear I will bite thee?"

"Uh, not exactly." It was her kiss that would devastate him
more! What would Fleta think, if he approached her in the company of this creature?

"We can be there by nightfall," she said, climbing nimbly into
the canoe.

Mach hauled his gaze away from her phenomenal profile and
wielded his paddle. If she spoke truly, he would not have to
spend a night on the road with her, in either her vampire bat or
luscious human form. He wasn't sure which of those worried
him more. They proceeded south.

Sure enough, as evening loomed, they approached the castle
of the Red Adept.

Suchevane inflated, and again Mach had to stifle a gape. "Hal-looo, Red Adept!" she called. "A bat brings a visitor!"

A hole opened in the hill at the base of the castle. They paddled in. There was a tunnel there, leading to the central chamber.

Therein was a troll. Alarmed, thinking himself betrayed, Mach started to backpaddle, but Suchevane got out and approached the troll without fear. "Adept, I be Suchevane," she said. "Of the flock thou dost protect. Long have I desired an excuse to meet thee."

The troll gazed at her, evidently struck by the same qualities in her that Mach had appreciated. He was as ugly as any of his kind, but evidently no threat. "This, then, be Bane's other self," he said.

"Aye," she agreed, smiling. "He be Mach, from the scientific frame of Proton, come to see Fleta the 'corn."

The troll faced Mach, though it seemed he would rather have faced the vampiress, as any male would.

"There be reason why this be not wise," he said.

"I know," Mach said. "I only want to bid her farewell. Then I must return to Proton."

"Aye. The Adverse Adepts seek to unite the Oracle, which now resides in Proton, with the Book of Magic, now in my possession. The only way to prevent that be to keep the two of ye in thine own frames, carrying no messages."

This was new to Mach. "What is so bad about those two things getting together?"

"The Book be the compilation of all the most basic and potent formulae, that underlie the laws of both magic and science. The Oracle, now called a computer, be the mechanism to interpret those formulae. The two together represent potentially the ultimate power in both frames. It were best that power not fall into errant hands."

"But Bane and I would not—"

"Not intentionally," the Adept agreed. "But there be ways of corruption, and the Adverse Adepts, hungry for that power, will practice those ways. It be best that contact between the frames be naught."

Mach had seen how the Purple Adept, and his counterpart in

Proton, acted. Certainly the man was up to no good! "But I think Fleta understands this. I just—I have to see her once more before I go."

The troll nodded. "She departed here four days ago."

"I must find her, to bid her farewell," Mach said.

"I promised her that none would interfere," he said.

Mach felt sudden apprehension. "Interfere with what?"

"That I may not say."

"O, I can guess!" Suchevane exclaimed. "She goes to die!"

"To die!" Mach cried. "That cannot be!"

"She knew that her dream could ne'er be," the troll said. "I could dissuade her not, so I gave her the enchantment she asked and let her go."

"What did she ask?" Mach cried.

"I may not—"

"Please, honored Adept," Suchevane breathed, leaning toward the Adept.

Mach saw the troll's face freeze in exactly the fashion his own had. Swayed, Trool yielded. "To be fixed in one form. More I absolutely will not say; I did promise her."

"But that shouldn't hurt her!" Mach protested.

Suchevane took him by the arm and turned him toward the canoe. "We thank thee, Adept," she called back over her shoulder. "Thou hast not betrayed thy promise. Fleta be our friend."

"I wanted not to do it!" the troll protested, as if accused.

"We know," Suchevane said. Then they were back in the canoe and stroking the air toward the exit.

Outside, Suchevane paused, turning to Mach. "I know where she goes. She and I have been friends long; I know her mind. I can show thee. But it be a day's hard run for a 'corn, and too far for me to fly without blood, and we cannot catch her in this canoe."

"A day? She left here four days ago! That means that three days ago—"

"Nay, she was locked in girl form, remember? So it would take her perhaps five days."

"That means she hasn't gotten there yet? If I can get there in one day—"

She shook her head. "I can show thee a shortcut, an this boat be able to float across chasms and lakes and trees. But even with two strong paddlers, it be at least two days."

He appreciated her offer to help, but it was obvious that she was not constructed for endurance paddling. How could he double the normal velocity?

"I must try magic," he said.

"Bane could be there in an instant," she said.

"But I'm not Bane. If I tried to travel like that, I could destroy myself and you."

She sighed. "I feared such. I know not what to do."

"Describe the route to me, and get clear of me, and I will try my magic," he said.

"Nay, she be my friend. I will chance thy magic."

This vampiress was easy to appreciate! "Then hang on; I'll try to give us strength to do it. That seems the safest course." For he remembered when he had enchanted his own potency, in order to survive Fleta's period of heat. That seemed to be safe magic.

He worked out a rhyme. Then: "Suchevane, can you sing?"

She made a moue. "That be not my talent."

"But can you try? I need supportive music to enhance my magic, or it goes wrong."

"I will try." She took a breath and began to hum. She was right: this was not her forte. But it was music of a sort.

Mach concentrated as hard as he was able, knowing that this had to work, or Fleta's life was forfeit. He hummed along with Suchevane. Then he sang: "Give us strength to work at length."

Fog formed, and swirled about them and the canoe, and dissipated. But Mach did not feel any different.

"I don't know whether it worked," he said. "But let's try paddling."

They tried paddling, and it seemed ordinary. The canoe moved northwest. So far so good; but if they tired—

They did not tire. It was as if they weren't working; each stroke was just like the first, without fatigue.

They moved out to a downhill slope. Before, the canoe had followed the contour of the land, but this time it held its elevation. Had he modified its behavior by his magic, or was this simply a matter of the operator's will? Or was the troll, evidently a creature of good will, sneaking in a little surreptitious help? Mach didn't question it; he just kept paddling.

But darkness was closing in. "We can't stop now," Mach said. "We have only one day to catch her!"

"I know the way; I can guide thee by night," Suchevane said, never halting her paddling.

They kept moving, and their arms did not tire, and their hands did not blister. His spell was effective, and for that he breathed constant thanks. Yet their progress seemed slow; certainly they were not doing double the velocity a person might walk.

Then he realized that a five-day walk presumed five nights of sleep. If they did not halt, they could double the effective travel time. It was possible to cover two days' distance in one!

On they went through the night. Nocturnal creatures sounded their calls, and there were sinister rustlings all around, but nothing bothered the canoe. Of course Mach had been sleeping in the forest during this journey and had not been attacked, but he had assumed that was partly luck and partly the secluded niches he chose. And partly the company: one night he had had a unicorn for company, and another a werewolf. Well, now he had a vampire; perhaps that was protection enough.

He became sleepy. "Mach!" Suchevane called sharply.

Mach snapped awake. "Did I stop paddling?"

"Aye."

"I fell asleep. It seems my magic gave me strength, but not wakefulness."

"Mayhap another spell?"

"I'm afraid I might ruin the one I have. My magic is so uncertain, it isn't smart to chance it."

"Then must the one keep the other awake," she said. "An thou sleep again, I will bite thee."

That brought him quite alert. They paddled for another hour. Then she flagged.

"Suchevane," he called. "Are you sleeping?"

She snapped awake. "Aye. Sorry."

"Do that again, and I'll—" He cast about for a suitable threat, but the only thing he could think of for a creature like her wasn't what he cared to say.

"That be no threat to me anyway," she said.

He felt himself blushing. "You read my mind?"

"The mind of any male be much the same."

In her presence, surely so. Then he thought of a suitable threat: "I'll whack you with my paddle and knock you out of the boat."

"I would change form and fly away," she said. But she remained awake, evidently not wishing to get knocked.

In such manner they kept themselves going through the night. As daylight resumed their sleepiness faded. But now hunger set in. "Dare we pause to eat?" he asked. "I have supplies."

"I think the time be very close," she said. "An we delay an hour, mayhap an hour too late."

And they couldn't risk that. So, hungry, they continued working.

And as the day waned, they approached the great White Mountain range. "The ledge of the unicorns be there," Suchevane said. "But still some distance. I know not whether we be in time."

"Can—can you change form and fly ahead, and see?" he asked. "I can keep the canoe moving meanwhile."

"That distance? Aye, now. But it will be slower for thee," she pointed out.

"I realize. But I've got to know."

"Aye." She shipped her paddle, changed, and flew up and ahead. Mach continued paddling, trying to put extra strength into it so as to maintain speed, but knew it wasn't enough.

The bat returned. It landed on the seat, and changed. "She be there," Suchevane said. "I did not approach, for that would have taken too much time; I returned the moment I spied her. She be trudging up toward the ledge, just a few minutes distant from it." She resumed paddling, and the canoe picked up speed.

"Then we're in time!" Mach exclaimed.

"Nay," she said sadly. "She will reach it before we do—and then we shall be at the bottom, while she be at the top. No way to stop her, unless perchance we call and she hear."

They paddled furiously, and the canoe fairly leaped along, but the spell of endurance had not allowed for this extra energy, and they were now tiring. Mach saw sweat staining Suchevane's black halter, and her hair was becoming a stringy tangle, and he himself was panting. But the high face of the cliff was coming into sight.

Far up, on the ledge, stood a tiny figure. Mach knew it was Fleta, locked in her human form. If only she waited until he could get close—

And what would he have to say to her, then? That he had decided to leave her forever and return to Proton! What glad news would that be for her?

There was a faint ripple in the air. As it passed through him, Mach thought he heard his name cried out with hopeless longing.

"Nay!" Suchevane gasped.

Horrified, Mach saw. Fleta had just leaped from the ledge, and was doing a graceful swan-dive into the pool of darkness below.

He could not reach her in time—and could not catch her if he were there. The height of the fall was far too great. She would be dashed into oblivion on the rock below.

As if it were in slow motion, he watched her plunge, her arms outspread. He knew it was for love of him she had done this, to free him from the need to be with her. But he could not let it happen!

He cast about for some magic to use to save her, but in the pressure of the eternal moment his thoughts were glacial. He could not make a rhyme, let alone sing it! And if he could, how could his puny magic prevail against that of an Adept? All he knew was that he loved her, and could not let her go. Not for any reason. And still she dropped.

"Thee!" he cried into the void that separated them.

The frame itself seemed to still, all the sights and sounds of it pausing in place as if listening.

"Thee!" he cried again.

A haze formed, an inward-drawing expectation, fogging out all the landscape beyond their canoe, the falling girl, and the line between them. Magic was coalescing.

"Thee!" he cried the third time, and all of his soul was in it.

The power of it jumped like a lightning bolt, from him to her, and struck her, and radiated out from her like sunrise, brightening the face of the cliff, the rocky ground, and the welkin above. A soundless explosion, striking iridescence from the environment and rippling on throughout the frame.

The face of the cliff was so clear it was mirrorlike, and the colors of the trees and sky were preternaturally bright, as though washed totally clean. The air was absolutely pure.

And she was gone. Where the falling human figure had been, there was nothing.

"The splash!" Suchevane breathed, and now her sweat was gone and her hair was sparkling; she was lovelier than ever before. "Ne'er before one like that! I love all everything!"

"But my love!" Mach cried in dawning horror. "What did I do to Fleta?"

They stared into the radiant emptiness before them, aghast.

Then came the sound of the hummingbird.

Almost afraid to believe it, Mach held up his hand. The tiny bird darted in and landed on it. The feathers of the folded wings were shining black, and the claws were golden.

"The splash!" Suchevane repeated. "It nulled the spell Trool put on her!"

"And her involuntary reflex took over," Mach said. "She saved herself!"

"But none hath power to null Adept magic!" the vampiress continued. "None save another Adept. Methinks thou must be—"

The bird hopped to the canoe, and abruptly Fleta was there in girl form, her sudden weight making the craft rock. She gazed at Mach for half a moment, her eyes brimming, then fell into his embrace.

He knew he could not leave her, no matter what the consequence. All the considerations of the welfare of the frames paled beside the truth of their love.

But that love was forbidden, in Phaze, and he could not take her to Proton. What were they to do?

A watery bubble appeared beside the canoe. The face of the Translucent Adept was in it. "Come to us, and we shall defend thy right to love whom thou dost please, and ne'er will the two of ye be parted," he said. And from him emanated a lesser ripple, in no way on a par with the one just past, yet it signified the truth of his utterance. The Adept had made a promise he would keep.

Now it occurred to Mach that either Stile or the Red Adept could have prevented Fleta's suicide, had they wished to. But what better way to discourage him from remaining in Phaze, than to let Fleta die! Suddenly he understood the nature of the critical mistake the Adept Stile had been fated to make: to let Fleta commit suicide.

Mach's will hardened. "We shall go with you," he said.

Suchevane turned an appalled countenance to them. "I know it be the only way," she said. "I cannot say nay. But O, what mischief be coming o' this!" And from her, too, came the splash of complete conviction.